T0315328

THE BIRD HOTEL

THE BIRD HOTEL

A NOVEL

JOYCE MAYNARD

ARCADE PUBLISHING • NEW YORK

Copyright © 2023 by Joyce Maynard

First paperback edition 2025

All rights reserved. No part of this book may be reproduced in any manner without the express written consent of the publisher, except in the case of brief excerpts in critical reviews or articles. All inquiries should be addressed to Skyhorse Publishing, 307 West 36th Street, 11th Floor, New York, NY 10018.

Arcade Publishing books may be purchased in bulk at special discounts for sales promotion, corporate gifts, fund-raising, or educational purposes. Special editions can also be created to specifications. For details, contact the Special Sales Department, Arcade Publishing, 307 West 36th Street, 11th Floor, New York, NY 10018 or arcade@skyhorsepublishing.com.

Arcade Publishing® is a registered trademark of Skyhorse Publishing, Inc.®, a Delaware corporation.

Visit our website at www.arcadepub.com.

10 9 8 7 6 5 4 3 2 1

Library of Congress Cataloging-in-Publication Data is available on file.

Cover design by Brian Peterson
Cover image by Diego Isaias Hernandez

Print ISBN: 978-1-64821-076-1
Ebook ISBN: 978-1-956763-74-4

Printed in the United States of America

FOR JENNY REIN

The country where this story takes place, though it bears a resemblance to various Central American locales, is an invention of the writer. So too are the lake and the volcano and the hotel, the inhabitants of the village, the magic herb, the fireflies that put in an appearance only once a year and only for a single night. Many varieties of birds described in these pages do not actually exist. You might call this story a fairy tale, or a fantasy, or just a dream. The part about the power of love—and the capacity of those who experience its effects to accomplish what might otherwise seem impossible— is real and true.

Dos besos llevo en el alma, Llorona,
que no se apartan de mí,
Dos besos llevo en el alma, Llorona,
que no se apartan de mí,
El último de mi madre, Llorona,
y el primero que te di.
El último de mi madre, Llorona,
y el primero que te di.
(I carry two kisses in my soul, Llorona,
that will never leave me,
I carry two kisses in my soul, Llorona,
that will never leave me,
The last one from my mother, Llorona,
and the first one I gave to you.
The last one from my mother, Llorona,
and the first one I gave to you.)

  —La Llorona, (The Weeping Woman), a traditional Mexican
 folk song about a mother who walks the earth grieving her dead children

Think of love as a state of grace, not as a means to anything, but . . .
an end in itself.

    —Gabriel García Márquez, *Love in the Time of Cholera*

One thing about hard times

I was twenty-seven years old when I decided to jump off the Golden Gate Bridge. One afternoon I had this great life. Half an hour later all I wanted was to be dead.

I took a taxi. It was just after sunset when I reached the bridge—rising up through the mist, that wonderful shade of red I had loved, back when I still cared about the colors of things, and bridges, and getting to the other side of them. Back when I cared about so many things that now seemed meaningless.

Before leaving my apartment that last time, I'd stuffed a hundred-dollar bill in my pocket. I gave this to the driver. Why wait for change?

There were tourists of course. Traffic heading in and out of the city. Parents with children in strollers. I used to be one of those.

A boat was passing under the bridge. From where I stood, preparing to jump, I watched it make its way under the pilings, men mopping the deck. Nothing made sense anymore.

I'd been dimly aware of an elderly man watching me. He might try to stop me. So I waited for him to move on, and after a few minutes he did.

Only I couldn't take that last step up onto the railing, over the edge.

"One thing about hard times," Lenny had said once, when our rent check bounced the same week Arlo got sent home from day care with head lice and I came down with mono and a pipe burst in our apartment that destroyed a stack of drawings I'd been working on for six months. "Once you hit bottom, things can only get better."

Standing on the bridge, looking down at the dark and swirling water, I think I recognized something about myself. Even though the place in which I now found myself was terrible, some small part of me couldn't let go of the world. The fact of grieving a vast loss, as I did, had to serve as some kind of reminder that life was precious. Even mine. Even then.

I stepped away from the railing.

I couldn't do it. But I couldn't ever go home either. I had no home anymore.

This is how I ended up at *The Bird Hotel*.

1970. From now on you're Irene

We heard the news on television two weeks before my seventh birthday. My mother was dead. The next morning my grandmother told me we were changing my name.

I was sitting at the kitchen table—yellow Formica with diamond-shaped sparkles, a pack of my grandmother's ever-present Tarrytons, my colored pencils laid out in their tin. The phone kept ringing, but my grandmother didn't pick it up.

"They can all go to hell," she said. She sounded mad, but not at me.

Odd, the things a person remembers. I held tight to my pencil. Newly sharpened. Blue. The phone kept ringing. I started to pick up the receiver, but Grammy said don't.

"People are going to be coming after us. They'll have a lot of opinions. It's better if they don't make the connection," my grandmother told me, reaching for a cigarette.

Opinions about what? Connection? What people?

"We can't let anyone find out who we are," Grammy said. "You can't be Joan anymore."

Truth to tell, I had always wanted a different name from the one my mother had given me. She named me after her favorite singer. (Baez, not Joni Mitchell. Though she'd loved them both.) I used to ask her to call me other names. (Liesl, for one of the children in *The Sound of Music.* Skipper, for Barbie's little sister. Tabitha from *Bewitched.*)

"Can I be Pamela?" I asked her.

There was a girl at school with that name who had the most beautiful hair. I loved her ponytail.

It didn't work that way, Grammy said. She had my new name picked out already. Irene.

Grammy had a friend from bridge club, Alice, whose granddaughter was the same age as me. I only met her once. *Irene.* She'd died a while back (I'm guessing from cancer but at the time nobody said the word). After that Alice stopped showing up for bridge club.

My grandmother said something I didn't understand about needing to have a paper with your name on it when you went to school to prove you were real.

"I am real."

"It's too complicated to explain," she said. We had to move someplace else now. I'd be going to a different school. They wouldn't let me into first grade without the papers. She had a plan for what to do about this. She'd seen it on an episode of *Columbo*.

That afternoon we rode the bus to a building where my grandmother filled out a lot of forms. I sat on the floor making pictures. By the time we left we had my new birth certificate. "It's official," she told me. "You're Irene now."

I had a new birthday too, the same one as dead Irene. Now I had two more months to wait until I turned seven. This was only one of many things that happened over the course of those days that confused me. "Don't ask so many questions," Grammy said.

My grandmother changed her name too, from Esther to Renata. To me she was still Grammy, so that was easy enough. Remembering I was Irene instead of Joan took a while. At the time I was working on writing cursive. I'd gotten my "J" down pretty well but now I had to start all over again with "I."

A box arrived. Inside were vinyl record albums. I recognized them of course. They were my mother's. The handwriting on the front of the box, hers.

A few days later the movers came. My grandmother had packed up all our things, not that we had much. After they'd carried out the last box—my Tiny Tears doll, a few books, my china animal collection, the ukulele my mother had given me for my last birthday that I didn't know how to play, the colored pencils—I stood at the window watching the men load the truck. Nobody had said where we were going. *Away* was all.

"See that man with the camera?" my grandmother said, pointing. "This is why we have to leave. They'll never let us alone now."

Who?

The paparazzi, she said. "The same people who made Jackie Kennedy's life so miserable she had to marry that ugly old man with the yacht."

I understood none of this. By the weekend we were unpacking the boxes in our new home, a one-bedroom apartment in Poughkeepsie, New York, where Grammy's brother lived, my Uncle Mack. He still called her Esther, but having met me only two times before, he didn't have a hard time shifting over to Irene. The first night he ordered Chinese takeout for us. I handed the little paper folded up inside my fortune cookie to Uncle Mack.

"The usefulness of a cup is in its emptiness," he read.

There was a paper umbrella on the table. *Open shut, open shut.*

Grammy got a job at a fabric store. Because my mother had never gotten around to signing me up for kindergarten the year before, she enrolled me in first grade at Clara Barton Elementary. After that I only asked about my mother one time. I got the impression I wasn't supposed to mention her so I didn't.

There had been no funeral. Nobody came by to tell us how sorry they were about what happened. If Grammy had any pictures of my mother, she kept them someplace I never saw. In the absence of any image of her, I drew one that I put under my pillow. Pink cheeks, blue eyes, rosebud mouth. Long curly hair like a princess.

When kids at school asked why I lived with my grandmother and why my mother was never around, I said she was a famous singer but I wasn't allowed to say which one. She was out on tour with her band, rehearsing for an appearance on *Hootenanny*.

"That went off the air," someone said. A boy named Richie who was always making trouble.

"I meant *The Johnny Cash Show*," I told him. "I always get them confused."

After a while there weren't so many questions, but now and then kids still asked, when was she coming back? Was I going to move to Hollywood? Could I get them her autograph?

"She broke her hand," I said. Her left hand, but she was left-handed. I thought that made the lie sound more convincing.

"I bet your mother isn't really famous," Richie said. "I bet she's really somebody dumb, like the grandmother on *Beverly Hillbillies*."

"My mother is very beautiful," I told him. That part was true, anyway.

My mother had shiny black hair that reached past her waist that I loved to brush. She had long, elegant fingers (but dirt under her nails) and she was so thin that when we lay on some air mattress together at one of the campsites we were always staying at, back in the old days, I could trace her ribs. The part I remember best was her voice—a pure, unwavering soprano. Her ear was so good (her instincts about music a lot better than her instincts about men) that she could hold the most complex minor key melody without a guitar to back her up, though it never seemed difficult for my mother, finding some handsome bearded folksinger with a guitar to accompany her.

People compared her to Joan Baez, but her boyfriend, Daniel— the one she was with the most for my first six years of life (off and on) till the month before the accident, said no, she was more like Joan's younger sister, Mimi Fariña. The prettier one with the softer voice.

She sang to me all the time, in the car late at night or lying in our tent together, sharing a sleeping bag the way we used to. She knew all the old English ballads—songs about jealous men who throw the woman they love in the river because she won't marry them, purehearted women promised to noblemen who choose a lowly commoner instead, only to find out he's the richest in the land.

She sang me to sleep every night. The songs were like bedtime stories.

"Twas in the merry month of May, when green buds all were swellin' . . . *Sweet William on his death bed lay, For love of Barbara Allen."*

"Can a person actually die from loving somebody too much?" I asked her.

"Only if they're a true romantic," she said.

"Are you a true romantic?"

"Yes."

Some of the songs my mother sang were more likely to keep me up at night than they were to put me to sleep.

"I'm going away to leave you, love. I'm going away for a while. But I'll return to you sometime. If I go ten thousand miles."

The part where she sang about going away used to worry me. The good part was when she sang about coming back, no matter what. "It's just a song," she told me.

But one of those old ballads scared me to death. It was "Long Black Veil." I'd lie there hugging the giraffe Daniel had got me at a carnival one time, when he popped five balloons in a row with darts, and even though I'd heard my mother sing that song a hundred times, there was a part at the end that I dreaded.

"Late at night when the north wind blows . . . *In a long black veil she cries o'er my bones."*

It was an odd choice for a bedtime song, but that was my mother for you.

"No more!" I'd call out from my bed—or whatever mattress she'd put me down on that night—when she sang "Long Black Veil," when

5

she got to that part. Then she'd stop singing, and I'd beg her to finish. I loved her voice that much. Even when the words gave me nightmares.

My mother wanted me to call her Diana. She said when I called her Mom or Mommy it made her feel old, like some character on a TV show wearing an apron. Or like my grandmother, which was worse.

She had graduated from Berkeley. She met my father at a sit-in protesting the Vietnam War at People's Park. She didn't know this yet, naturally, but by the time they headed back over the bridge Diana was pregnant with me.

My father got his draft notice that fall. They ordered him to report to duty around the time I was due to be born. He went to Canada instead. He sent Diana a letter every day—two a day, sometimes—begging her to join him there, but by this point she had gotten together with someone else—a banjo player named Phil who reminded her of Pete Seeger, but sexier. My guess is that Diana was more in love with heartbreak—whether in life, or in songs—than she ever was with my father. Then she and Phil broke up and she sang a lot of sad songs. Well, that was always the case.

She met Daniel the day she went into labor with me. This was her pattern. She was a person who needed a man at her side, and she never had any trouble finding one.

Daniel had been her nurse in the delivery room—an unusual job for a man in those days, but Daniel loved babies, and, as he told me once, he loved helping women give birth. He'd coached Diana through thirty-two hours of contractions, followed by six of pushing. The story went that by the time I was born the two of them were in love.

My memory of what I think of as the "Daniel Years"—with frequent guest appearances by various others—centers mostly on the music we listened to at the time, a record Daniel had bought me of Burl Ives, who seemed like exactly the kind of grandfather you'd want to have, if you had a grandfather, and an album of Woody Guthrie's songs for children. Unlike Burl Ives, Woody Guthrie always sounded a little crazy, but his songs were the funniest. I made Diana and Daniel play the Woody Guthrie record a dozen times a day—my favorite of the songs being one about riding in a car, accompanied by a lot of funny noises you had to make with your mouth. This is one of my strongest memories of Daniel, how he thrummed his lips to mimic the sound exhaust pipes make on very old vehicles, which sounded exactly like the exhaust pipe on our very old vehicle. I thought every car made noises like that.

We spent a lot of time in the car—a succession of them. Whatever old and problematic vehicle we drove generally gave up the ghost on a highway headed to some peace demonstration or concert or back home, times when we had a home, or back to the motel or the campsite, or the apartment of some guitar-playing friend of my mother's when we didn't. Diana and I spent hours standing by the side of the road while Daniel or some other boyfriend worked on the car. Most of them blend in my memory—long hair, funny smell, jeans that dragged in the dirt—but one who stands out went by the name Indigo. He called me Kid and liked to tickle me even after I told him I hated tickling. One time when we were staying at a motel with a pool, he'd thrown me in the water.

"Joanie can't swim," Diana yelled. Indigo just laughed. I could feel myself sinking to the bottom of the pool. I opened my mouth. No air. My arms were flailing but there was nothing to hold on to.

Then Diana was there. She'd jumped into the pool in her denim skirt. She was pulling me to the surface. Then I was coughing and gasping, water pouring out of me. That was the last time I ventured into a pool.

My mother and her boyfriends brought me along to a lot of concerts. My chief memory of those times features the smell of the Porta-Potties that I was always scared I'd fall into, and of marijuana and musk oil, and the warm feeling I got when my mother climbed into the tent with me and whatever boyfriend she had at the time, late in the night. Later came the sound of the two of them whispering and laughing softly in a way I now recognize as part of their lovemaking, when they thought I was asleep. At the time, it was just the soundtrack of my life, no different from old ballads and Kumbaya.

Often there would be speeches still going on outside blasting over a crackling PA system. I liked the nights best when Diana sang to me as moths circled our heads in the light of our Coleman lamp. Times when she and Daniel were together, he used to sit just outside the tent with his flashlight reading the textbook for an exam he was going to take so he could get to be the next level of nurse or smoking a joint or whittling the same piece of wood he'd been working on for as long as I could remember. It wasn't in the shape of anything I could recognize, but it was so smooth I liked to hold it against my cheek. I imagined my mother's hand stroking me that way, but she was usually off doing something else.

The three of us lived in San Francisco for a while. We got an apartment, even, and a couch, and a real bed for me. Daniel's sister sent him a sourdough starter. For a while there, our apartment smelled like bread, and I actually thought we might stay put for once. But in the summer of 1969, when I was six, my mother and Daniel made a plan to drive across country to attend a music festival, Woodstock. Her idea, probably, but Daniel went along with it.

They packed the car—that summer, it was a silver Renault—with everything we owned in the world, which wasn't much: a few tie-dye shirts and blue jeans and my ever-present pencil set, my giraffe, a patchwork quilt my grandmother had made for us and my mother's prize boots, with roses tooled along the sides, Daniel's books from nursing school. Tucked into the trunk was a crate containing Diana's precious collection of vinyl records. When we were someplace hot like Arizona she worried they might melt. One time she bought a cooler and put some ice in it to keep the records safe. The thought had not come to me at the time—only later—that Diana took better care of her records than she did of me.

8

Mostly we camped out, though not in national parks because they cost too much. A week before the festival was due to start, our car began making noises like the ones in the Woody Guthrie song, so we never made it to Woodstock. We ended up at a festival in some little town near the Canadian border where a man Diana started dancing with who was on an LSD trip gave her the keys to his VW Bug, which was orange. We left the concert and drove away in it before he came down from his trip enough to change his mind.

Three days later, possibly in response to Diana's dancing with the Hare Krishna man, my mother and Daniel had one of their fights at a rest stop in New Jersey—the last one, as it turned out. I have only a dim memory of the next part. Diana and I sat in the front seat of the Bug while Daniel stuffed his clothes into his duffel bag, along with some albums that my mother said she wouldn't want any more, because they'd remind her of him (Burl Ives was one of these. Woody Guthrie, another) and the sourdough starter that he kept in a jar. That piece of wood he'd been working on was the last item Daniel placed in the bag.

"You're a great little kid," he told me, just before he headed out of the rest stop parking lot. We passed him a few minutes later, standing by the side of the highway with his thumb out. He looked like he was crying, but my mother said it was probably just allergies. I felt like crying too. Of all the people I knew during those years, Daniel was the only one who seemed dependable.

Gassing up the car somewhere in New York—not filling the tank all the way—Diana struck up a conversation with a man named Charlie who was a member of a group he called the Weather Underground. That name stuck with me, because the idea had seemed confusing— how could there be weather underground? It seemed to me it would pretty much always stay the same.

Charlie invited us to move in with him and a group of his friends on the Upper East Side at a house on East Eighty-Fourth Street belonging to the parents of one of them. Next thing you knew we were crossing a bridge into New York City.

The house was brick, with a pot of geraniums on the front step that nobody had watered in a while from the looks of things. Inside, Charlie and his friends played a lot of records whose jacket covers I studied, since I didn't have any books—Jefferson Airplane, Led Zeppelin, Cream. My mother still had most of our albums in the crate of course, but nobody ever wanted to hear those. Songs like "Silver Dagger" and "Wildwood Flower" seemed out of place at Charlie's friend's parents' house.

I knew, even then, that Joan Baez and my grandmother wouldn't have liked this place or approved of the way things were going there. The music Charlie and his friends favored was different—loud, with a lot of yelling going on and guitars that sounded like people crying. We ate a lot of peanut butter and Cocoa Puffs and sometimes we had ice cream for dinner, which might have seemed really great but wasn't. A girl who came over one time, Charlie's friend's stepdaughter, a couple of years older than me, had a Barbie doll that she kept in a special case. I'd known enough about my mother's opinions not to ask for a Barbie, myself, but I loved it that the girl let me dress her up in all the outfits.

On that last trip across country, Daniel had read me a chapter of *Charlotte's Web* every night in the motel room or the tent or wherever we'd ended up. He must've taken the book with him when he left, and we had three more chapters to go, so I never knew what happened in the end to Fern and Wilbur and Charlotte, and I worried about them. I was confused why my mother's friends all hated pigs. If Wilbur was a typical example, pigs seemed pretty great.

I didn't understand a lot of what Charlie and his friends were talking about, except the Vietnam War was a big part of it—not that I knew what this war was, or where. I knew they were building something in the basement that required a whole lot of nails. One time I went down there to see, and everyone got mad, especially Charlie, who called me a brat.

After that my mother decided it wasn't a good idea for me to be sticking around in the Upper East Side house, so she brought me to my grandmother's apartment in Queens. "Charlie's not my type of person," she said. "I'm getting out of there." She was just going back for her records, she'd come for me in a few days. We'd find a cozy little house someplace in the country and plant a garden. She was going to find someone who could teach me how to play my ukulele (odds were good, this would be a man). She had this plan of cutting an album. Some guy who met Buffy Sainte-Marie one time had given her his card.

2

No evidence of survivors

My grandmother was making grilled cheese sandwiches with the news on in the background when we heard about the explosion. The newscaster kept talking about this place called the Weather Underground house on East Eighty-Fourth. "Total destruction," the newscaster said. Two people on the street outside the building had been killed when the house blew up. One of them was an off-duty policeman, father of three daughters and a ten-year-old son.

There was nothing left of the building, after, but they showed a picture of how it looked before, and I recognized the steps out front and the red door. "No evidence of survivors," the newscaster added.

Some reporter out on the street, standing in the wreckage, was interviewing a bystander. "Bunch of murderers," she was saying. "Good riddance to bad rubbish."

After she turned off the news my grandma put me to bed, but I could hear her through the wall between the living room where I slept and her bedroom. That was the only time I ever heard Grammy cry.

They didn't release the names of the people who got blown up in that house making the bomb until the next day, but by that time we knew. My grandmother didn't tell me that part, but I heard the report on someone's radio, and when I did all I could think about was Cocoa Puffs shooting out all over the place. I pictured that record album cover of the Beatles with the bloody baby dolls on their laps, and another album cover by King Crimson that used to give me nightmares, even before the explosion: of a man's face up so close you could see into his nostrils, with his eyes open very wide like he was screaming. I pictured pieces of black vinyl scattered all over the street in front of the house and Diana's boots with the roses hand-tooled on the sides that she took with her every time we moved, even times we hardly took anything else. (My glass animal collection, for instance. I'd left them all at the house that exploded. In my head, I imagined my animals, one by one, flying through the air and out into the street. *Horse. Monkey. Mouse. Unicorn.* I'd taken such good care of them up till then.)

The truth was, there was nothing left for anybody to recognize, though one TV reporter mentioned the police found a piece of somebody's fingertip. When she heard that Grammy turned off the set.

"How did the fingertip come off the person's hand?" I asked my grandmother. "After they found it, what did they do with it?"

In one of the news reports they broadcast in the days that followed the explosion, a picture of my mother from her high school yearbook came on the screen. She was a lot prettier in real life than in the picture they showed on TV. A reporter stuck a microphone in front of a woman who turned out to be the wife of the dead policeman.

"I hope she burns in hell with the rest of them," the woman said.

It was around this time that we changed our names to Renata and Irene.

After that I stayed with my grandmother—first in Poughkeepsie, then North Carolina, then Florida, then Poughkeepsie again, then back to Florida. I'd never actually met my father, Ray, but a year or so after our first move or possibly our second, my grandmother tracked him down. In case he hadn't heard the news about my mother, she thought he should know. She made him promise not to tell anyone our new names or where we were.

Ray was living on an island in British Columbia with his wife, who had recently given birth to twins. He told my grandmother I was welcome to visit sometime if we were ever in the area.

"I'll always remember sitting in the park that summer, singing all those crazy old songs," he'd written. "Say what you will about Diana, but she had a beautiful voice."

Sometime around third grade Daniel showed up at our apartment in Florida. He must have passed the test that made him a higher level of nurse because he drove a regular-looking car. He was working at a hospital in Sarasota. Ray had broken his promise about keeping our secret, evidently.

"Your mother was the love of my life," Daniel told me. He started to cry. I think the idea was that he'd come to comfort me, but I ended up comforting him. "I don't think she ever meant to hurt anyone," he said. "She probably didn't get what the rest of them were up to. All she really cared about was singing."

What about me, I wanted to ask him.

"Diana probably wouldn't approve of this, but I brought you a doll," he said. It was a Barbie, and of course he was right. My mother never would have let me get a Barbie, not even the Black one.

My grandma and I walked Daniel out to the street to say goodbye. He opened his trunk. I could tell from the way he lifted the box out that whatever it contained was something very precious to him, not easy to part with. It was a stack of vinyl record albums—the ones my mother had let him take that day we left him at the rest stop—Woody Guthrie, Burl Ives, the first Joan Baez album, badly scratched. I still knew the words to all the songs: "Mary Hamilton." "House of the Rising Sun." "Wildwood Flower." All those old songs we used to sing in the car together.

"I was the first person that ever met you," Daniel said as he got into the driver's seat. "I cut the cord." It took me a minute to understand what he was talking about. He'd been the nurse in the delivery room with her that day. The job had fallen to him.

"I would have loved to be your father," he told me.

"That probably would have been good," I said.

With the exception of Daniel—and Ray, my father, who my grandmother had sworn to secrecy, same as me—nobody from our old life tracked us down after the explosion. But Grammy lived in fear of being discovered. As the years passed, I could never understand why it seemed like such a big deal to her, but a week never went by that she didn't remind me of my promise that I'd never tell anyone what had happened or who we were before.

"This is our secret," she said. "We take it to the grave." This made me think about being dead, which made me think about the long black veil song, which still made me shiver.

Take it to the grave. What did those words mean to a ten-year-old? It was the mantra of my childhood. *No one must ever know who you are. You have to promise me. You'll take it to the grave.*

I had nightmares about what would happen if anyone found out who we were.

My grandmother took many jobs over those years. Not having a Social Security card was a problem. She had to know somebody personally to get hired, or do something like babysitting where they didn't ask.

I was eighteen years old, newly graduated from high school, when my grandmother received the diagnosis. Stage four lung cancer. Those Marlboros caught up with her.

I spent that summer taking care of her. The last week, when she was in hospice, she made me promise, again, to keep the secret of my mother.

"I've never told a soul, Grammy," I said. "But even if I did, it wouldn't matter anymore." By now I understood much more about what had happened, and about what it was that Charlie and the rest of them were doing in the basement of that Upper East Side townhouse that day. Sometime around my sixteenth birthday I'd gotten curious and spent a day at the library researching the Weather Underground. I had probably never wanted to know, before, how it was that my mother died, but once I read the stories I couldn't get the pictures out of my brain. Shattered glass all over the street. That one fingertip. A woman's.

"Just promise," Grammy said. "Never tell. It could make for trouble in ways you don't understand."

She was on a lot of medication by this time, so none of the rest made much sense, but she started muttering about the FBI then, and some new kinds of tests they could perform now to track people down based on nothing more than your saliva on a coffee cup or a strand of hair from your brush.

"If anyone ever asks you about Diana Landers," she whispered, "you never heard of her."

3

A man from the sunny side of the street

It didn't take that long clearing out my grandmother's apartment, she had so little. She'd wanted to be cremated, with her ashes spread—at her request—at the foot of the Unisphere from the 1964 World's Fair that she brought me to when I was a baby. Her life savings, after I paid the last of her bills, came to a little over eighteen hundred dollars. My legacy. I used the money to get a studio apartment and a turntable to play my records.

You have to live a whole different kind of way when you're keeping a secret, particularly if it's as big a secret as how your mother died, and that the name people call you isn't the one you were born with.

For a person carrying a secret, it's easier if you don't get close to anybody, and for a long time I didn't. For all my years in high school and into my art school days, I never had a boyfriend, or a close girl-friend either. Apart from when I was at art classes and my waitress job at a diner in the Mission, I kept to myself.

I was always drawing. I tacked a picture of Tim Buckley on my wall, partly because he was so handsome, but also because he died young, and tragically, like my mother. I played "Once I Was" so many times I had to replace the album. Any time I wanted to get myself into a particularly dramatic mood, all I had to do was put on that song.

Then I met Lenny, a man without the slightest air of tragedy around him. If I had only one sentence to describe Lenny, it would be this one: *He walked on the sunny side of the street.* Meaning, he was the last person I'd ever picture myself falling in love with, the last person who'd ever fall in love with me. Only we did.

Shortly after I graduated from art school, I'd been chosen to participate in a show in San Francisco at a little cooperative gallery in the Mission. The artists took turns working there, setting out plates of saltines that we'd squirt with cheese from a can when someone walked in to take a look, which didn't happen all that often.

Most of the other artwork in the show was abstract or conceptual. One guy's art piece was a slab of meat lying in the middle of the room. By day 2 there were flies circling it, and by day 4, the smell of rotting flesh filled the whole gallery. "I think you need to take this away," I told him when he came by to do his stint handing out the saltines. No problem, he said. He'd brought a fresh piece of meat. A cheaper cut.

My work hung in the corner. Unlike virtually every other artist displaying their art in the gallery at the time, I made highly realistic drawings in pencil, inspired by nature. This had been an interest of mine since I was very small, dating further back than when I moved in with my grandmother, though it was probably after the disappearance of my mother that making pictures became my obsession. When I took out my pencils and got to work, the rest of the world went away.

I'd had phases over the years when I spent my days in the woods— or, when I couldn't get to the woods, in the park—sketching mushrooms and fungus or lifting a rotting log to study the teeming community of insects revealed underneath and drawing them. The spring my grandmother died, I'd taken off for the Sierra for a couple of weeks, where I hiked and slept in my old tent and filled my sketchbook with images of the wildflowers I found there. It had been that sketchbook that earned me my scholarship to art school.

At the time of the gallery show, I was mostly drawing birds. The pictures displayed on the wall that day featured a species of parrot known as conures, who'd taken up residence in the city.

The story went that sometime in the mid-1980s, two or three rare and beautiful conures had escaped from an exotic bird pet store in southern California, eventually making their way north to San

Francisco, where they had mated with surprising success. Soon a flock of brightly colored birds could be seen perched on trees all over Telegraph Hill.

In a city whose bird population was largely made up of pigeons, sparrows and jays, the red and blue and yellow plumage of the parrots of Telegraph Hill was impossible to miss. From the window of my little studio on Vallejo Street I could stand with my cup of coffee, taking in the sight of them as they swooped over the Filbert steps toward Coit Tower. The photographs I took of these exotic birds that I tacked on the wall over my drawing table—so unexpected in the gray mist of the Bay Area—became the basis for the series of drawings I was exhibiting at the gallery the day Lenny walked in.

He looked around my age—a man of average height and build. There was nothing particularly outstanding about his appearance, except that he had the kindest eyes and looked like a person who was comfortable in his skin. This probably stood out because I could not have said the same of myself. He was wearing a San Francisco Giants jacket so beat up that most people would have thought it was time to throw the thing away, which made me understand he was either totally broke or extremely sentimental about his team. Both were true, but Lenny loved the Giants almost as much as, ultimately, he loved me.

He walked right past the other pieces in the show—the sculpture of a giant eyeball with the words "BIG BROTHER" written across the pupil, a painting of a young man holding a gun against his head that I knew (as others would not) bore a strong resemblance to the artist who'd made it, who'd been in my figure drawing class and suffered from depression. When the time came for the artist responsible for the gun painting to put in his time greeting visitors at the gallery and pass out crackers, he'd said this was impossible. He couldn't get out of bed.

You knew, the moment you met Lenny, he had an extremely positive outlook on life. He ignored the rotting skirt steak on the floor. He made a beeline for my drawings of the Telegraph Hill conures.

"These are great," he said, standing in front of a drawing of a pair of conures perched on a branch. He had a saltine in his mouth, and two more in his hands, and he was smiling. Later I learned that he'd come into the gallery with the hope of free food. What ended up happening had been a surprising bonus.

"I made those," I told him.

"My family had a parrot when I was a kid," he said. "Jake. I taught him how to say 'Beam me up, Scotty' and 'Go ahead, make my day.'"

That was Lenny for you. He was a man who formed his attachments—to a song, or a picture, or a place—based on happy associations from what had been, up until now, a singularly happy life. Not only did he have a parrot, growing up, but he had two sisters who adored him (one older, one younger) and a dog—also uncles, aunts, cousins, friends from summer camp with whom he still got together regularly, and two parents still married to each other and still in love. He'd had a bar mitzvah where his family had carried him around the room on a chair, singing. He was on a bowling team and actually owned his own bowling shoes and a shirt with his name stitched on the pocket. He was in his first year of teaching in a pretty rough part of the city, coaching T-ball on weekends. To a person like me, he might as well have come from Mars.

"I really admire artists," he told me. "I can't even draw a straight line."

"You probably have all kinds of other talents," I said. "Things I'd be terrible at." It wasn't the wittiest line, but for me, even saying this much to a man—not a wildly handsome one, but nice looking, around my age—was highly unusual. After I said the words I worried they might come across as sexually suggestive, which he later agreed they had.

"How are you at throwing a baseball?" he asked me.

"Guess."

"I'll take you to a game," he said. Just like that.

"Where?"

"You aren't going to tell me you've never been to Candlestick Park?"

"I won't tell you, then."

After that we were together all the time. At the game—my first professional sports event ever—he took time explaining box scores and what an RBI was and a forced error. Somewhere in a late inning, when one of the Giants made a hit that sailed high over the head of the pitcher, I'd turned to him and said something along the lines of "Great!"

"We call that a pop fly," he told me. "It's not a good thing." He said this kindly. Then kissed me on the mouth. It was a great kiss. That night, back at my apartment (mine, because Lenny had a roommate) we made love for the first time. For me, the first time ever.

I was twenty-two years old, six months out of art school. I had a part-time job as a medical illustrator, which meant there were always pencils laid out in rows, by color family, on the kitchen table of my apartment on Vallejo Street and pictures of the major medical organs and drawings of the reproductive, circulatory, lymphatic, digestive, and skeletal systems tacked to the wall. Some years earlier, while I was still in art school, I had tacked up, next to my medical diagrams, a postcard of a painting I loved, by Chagall—a man and a woman, in a small apartment somewhere in Russia, with a cake on the table and a bowl of what appeared to be berries, and a row of neat, identical houses visible out the window, a chair with an embroidered pillow, a single backless stool.

The painting is all about the lovers who occupy this room. The woman wears a modest black dress with a ruffled collar, with black high-heeled shoes on her impossibly tiny feet, and she's holding a bouquet. The man and woman are kissing, and their feet don't touch the ground. Nothing touches but their lips, in fact, though to accomplish this requires an act of astonishing gymnastics on the part of the man. To make this kiss possible, he has twisted his head a full 180 degrees, as—as my anatomical charts reminded me—the head of no human ever could. Never mind the flying part. Only love could allow two people to take flight this way.

There's something incredibly tender and innocent about the two figures in the painting, but at the same time, it's erotic. All they need, to lift themselves off the ground, is the touch of their lover's lips against their own.

The day after our baseball date, Lenny brought me a postcard identical to the one I'd kept on my wall. He'd slipped it under my door with a note that said: *I think I'm in love.*

When he picked me up for dinner that night—bearing roses—he looked like the guy on my grandmother's favorite show, *Jeopardy!*, when he won the all-time jackpot. If any mortal humans could have taken flight that day, it would have been the two of us. I might not have said, yet, that I loved this man, but I knew I would soon enough. We were like those two people in that painting, Lenny and me. It was as if we'd invented love.

He taught second grade at Cesar Chavez Elementary School. He loved his students. Every night over dinner he told me stories about what happened that day in class, which student had a hard day, the one who finally figured out subtraction. I came to know all their names.

He was, from the beginning, a romantic man. In that brief period before he moved in with me—also after he did—he never showed up at my door without flowers or a chocolate bar or some goofy present like a yo-yo. He copied poems out of books and read them out loud to me. He loved songs like "I Think I Love You" and "Feelings" and "You Light Up My Life," because they expressed so perfectly how he felt about me. If a song he loved came on the radio when we were driving, he'd turn up the volume and sing along. One time he brought over an album of the Kinks. There was this song he had to play for me that reminded him of us. "Waterloo Sunset."

For me the best moments with Lenny—the ones I'd think about, after—were never these. What got to me were the most ordinary things that Lenny took for granted—a time I got a cold, when he ran out and bought me cough medicine, the time he came home with a pair of shoelaces for me—not roses, shoelaces—because he'd noticed mine were so frayed it was hard getting the ends through the holes in my sneakers. It never got that chilly in San Francisco, but on rainy days he warmed up the car for me and, one time, knowing I'd be borrowing his Subaru to drive over the bridge for a dentist appointment, he checked the tire pressure the day before. Then there was the time, on a weekend getaway to Calistoga, when he'd sat beside me for two hours on the edge of a hotel pool, trying to help me get over my fear of the water. "I'll never leave you," he said. Possibly the one thing he told me, ever, that wasn't true.

Later, when we were trying to have a baby (a decision we made about a week after we'd met), he made a chart that he put on the refrigerator, tracking my temperature every morning so we'd know when I was ovulating, with a box next to every day to check off that I'd taken my folic acid.

We hardly ever argued about anything, though it hadn't gone over well when, as a joke, I mentioned that since I'd been born in Queens, I should probably be a Yankees fan. "We'll work on that," he told me.

Virtually our only point of tension lay in my reluctance to meet Lenny's family.

Because he was Jewish, Christmas was not an issue, but there were all these other holidays. Thanksgiving, Lenny's birthday, his mother's birthday, his grandmother's, his aunt's, his Uncle Miltie's. He wasn't observant, but he fasted on Yom Kippur in honor of his grandfather, who'd died a few years before we met. As was true of just about every one of Lenny's many relatives, he'd loved this grandfather deeply and carried wonderful memories of going to the ballpark with him as a kid.

Partly I loved hearing Lenny's stories of his happy childhood, his happy life. But sometimes, too, the stories of life on the sunny side of the street—Lenny's side—seemed to separate me from this man I loved. It was as if the two of us spoke different languages, and except for the part about being crazy about each other he would always seem to me like a kind of foreign traveler paying a visit from his country of origin, same as I must to him. As much as we shared, there was this gulf between us. His experience of the world gave him a sense of hopefulness and security, where I could easily spot trouble and anticipate loss before it even happened.

Lenny's parents lived in El Cerrito, just over the bridge from the city. The first year we were together, he'd assumed I'd go there with him for his family's Passover seder. I made an excuse—something about an assignment for my painting class—but he knew better.

"I have a hard time being around families," I told him.

He had asked about my family, of course. I'd told him only the basics—that I never knew my father and my mother had died when I was very young, that my grandmother raised me, and that after her death four years earlier, there had been nobody else.

Being Lenny, he wanted to hear more—how my mother died, how it had been for me. "We should visit her grave," he said. He wanted to know the date of her death so when that date rolled round we could light a candle for her.

I couldn't tell him there was no grave. How do you bury a fingertip?

"I don't want to talk about it," I told him. "It's better that way." He was my family now, all that I needed.

Then along came one other person. Our son.

Arlo was born just over a year after Lenny and I got together. The World Series was on that night—a matchup of the Mets against the Red Sox, leaving Lenny no choice but to root for Boston. But that night he was thinking of nothing but our baby, and of me. Not even the Mets' rally from a two-run deficit in the tenth inning to win the game and, ultimately, the championship, could distract Lenny from his place at my side for every minute of the twenty-three hours it took for Arlo to enter the world. "Can you believe it?" he said, when the nurse put our son in my arms. "We made a baby."

I'm a dad. Over and over, those words.

I used to say he was the best dad ever, also the best husband. He brought me coffee in bed and came home with odd, funny presents for no particular reason: a fountain pen, a pair of socks in Giants colors, a rhinestone tiara. He took Arlo to the Y every Saturday for parent-child swim classes—the only father in a pool-full of mothers holding their babies, while I sat on the edge, the memory of the time my mother's boyfriend Indigo threw me in that motel pool having left me with a terror of the water. When Arlo cried in the night, it was always Lenny who jumped out of bed first to bring him to me, and Lenny who bathed and changed him whenever possible. Until then, he had loved his teaching job, but now he hated going off to work. "I don't want to miss anything," he said.

The part about Lenny's family—his parents in particular—was a sore point. By this time I'd agreed to occasional visits with Rose and Ed, but nothing like what they would have hoped for with their first grandchild, or what Lenny would have wanted for them.

Not surprisingly, considering their son's outlook on life, Rose and Ed were wonderful people. All my life I'd wished I was part of a big, loving family but now that I'd been welcomed into one, I felt like a misfit. When we got together with Lenny's family everyone talked nonstop, and loudly—interrupted each other, offered many opinions, expressed emotions freely. There was always a lot of laughter.

I said little during these visits, but so much else would be going on it didn't matter. I sat on the couch feeding Arlo and accepting the offerings of food that seemed never to stop. Sometimes I brought a drawing pad along and made sketches of everyone. "Our family Michelangelo," my mother-in-law called me. (*"Our family,"* she said. In Rose's eyes, if not my own, I was part of this happy circle.) She and my father-in-law had framed every drawing I'd ever made at their house. They hung alongside the photographs of all the relatives—me, included. My photograph had never hung on anybody's wall before.

"So when are you two having another one?" Rose asked me, the day we celebrated Arlo's first birthday. I wasn't accustomed to questions like that. I'd learned, young, to keep my cards close to the chest.

On the drive home from El Cerrito that day, Lenny was quieter than usual.

"Don't mind my mom," he said. "That's just her way. She loves you so much. "

"I didn't know what to say," I told him.

"I know it's hard for you," he said. "Maybe one day you'll be able to tell me why."

I couldn't. I'd made a promise to my grandmother.

We got married a few weeks after Arlo's first birthday, on the top of Mount Tamalpais, at a funky old hiking lodge called the West Point Inn, with no electricity. There was a big old piano in the main room of the lodge where Lenny's sister Rachel played for us—show tunes, American Songbook, the Beatles—accompanied by an assortment of family members with bongo drums and a tambourine and Lenny's Uncle Miltie on accordion. Lenny's mother and sisters baked for days in preparation. They hauled everything including Arlo's high chair up the mountain along the fire road. Arlo had just started walking at this point. He ran around in circles, beaming.

In the weeks leading up to the wedding, Lenny had kept returning to the question of who there might be from my side of the family who should be invited to the event. To Lenny, the idea that a person he considered as lovable as me would have nobody in her life who'd want to be present when she spoke her vows had been inconceivable.

At art school, I'd maintained casual friendships with my fellow students, but nothing of any seriousness. Though I couldn't explain this to my future husband, it was that old curse of secret-keeping—my inability to say who I really was—that made it impossible to get close to anyone, other than Lenny.

"What about uncles, aunts, second cousins?" he asked me. "There has to be someone."

In a weak moment, I'd mentioned that the last I heard—meaning, almost twenty years before—my biological father lived on a very small island in British Columbia. That was enough for Lenny.

"I never even met him," I reminded Lenny. "All I know is he's called Ray and he's the father of twins."

This was enough for my future husband. He tracked Ray down. I was in the room when he made the call.

"You don't know me," Lenny said. "But I'm in love with your daughter. We're getting married next month in Marin County California. It would mean the world to us if you came to the wedding."

Years before this, the US government had announced a policy of amnesty for Vietnam war draft resisters who'd fled to Canada. No danger existed for Ray of getting apprehended at the border if he came south for the ceremony. But it was clear from the half of the conversation I took in—Lenny's half—that my biological father was about as interested in attending my wedding as he would have been in participating in a tax audit.

My future husband's voice with the man he spoke of as his future father-in-law remained friendly, with no hint of accusation or any attempt to inspire guilt.

"I know it's a long trip, man," Lenny was saying. (One hand on the receiver, the other around my shoulders.) "I'd be happy to pay for the flight. My folks would put you up. It would mean a lot to Irene."

Years before, Ray had been informed of my name change from my grandmother. Not that he'd spent any time calling me by my original name anyway.

"I hear you," Lenny was saying, his voice very quiet now. I knew how hard he was trying to keep anger at bay. "I understand. Maybe you'll think it over."

Then, finally, his last words before the conversation ended. "You've got a beautiful daughter, Ray. If you ever met her, you'd love her."

From what I gathered from the look on Lenny's face, the line went dead at that point.

4

One way to find your family

For the first time in my life, probably, I was happy. But there was always the secret—the fear my grandmother had bequeathed to me, with her Hummel figurines and her Betty Crocker cookbook, that someday someone would find out whose daughter I was and come after me.

That winter, curled up on the couch watching television after getting Arlo to bed, a segment came on one of those magazine shows about new technologies that were helping to solve crimes. The episode followed a case in England involving two teenage girls who'd been raped and murdered. A boy in their village had been charged with the crime but exonerated through the use of DNA testing. The same kind of testing had ultimately identified the real killer, when police in the area set up voluntary testing sites to collect blood samples of every man living in the area. Only one had refused the testing, but it had come out that another local man, reluctant to undergo the testing, had persuaded his friend to submit a blood sample under his name. When the police finally obtained a sample, his DNA had matched that of the rapist. The program Lenny and I watched that night followed the story of the man's conviction and sentence to life in prison.

Lenny loved science, and he loved detective shows. That night, lying in bed, he was still talking about that story. As a person for whom family meant so much, he was excited by the idea that maybe, through DNA testing, I might find relatives I didn't know I had— someone besides my birth father, Ray, who'd taken no interest in knowing me.

"Even when they're a little annoying," he said, "it means so much to me, having my parents and my sisters, and my Uncle Miltie and all the rest of them. I wish you had that sense of connection."

"I've got you and Arlo," I told him.

My husband wasn't ready to let it go.

"This DNA stuff is amazing," he insisted. "I can't believe how they can take one strand of a person's hair or some piece of evidence locked up in a lab for thirty years and solve a case with it."

Like a fingertip, I thought, though I didn't say this. Not that I really believed it would tell me anything I didn't already know about what happened to my mother almost twenty years before. That story was finished. I didn't want to think about it anymore.

Then something happened that made me go there. My drawing teacher from art school, Marcy, called me up. "This will sound nuts," she said. "But I got a call from some kind of detective, asking about you. He was talking about some terrorist activities in New York City where a policeman got killed. Nothing he said made any sense. The date he mentioned when this event took place, whatever it was, you would have been a little kid. I told him he must have the wrong person.

"He didn't even have your name right," Marcy said. "He kept referring to you as Joan."

I could feel sweat on my palms, holding the receiver. In the eighteen years since the explosion, I'd kept my promise to my grandmother to never speak to anyone about what happened, or my connection to it. Only two people ever learned where we had been: my biological father, Ray, and Daniel.

Daniel would never tell. Ray was another story.

"Did this detective say anything to you about where he got this supposed information about me?" I asked my teacher. This had to be the FBI, of course. They were looking for me.

"The whole thing was crazy," she said. "He told me something about a trip he'd made to British Columbia. Some Vietnam War draft resister."

"They must have me confused with someone else," I told my friend.

For a few days after that I kept waiting for a federal agent to show up at our door, but no one ever did. Still, I knew it was time to tell Lenny the truth.

I was getting ready to do that. But it was October, and the Giants had made it to the World Series, against the Oakland A's. Lenny was on cloud nine. I told myself nothing should interfere with his rapture. I'd tell him the truth I'd been hiding all this time once the games were over.

5

Orange and black balloon

Giants versus A's. My husband's dream. In honor of Arlo's third birthday, Lenny's sisters had gotten together to buy us tickets for Game 3. The plan was for Ed and Rose to take care of Arlo while Lenny and I were at the stadium.

The day before the game—with Oakland leading the series—Lenny made a decision.

"My dad's been a Giants fan even longer than me," he said. "Seeing this game at Candlestick would mean the world to him. Let's give my folks our tickets. I don't really want to watch the game without Arlo anyway."

So we stayed home, which was fine with me. We'd watch in our apartment on TV. I didn't need to be with fifty thousand people. Two was enough, so long as it was those two.

A half hour before the game was due to start, Lenny decided we should have peanuts, like at the ballpark. The three of us ran down the street to pick them up, along with a six-pack of beer. "Go Giants," the woman behind the counter, Marie, had said to Lenny as she handed him the change. Everyone in our neighborhood knew my husband and knew how he felt about the team.

At the store, Arlo had spotted a helium balloon. Giants colors, orange and black. Marie had given it to him.

The next eight minutes have played over in my head a thousand times, like that film footage of the *Hindenburg* exploding, the bomb cloud over Hiroshima, the Kennedy assassination.

Arlo wanted to hold the balloon but Lenny said that wasn't a good idea. "You don't want to lose your balloon, buddy," he said. "Let's wrap the string around your wrist to keep it from getting away."

Arlo asked for a peanut. "Let's wait till we get home," I said. He spotted a piece of shiny paper on the sidewalk from the inside of a cigarette package and picked it up. A woman walked by with her dog. Arlo wanted to pet him.

Lenny was talking about the game, of course. The A's had won the first two games in the series, but Don Robinson was pitching that day. My husband had high hopes our team would make a comeback.

"You need to remember what happened in '86," he said, though I didn't. "The Mets were down two games and they ended up taking the championship."

We were halfway down the block, Lenny trying (but gently) to get Arlo to go faster so we'd make it back in time for the start of the game. I bent down to pick him up but he shook his head. "No, Mama." Our son wanted to walk on his own.

He hopped along between the two of us, Lenny and me each holding one of his hands, the balloon over our heads like a thought bubble in a cartoon. Arlo was singing a song I'd taught him from my old Burl Ives record, "Little White Duck." He had a sweet high voice and even then knew how to carry the tune, which made me think—though I never said this to Lenny—that he must take after my mother. In that one way at least.

"Little white duck, sitting in the water.

Little white duck, doing what he oughter . . ."

"I can just picture my parents at the ballpark right about now," Lenny said. "My dad's probably wearing those awful orange pants Mom gave him for his birthday."

"It was really something that you gave your folks those tickets," I observed.

"It was really something my sisters got them," Lenny said.

33

That was a family for you. His family anyway.

They were mine too, in Lenny's eyes anyway. At just that moment I remember thinking how perfect everything was. I had married this wonderful man and we had this beautiful child bouncing down the sidewalk between us, heading home to watch a ball game—a round orange balloon hovering over our heads as if the sun itself were shining down on the three of us.

We had just reached the curb half a block from our apartment when the string wrapped around my son's wrist came loose. Before either of us could catch it, Arlo's balloon began to drift away overhead. Just a balloon, but to Arlo at that moment it was the world.

He let out the most piercing cry. "Come back!" To a three-year-old, the idea of a lost helium balloon reversing direction and returning to him would not have seemed impossible.

A gust of wind must have caught the balloon then, and for a moment it seemed we might actually retrieve it. The balloon dipped lower, directly in front of us, but it was moving out over the street. Arlo, seeing this, broke free of our hands. He wanted his balloon back.

The light turned green. A minivan rounded the corner—Giants flags attached on either side, its driver going faster than normal on account of the game about to start, probably. Like us, he wanted to get home. My son must had taken in nothing but the balloon. He raced into the street.

Seeing this, Lenny threw himself in front of the car like a man shot out of a cannon.

I can still hear it: a woman's voice—my own—screaming. My husband diving for our child. The sound of screeching brakes.

Then Lenny was on the ground. Both of them were.

There was wailing in all directions—the only one making no sound, our son, lying motionless on the street. Lenny lay next to our boy, blood leaking out of him.

"I'm so sorry," he said. "I couldn't—" Then nothing more.

I can still see my husband lying there. His face bore an expression I had seen once before, in a photograph: a citizen of Pompeii, frozen in time and petrified in his moment of greatest horror—mouth open, eyes wide, as the dust of Vesuvius rained down on them, as if it were the end of the world.

6

The earth opens up

Later, I learned an earthquake hit the city of San Francisco that day. Loma Prieta, they called it: 6.9 on the Richter scale. A part of the Bay Bridge collapsed, also a stretch of road known as the Cypress Freeway. Sixty-three people were killed. Game Three of the World Series was canceled—rescheduled ten days later.

I never watched another baseball game, but at some point I heard the Oakland A's took the championship that year. This would have devastated Lenny if he'd lived to learn the news. None of that mattered to me anymore. In the space of an instant everything I had loved in the world floated away—the two people on the planet who had my heart.

I might have found solace with Lenny's parents then, as families do in such times. I might have made my way over to El Cerrito to sit in the living room with Rose and Ed and Lenny's sisters. They called me many times, and his sister Miriam showed up at my door, but I had nothing for them anymore, and though I wished it were otherwise, they had nothing for me. I knew of course that the family would sit shiva for my husband and our son. People would bring food. Given the opportunity, Rose would have put her arms around me, and we could have wept together on that familiar couch. But I knew nothing of how it worked, being part of a family like theirs. My two big losses until then—my mother, then my grandmother—I had suffered alone, without words of comfort or embrace. All I knew of death was to keep it secret. Soldier on.

No doubt I offended those good people, Ed and Rose—also Lenny's sisters, Rachel and Miriam—by my failure to appear at their home in those terrible days. The Bay Area was still reeling from the earthquake, of course, but there was more to my absence than the difficulty of making my way across the bay to the home of my in-laws. What difference did it make in the face of loss vast as theirs, whether or not a minor character like me showed up at their door? The earth had opened up that day and swallowed everything that mattered. If I could have, I would have been swallowed up too. The worst thing was being left behind.

Six months after the accident—springtime now, a whole new year—I made a decision. It came to me one afternoon in our little apartment on Vallejo Street that had become unbearable to me. I was looking out the window as I had so often, at the conures perched on a nearby branch, one in particular. It seemed to me that that he was looking me directly in the eye, and as he did so, that he was telling me something. *Fly away. Go.*

I could spend the rest of my days looking out the window. Or I could be like the rare exotic bird and escape. Like the woman on my Chagall postcard, I might let my feet lift off the ground and my body take flight. No longer for the promise of a kiss. Just the promise of release from the relentlessness of my grief.

I packed up my pencils. I emptied the contents of my desk drawers in a trash bag, then filled a second with my underwear, on the theory that there are certain items no stranger should have to sort through or dispose of, and a drawerful of old underpants and bras qualified as such.

My vinyl record albums had meant a lot to me. Now I placed them in a crate that I carried out to the curb. By the time I was back in my apartment, I could already see, out the window, a kid on the sidewalk below, flipping through them. Wait till he got to *The Freewheelin' Bob Dylan*, the original Beatles cover for *Yesterday and Today* with the bloody baby dolls. Would he be smart enough to recognize the Woody Guthrie record for the treasure it was? Doubtful.

I took down the drawings I'd tacked up, crumpled them in another bag, along with Lenny's postcards. The refrigerator was empty already, except for a bag of carrots and a half-eaten tin of tuna. Those, too, I carried out to the curb. As I set them down, I felt a surprising calm.

Hardest to throw away were Arlo's toys—his blanket, his Hot Wheels collection, my old carnival giraffe from the Daniel days that my son had slept with. Then Lenny's baseball cards. His glove. The baseball signed by Willie Mays. I set these on the sidewalk alongside the rest.

I made one last trip upstairs to turn out the lights. I figured I should have some form of identification on me, for later, so I stuck my passport into my pocket. I set my keys on the table. Pulled the door shut.

Within a couple of hours of when the conure and I had met each other's gaze, I was out on the sidewalk hailing a cab. It was just after sunset when I reached the Golden Gate Bridge. I looked down. If I climbed over the railing now, everything could be over in less than a minute.

I thought about who there might be to register dismay over this news. There'd be some brief mention in the *Chronicle*, possibly—and maybe, if someone on the news desk were on the ball, they might even link the event to the tragic death of a young father and his three-year-old son last October in an accident on Vallejo Street the day of the Loma Prieta earthquake.

Besides Lenny's family, who were consumed by their own grief, it was hard to think of anyone whose day would be ruined by the news. As suicides went, mine would leave less in the way of heartbroken survivors than most. I had not yet reached my twenty-seventh birthday, but I believed my life was over.

I could still picture the first night Lenny took me to a ball game—sitting on the bus that would bring us to the ballpark, Coit Tower glittering on the horizon, and beyond it, the water, sailboats dotting the bay, the air perfectly clear.

From someone's radio on the seat behind us, a song came on that Lenny and I both liked. It was Dolly Parton singing "I Will Always Love You." If we hadn't been in a public place at the time, Lenny would have belted out the words along with Dolly.

"This is our song," he told me.

"What about the part about 'bittersweet memories'?" I asked him. "What about the place where she says 'I know I'm not what you need'?"

"When I sing it at our wedding I'll skip over that," he said. "I'll come up with some more appropriate lyrics." This was Lenny for you, a man so determinedly hopeful that he had failed to understand a heart-break lyric when he heard one.

"But that's the whole point of the song," I told him. "The idea that there's this woman who loves this man so much, but she knows she can't be with him anymore."

"That's just crazy," he said. "Who ever heard of two people that much in love who can't work things out. You can always work things out."

That was Lenny for you. The perpetual optimist. Not just when the Giants were down six to nothing in the eighth inning, and he still told me they were going to come back and win it. But in life as well as base-ball. Whatever the problem was—not that he'd ever faced one as terri-ble as this—he held the conviction that you could make things better, and though I had no such faith myself, it suddenly seemed not simply wrong, but disloyal to my darling husband and our precious son to throw away my life because they'd lost theirs.

I stepped away from the railing.

I didn't go back to our apartment. That chapter was finished. I didn't know where I was going. I just walked: To the foot of the bridge, and beyond, up Lombard Street, and beyond that, along the marina to

North Beach, past the Italian restaurants where couples (I used to be part of one of these) sat on the sidewalk over a plate of pasta, and the City Lights bookstore, where a sign announced the reading of some poet from the sixties, and across Broadway to the flashing lights of the strip shows, and through Chinatown, where old women pushed carts full of vegetables and laundry hung out the windows and the air smelled of rotting vegetables and fish. My world as I'd known it. It amazed me, that it all looked the same, even as everything was different now.

"I wandered lonely as a cloud." Words to a poem I'd memorized at school once. As many years as I'd lived in the city, I was lost now, the streets no longer familiar. I passed a woman sleeping in a doorway, covered in a blanket printed with images of Disney princesses, with a dog alongside her, and a shopping cart full of discarded dinner rolls. There was a man in the middle of the street tossing juggling balls in the air and a couple of boys who didn't look older than thirteen, skateboarding on a set of church steps. I could not look at children. Teenagers were hard enough. Also Giants fans.

From inside a bar I passed, I could make out the sound of someone playing an old jazz ballad and a woman's voice calling out over the music, "Hasn't anybody around here ever heard of a happy song?" Lenny used to say words to that effect when I played my old records of sad English ballads. He'd always gravitated to the major key.

Then I was on a smaller street I'd never been before, a steep uphill climb that left me short for breath, probably because a long time had passed since I'd walked as far as this. I was wearing the wrong shoes for walking. All I had intended to do that day was jump.

It was dark, and where I was now there were fewer people out on the street and surprisingly few cars. But up ahead my eye was caught by the sight of a beat-up looking bus with a bunch of people—some young, some not so much—lined up alongside preparing to get on, from the looks of things. Someone—the driver, maybe, though he wore no uniform, only a tie-dye shirt and jeans held up with suspenders—was loading an assortment of backpacks and duffel bags into the luggage compartment.

I stood watching as the motley assortment of passengers boarded the bus. It was painted green and decorated to look like a turtle.

"You joining us?" the driver said. He had a striped hat on, like something out of Dr. Seuss, and Converse sneakers, and when he opened his mouth to smile it appeared that a number of major teeth were missing.

At that moment the thought of getting on a bus driven by a stoned-looking man in a tie-dye shirt seemed as good an idea as anything else, as close as I could come to disappearing.

"Remind me where we're going?" I asked him.

"You got a head start on the weed, huh?" He grinned.

"Arizona. Texas. Mexico," a woman told me. She had a child holding on to the fringe on her macramé purse who looked around five years old—reason enough not to board the bus—and from the looks of things she was pregnant.

"Someplace warm is all I care about," said the pregnant woman.

"You should come," the driver motioned to the doorway. The last passenger was just getting on. The doors closing.

"I don't have a ticket," I said. Or money. Or a change of clothes even.

"It's all cool," he said. "You look like someone that could use a vacation."

His name was Gary. The other driver, Roman, was taking a nap in the luggage rack, preparing for the night shift.

I stepped on board.

7

Riding the Green Tortoise

Inside the bus there were no seats. The floor was covered with mat-tresses, and the luggage storage racks had been turned into bunks. By the time I stepped on board these were occupied. The only open spot on one of the mattresses was one next to the pregnant woman—the last place I wanted to be. She had laid out a blanket for herself and her daughter, whose name turned out to be Everest. The little girl was already curled up with a stuffed pig and a bottle of juice. On one side of us, a man picked out a Bob Marley song on a guitar and on the other, a man with a long orange beard was reading *Siddhartha* with a flash-light. Bumpy as it was navigating the road in a vehicle that appeared to have little in the way of shock absorbers, I couldn't have imagined reading on a bus like this without getting sick, and as it turned out I was right. We were not yet out of San Francisco when he reached into his backpack and took out a plastic sack.

"My trusty barf bag," he said. "I never go on one of these trips with-out it."

So much of my early childhood had been spent like this—in the back of some old vehicle or other, staring out the window for hours at a time in a cloud of smoke with a never-ending soundtrack from a scratchy radio. Over those years with Diana and Daniel (Indigo, Julio, Ocean, Charlie . . .) I'd gotten good at endless hours on the road, and in the days and then months since the accident I'd reclaimed the skill of turning my brain to a blank, letting the hours wash over me. This served me well on the green bus. Out the windows—not that we could see much, with all those sleeping figures in the luggage racks—cars whizzed past on the highway. I took in the names on the exit signs. Now and then the lights of some city, but fewer and fewer of those the farther south we went.

Some people on a long trip like this might be looking forward to their arrival at some destination. But I was headed nowhere in particular. When there's no place you want to be you're in no rush to get off the bus.

A night passed. My fellow passengers paid little heed to any discernible rhythms—when the sun came up, when it went down. There was always someone playing a guitar or a harmonica, always someone sleeping, someone smoking, someone holding forth about astrology or hydroponic marijuana cultivation or the hidden messages you divined by playing Pink Floyd backwards. *The Wall.*

There was no bathroom on the bus. Just as well, considering how difficult it would have been, making one's way over the bodies on the mattresses to get there—so Gary or Roman, whoever was on duty at the time, pulled over every few hours. Sometimes we stopped at a gas station but when possible, at some scenic location, where those of us who chose would step outside, execute a few sun salutations, snap a picture, buy a snack, visit the restrooms, and get back on the bus. Early on, my fellow travelers appeared to recognize that I had no interest in conversation. They referred to me as "the Thinker," but I was the opposite. I didn't want to think about anything.

The fact that I had no money proved less of a problem than one might think. There was always someone willing to share a bag of chips or half a banana or a handful of nuts. I wasn't that hungry.

One night, asleep on my section of mattress, I felt something warm on my leg. A hand. Then another hand on my belly. Warm breath in my ear. Then a tongue.

Turning around, I was face-to-face with Artie, one of the half dozen guitar players. "Hey babe," he said. "Feeling romantic?"

In another circumstance, I might have had a lot to say about how totally unromantic it was for a man to start pawing a woman in the middle of the night on a crowded bus with no air conditioning, somewhere in the Arizona desert. I might have reported him to the bus driver, Gary, if the other bus driver, Roman, weren't doing roughly the same thing with a different woman.

As it was, I just looked at him. I imagined I was a conure, bearing down on him with my beady eye. That was enough.

We passed through Tucson. Then a very long stretch of highway with nothing but cactus and dirt on all sides, and the occasional burnt-out vehicle, and one time, a falling-down roadside stand with a sign out front that said FRESH BEEF JERKY. If there had been anyone with whom I felt like sharing the thought, I might have observed that this struck me as a contradiction in terms, but none of the sleeping or stoned figures around me were likely to get it.

My main companion on the trip turned out to be the person I'd most wanted to avoid—Everest, the five-year-old daughter of the pregnant woman, Charlayne. ("I named her that because I was high when I got knocked up," Charlayne told me. "You might call it an in-joke.") Charlayne slept more than most people on the bus, unlike her daughter, who just about never did. Everest asked a lot of questions. I seemed to be the only person prepared to answer them.

She wanted to know if Gary was the boss of us, or if Roman was. "Nobody's the boss," I told her. Nobody was in charge here, that was for sure.

She wanted to know if there would be kittens in Mexico, or bunnies, her two favorite animals. She wanted to know if there were other kids where we were going. She wanted to know my favorite color. Most girls liked pink, she told me. But hers was yellow.

"I'm getting a baby sister," she said. "My mom's boyfriend wasn't too happy about that. But he's not around anymore."

She wanted to know if I had any kids. I shook my head.

"Don't you like kids?"

"I like you."

"If you had a kid I bet you'd like her a lot," she told me.

"You're probably right."

"So why don't you have a kid?"

No answer.

"Maybe you're scared it might hurt to have a baby," she said. "Maybe you just need more time to think about it."

It hurt, but not the way Everest was talking about.

She seemed so determined to stay on this subject I might have moved to another spot on the bus if that was an option, but there was no other space on the mattress. We were jammed together like sardines in a tin.

"Maybe you'll change your mind someday," Everest said. "You might really like being a mom. You never know."

Only I did. It was something I'd known since the day of the accident. I was never going to be anybody's mother ever again.

8
Bus to nowhere

Somewhere in Arizona the bus started making an odd, grinding sound. First just a little, then louder. Roman, who was driving at the time, pulled onto the shoulder.

"Okay, everybody," he said. "Looks like we're taking a break." He hopped out to inspect the engine. For no discernible reason, Gary set off on foot down the highway.

Roman worked on the engine for a few hours—an oddly familiar sight that brought back memories of that long-ago cross-country trip to Woodstock with my mother. This was the heat of the day. A few of our group found a thin strip of shade under a cactus. Most just lay on the dirt. Everest took off her dress and practiced her skipping. I had to look away at that point. Arlo had longed to skip but couldn't figure out how. "When you're four you will," I used to tell him.

It was late afternoon when Roman got the engine going again. Just at that moment, Gary reappeared. He'd found a casino up the highway and took the opportunity to play the slot machines.

He'd hit the jackpot. Five thousand dollars in quarters, that he'd traded in for bills. Now, as we regained our seats on the mattresses, he made his way down the length of the bus, passing out money.

When he got to me, he bent low, close to my ear.

"Don't let anyone know," he said. "But I wanted you to have a little something extra. I get the feeling you could use it."

Before I could say anything he'd stuffed a wad of bills in my jeans pocket. It was hours later, somewhere near the Mexican border—

Roman at the wheel again, most of the others asleep, Everest's small, warm hand draped across my chest—that I took the money out to look. Our driver had presented me with fifteen hundred-dollar bills.

The only reason I'd taken my passport with me that day I headed out to the bridge was so someone could identify my body, later. But as things turned out, it was a good thing I had it when we reached the border. One of the passengers in our group, Chuck, had forgotten he needed any documents for the trip. We had to leave him at Nuevo Laredo.

Then we were in Casa Grande. Chihuahua. Jiménez. Torreón. Querétaro. Tiacala. The names blended, one into another.

We'd probably been on the bus close to a week when we reached Tapachula. Everyone got out there.

Charlayne had heard about a commune not far away where there were midwives who could help you have your baby. You got to stay in a yurt in exchange for working in the garden. One of the guitar players, Artie, took off hitchhiking. Roman, the night driver, decided he'd had enough of buses and headed into town in search of a motorcycle.

I stood in the dirt with no idea where I'd go and no particular concern, one way or another.

Across the street from where the Green Tortoise let us out there was a taqueria and a bodega, and down the block, another taqueria, and a place called Hotel California advertising rooms by the hour. There was a store selling dresses and a stand with piñatas and quinceañera dresses. I figured I'd keep walking.

I'd probably covered a mile when I reached the airport. You couldn't call it that, exactly. It was more like a bus station, but with a single runway alongside and two propeller planes parked at either end, neither of them even close to new. A sign attached to the roof of the cinder-block building said Aeropuerto. I drifted inside.

There was a flight leaving in ten minutes. Destination unclear. Fine by me.

My Spanish was limited. I laid one of the bills Gary had presented to me on the counter.

The flight to the capital city of San Felipe was a bumpy one. Our plane flew low enough to offer a clear view of the countryside, which was nearly entirely uninhabited from the looks of things, with the exception of the occasional very small village, and a few narrow trails that cut over the mountains. We passed above a volcano at one point, and then another. Then a city came into view. No high-rise buildings here, but for as far as I could make out, small, impermanent-looking structures dotted the mountainside, their roofs made of sheets of wavy plastic lamina, each structure pressed close against another, every one painted some bright color. People might be poor in this place, but that didn't mean they couldn't paint their home orange, or green, or purple. All the more reason.

Then we were coming in lower, low enough that I could distinguish the sight of laundry hanging in the dirt yards of the houses and men tending crops and children gathering sticks and women doing laundry at outdoor sinks and hanging it out on the ground to dry.

If I hadn't been a person who'd planned on killing herself just seven days earlier I might have felt terror at the way the pilot brought us in for the landing, but as it was, I felt a curious detachment. *Maybe this is how it will all end up*, I thought. *If so, fine.* But a minute later we had taxied to a stop and a minute after that I was on the ground in an airport only slightly larger than the one from which we'd taken off, though greeted by a marimba band this time, and a variety of women offering to sell me hats, purses, necklaces, gum.

I made my way through customs—the lone North American in the line—and out to a dusty sidewalk where a beggar with no legs tried to sell me a keychain and a group of young white people in strangely out-of-date suits and bonnets clutched their Bibles, and an old woman in an apron wept at the sight of a man—her son, no doubt—in a cowboy hat and an Oakland Raiders sweatshirt, returned home after what must have been, from the looks of things, a very long absence.

One thing that always used to get to me at airports was the sight of two people reuniting as one of them got off a plane. Many, of course— the majority—just brush lightly up against each other before heading to the baggage carousel, or pat each other on the back and ask what always struck me as the most meaningless question, "How was your flight?"

But every once in a while you see some traveler, spotting the person who's been waiting for the first glimpse of their well-loved person (son, daughter, husband, wife, brother) and the two of them practically keel over, they're so happy. For me at least, it used to be like watching the best movie ever when I'd see one of those reunions, because it was real. For the first twenty-two years of my life when I'd watched family members meeting each other at some airport or bus station I'd done so as a person without a family. Too briefly, I'd known what it was, myself, to have someone in your life (two of them) whose face lit up every time he laid eyes on you. In the case of Lenny and me, from the day we got together we'd never been apart more than a night, but just watching him walk in the door after a day at work (or him, watching me do the same) had been enough to make us throw our arms around each other in the way certain lucky people did at airports. That afternoon, studying the mother and son, was one of those times. The two of them must have held each other for a good three minutes. I probably stood there for just as long myself, watching them.

I had traveled three thousand miles at this point. I hadn't had a shower or slept in a bed in a week. Nobody was there to greet me in this place, and there was nobody in this country who knew my name. It occurred to me, as I stood waving away the offers of cab drivers to take me to a hotel and small boys selling tassel pens, that if I died here no one would know, and if they did, what they would do about it?

A bus pulled up, with a sign on the front that read Jesús es El Señor! For the third time in eight days—and for no better reason than because it was there—I let myself be carried along with no greater sense of volition than a stick floating down a stream or a piece of milkweed drifting in the wind.

I took my seat next to a woman wearing an apron and an embroidered huipil, holding a box of fried chicken. She nodded at me. I gathered she was saving the chicken for later to share with her family at our destination, the place whose name was lit up on the front of the bus, Lago La Paz. Peace Lake.

For the first hour we made our way through the city, where the air was thick with the smell of diesel fuel and every time the bus came to a stoplight, crowds of people reached out their hands toward the windows, with plastic bags of some kind of drink to sell, and pork rinds and Chiclets and slices of fruit. In the time required for a red light to turn green, one man took a large gulp of what must have been kerosene and lit a match in front of his mouth in such a way that flames leapt out. Only one person on the bus gave him a few coins.

We made it outside the city limits, finally, to open land—fields of cabbages and broccoli, onions and potatoes—and beyond that, mountains studded with tiny villages where skinny dogs shambled through discarded plastic and shivering barefoot children lined the roadway with bouquets of calla lilies for sale and ceramic pots. We passed an overturned truck that looked as if it had been there a long time, and many white crosses bearing Spanish names. *Emilio. Santos. Maria.*

At a stop we made for the driver to buy gas, a boy who looked around four years old had set out rows of small handmade sheep made from wrapping wool around twigs. In spite of my plan to steer clear of all children, I knelt to study his wares. All I had were US dollars, so I gave him a hat I'd picked up a few towns back, which was too big for him of course, but he put it on.

Then we were climbing higher into the mountains—our bus careening over switchbacks no North American highway engineer would have deemed safe or acceptable, more children lining the roadway as our driver's plastic Madonna swung wildly from the rearview mirror. Another bus had entered the lane of oncoming traffic—attempting to pass a truckload carrying a dozen or so passengers and a great many carrots—and now loomed dead ahead.

Nobody on the bus but me seemed to take notice. On the radio, a man was singing about his *corazón*. If Arlo had been on this bus, he would be asking if we were there yet and if not, why. We'd have a Wee Sing tape in the cassette player, of songs he loved. He'd have a stack of picture books to occupy him and a bagel on a string around his neck, or a necklace made from Cheerios to snack on—and even so, he'd be restless.

Not one of the babies on this bus made a sound for the duration of the journey. You wouldn't have known they were on the bus at all, except for the bulges their heads made—their bodies wrapped in shawls against their mothers' breasts. This was not a country where children complained.

Four hours later—the chicken in my seatmate's box still untouched, the Madonna dangling from the mirror spinning more wildly than ever—the bus made its way down the steepest portion of road yet. Around one bend, there was a car suspended in some tree branches—the vines so thick they held it suspended over the canyon below—and alongside the car, another group of white crosses. Beyond the floating car I caught sight of a vast expanse of turquoise water. Here was the lake.

We came to a stop at a long wooden dock. The woman with the box of chicken seemed clear I should get off here, so I did.

For the first time in all my days on the road, it occurred to me to ask where I should go. The woman didn't hesitate.

She spoke with surprising firmness. "La Esperanza," she said. The word meant hope.

9

A seven-year-old tour guide

This was Lago La Paz, stretching out as far as I could see in every direction—miles of clear turquoise water, around the edges of which I could make out a dozen small villages. The lake was dotted with no more than a handful of small fishing boats. The shoreline was green.

For some people, landing in a place like this one would probably feel disorienting. Everything looked so unfamiliar. To me, this provided a comfort of sorts. Except for the sight of little boys, or couples walking hand in hand, there was so little here to remind me of where I'd come from.

One aspect of the landscape in particular was utterly unlike anything I'd known before.

Wherever a person might find herself, the volcano dominated—a dark and silent presence, neither ominous nor inviting. The volcano loomed over everything—its sides deeply ridged from a few thousand years of erosion, probably, its peak obscured by a single perfectly shaped cloud.

Whatever else might change—weather, seasons, children growing up, old people dying, or my own particular brand of tragedy that I could not bear to name, this was the constant. For a person like me, who had never known what it was to live in the shadow of a volcano, the sight could take your breath away, but for the people who lived around Lago La Paz, who had never known what it was to live without a volcano looming over them, its presence across the water was as much a part of the fabric of life as rain, trees, corn fields, air.

"El Fuego," a man offered. "*Nuestro volcán.*"

Our volcano. He spoke the words as if everybody had one.

If this had been the United States, or any other so-called first-world country, a lake of this scale would have been lined with high-rise hotels and tourist attractions, with umbrella-dotted beaches and big power-boats and Jet Skis wailing across. But there was none of that. Just sky, water, and volcano.

Together with a half-dozen other travelers—a motley crew of coun-terculture types, a few aging hippies, and a stunned middle-aged couple who looked as though the realization was dawning on them, fast, that they should have booked that trip to Hawaii instead—we made our way to a single open-air passenger boat that was tied up alongside the dock. A man gestured to me to get on.

As was my practice now, I asked no questions, just handed him one of my smaller American bills, recited the name of the town my seatmate had instructed me to go—La Esperanza—and stepped into the boat.

It was late in the day, the sun low over the volcano. A flock of birds swooped over us and a man passed, standing up in his small wooden boat, paddling toward shore. From deep inside the shawl of the woman sitting next to me, I heard the sound of a baby at the breast.

We reached a village where the family with the basket of fish got out, and another family with a basket of eggs got on. Then three more stops—one at a small hotel where the the old hippies disembarked, and then a rickety-looking dock with a shack-like structure in front, where the old American man got off, a smell of sour beer and a week's worth of sweat filling my nostrils as he brushed past.

The *lanchero* had indicated to me that mine would be the final stop. By the time we reached the town of La Esperanza, I was the only pas-senger left. This was the end of the line.

As I stepped onto the dock in the fading light—the sky pink now behind the volcano—a half dozen skinny boys—barefoot, mostly—surrounded me, all vying for the role of my guide. One hung back a little, and for this reason, I chose him.

"I'm looking for a place to stay," I said. As limited as my vocabulary was from a couple of years of high school Spanish, he got the idea.

He looked around in search of a suitcase. I shook my head.

His name was Walter. He said he was seven years old but could have passed for five. His voice, when he spoke—and he had a lot to say, it turned out—had a surprisingly manly air, not only because it was deeper than you'd expect but because of the tone he conveyed of being in charge. He took my hand, not in the way my son would have done, for guidance, reassurance, comfort. More as my husband had, with an air of protectiveness. For a person who had made the vow, recently, to stay away from all children, I was doing a poor job of sticking to my plan.

Walter appeared to know a few words of English, learned from assisting tourists, probably. When he spoke, it was in a combination of languages—more Spanish than English, with lots of hand gestures to fill in the blanks.

"Be careful of him," Walter said, pointing to a man asleep in the yard of a particularly ramshackle house. "He says he takes you on a volcano tour, but he'll steal your money. He's a *borracho*." Based on what I had witnessed, I figured that meant a drunk.

"Good tamales," he said as we passed a food stand I would probably not be patronizing. He eyed them longingly. I bought him one.

Our journey brought us down a stone path—wide enough for no more than two people, if they hadn't eaten a lot in recent years. We dodged a pack of dogs on our way, who looked about as sparsely fed as my new guide, though two of them appeared to be nursing mothers. We passed a child sitting by herself who looked to be three or four. (But who could tell? She might have been six—just small, like everyone else in this place.) No sign of a parent watching over her. She carried an assortment of headbands and tried to sell me one. I bent to offer her a banana.

Walter and I came to what I gathered must be the center of town, based on the presence of a basketball court and a church and a cart from which emanated a smell of fried chicken and rancid oil. A couple of *tuk tuks* sat waiting for passengers but Walter waved them off. Maybe he worried that if we made our journey to my destination any other way but on foot, his fee for the job might be reduced. I followed along on the dirt road behind my young guide, making out most though not all of what he was saying to me.

By now the sun was low on the horizon, disappearing behind the volcano. Not knowing how much farther we had to go, the growing darkness gave me pause. The road was dirt and full of rocks. For a moment the thought came to me that only days before, I'd been planning to end my life, but now the thought of turning my ankle worried me.

"I'm taking you to the most beautiful place in the village," Walter told me.

10
Stone egg

Five minutes later we were standing in front of a large wooden door with a sign over it, hand-carved, bearing the name La Llorona. Mounted on a post by the door, an ancient-looking buzzer.

The gate swung open. A woman stood there. She wasn't unfriendly but didn't smile. She spoke briefly to Walter, handing him a few coins and indicating that his service was now complete.

I had thought I'd ask if she had a room available, and if so what it cost, but no such exchange occurred between us. She looked around for a suitcase but displayed no visible surprise at the absence of one.

"We need to make it down the steps before we lose the light," she told me.

The steps were stone. A hundred of them, at least.

"I'm Leila," she said. She was American, evidently.

"Irene," I told her. For one crazy moment my old name, Joan, had come to me. The one I never spoke.

It was hard to guess Leila's age. Sixty, possibly. But she might also have been seventy-five. She was very thin. Her hair was dead-white and her hands suggested decades of hard work, but her face, though not unlined, had a kind of glow that made me wonder if some magical plant grew in her garden, the secret ingredient to a serum that reversed the aging process.

Leila displayed no difficulty navigating the long descent to the house, though for me it presented a challenge. The path was thick with vegetation—plants known to me, if at all, only from the pages of some book or a visit to a botanical garden.

Having left my San Francisco apartment with no expectation of a future of any kind, I had not brought my drawing pencils with me. Now it surprised me to realize that I missed them. If I could, I would have wanted to draw this wild, fantastical garden.

Everything seemed to grow on a whole other scale in this place. Vines hung down over our heads, and bananas; orchids clung to the trees. At one point we came to a stand of bamboo; at another, a carving—life-sized—of a monkey. At another: an even larger carving, in stone, of a giant egg. It was a surprising choice for the subject of an artwork.

"There's a man in this town, Otto, who makes carvings out of the stone here," she told me. "I've bought a lot of his work for my property over the years. One day he showed up at my house carrying this egg. It has to weigh two hundred pounds, at least. He'd carried it all the way from the village."

"He wanted you to buy it?" I asked.

"He wanted to know if I'd lend him money to take the bus to San Felipe to find someone who might want his creation," she said. "Thirty *garza* for the ride to the city and back. Eight hours of travel, total. So I asked him what he hoped to get for the egg. A hundred *garza*, he said. Roughly ten dollars."

"So you bought it."

Leila had a brisk, matter-of-fact air as she spoke, a striking lack of sentimentality or even softness. "I only did it to save him the long trip," she said.

When we neared the bottom of the long run of steps, the house came into view. The roof anyway; we had not yet fully descended the property, but I could make out an expanse of thatch and the glow of lights through a window, and beyond it, the lake, glittering in the last rays of daylight.

"Maria will have dinner for you," Leila told me. She was speaking of the cook, evidently. "I hope you like dorado." A local fisherman, Pablito, had caught it in the lake that morning. With a harpoon.

57

"Will the other guests be joining us?" I asked her.

"No other guests," Leila said. "It's just you."

We had reached the door to the house now—blue, with birds carved into it and a wooden handle in the shape of a fish.

Leila opened the door.

How can I describe La Llorona, as it looked to me that day—a vision of paradise before me at the darkest time I could ever have imagined?

The hotel was like someplace you'd see in a fairy tale. Wherever I looked my eye landed on some extraordinary detail, no doubt Leila's creation, or that of the workers of the village here: not just stones transformed into monkeys and jaguars and eggs, but vines trained to form arbors dripping with flowers whose blooms resembled the imaginings of somebody's wildest LSD trip and little man-made streams winding through the gardens, tumbling over smooth round stones—some of them green, in certain lights anyway, some almost blue. There was a stone bench built into a hillside, and there was also a chaise lounge that appeared to be fashioned from a single tree trunk. An old wooden fishing boat piled with cushions hung from a tree, with a half dozen different varieties of orchids sprouting from its trunk, and a wooden owl carved from a burl.

There was a grove of fruit trees bearing lemons, pomegranate, papaya, and tall, spear-like ginger plants with brilliant red blooms, and bird of paradise flowers, and bougainvillea, and jasmine plants, and gardenia, and *bella-de-noche*, leaving a perfume in the air so potent you could be blindfolded and know where you must be standing in the garden just from the smell of the blooms in that spot. I had never seen anyplace so beautiful, or one offering greater evidence of love on the part of its creator.

But the property was falling apart. Wherever you looked, alongside the beauty lay evidence of decay. The stone walls were crumbling, the steps we'd descended to get to the house precarious, the railing rotted in a dozen different places. The rose plants were stunted from encroaching weeds, the fish pool dark with algae, and when the wind blew, a stink of rotting fruit rose from the compost pile. A mountain of old wine bottles lay under a lean-to behind the house, and beside them, a pile of broken dishes, tools, chairs missing rungs that someone must have set aside at some point to repair, but never got around to. The paint on the door was flaking off, and the door itself, when Leila pushed it open, made a creaking sound. The lamp mounted alongside it to welcome guests had been fashioned from pieces of colored glass—from old wine bottles and beer bottles, probably, with stones and shells and beads and pieces of broken plates mixed in. It would have made wonderful, rainbow-colored patterns on the doorstep if it worked. But the bulb was burned out, and my best guess was that this had been so for a long time.

"We're a little behind on repairs at the moment," Leila said as she led me into the gallery. "When I was younger I did a better job of keeping up with things."

The ceiling was high, the windows covering most of the wall looking out to the lake—but in need of cleaning, like everything else—and from the center of the room, a giant wagon wheel had been suspended, lit with a dozen small lights, filaments glowing, like something from Thomas Edison's day. Some functioning, most not.

Along the back wall, facing the view, there was a couch made from a single massive tree trunk, hollowed out—hard to imagine how they'd got it in the door—with cushions piled over it of a fabric that appeared to have been woven by hand a long time ago. It reminded me of the embroidered pillow in the Chagall postcard I'd tacked up on my wall back in San Francisco. The rugs were handwoven too—covered in images of birds again, and jungle animals, with bare spots where the floor showed through.

There was a long slab of a table whose legs were formed out of thick, twisted vines—piles of books in every direction, a fire glowing in a

fireplace built into the far wall. (As warm as the day had been, the evening air offered a certain chill.) On every wall were paintings—of
women and calla lilies and birds. One very large canvas that seemed to
depict every conceivable variety of disaster. When I moved closer to
study it, I could make out, in one corner, a group of characters partially
submerged in roiling waters from what appeared to be a flood; else-
where, an erupting volcano with glowing lava pouring down over a
huddle of desperate villagers wearing the kinds of embroidered indigenous clothing I'd seen that afternoon on the boat ride across the lake.
Another corner of the canvas featured what appeared to be an earthquake—the ground giving way, women and children falling into a
bottomless crevasse, and a swarm of bees, a pack of rabid-looking
dogs, a *tuk tuk* crash, a church steeple toppling in a deluge, a drowning
fisherman ejected from his boat, a horse galloping off the edge of a
cliff, his rider in free-fall.

I could have studied the painting a long time, but Leila was gesturing me to move on down a long corridor lined with doors, each one
carved with a different Mayan symbol.

Mine was the last door at the end of the hall.

"You'll stay here," she told me. I placed my hand on the knob—not
a doorknob at all, but a carved jaguar made of some very smooth, dark
wood that must have known many hands before mine. Touching it, the
memory came to me of Daniel, whittling outside our tent.

It wasn't easy opening this door. There was a weight to the wood. It
creaked as it opened, as if a long time might have passed since the last
occasion anyone ventured past this point.

Inside was a small bed covered in a woven white cloth. Like everything else in the place, these showed the signs of wear. There were
places in the bedspread where I could see the blanket beneath it.

Here, too, a fire had been lit in the fireplace. (How did my host
know I was coming?) A row of candles burned on the mantel. The
nearly overpowering smell of some flower I'd never encountered hung

in the air, that made me want to breathe deep and turn away, both at the same time. A large curtainless window stood open to the outdoors, so I could hear the sound of the lake water. It lapped against the stone foundation of a long, broad patio, covered by a vine-festooned lattice from which hung a wall of brilliant, jade-colored blossoms—thick as a curtain, nearly fluorescent in the darkness that enveloped us now.

"You probably want to change your clothes before dinner," Leila said. Maybe she figured out from my lack of luggage that this would pose a problem. "Wait just a minute," she told me, disappearing down the dark hallway.

When she returned there was a dress draped over her arm, full length, in the shade of blue I favored back when I cared about those kinds of things, with a matching shawl.

"I'll see you at dinner," she said and disappeared down the long hallway.

I slipped off my jeans and T-shirt, took my hair out of its clip, and stood in front of the mirror. *Memorize this,* I told myself. *Before this is over—but who knew what "over" would look like?—you may not be the same person you were anymore.*

This was not bad news.

I turned on the shower then and stood under the water for a long time, washing off the dirt.

11

The only thing that lasts is the volcano

An hour later—dinnertime now—we met up again by candlelight on Leila's patio. A blue ceramic platter sat in the center of a tablecloth strewn with rose petals.

"Our friend Pablito brought our dinner in from the lake this morning," Leila said. "Fish caught with a harpoon tastes nothing like the kind they harvest with a net. A fish caught in a net takes his time dying, and the flesh goes tough. A fish stabbed in the heart dies instantly. That's why it melts in your mouth this way."

Leila introduced me to her workers—Luis, the chief overseer for the property, and his wife, Maria, the chef. Off in the garden, she pointed out a young man—no more than sixteen from the looks of him—scrubbing a reflecting pool. This was Elmer, the couple's son. "Elmer's been working for us since he was eight years old," Leila said. "He's the closest thing I have to a grandson."

"And this"—she gestured in the direction of the young woman setting a platter of steaming vegetables before us—"is Mirabel."

About the same age as Elmer from the looks of her, she had a heart-shaped face and the shiniest black hair, tied into a thick braid—large dark eyes, beautiful dark skin, the bearing of a queen. In her embroidered huipil, a belt around her waist, her long skirt wrapped around her body, she had that kind of beauty that seemed to glow from within. She had disappeared into the kitchen briefly. Now she was back with a platter of fish that she placed on a white linen cloth in the center of the long table.

Buen provecho, Leila said. *Salud. Dinero. Amor.* Health. Money. Love. I lifted my fork to my lips. It was the first meal I'd had in over a week that hadn't been eaten on a moving bus while inhaling the fumes of diesel fuel.

The flesh fell off the bone, as moist as if it had been lifted out of the lake that morning, which it had been. Leila reached for a crystal decanter. "Most of the wine here comes from Chile," she said. "But this one's from France.

"So, what brought you to La Esperanza?" she asked.

"It was a spur-of-the-moment decision," I told her. I left out the green bus, the propeller plane that happened to be taking off just when I'd found myself at that narrow, dirt-covered landing strip. I said nothing of San Francisco. The bridge. My husband. My son.

"I don't advertise La Llorona," she said. "The people who are meant to come here find their way."

Maybe I worried that she'd ask me questions about myself. I steered the conversation swiftly in another direction.

"You must meet some interesting people. Being . . . off the beaten path this way."

A look came over Leila's face, as if she were remembering some of them—a few decades' worth of visitors, a few hundred stories.

I asked her, had she always run the hotel on her own? I didn't ask, had she been married. But I wondered, of course. This was a lot of property to care for, even with the team she'd introduced to me. A lot for a woman on her own.

"Men came and went," she said, as if she'd read my mind. "The only thing that lasts is the volcano. And even the volcano—" She stopped herself.

It began that night, the telling of her story. I didn't understand this, but there was a kind of urgency in Leila to impart to me—a stranger who'd shown up unannounced, not two hours earlier—the story of her life.

There had been a Mayan scholar a few years back, she told me. His journey to the lake represented the culmination of a few decades of study of ancient shamanic practice and Mayan ceremonies.

"Benjamin was brilliant, romantic, mysterious. I knew from the beginning that he was haunted by his old losses. He came to the lake, as many do, to address his own demons. No doubt I had a few of my own."

Why was she telling me this story? Did mine reveal itself on my face?

"He climbed the volcano with Luis and Elmer one day," she said, taking a sip of her wine. "Then he asked them to leave. It feels like the top of the world up there. He wanted to be alone."

"We heard nothing more of Benjamin for a long time. Then one day—six months after his disappearance—a guest who'd made the volcano hike told me she'd spotted him up there, praying. Nobody ever laid eyes on him again, but people think he jumped into the crater. Life on earth was too much for him. Perhaps you understand."

Better than she knew. Or maybe she did.

"The volcano's active?" I asked.

"Oh yes. Sometimes at night we see it glowing, and sometimes smoke pours out. But there hasn't been an eruption in a few hundred years.

"It will happen one day, of course," she said. "But I like to think that living this way, in the shadow of an active volcano, serves as a daily reminder of the preciousness of my days. One day I'll be gone. We all will. Why worry about that? In the meantime, let's make sure the fish is cooked just right, and that the wine is French."

12

I remember food

In the weeks, then months, since the accident, my sleep had been over-taken by nightmares. I'd replay the moment the minivan tore around the corner, when my son broke free of my grasp. Sometimes pictures of things that never happened came to me, but in the night they seemed as real as those that did. Lenny came to me one night. "I have to go away," he said. "I can't live here with you anymore."

I'm going away to leave you, love. I'm going away for a while. The words came back to me from the song my mother used to sing to me, nights in the campground.

In my dream, Arlo was on a little boat, alone in the ocean, calling out to come get him, but the undertow kept pulling me back to shore. I'd hear his voice. *Mama, I need you.*

I'll save you, I called back. Only I couldn't.

That night at La Llorona I slept undisturbed for the first time in six months. I was up with the sun. Partly it was the light streaming in through the glass that woke me, but more so it was the birds. In among the vines and branches, the palm fronds and cascading strands of blossoms in colors I couldn't even summon names for—and the bird of paradise flowers, and the ginger plants—a whole chorus of birds began singing the moment the first glimmer of morning light appeared behind the volcano. Lying in my bed looking out at the patch of sky framed by the window—the volcano perfectly centered there—I could make out the songs of at least six differ-ent varieties of birds, some seeming to answer each other, with one bird calling out from his branch to a different bird, perched on another tree, who answered back with a song of his own.

I could hear the water too, and a lancha boat passing by, bringing workers to their jobs and tourists to the hotels. From the kitchen, I could make out voices, though not the words they were speaking. The sky was pink, then red, then orange.

The day I lost my family the world went from color to black and white. My skin went numb. I seemed to lose my sense of taste and smell. Now here in this otherworldly place, a strange and wonderful scent filled the air, coming from the blossom of a flower I didn't recognize in the vase next to my bed. Then came another smell drifting up from the terrace. Freshly ground coffee. A bell rang, announcing that breakfast was served.

The idea of actually wanting a meal, as I did now, came as a surprise, like a rekindled memory from a time long ago though only a few months had passed since my own personal earthquake. *Oh yes. Food. Now I remember.*

Leila had left a robe on the hanger but I put on another dress she'd left for me—this one green—and made my way to the patio where the table was set. A plate of freshly cut fruits—some I knew, many I didn't, one in the shape of a star—was laid out on a woven cloth alongside a ceramic pot of good strong coffee.

There was a basket with a cloth inside, folded over a stack of blue corn tortillas, still warm, on a hand-painted ceramic dish. Local cheese, and black beans and fried platanos, a glass of orange juice, fresh-squeezed. Maria had waited until my arrival at the table to cook the eggs. Now I heard them sizzling on the pan.

Taking my seat at the table that first morning, I looked around for my hostess but Leila was nowhere in sight. Somewhere on the property someone was running a garden hose, this being the dry season. Out on the lake, a handful of fishermen sat in their small wooden boats, nearly motionless except for the rare moment when one of them reached into the water and pulled something out. A fish no doubt. A crab, maybe.

Mirabel explained that Leila always had breakfast in her room. She never emerged until midmorning.

A hummingbird appeared, hovering by the trumpet-shaped blossom of another flower I didn't recognize, whose blossoms were twice the size of my hand, looking like something out of a Georgia O'Keeffe painting. Deep red on the outside, pink deeper in. Layers of petal folded in on each other.

I ate like a person starved for a very long time. I felt guilty loving this meal as much as I did, but there was never a more delicious plate of scrambled eggs—their yolks a color of gold I'd never seen—or sweeter orange juice, richer coffee. I could have slathered the butter and jocote jam on my fingers and licked them clean. How could a woman who'd lost her husband and child consume a meal with so much pleasure?

After, I explored Leila's gardens. It would take days, maybe weeks, to discover all the secret places she'd built—the little altars and reflecting pools, mosaics and ceramic animals set into the stonework, vines trained into the shapes of hearts or crescent moons, weird, twisted cacti that seemed almost like a strange new species of man rising up from behind a terraced wall.

I was standing in front of one such spot, taking it all in, when I heard a voice behind me. Leila's.

"When I got this place there was nothing here but weeds and underbrush," she said. "Every plant you see, we brought to this land and planted here."

In the old days, Lenny and I used to visit the Japanese Garden in Golden Gate Park, and once, on my birthday, he'd taken me to the San Francisco Flower Show. But those places offered nothing like this. The wildness, the lushness, the way the plants practically exploded over each other.

"Your garden is an artwork," I told her.

"For a long time I never went anyplace without a pair of scissors in my bag," she said. "I'd see a plant by the side of the road that we didn't have here, and I'd stop and take a cutting to bring home. Everything grows so easily here, all you have to do is stick a branch or a twig in good soil and water it."

Except for the orchids. Those you had to dig up. They grew in the mountains.

"I had this lover once," she said. "Pascal, a botanist from Belgium. The two of us would disappear for a week at a time and come home with a sack full of plants nobody ever saw before."

I might have asked what happened to Pascal, but it seemed obvious enough he was long gone. "Gardens last longer than most love affairs," she said. "It's safer to bet on orchids than men."

I asked if she still went up the mountain searching for plants. She shook her head.

"I have this little problem now," she said. "There's some kind of nasty blood clot lurking in my arteries, nobody can figure out where. Sort of like a mugger, hiding in the shadows. You never know when he might jump out and get you. Meanwhile, strenuous exercise is not recommended."

I was dimly familiar with the syndrome Leila described, from my days of making medical illustrations. I figured she was probably talking about a condition known as AVM—arteriovenous malformation. I'd created a series of drawings about it for a textbook. I still remembered the pair of images—one of a set of normal arteries, the other a tangled-up clump that made the circulation of blood difficult and sometimes impossible. I remembered something about seizures and strokes as a possible consequence. Or death.

"It doesn't matter that much," Leila said. "I had my time on the mountain."

I stretched out in a hammock. I had no plans—no need to engage in the usual tourist adventures or look for trinkets in the market to bring home. I had no home, and no desire for anything except what I could never get back. Lying there staring at the sky and the volcano, I must have fallen asleep.

I woke a few hours later to Leila's voice. She was standing over me, holding a trowel and a bucket of what turned out to be grout. She'd spent the morning laying tile in front of the sauna, she told me. She held one out to me, a circle of fishes in bright blue glaze.

"You can come with me to the market if you like," she said. "We're almost out of avocados, and today's the day one of my favorite fishermen comes from the coast with *camarones*."

"I'll put on my shoes," I told her.

13
Shrimp as big as your hand

It was a ten-minute walk along the dirt road to the market, where a gathering of local people displayed that day's offerings: gorgeous young eggplants and peppers, baskets overflowing with tomatoes, chard, potatoes freshly dug, bouquets of spices.

I followed Leila in silence. I had many questions but saved them.

A man approached me with a blanket to sell. I made the mistake of stopping to examine it for no particular reason. "I'll make you a good deal," he told me. He followed me down the path, calling out, offering ever lower prices.

Another man, younger—strikingly handsome but something about him was unsettling—said something to me in English about Mayan astrology. A reading. My energy. My future. My soul.

"Keep moving," Leila told me. "That's Andres. You don't want to have anything to do with him."

There were dogs of course. And babies wherever you looked. For some reason, here in this place the sight of children—even small boys, whom I'd taken particular care to avoid—didn't make my chest constrict as it had back home. I was in a whole other world where none of the usual rules applied, including the timetable for grief, if there was such a thing.

This wasn't the kind of destination Americans with money and two weeks of vacation time—middle-class Americans expecting margaritas and Jimmy Buffett songs—were likely to choose. Passing one taco joint frequented by an assortment of hippie travelers, I made out the strains of a Bob Marley song, but mostly the foreigners here favored their own drums and guitars or the vague, rhythmless pulsing of ecstatic dance music, as they floated down the path with their feather earrings and studded noses and puppies they'd adopted the day before (and would abandon three weeks later, Leila told me), skipping and hugging each other and passing out slices of watermelon.

We found the *camarone* man. I had never seen shrimp this big, brought early that morning from the coast in an ancient pickup with tires so bald they could have rolled over soft mud without making an imprint. *Camarones* big as your hand.

We ate them on the patio that night, as always, with a row of votive candles featuring images of the Virgin of Guadalupe laid out in the center of the cloth and good crystal glasses. As always, Leila took her seat at the head of the table, wearing a blouse of handwoven fabric covered with the most intricate and fanciful embroidered birds. Her long white hair was piled on her head and held with a mother-of-pearl comb. She looked me in the eye in a way that reminded me of that conure outside my window back on Telegraph Hill.

"So what happened?" she said, filling my wineglass. "What brought you to my door?"

I studied the face of my hostess—deeply lined, once beautiful. Her eyes suggested a woman who had seen more than the usual measure of pain as well as joy. There was enough of a moon that night that you could make out the tiny gemstones on the necklace circling her long, elegant neck. Her silver bangles—some heavy, some very thin—made a sound like a windchime. Her wrists looked impossibly thin.

"Nobody who comes here does so without a story," she added. "It's seldom an easy one."

"I can't get into it," I told her.

A look of surprising kindness came over her. "You don't have to say anything," she said. "It's not important what took place before. It's what you do now that matters."

The past was important, though. The past was all I had. "Some kinds of trouble never leave you," I said.

A bomb in a basement, for instance. My mother blown into a hundred pieces (one of them a fingertip). Nails shooting out in every direction, pieces of shattered glass and metal flying out over East Eighty-Fourth Street, one of them lodging in the brain of an off-duty policeman.

An orange balloon that slips from a child's hand. A minivan with a San Francisco Giants flag attached to the side mirror. A bag of peanuts scattered on the road.

"You probably wonder what brought me here," Leila said. I think this was an act of kindness on her part, shifting the conversation as she did. She tossed the head of a particularly large shrimp across the table, into the lake, lifting the body to her lips as she did. Sucking the moist, garlic-buttered flesh.

"I have my story too, of course," she told me.

14

How to make macarons

Leila was born in Nebraska. "Where I come from, it's so flat you can drive a hundred miles straight without ever turning right or left or going uphill," she told me. We were sitting on deep cushioned chairs on her patio as we talked, the sun about to disappear behind the volcano in a way that had turned the sky the most brilliant shade of orange.

She grew up in a town called Assumption. Her father raised seed corn, strictly a small-time operation. When they had a good season, the money he made on one year's crop got them through to the next. When they didn't, they took out a loan. Her mother worked at the post office. They had a two-bedroom house. She shared a room with her older sister. Her grandmother slept on a cot they'd set up in the living room, with a screen for privacy.

"Grandma had this straw hat with silk flowers that her unmarried aunt had given her for a high school graduation trip to the state capitol in Lincoln," Leila said. "She kept it on her bureau in the corner of the living room, with a Degas painting of a ballerina nailed to the wall above it. To me, those two things—the hat and the ballerina picture—represented the opposite of everything about our life on the farm. I wanted a life like that, where I could wear a hat with a flower and see a ballet." Not that she would end up achieving either of these goals, but the part about getting out of Nebraska had been what mattered.

That was the main thing.

She had an uncle, Timmy, a soldier. These were World War II days, France. Timmy was Leila's favorite, a lanky guy who taught her Morse code and did magic tricks and cut out comics from the newspaper that he sent her from the base to color in.

While he was on leave in Paris he met a young woman named Noemi. Never mind that the only words of French Uncle Timmy knew were "*Comment alle*ɀ-*vous*" and Noemi's English was about on par. They fell in love, or thought they did anyway, and by the time Timmy's eight-day leave was over, they'd gotten married. He was twenty-one years old. She was eighteen.

Uncle Timmy had sent a picture home of himself in his Army uniform, Noemi next to him in a polka dot dress and a red patent leather belt around her tiny waist. Timmy stood straight, facing the camera with a look on his face as if he still couldn't believe he'd convinced this goddess to marry him. Noemi had struck a pose like a movie star. They were standing on the banks of a river with a bridge across it.

"I took one look at that picture," Leila said. "And I wanted to be Noemi on that bridge. I wanted to have a polka dot dress and live in Paris."

The army had sent Uncle Timmy to England on a top-secret training mission, in preparation for what would become the D-Day invasion. Timmy was one of a platoon of soldiers chosen to participate in Exercise Tiger, a weeklong training set to take place in the town of Slapton Sands in Devon, a place chosen for its physical similarities to Normandy beach, the ultimate destination for the invasion scheduled to take place a few weeks later.

Though the Allied troops had arrived under cover of darkness, a group of nine German U-boats had spotted them. Another boat—this one with the Royal Navy—recognized the enemy presence and sent a warning to the commanding officer of the Allied troops, but the warning had been scrambled as the result of a typographical error. The soldiers of Exercise Tiger never knew they'd been spotted. When the Germans attacked, the Allies were caught totally off guard. Seven hundred and forty-nine soldiers died that night. Uncle Timmy was one of these.

When the call came to the small Nebraska farmhouse where Leila and her family lived, delivering the news, his sister—Leila's mother—had been so overcome she didn't get out of bed for two months. Leila's grandmother, Timmy's mother, had taken over running the house-hold, cooking for the family and helping Leila's father out, milking their eight cows. Leila's sister Roxanne occupied herself with school-work. Leila spent her days in the library reading everything she could about Paris. *Escape.*

One day a young woman showed up at the door, having ridden to town on a bus all the way from the train station in Chicago and before that, a plane from France. It was Noemi, Uncle Timmy's bride and widow. She was carrying a single suitcase and wearing the polka dot dress from the wedding picture. She told them she was four months pregnant.

Although she had lived her entire life in a small village outside of Paris, Noemi had no family to speak of, no one to take her in, and no money besides the United States Army widow's benefit that had pro-vided just enough for her to buy a plane ticket to America.

In the package of his belongings sent to her following Timmy's death there was a collection of letters from home written by Leila's mother and grandmother, and Leila herself. From these, Noemi had learned the family's address in Nebraska—a place as unknown to her as the moon. For all she knew when she'd boarded the plane that day at Orly Airport, she might have been heading to a great American city like New York, or maybe Hollywood. She had definitely not been bar-gaining on ending up in a place like Assumption, Nebraska, with its population of nine hundred and twenty-four citizens. Not one of whom spoke French.

The family took her in. It was the least they could do to honor Timmy. The girls—Leila and her older sister, Roxanne—already shared the living room, with Grandma on the other side of the screen, but now they added a cot for Noemi. Leila's father found a book of helpful phrases in French and, to cheer up the young widow, Leila drew a picture of the Eiffel Tower and another of the Arc de Triomphe, based on her library research, that she tacked on the wall above the mantel alongside the reproduction of the Degas painting cut out of a magazine. Still staying in bed mostly, her mother reminded them all of the importance of good nutrition for a pregnant woman, so they'd stocked up on Spam.

Roxanne wasn't even remotely enthusiastic about the addition to their family of their new French aunt and the baby on the way. Beyond her one suggestion concerning nutrition, Leila's mother was too depressed to do much about Noemi's presence, and her grandmother and father were just too busy all the time. But Leila had befriended Noemi.

Every day, the two of them sat at the kitchen table for English classes. (English and French. The lessons went both ways.) Leila taught Noemi the names of the states and the presidents and certain key facts of Nebraska history—in particular, that the land now incorporated into the state had once belonged to France, until it became part of the Louisiana Purchase. Not only that: Nebraska was where Kool-Aid had first been invented, in the town of Hastings, in the year 1927.

"*Qu'est ce que c'est, Kool-Aid ?*" Noemi had asked her.

A drink.

"*Comme du vin?*"

No.

"Noemi was always looking to expand her horizons," Leila told me. "She took every class they offered in the adult education program at the high school—how to fold napkins in fancy shapes. How to make a cover for your toilet paper rolls that looked like a Southern belle in a hoop skirt."

Because Noemi spoke so little English, and for plenty of other reasons as well, Leila was her only friend in Assumption. The two of them spent a lot of time together. Noemi was sad about Timmy of course, though not as sad as Leila's mother believed she should be. Though she'd adored her uncle, Leila forgave Noemi for not doing a better job of acting like a heartbroken widow. At the point Timmy left for England, she had only known him for eight days. Leila did make the suggestion, to Noemi, that it would probably be a good idea not to tape a picture of Jimmy Stewart in the bathroom, that she'd cut out of a magazine. As basic as Leila's French skills were at this point, Noemi understood and took it down.

Noemi had loved Uncle Timmy, but she was also nineteen years old, with a zest for life. In addition to teaching Leila the lyrics of Édith Piaf songs, she decoupaged the cabinets and made a bunch of Southern belle toilet paper covers to sell at the church bazaar—the proceeds from which had gone to her occasional purchase of the only item at the A&P in Assumption that seemed remotely French: a brand of cheese that vaguely reminded her of Camembert. Evenings at their house, she rolled up the braided rug in the living room, and for as long as she could fit into it she put on her polka dot dress from the wedding picture and taught Leila how to dance like a girl in the Folies Bergère.

When Noemi turned up at the family's Nebraska farmhouse she had been sixteen weeks along in her pregnancy (the dates easy to calculate, given the number of days she and Timmy actually spent together).

As the weeks passed and her body changed, it became clear that Noemi needed some new clothes. Leila's father volunteered to give her a pair of overalls, but Noemi was Parisian after all. Poor or not, overalls weren't her idea of suitable attire, even for a trip to the drugstore in downtown Assumption.

In the end, Leila bought some fabric and a pattern, and the two of them had made three shift dresses, roomy enough to get Noemi through her pregnancy. (No woman should have fewer than three dresses in her closet, Leila told me. This was the very number of dresses with which she had provided me, after my arrival at La Llorona.)

A couple of months into her stay with the family, Leila's father had sat them all down. The topic was their finances. It had been one of their worst growing seasons ever, and having one more mouth to feed (two, soon enough) was a big problem.

"I wouldn't expect you to get a fulltime job," he told Noemi—with Leila, who spoke only the most rudimentary French, serving as translator. "But Evelyn and I" (he was referring to Leila's mother) "were thinking it would be good if you could, I don't know . . . pitch in a little. Contribute a few dollars to the grocery fund."

"Pitch in?" Noemi asked. She looked at Leila here. Leila had recently introduced her to the sport of baseball. Now she was confused.

"Maybe you have some particular talent," Leila's father said. "Something that could earn a little cash."

She did, in fact. All this time, she had never mentioned it but now was the moment. Noemi made macarons.

"Beg pardon?" Leila's grandmother said. "Macaroons? Mackerel?"

"Macarons."

"Je pourrais les vendre," she said.

That afternoon, Leila and Noemi set off for the grocery store. For a project meant to generate income, the ingredients proved pricey, but the two of them promised Leila's father that once Noemi got into macaron production, they'd be raking in the cash. These macarons would sell like hotcakes.

The next day was a Saturday. No school for Leila. Though generally Noemi slept late (one of the many aspects of Noemi that wore on the family's nerves), she got up early to get going, laying out the ingredients. Butter, flour, cream, food coloring, confectioners' sugar, eggs.

Noemi's mother had been famous for her macarons, evidently. Though Noemi had been only nine years old when she died, she had taught her daughter the trick to producing the silkiest buttercream, the lightest cookies. Time was, people came from all over Paris to buy Noemi's mother's macarons. Now, perhaps, they'd come from all over the state of Nebraska.

By three thirty, the two of them had created ten dozen macarons— pink, blue, green, violet, and yellow. Noemi had waited until the last macaron was assembled before sampling one. She closed her eyes first, taking in the taste of the cookie—the crisp outside layer, the smooth, creamy center. As she began to chew, a tear formed in each eye, then they slowly made their way down Noemi's cheeks.

This was a good cookie, all right, but there was more to it than that. As she chewed, Noemi was tasting Paris, unencumbered youth, good cheese, the memory of fitting into her polka dot dress. She was in France again. She was home.

She might have sat there a long time, weeping—possibly for Timmy, more likely for everything else—but the two of them had work to do. This was a cookie best eaten fresh.

Not having containers for the macarons, Leila and Noemi had laid them out in shoe boxes Leila's grandmother had been keeping to store coupons, which they now dumped out into a grocery bag. Then they set out with their wares with the plan of selling the macarons door-to-door.

Noemi had suggested a price of three dollars a dozen for the macarons, on the theory that they were not only delicious macarons but also the only macarons in the state and possibly the entire Midwest. Leila had suggested a somewhat lower price, using—as the basis of comparison—the cost of a pack of Oreos or Fig Newtons, both under fifty cents.

Oreos? Fig Newtons? Leila was missing the point, Noemi told her. They were talking about *macarons* here. How did you put a price on a baked good that could transport a person across the ocean, to the banks of the Seine? This assumed, of course, that the person in question wanted to be transported to such a place. For the citizens of Assumption (all except Leila, anyway), the answer was, probably not.

The two of them—the unlikely pair of a nine-year-old girl and her nineteen-year-old pregnant French aunt—spent the next three hours walking the streets of their small Nebraska town, knocking on doors with their basketful of gourmet cookies. They sold a half dozen to a woman who'd traveled to Paris long ago on her honeymoon with a husband long dead. A couple of people asked for free samples.

That evening, when Leila and Noemi got home, they had a dollar fifty, and nine and a half dozen beautiful, pastel-colored macarons.

That was the end of Leila and Noemi's macaron business. But not the end of Leila's macarons. Sometimes, still—if her father was in a good mood, and her grandmother wasn't busy in the kitchen herself, making something more sensible like tuna casserole or Spam fried rice—the two of them would whip up a batch of macarons just for themselves.

"Someday," Noemi told Leila on one of their baking afternoons— winter now, Noemi's enormous belly pushing against the fabric of the largest among the dresses they'd sewed to get her through her pregnancy—"we'll go to Paris together, and I'll take you to my favorite *pâtisserie*, and we'll order an espresso and a plate of macarons." In these fantasies of the future, Noemi's baby was never mentioned.

They'd go to the Eiffel Tower, and the Louvre, and see the painting Leila's grandmother loved, of the ballerina. Leila would speak French; she had gotten pretty good at it by now. They would ride bicycles along the Canal St. Martin.

The baby was born that January—a cold spell so bitter Leila's mother had stuffed a couple of hot baked potatoes inside Noemi's coat for the drive to the hospital. Everyone expected her to name the baby Timothy, but she named him James instead, after Jimmy Stewart.

Late the next summer, Noemi met a very nice man (Marvin, a Bible salesman) in a class she was taking on photography (never mind that she didn't own a camera; it was the best class in the adult education program for meeting men) and within a couple of months they were engaged, and a couple of months after that, they got married. Marvin adopted James and the three of them moved to Wichita, but not before Noemi gave Leila her patent leather belt and wrote out the instructions for macarons, in French, in case she ever forgot them, which she never would.

The following spring the 4-H club sponsored a baking contest, and Leila's macarons won first prize. Their church youth group held a polio fundraiser whose theme was Gay Paree, and again Leila was drafted to make macarons.

When Leila was eighteen, newly graduated from high school, with no particular prospects, her mother saw a notice in the paper for a contest called the Pillsbury Bake-Off. Finalists would be flown to New York City where they'd be put up at the Waldorf Astoria Hotel to compete in the nationals for the grand prize of five thousand dollars.

The macarons got Leila to New York, where she went to the top of the Empire State Building and rode a subway train. It wasn't Paris, but it was pretty good.

She didn't win first prize—probably (though Leila would never have said this at the time) because Pillsbury flour was an inferior substitute for the almond flour in Noemi's recipe. Leila won second place: a lifetime supply of Pillsbury flour and seven hundred and fifty dollars. She didn't care that much about the flour—though her mother and grandmother would. But the money bought her a ticket to Paris.

By this point in Leila's story we'd finished off the *camarones* and the rice and the mango parfaits Maria had set in front of us. I was still waiting to see how all of this was going to get Leila to Lake La Paz, and grateful, most of all, that Leila's story had allowed me to turn my focus from Lenny and Arlo to a cast of characters who'd never break my heart.

Leila didn't know a soul in all of France. (Noemi, who had given birth to two more sons by this point, was off in Kansas with Marvin.) She found a rooming house on the Left Bank. The next morning, as soon as she'd taken a walk along the Seine and located the bridge from the photograph she still kept in her wallet, of her uncle Timmy and his new bride, she applied for bakery jobs. She listed her specialty as macarons, but nobody took her seriously, as an American, until finally she bought herself the necessary ingredients and, late one night in the rooming house kitchen, she made a batch—from Noemi's specifications, naturally. Next day she returned to the first of the bakeries whose owner had turned her down before. He hired her on the spot.

Normally she worked in the back, piping the batter for the cookie portion onto baking sheets, beating up batches of butter cream, swirling in the colored paste. But on this one day, a couple of years into her time in Paris, her coworker Anny had failed to show up, and her boss put her behind the counter.

A customer came in. He wanted two pistachio macarons. One hazelnut. One lemon. Under his arm was a beat-up copy of the poems of Rimbaud in translation.

All that morning he sat at the one table they had, off in a corner, sipping coffee and smoking and eating macarons. Three times, Leila asked if he wanted another coffee, which he always did. Also more macarons. From the book he was studying she knew she could have spoken to him in English, but she preferred French.

After he finished his coffee and got up to go, he stopped back at the counter. "You want to get a drink later?" he asked. She explained that there were three hours to go before she got off from work. He said he'd wait. He sat in the corner, still reading Rimbaud.

Her coworker Arlette emerged from the back of the shop, looking as if she might faint.

"Did you see him?" she said.

"Who?"

"In the corner. With the book. Marlon Brando."

Never that much of a moviegoer, Leila had failed to recognize him.

He took her to a café around the corner, a table in the back where people might not notice him, but they did. It turned out that like herself, he'd grown up in Nebraska. After, they walked the streets of Paris most of the night. Then they went back to his hotel—a very different kind of place from the rooming house where she lived. There was room service. Champagne.

It rained all that week. No matter how many glasses of red wine they drank, they were always cold, except when they kept their bodies pressed against each other, which they did, for hours.

Leila had known Marlon Brando exactly six days when he told her he was thinking about buying a piece of land somewhere that people would leave him alone. A man he'd met on a movie set told him about a lake with a volcano looming over it that he'd been to once, somewhere south of the equator. He wanted to check it out. He was leaving tomorrow, actually, on his private plane.

"If I stay in Paris much longer, I'll get fat on those cookies you make," he told her. "Come with me."

She thought about Noemi, back in Kansas with her salesman husband and a clothesline hung with diapers. Noemi, who kept a stack of movie magazines next to her bed and, every May 20, sent a birthday card to Jimmy Stewart. If Marlon Brando had invited Noemi to fly away with him—anywhere—she would have hopped on that plane without a backward glance.

But Leila hesitated. She loved Paris. She had just bought a mattress and a blue teapot and a yellow mug. She had her job, and a beret even, though within hours of buying it she realized the only people who wore those in Paris were tourists.

In the end, she agreed go away with her movie star lover. She took one overnight bag containing a couple of books she loved and her three dresses. Somewhere over the Atlantic Ocean, Marlon Brando presented her with an extremely large diamond ring.

The whole thing was over by the following weekend. "Marlon had a certain appeal," Leila told me. "But that wasn't my big love story."

From the moment their plane touched down—on a rare piece of flat land, a cornfield outside of La Esperanza—Leila felt strangely at home. The lake was a shade of turquoise she had supposed a person only saw at the bottom of a swimming pool, but here it was real. The air felt thick with the smell of jasmine and gardenias. Birds sang as if she were inside an animated Walt Disney movie. Children ran up to her (didn't I know? The sight of them could tear my heart out), offering cardamom chocolate and woven bags and necklaces. Nobody recognized her lover in this place, but little boys ran after the two of them, laughing and calling out, performing cartwheels.

Then there was the volcano. "If I live to be a hundred," Leila said, with a look on her face suggesting that she knew she would not, "I'll never tire of seeing it there, rising up from the lake, with that one odd little cloud perched over the top."

Two days after Leila and Marlon Brando landed at Lago La Paz, he decided where he really wanted to be was an island in French Polynesia. He assumed Leila would join him. She said no.

"I had fallen in love," Leila told me. "But not with a man. I had fallen in love with a volcano and a lake and a village."

At the time, the only people who lived in La Esperanza were indigenous Mayan farmers, a few weavers, a small band of missionaries, a couple of American nuns. After saying goodbye to Marlon Brando, she

rented a room for a dollar a night. On her third day in the village—
swimming in the lake—she spotted a piece of very beautiful undevel-
oped land with nothing but a tiny adobe hut on it on the edge of the
water, and a For Sale sign on it. Wherever she looked, she saw birds.

Leila had $525 left over from her Pillsbury prize money. The price
of those two acres of waterfront land came to five hundred US
dollars.

As soon as the papers were signed and the land was hers, she got to
work making her garden.

"You know the funny thing," she told me. "I've never been back to
Paris."

15
No return address

On my third day at La Llorona I woke up thinking about Rose and Ed and Lenny's two sisters, Rachel and Miriam. As much as I'd resisted it, they'd welcomed me into their family. Maybe they even loved me.

Like me, Rose and Ed had lost their son. Also their grandson. And though in the scale of those losses my disappearance from their lives was minor, it weighed on my mind that I hadn't said goodbye.

Sitting at the little avocado wood desk in my room, looking out at the lake, I wrote a letter to Lenny's parents.

The letter occupied no more than a page. I wanted to thank them for everything they'd done for me—and for Arlo of course. I wanted to tell them what wonderful parents they'd been to Lenny, how much he'd loved them.

"I'm sorry I didn't say goodbye," I wrote. "I didn't know what to say. I had to get away from every single thing that reminded me of Lenny and Arlo. I never wanted to hurt you."

I was a person, myself, who'd known the feeling you're left with when someone you love fails to tell you goodbye. I didn't want to do that to anyone else.

I said no more. I didn't tell them about the bus and the plane, the boat, and the place I was living now, on the shores of a turquoise lake that looked out over a volcano, the hummingbird hovering over a thunbergia flower outside my window, the hollow feeling that never went away.

Rose and Ed would see a foreign stamp on the envelope, but I offered no return address.

I did not say—because it wouldn't have been true—"I'll see you again." I told them I would be forever grateful for the love of their son, and the child we had so briefly gotten to raise together. "I hope you can forgive me," I wrote. Nothing more.

16

A hand-beaded belt

Maria and Luis had started working for Leila not long after she'd bought the land. They were all young then. They were old now.

Luis still put in long days of hard physical work—repairing walls, hauling wood, mixing cement, climbing an ancient ladder to trim branches in the jocote tree, tending the garden—but he moved like a man whose back hurt. Maria took care of meals, and though the food she produced was invariably delicious, she moved slowly through her tasks, lingering long minutes over the act of peeling a mango or chopping a bulb of garlic.

Elmer, the couple's son, helped out wherever he was needed, but he was still a teenager, and got distracted easily. Most particularly what distracted him was Mirabel, the young woman who helped Maria out. She cleaned the rooms and took care of the laundry and every day, just at sunset, whipped up a drink for me in the blender made from fresh fruits and coconut milk and some mysterious assortment of spices (cardamom, maybe, and ginger?) that had become her trademark at La Llorona. Many guests, over the years, had begged for the recipe, offering to pay her to share it, but Mirabel just smiled and shook her head. "It's different every time," she said. "There is no recipe. I just get a feeling for what to put in that day."

Like Elmer, Mirabel had worked at the hotel since she was a child, ever since the death of her mother when she was nine or ten, when she'd presented herself at Leila's gate asking for a job. Sixteen years old now, she had an almost otherworldly beauty—honey-colored skin, the largest brown eyes—but it was the fine intelligence revealed behind her eyes that made you take particular notice.

Mirabel wore her hair in a single long braid down her back, with a ribbon woven through it (different colors, depending on the day) and the traditional skirt of women in the village—a single length of hand-woven fabric, wrapped around her body and held up with a belt. For most girls, the traditional belt would be made from a single color of thread, or embroidered with a simple pattern, but the strip of fabric wrapped around Mirabel's tiny waist was encrusted with elaborate beadwork that featured calla lilies and orchids and hummingbirds, all made from tiny beads that caught the light as she moved. She told me, when I'd complimented her on the belt, that she had spent over a year making it.

Watching her as she tended to her work—swift, efficient, but never hurried, and taking great care in everything she did—I could see why she had such an effect on guests. But of all those who took notice of Mirabel, none was more transfixed by her presence than Elmer. Every time Mirabel came into view over the course of the day—stripping a bed or hanging up laundry, beating rugs with a broom to get the dirt out of them—he'd pause in whatever job he was tending to take in the sight of her. He barely spoke, but sometimes, when she walked past Elmer in the kitchen or the garden, I'd hear a long, low sigh come out of him before he picked up his tools again and got back to work.

With no guests at the hotel, besides me, it seemed crazy that Leila continued to employ a staff of four—cleaning bedrooms nobody slept in, serving wonderful meals for nobody but the five of us. But I understood, from my earliest days at La Llorona, that Leila was not a woman to pay particular attention to the balance sheet. Loyalty to her staff, on the other hand, was a central concern.

A strange thing was happening to me at Leila's hotel. I hadn't shaken my bone-deep sadness, but in small ways, I was coming back to life.

My body, that had gone numb, began to feel again. Sun on my skin, good food, something as simple as the smell of the freshly squeezed orange juice Mirabel set in front of me every morning and the sunset elixir I now looked forward to every late afternoon, as I watched the sun dip low behind the volcano. This was followed, every evening, by the most marvelous meal.

Over our dinners together on the patio, Leila told me many stories of her decades of hosting visitors at La Llorona. For reasons I did not understand, she seemed to want me to know what she'd witnessed. Most of all, what she'd learned.

"There was this one time . . . " she'd say, as we sat down for a meal of tamales, or chicken pepian, or a bowl of Maria's fish stew, seasoned with some herb I'd never encountered before. Then she'd launch into another story.

"Foreigners who come often try to make money off of this culture," Leila told me. "Sometimes they actually do. But the true beauty gets lost in the translation."

One night she told me about a woman who called herself Ariadne who came to the lake in search of antique textiles. After checking into the hotel, Ariadne went around the village searching out examples of particularly beautiful embroidery, and when she spotted a huipil she liked she'd offer to buy it then and there off the back of the woman wearing it. The money she offered—though it was nothing in the world Ariadne came from—seemed like a fortune to the women of the village. Ariadne had told them of her plan to return to the village the next fall with fabric and embroidery thread for them. She'd rent a workshop for the women and pay them handsomely for more of their handiwork.

Ariadne brought trunksful of huipiles made by local women back to New York City, where she created a line of clothing. No doubt this made her a lot of money. That winter a six-page spread appeared in *Vogue* featuring Ariadne's line of clothing, integrating traditional embroidery, modeled by tall, thin, gorgeous women, pouting into the camera. The women from the village who'd sold their handiwork to Ariadne had gathered around to study the photographs, pointing out the pieces of embroidery they'd created now on display in the magazine, laughing and hugging each other at their good fortune. They hoped they might develop an ongoing relationship with Ariadne, selling more of their work over the years. But a year later she was on to something new.

As Leila told me the story, Mirabel appeared on the patio wearing a beautiful huipil of her own. She cleared away our plates and refilled our glasses. I watched her as she disappeared back into the kitchen. She set an orange cake in front of us and floated off like a dancer, as Elmer, stoking the outdoor fire, stood mutely watching her. On his face was a look I still remembered, from a time not so long past, though it seemed now a hundred years ago.

Love.

17
Seekers

Every night I sat on the patio with Leila. Every night, from her chair at the head of the table, she shared more of her days at La Llorona. There was more going on for her than simply entertaining me. I could feel an urgency in her story.

She seemed to need someone to know her story. That person appeared to be me.

"I'll tell you about Fred," Leila began one night. "He came from somewhere in the Midwest. Sold insurance. Except for one trip to Canada, he'd never been out of the United States. Then he read about the potentially mind-altering properties of cacao and he wanted to experience them."

Mayans had held cacao ceremonies for centuries, she explained. But Fred had recognized a profit-making potential.

"I wanted nothing to do with this project," Leila told me. "When I heard what Fred was up to I turned him away from the hotel. But someone in the village sent him to the coast to procure the cacao, and after he came back with a few hundred pounds of the stuff, he made quite a business for himself. Created this cacao drink, ripped off from a traditional Mayan formula, that supposedly possessed the power to expand a person's consciousness. He'd changed his name to Federico and he was calling himself a shaman. He started holding ceremonies for travelers for a hefty price. Pretty soon American travelers were flocking to his doorstep to partake of his mind-expanding drink."

"Tourists, not locals, I guess?"

She laughed. "What do you think? We get a lot of seekers here. People on the run from their old lives. People in search of answers, without necessarily considering the questions. *Sip a drink and learn the secret of the universe.*"

Federico the Cacao Shaman had developed quite a following among the young hippie travelers who flocked to the village every winter. He'd built his own place now, the Cacao Temple, where people came from all over to participate in ceremonies and partake of Shaman Federico's cacao drink, whose recipe he kept top secret. "You might think the local indigenous community would have taken offense at a North American's appropriation of their ancient traditions and how he altered them to suit the interests of a bunch of gringos," Leila added. "But most people in the village were simply amused."

She took a bite of fish. "The people born into this culture will be around long after Federico's gone," she said. "The last I heard, he'd bought a powerboat and was taking flying lessons."

Not every one of Leila's stories was troubling. Another night she told me about a logger who had come from the prairies of Canada. Forty years old, never married, Arthur had lived in a logging camp much of his life. He'd dreamed he'd find his true love somewhere near a volcano. He showed up one day at La Llorona hoping to find her.

"The week he arrived, a young widow from the village came by selling banana bread," Leila said. "Thirty years old, she was living in the home where she grew up, taking care of her three sons and her mother. She and the logger fell in love. They run a health food store across the lake now. They had four more children. Everyone's happy."

Leila looked out over the water. It was pitch dark now. I had never seen so many stars.

"Many stories have unfolded in this place," she told me. "Some very good ones and some that could break your heart. Everyone I ever met who came here was on some kind of quest. They didn't always find what they were looking for. But they usually find what they need."

The name she'd chosen for this place, La Llorona, came from an old Central American legend about a woman who, having seen her husband in the arms of another woman, flew into a blind rage and drowned her children in a river. Immediately regretting her actions, she threw herself into the river after them but could not save their lives. Forever after she lives in purgatory, roaming the earth looking for her children and wailing every night. People speak of her as La Llorona—the wailing woman.

"You might say it's an odd name for a travel destination," Leila said. "I suppose I'm an odd person."

At just this moment, a sound like a shriek rose over the lake. "A heron," Leila said. "Beautiful bird, awful voice."

"I never saw so many birds as I did on the lancha, crossing the lake," I told her. "Birds in the trees, birds swooping over the water, diving for fish. Birds everywhere."

(No conures, strangely enough. But a hundred other species, as brightly colored as the ones out my window back home. What used to be my home.)

"Wait until morning," Leila told me. "That's when the choir comes out. Sometimes I think I should have called this place *The Bird Hotel.*"

Leila's stories filled my head. As a person on the run from her own story, they offered blessed relief. So long as the two of us could sit on that patio—Leila talking, me listening—I could leave my grief for a while.

That night, I hung up the blue dress in the handmade wooden armoire. Out the window, the wind had died down. The sound of the water lapping against the rocks had quieted. Moonlight poured in the room. In the fireplace, a few embers still glowed.

"Everyone who comes here is on a quest," Leila had told me as we sat on the patio that night. "You may not even know it, but you are."

"I'm not really looking to find anything," I told her. "I think I know my story pretty well already."

"One story, maybe," she said. "You'll have others."

At the time it was impossible to imagine this, or to believe that anything I might do, anyplace I might go or stay, could alter the immutable fact of my own unspeakable losses. I would have said, when I got on that green bus, that all I wanted was to get away from where I'd been. The idea of ever getting to someplace else—someplace where things might be better, or simply different—would not have occurred to me.

18

A good place to disappear

There had been another reason beyond the deaths of my husband and child that had compelled me to believe I had to disappear—off a bridge, or onto a bus, and finally to the kind of place where I imagined nobody would ever track me down.

Sometimes in the night, alone in my bed, I'd think about that call I'd received, back in that other lifetime, from my art teacher, telling me someone was looking for me and asking questions. The FBI maybe, or the police. When I thought about getting called into some federal office to answer questions about my mother—and the news stories that would follow, and everything else—I could hardly breathe. If Lenny were alive, he'd put his arms around me. If Lenny were alive, I'd tell him the truth about myself now. I'd missed my chance for that.

Where I was now, I believed, no one could find me. When I got on the green turtle bus, I'd revealed to nobody who I was or where I was headed. I didn't know the answer to that one, myself.

"A person can start off fresh in this place," Leila had told me that first night. "For anyone who ever wanted to escape their life, there's no better hotel to check into than this one."

19

Have you ever met Spider-Man?

It had been a fact of my life since I was six years old that I must not speak to anyone concerning the truth of what happened to my mother. Until meeting Lenny, I accomplished this by avoiding close friendships. With Lenny, I lived in the present. The words we shared were real and true and intimate. I simply cut off all connection to the past, and though in our early days my husband tried to get me to tell him more, he recognized the discomfort I felt every time he raised the subject of my past. After a while he left it alone.

Now, strangely—in this place so disconnected from anything I'd known or anyone who'd known me—I felt a sudden longing to share my story. Sitting with Leila on the patio as she regaled me with her story, I'd imagine how it might feel to tell her mine—not only about Lenny and Arlo, but about that day I'd learned the news of my mother's death from a TV news broadcast, and everything else. If I'd grown up with a mother, rather than a grandmother who made it clear that I must never speak about what happened, maybe I'd know the feeling of confiding in this way.

"I need to let you know something," I'd say to Leila. *"I had a husband named Lenny. We had a son, Arlo. They were everything to me. They died."*

"What about the rest of your family?" she'd ask. *"Your mother?"*

Even Leila—as tough as she was, and unsentimental, and not inclined to large displays of emotion—would feel sorry for me. I couldn't bear her sympathy. Worse yet, her pity. But a change had come over me. After all those years in which all I wanted was to keep my cards close to the chest, I yearned to tell someone the truth.

Walter, the boy who'd met me at the dock that first afternoon, showed up at the gate. Had I heard about the waterfall up on the ridge? Would I like him to take me there? I'd never find the place on my own, but for a few *garza* and maybe a taco, he'd serve as my guide.

The hike was beautiful, and Walter—though small for his age—served as an excellent guide, pointing out varieties of plants and insects along the way. At one point on our hike he indicated a couple of young men—in their early twenties, probably, and brandishing machetes. "Very dangerous," he said in Spanish, his voice deepening even more than normal. "But they won't bother you so long as I'm here."

Once we reached the waterfall we explored a bat cave. Then Walter brought me to the house of a woman who made fine baskets out of *tul* reeds and a blind man who carved wooden slingshots in the shape of monkeys and iguanas and another man who prepared a drink that appeared to be moonshine. (I chose not to sample his wares.) When Walter and I passed a tienda selling orange soda, I bought him a bottle. He spotted a particularly interesting rock and presented it to me as ceremoniously as if it had been a jewel.

As few words of English as my small guide possessed, he used them to great effect. He was going to be rich someday, he told me. He would marry a very beautiful woman. They would have a house with a refrigerator and a flush toilet. He'd drive a sports car like the one on *Miami Vice*, a show he'd seen on the television set in a gringo bar in town.

A curious ritual developed between Walter and me. He'd speak to me in Spanish. I'd answer in English. I might only understand 10 percent of what he said to me, but I let the words flow over me. I figured that Walter understood even less of what I said back. But it was oddly comforting, talking with him. It occurred to me that his having no idea what I was talking about much of the time was not so much a problem as it was an advantage.

"Have you ever eaten Pollo Campero?" he asked me, in Spanish as always. For most people in the village, a meal from that fast food chain, whose name I remembered from the box of my seatmate on the bus that brought me to the lake, represented the ultimate feast.

I prefer fish, I said in English. The part about *pescado* he understood.

"The capital of Massachusetts is Augusta, yes?" he asked me (still working on his state capitals).

That's in Maine, I told him. The capital of Massachusetts is Boston.

"Who's your favorite soccer star?" he asked me one day, on one of our walks. He called it football.

I tried to come up with a name. Baseball players, I knew, thanks to Lenny of course. Soccer not so much.

Pelé? I said. The one name I knew from the world of soccer.

"In your time in America," he asked me, "have you ever met Spider-Man?"

I confessed I had not.

We walked in silence for a moment. I could see from his expression that Walter was working hard to come up with a new conversational topic.

"Could you be loved?" he said. In English this time. At first this took me aback. Then I realized he'd heard it in the Bob Marley song. *"Don't let them change you or even rearrange you,"* he said, in English again. He spoke the words, it sounded more like *done lettemchangoo orevenrearangoo.*

Could you be loved? Would you be loved? He probably had no idea what it meant. He just liked the song.

"Where you come from, what are your volcanos like?" he asked me.

How to explain that there were none? I might as well tell him there was no sky, no air.

With Walter, I never felt a need to fill the silence with idle conversation. But now, as the two of us made our way along the dirt road into town—I with my basket, to hold the vegetables I'd promised Maria I'd pick up for her in the market—I felt the urge to speak something real and true. Walter wouldn't understand me anyway. His presence offered the comfort of a confessional.

"I was so sad before I came here, I wanted to die," I told him. The road was dusty. A swarm of bees circled us, buzzing from the wildflowers in bloom. Walter kept his eyes on the road ahead, looking out for the banditos against whom he was prepared to defend me, should the need arise.

"I was going to jump off a bridge," I said, very quietly. Not that anyone could hear. Not that they'd understand if they did. "I'm glad I didn't."

Walter said nothing. He had found a candy bar wrapper that someone had left on the path. He bent to pick up a piece of shiny paper from the packaging, and stuffed it in the pocket of his falling-down pants. For a minute, neither one of us said anything.

"Have you heard of multiplication?" Walter asked. No doubt the fact that his attendance at school was rare—a function of his job responsibilities—had not done much for his grasp of arithmetic. "I don't know how to do it."

"Let's sit down," I told him. "I can help you."

Together, we assembled a pile of small stones. Out of these I made a smaller grouping of three pebbles, and beside that, two more groupings of three pebbles each.

"Three times three," I said, gathering the three small groups of pebbles into a single pile. "Now count them."

Uno. Dos. Tres. Cuatro . . .

"That's multiplication," I said. "My son Arlo was just learning how to count."

Arlo, said Walter. So far from home, so long since I'd held my son, it felt good speaking his name.

"*Dónde está Arlo?*" Walter asked me.

"*Muerte.*" I said it in Spanish. A look came over Walter's face.

He took my hand.

The two of us walked together on the trail—Walter's thin frame bouncing along on the dirt, cutting away low-hanging brush to clear the path for me. His pants were held up with a piece of rope and his shirt was torn. He was barefoot. I'd bought him a pair of sneakers, but he was saving them, he told me. So they wouldn't get dirty.

I could love this child. But I wouldn't let myself.

20
Unlikely demographics

When Leila had arrived in La Esperanza—fresh from Paris in the company of a movie star, with what was left of her earnings from the Pillsbury Bake-Off—the village had consisted of little more than a single tienda, the Catholic church, a few coffee fields and hillsides dotted with small family patches of maize, and a hotel with a single room, offering a sagging mattress with a bathroom down the hall and a rooster out the window who started crowing every morning just before five a.m. This was where she had stayed, briefly, with Marlon Brando.

It had not broken Leila's heart when the movie star in question had taken off for an island in the South Pacific three days later. That was enough time for Leila to know she wanted her own piece of land in this place—long enough to know that this would be her home for life.

Though the price she got for the Marlon Brando diamond ring at a pawnshop in San Felipe, shortly after her arrival here, must have fallen far short of its real value, the money had been enough to fund the purchase of just over a hectare of prime lakefront land facing the volcano but also the construction of a simple adobe structure with a room for herself, a room for Maria and Luis, the couple she hired to work for her, and two additional rooms that she rented out to travelers. Within a year the income from those rental rooms had allowed Leila to expand the property again.

Five years later, with a crew of men from the village overseen by Luis, they'd built the larger and far more beautiful structure that became the hotel. Along the way, Luis and his crew kept building stone walls and steps that wound through the property, while Leila filled the gardens with cuttings from other people's gardens. Then came rose arbors, the lily pond, the sauna, the waterfall. Then guests.

For the first few years of her time in La Esperanza, Leila was among a handful of foreigners living around the lake. At the time, La Esperanza had been a town of no more than a few hundred indigenous families who proudly maintained the ancient Mayan traditions, including a language separate from Spanish, a largely agrarian economy, augmented by a little fishing, and a connection to family so deep that parents lived all their lives with their children and, later, grandchildren, often in the space of a two-room adobe structure without electricity or running water.

The people in La Esperanza lived on very little. They did not measure their lives in terms of worldly successes or material wealth, but by the well-being of their families—the children, the elders. They probably did not spend much time, if any, considering the question of whether or not they were happy. More important was the question: Would their crops do well? Would the hurricanes spare them? Could they feed their families? Would God grant them another year of life, and if he did, another year after that?

This was the world Leila had chosen to make her home. But that world had changed over the years, and it was the arrival of the foreigners—with their money and their ambitions, their building projects and businesses designed to bring more foreigners here—smoothie bars, wood-fired pizza parlors, healing centers, yoga retreats—that changed everything.

A few years after Leila arrived, others began showing up from the United States, France, Germany, Switzerland, South America, the Netherlands, England, and Canada. They were a diverse group—young and middle-aged, a few married, most not, none rich, though in a couple of cases, they had been rich once but had lost everything. Each of them had arrived independent of the others, each with a different story, whose one common theme appeared to have been the desire to leave behind everything from the past and start over new. They all fell in love with the beauty of the village. And the first thing they did, once they settled in, was set out to transform it.

They'd created businesses—restaurants, hostels that had depended on the presence of travelers, particularly younger hippie travelers whose numbers had multiplied dramatically over the years.

When they'd built their businesses, it had been an act of faith that anyone would ever show up to frequent them. Then the travelers began to come. Word spread on the hippie circuit—the route traveled by a few thousand young people every year, in search of cheap places to live with good weather and easy access to music and drugs, and other young people in search of the same. La Esperanza was a place where you could find these things. Then came another wave, the seekers of new age wisdom.

The town grew fast. More gringos arrived. The indigenous community, the young ones at least—newly exposed to their ways, and to their needs for places to stay, places to eat, things to buy, and tourist-friendly versions of their ancient customs—adapted to serve them.

Meanwhile, the old guard among the gringos—Leila among them—stood back with a certain regret and resignation, watching what had become of their little paradise over the years. No longer young themselves—in their forties and fifties now, or, like Leila, older. The new expatriate settlers had seemed to float in like a puff of smoke, with as little awareness of this place or the people who'd made it their home for centuries as a swarm of locusts. Some floated off again, soon enough. Others stayed, to hang out their shingles as healers, jewelry makers, builders of flutes and drums and tie-dye clothing for the next wave to step off the boat. Few bothered to learn Spanish.

As much as the stories varied, of the unlikely, ragtag assortment of foreigners who'd chosen to make La Esperanza their home in the early days of what I thought of as the Gringo Invasion—men and women, no longer young, who'd arrived from France and Germany,

Switzerland, the Czech Republic, Brazil, and the United States of course—it was not so difficult to recognize a common element among them. With rare exceptions, they were people fleeing their past and trying to write a new story. Concerning who they had been or what they'd done in the country they came from, most said little, if anything. That was the point. It didn't matter anymore, what had happened before.

The most powerful member of the old guard was Andromeda, founder of the meditation center whose monthlong, life-altering course, "Sanacion Espiritual," had been attended by a few thousand questing travelers over the years. The center occupied a large swath of land running from the lake and halfway up the path to the center of the village.

Andromeda's house stood at the far edge, overlooking the lake, surrounded by couple of dozen small, pyramid-shaped structures, just big enough to house a mattress and a candle, and tall enough for a person to stand up in at the center, though no place else. These housed the students in the courses offered at the center. Participants mostly gathered on the grounds, which included an herb garden and a meditation temple. The challenge of providing meals was significantly diminished by the fact that most participants in the program fasted, or limited their consumption of food to nuts and papaya slices.

Katerina was among the early settlers. Back in her California days she'd been Kathy, but like most who'd moved to La Esperanza, she'd chosen a new name more in keeping with her life here.

Kathy had moved to the village sometime in the seventies. In her late fifties now—with long gray braids, still sporting sandals—she'd held on to the politics of her college days.

Katerina set up shop with a small business, exporting woven bags back to the United States. They'd been big sellers at Grateful Dead shows, back in the glory days.

Katerina operated her export business as a nonprofit, the proceeds going to fund a kitchen in the village providing free lunches to those who needed them. On the side, she wrote songs that she performed on guitar, whose lyrics (delivered in English, or rudimentary Spanish) generally had to do with the rape of the environment, the nobility and suffering of the Mayan people, the importance of love and the evil of war. She still featured, in her repertoire, a song about the Equal Rights Amendment, and another about Leonard Peltier.

Then there was Wade. Back in his old life, Wade was rumored to have been a highly paid attorney in Chicago, until he ran into some kind of trouble with the law.

The structure Wade had built here—on a steep path rising a half mile or so out of town—was a vast temple-like building with a fountain in front and a statue of a naked woman that had most definitely not been rescued from a sixteenth-century church or cathedral.

A key element of the menu at Wade's restaurant—El Buffo—was roasted rabbit. Rabbit was not just on the menu at Wade's restaurant. Rabbits featured as the chief decorative element of the place. All four walls of the dining area were lined with small wooden cages, each of which housed a rabbit. Some, very large, were no doubt imminently on their way to becoming dinner. Others were merely bunnies, though for them, too, the future seemed clear.

Even for someone who was not, like Katerina, a vegetarian, it was an unsettling sight.

An evening at El Buffo required a person to come face-to-face with the relationship between the decor and the dinner.

Then there was Il Piacere, whose owner, Rosella, possessed all the style and gift for creating a magical setting for a meal that the creator of El Buffo lacked.

Rosella had to be the most beautiful woman among the gringo settlers of the village. She'd shown up in the village after leaving a bad marriage back in Italy.

If you'd stripped away all the decorative touches provided by Rosella, her restaurant might not have looked like much, but because of Rosella, it was a jewel. She had filled the garden with religious stat-uary rescued from churches destroyed in the 1978 earthquake and before, along with gaslights and hand-built coffee wood tables tucked into a forest of giant ferns. Tiny white lights and even smaller bells hung from the trees, and in the center of the garden, a wood fire glowed in an old cast iron stove.

A lover of Italian opera, Rosella played nothing in her restaurant but recordings of Franco Corelli and Enrico Caruso and Leontyne Price, and her favorite, Maria Callas. Her choice of musical selections may have discouraged the young hippie travelers from frequenting Il Piacere. Very likely this was precisely what Rosella had in mind.

21

Only money

For all the details Leila shared with me over those nights we spent on her patio together, the subject of how she paid for things remained vague. Every time I raised the question of what I owed her for my room, she waved her hand—her silver bracelets jangling as she did so. "Now is not the time to talk about that," she told me. "We'll work it out later."

There had been a time when La Llorona was a thriving hotel. The author of a guidebook about Central American travel featured the place with a full-page write-up. "Unforgettable experience," she'd written. "Five stars."

Within a few years of opening its doors, the hotel was booked months in advance. Leila focused her energies on the garden, mostly, and on acquiring beautiful objects and textiles to decorate the house—antique relics of saints and Madonnas from old churches, wood and stone carvings, artwork, chandeliers made from gourds, a swinging basket chair, a marimba. Maria ruled the kitchen, arranging the meals she created like works of art on Leila's hand-painted ceramic plates.

Nights on the patio, or afternoons we walked into the village together, Leila told me about the old days: how the tables glimmered in the candlelight as guests shared stories and clinked their glasses under the stars, looking out across the lake at the fireworks people let off every time a baby was born. One night, a pair of visiting tango dancers had performed on the dock. Another time, a violinist and his flute-play-ing wife had stayed at the hotel, playing for the guests in lieu of pay-ment for their room. The music they made that night had floated out over the water. When they finished, you could hear people clapping and cheering from nearby houses all around the lake.

"If there was ever such a thing as paradise," Leila told me. "It seemed like we'd created it here."

"What changed?" I asked her.

"Ah well," she said. "I don't like to dwell on it. There was a man in the village—a foreigner, not local—who did a lot of work for me. I trusted him. You could say I was foolish and you wouldn't be wrong. I never paid much attention to the ledger. It turned out he'd been robbing me blind. I never even told Maria and Luis. If I had, Luis might have gone after him with a machete.

"My poor judgment left me with a mountain of debt," she said. "That was when everything started to go downhill.

"It's only money," she said.

Maybe, Leila speculated, she had allowed herself to be taken advantage of as she had because she felt guilt over having such a large and beautiful property in the first place—a place so much grander than any other in the village. She understood the contradictions, and the fine line she walked that separated benevolence from exploitation. She was a rich woman in a town where local people struggled to feed their families, and though she provided jobs to many, she understood that in the eyes of some, the world she'd built within the walls of La Llorona seemed wildly out of touch with the lives of the people she employed.

The presence of gringos in the town—though it had created a tourist industry—had also thrown the culture out of balance. People from the United States were buying up land, offering prices that seemed like a fortune in the indigenous community. Once the money was gone, the reality of selling the property that had been in their family for generations hit home. The next generation no longer inherited land to make homes for their families and cultivate their crops.

"I try my best to do more good than harm here," Leila told me. "But the thought has not escaped me that the people of La Esperanza might have been better off if none of us ever showed up here in the first place."

Mirabel appeared, holding a hand-blown glass pitcher, having whipped up a papaya drink with ginger, mint, limes, and lemongrass. A little way off, Elmer, watering the roses, looked up as he always did when Mirabel came into view. He stood there as water flowed from the hose—a pool forming at his feet, a look in his eyes of unadulterated adoration.

Leila, seeing me observing this, nodded. "That boy's been in love with Mirabel since he first started working here. Even then he told his parents he'd marry her someday."

It made no sense that Leila continued to employ Mirabel at a hotel with only one guest, but viewed strictly in financial terms, many things Leila did made little sense.

"How could I let Mirabel go?" Leila said, as if she'd read my mind. She sipped the last drop of her drink and licked the rim of her glass. "She supports her younger brothers and sisters. She counts on this job. Not to mention, that girl's an enchantress."

One thing was for sure: Elmer was under Mirabel's spell. Every time she walked past to pick herbs or flowers for the table when he was working in the garden, he seemed to forget everything else but her.

22
Bankers come knocking

By my second week at La Llorona I realized two things. First, that this was a place of extraordinary beauty—heartbreaking beauty, you might say. Heartbreaking, because the place was falling apart. Wherever I looked there was something magical. And something broken. It was the broken part that allowed me to feel at home in this place. Without the sense I had that painful events occurred here, and that things were far from easy, I could not have seen myself as belonging here.

Though I never spoke of my losses, I knew from my conversations with Leila—and, as my Spanish allowed, with Maria—that it was a rare parent here who had not lost a child at some point, or a partner. Every one of them grieved as much as I did, but differently. Here in La Esperanza, death was a part of life. When hotel guests said goodbye to Maria or Luis by saying "I'll see you next time," they always responded with the same words. "*Si Dios me concede un otro ano de vida.*" If God grants me another year of life. A baby might be healthy one day and dead from an infection a week later. A boulder might fall down the mountain and crush you. A gust of wind might tip a fisherman's cayuco boat and send him to the bottom of the lake. Even the youngest among the people of the village took nothing for granted.

The second realization that came to me over the course of those early days after my arrival at La Llorona was the harder one. For all her seemingly abundant energy—the way she went up and down those crumbling stone steps without breaking stride, her careful selections of just the right fish at the market, her perfect arrangements of flowers, stones, wind-chimes, candles—Leila was tired. Quite apart from the money required to keep up a property like this one—money Leila lacked—the task required vast stores of energy, strength, and devotion, and though the devotion of my hostess to this place was evident, her energy and strength were not what they had been.

"Luis and Maria are getting older too," she told me. "And Elmer and Mirabel are still so young. We can't keep up with everything anymore."

Once, coming into the kitchen, I'd spotted Leila leaning on the counter, her head slumped down, one hand over her eyes, as if the prospect of listening to one more guest asking her about the volcano hike or whether it was safe to eat the tomatoes here was more than she could take in. Sometimes, when she wasn't aware of this, I'd catch a glimpse of Leila leaning back in her chair, her eyes closed, her jaw slack—and suddenly she looked like an old woman.

Then there was the problem of money. The week I arrived I was the only guest at the hotel, same as I was the following week, and from all I could determine, this was standard occupancy for La Llorona. Mirabel endlessly washed and rewashed sheets and hung them up to dry, but nobody besides myself ever slept on them. Luis might keep the fire lit in the gallery, and Maria still served her beautiful meals at a table perfectly set by Mirabel—the candles always lit—but we were the only ones around to consume them.

One time, when I was alone on the patio, I could hear Maria and Luis speaking in the kitchen. "The man from the bank came to the gate again," Maria said. "The third time this week. I told him the señora was not home."

"He'll be back," Luis said.

"When he returns," Maria said, "we'll send him away again."

23
Health problems, and a bag for carrying potatoes

More than once, times when I'd observed Leila stopping to catch her breath in the middle of a task—in the kitchen, or the garden, or climbing the steps to the gate—I'd observed a worried look passing over Maria's face.

"I'm worried about Leila," I told her.

"Luis and I have tried to convince the señora to see a doctor many times," she said. "She'll never go."

Every afternoon, I walked into town with Leila to buy vegetables for that night's dinner. One such trip, I bought a hand-crocheted bag from an old man who could be found every day, sitting on a stone under the giant ceiba tree in the square, crocheting. My bag had cost a few hundred *garza*—more than some vendors charged for a woven mat or a handmade skirt, but something about the bag, and even more so, the man selling it, had seemed unusual.

"You made a wise choice," Leila told me, fingering the crochet work.

On every one of our walks to the village, Leila seemed compelled to educate me.

Bags like mine were called *morales*, she said. They were made from the threads of the maguey plant—part of a dying art.

"So much that I love is dying off here," she said. She shook her head.

Only the oldest men in the village still knew how to make a *morale* bag the right way, Leila told me. It was a long, slow process. As most things were, that were worth doing.

The man who'd sold me my maguey bag, Israel, was one of the last of those who knew the art, Leila explained. You could see him out by the rocks most mornings, along the edge of the lake. First he'd chop a maguey leaf from the plant—a leaf long as a saber, and almost as sharp. This he'd place on a rock, and with another rock, a large one, he'd begin to smash the maguey leaf in such a way that slowly, very slowly, the individual fibers of the plant loosened from its flesh, until what he had was a skein of very long, very strong threads, stronger than any string or twine you could buy at a store.

The old man wasn't done yet, though. He had to soak these maguey threads in lake water for at least a week. Then dry them. Then twist them so the individual fibers would come together. Only then could he get to work on constructing a bag like the one I now used to carry my daily purchases from town—crocheted, with a thick leather strap. Mostly what I carried in the bag were vegetables and—though Leila didn't think much of what they sold in the stalls in town—the occasional bottle of cheap Chilean wine. But I could have carried stones in that bag, and the woven threads still wouldn't have given way.

"You'll be carrying potatoes home from the market in this bag fifty years from now," Leila told me.

24

Serpent in the garden

There was a phenomenon Leila explained to me that invariably occurred when people came to Lago La Paz for the first time. "It's like the early days of a love affair," she said. "All you notice are the beautiful parts. Every bird, every flower, every insect."

I was experiencing the phenomenon myself. It was as if some kind of magic spell had been cast over the property, intoxicating as a night-blooming flower. And not only the property where the hotel was situated, but the entire town of La Esperanza: The laughter of the children on the path—small girls gathering firewood for their family's cookstove, small boys, as if transported from another century, rolling hoops. The crinkled faces of the old women selling the banana bread and young ones, in their brightly embroidered *traje* and plastic shoes (that they wore out on the basketball court, even), with their hand-beaded belts tied tight around their narrow waistlines, their hair shiny as patent leather. And the babies of course. Always those. One year, a girl wore her belt cinched tight. The next year, looser, with a shawl wrapped around her (in the front, if she were nursing, in back for walking), nothing but a tuft of hair showing and maybe not even that much. The babies born to the young women of this village had to be the most irresistible of any babies, anywhere.

All but the one to whom I'd given birth.

"It's all so beautiful," Leila said. "At first."

Later, she added, the seams start to unravel. Everything about the place that you'd fallen in love with was real but you began to notice the rest. But by the time you did—and this, too, resembled a love affair—you were too deep in to turn back.

Though I had not intended this to happen—had not supposed, when I'd boarded the bus in San Francisco that day, that I could care deeply about anything that happened to me anymore, had supposed I was just marking time now—within days of my arrival I was in the love phase of my time in La Esperanza, myself.

There was plenty to love. Not only the birds out my window every morning—and again, right around sunset, when whole flocks of them swept across the lake just above the surface of the water to wherever it was they'd bed down for the night. There were the sunrises, and equally wonderful, the sunsets, and the starry skies that came after them and the first bite of a mango fresh from the tree, the murmuring voices of the fishermen out on their cayuco boats with the first light of day, winding strips of *tul* grasses around the bodies of the crabs they caught—still alive—so they couldn't crawl away, or bite. There was even a word assigned in the language here for this particular time of day, just after the sun first showed itself over the volcanos, but before the world was fully illuminated. *Madrugada.* Where else would there be a place where the people had given a name to a particular angle of morning light?

"I never knew a place like this could exist," I said to Leila. "This peaceful. This safe."

For the first time since the day I lost my husband and son, I could sleep through the night again. My old dreams in which Arlo was calling out to me no longer haunted my nights.

"I love how simple life is here," I said to Leila. She turned her face to the night sky, as if considering how to respond.

"I'm glad you've found some respite," Leila told me. "But things in La Esperanza may not be quite as uncomplicated as you think now. It's best you know that from the beginning.

"You remember the story of the Garden of Eden?" she said. "Every paradise has its serpents."

25

Scorpions

That night, over a dinner of chicken in *mole* sauce and roasted vegetables, Leila told me the story of her hotel's most recent visitor, a man named Carl Edgar, from Dallas.

"I should have known from the first time I heard his name that this person was not my kind of guest," Leila told me. "He had a secretary book the room, and he wanted to arrive by private car."

Leila had strong ideas about how a visitor to La Esperanza should arrive at the town. By boat. In the glory days, there had been a dock in front of the hotel where the lancheros pulled up to deliver guests. The posts supporting the old dock had become so rotten that Luis had finally taken it down, which meant that now guests coming to La Llorona had to be dropped off at the public dock in the village, where young boys—my young friend Walter the most enthusiastic among them—accompanied them along the road to the hotel on foot, carrying their suitcases. This made it possible for the boys to pick up a little money, which was Leila's plan, no doubt.

But Carl Edgar had arrived in a black Land Rover. When Leila met him at the gate he was wearing a suit and carrying a briefcase. He had his camera out, and he was taking pictures, but not of the plants or the trees or the birdlife. He seemed interested in the road and the power lines. His first question: Did they get television service here?

Leila wasn't even all the way down the steps before she regretted accepting Carl Edgar's reservation to stay at the hotel. Never mind that at the moment of his arrival, not a single other guest was staying there, or that five weeks had passed since they'd had a booking. Leila did not want Carl Edgar on her property. She did not want Carl Edgar eating Maria's food. She did not want him sleeping in the Jaguar Room, or any other room at La Llorona. Leila didn't want to be breathing the same air as Carl Edgar.

"You've got quite a place here," he said. "It must be a lot to take care of, on your own."

She showed him to his room. She had hoped their interaction might end there, but Carl Edgar told her he wanted to talk about something. "I've come here to make you a proposal," he said. "It's something I think you may find highly interesting."

There was not one aspect of Carl Edgar that Leila found remotely interesting, and she strongly doubted that anything he contributed in the way of further discussion was likely to change that. But she sat down on the terrace with him, just as I was sitting with her now, as she told me the story. She refilled my glass of wine before she began. At just this moment, a flock of doves assembled in a semicircle around us on the patio, almost as if they, too, chose to listen.

Carl Edgar wanted to buy the property. With the instincts of a vulture, he had picked up the smell of trouble. For him, the beauty Leila had created in every direction was immaterial. All he saw was a failing hotel, a balance sheet that would soon bring its owner to bankruptcy. Now was the moment to swoop in.

Leila had recognized this, of course. She was not about to let this person destroy what she had spent the last four decades creating.

The two of them took their seats at precisely the hour Leila considered the most beautiful of the day, with the sun going down and the lake bathed in a golden glow, and the fishermen paddling in to shore with their day's catch. Carl Edgar appeared to notice none of this, though he had taken out his camera again. He was taking a picture of the roof, which—like everything else on the property—stood in need of repair, with large patches of thatch giving way, requiring the placement of buckets on the floor below during rainy season.

"I'm here representing a major hotel corporation in Texas," he told her. (He said the name; she just chose to forget this as swiftly as he stated it. Call it the B.W. Corporation. For bigwigs.)

Over the past eighteen months, Carl Edgar told her, the corporation for which he served as an executive had been conducting an in-depth survey of Lake La Paz, and specifically the town of La Esperanza.

To put it in layperson's terms, Carl Edgar told Leila, his company was in the business of developing new destinations for the high-end tourist market to meet the needs of a population not yet ready for retirement but beginning to think about it. To that end, the B.W. Corporation was looking to buy up property that would become the site of luxury condominium housing for wealthy retirees in search of exclusive, prestige property.

"You've got your Cancún and your Acapulco," he said. "Costa Rica, naturally. The Caribbean. The problem with those places is they're basically saturated. The good land's gone, even for our kind of client—the people of means. If a wealthy couple wants to build in Costa Rica today, they're going to be talking second, third tier now.

"But the worst is the red tape," he said. "The government's got us developers by the *cojones*. Excuse my French. Five years ago, down in Costa Rica, we tried putting up a simple fifty-unit development and let me tell you, after all this time, with five lawyers on the case, we're still all tied up in permits and environmental requirements. Hemorrhaging money. *Hemorrhaging.*"

"This place has it all," he said. "Fabulous vistas. Zero existing development. No organized resistance. Minimal government regulations, and nothing that can't be overcome with a few shekels crossing the right palms.

"No golf course, unfortunately," Carl Edgar added. "And the terrain's a little hilly. All we need is a few bulldozers and we'll take care of that."

"What are you saying?" Leila asked him.

"We're prepared to make you a very generous offer for your property here," Carl Edgar told her. "I have the paperwork in my briefcase." He patted it, as a certain kind of person who is not particularly interested in children and animals might pat a baby or a dog.

"My hotel isn't for sale," Leila told him.

As Leila recounted the conversation, this was when Carl Edgar's smile disappeared. He had a look, she said, like an iguana. "The matter may be out of your hands. There's the issue of your bank loan. It appears you're significantly behind in your payments."

It surprised me that Leila, a woman I'd just met, would share with me the intimate financial details of her property. Maybe it was the wine that inspired her to do this. Perhaps she just had to talk with someone, and who else might it be? In my brief time at the hotel, it had become clear she'd chosen to make me a kind of confidante, and a repository of information about the place.

It was true, she said. Some years earlier, at a time of particular financial stress, Leila had taken out a large mortgage on her property. She had been so desperate then she hadn't paid particular attention to the details, but the interest rate was astronomical. The bank maintained the right to foreclose at any point and had been threatening to do so. What do you know? Carl Edgar's company were shareholders in the bank.

"I don't want to ruin anybody's life," he told her that night. "This time tomorrow you could be out of debt, with enough cash left over to buy yourself a sweet little condo someplace. Take it easy."

There was more, though she barely took it in: The Bigwig Corporation's plans for a private airport—just a single runway to start out with, until they got going with Phase Two. The tennis compound. Down the line, a medical facility catering to those in search of cosmetic surgery at prices well below what a person would pay up north. The company had their eye on a number of other properties contiguous to hers—far enough outside the village that their clientele wouldn't have to rub shoulders much with the locals—but this place—he waved his arm again, even more expansively this time—this place was the linchpin.

She already knew the answer of course, but she had to ask. What did Carl Edgar propose to do with the existing structure of her hotel? The terrace. The gardens. The orchids. The citrus grove. What about the jobs of the people who worked for her?

A pained look crossed his face then, though only fleetingly. "Listen," he said. "It goes without saying you've built yourself a fabulous little place here. But to expand the footprint for cutting-edge amenities and maximize the revenue benefit we'd be looking at putting a larger structure on the property."

"You want to tear down my hotel?" Leila asked him.

"A certain upgrade would be called for," he said.

"And what about the people who work for me?" Leila asked. "Maria. Luis. Their son, Elmer. Mirabel. They all count on their salaries."

"Regrettably," he said, "we'd need to staff the new facility with English speakers—the kind of person our guests could relate to. While still maintaining the integrity of the original concept, naturally," he added. "An oasis, if you will. The garden of Eden, practically." In fact, this had been one of the CEO's suggestions for renaming the property. *Eden.*

At this point, Carl Edgar had taken a cigar out of his briefcase. A long, fat Montecristo.

"I don't want to offend you in any way," Carl Edgar added. "But our research indicates you're eight months behind in your payments and, no offense, but your place here is in serious need of repair."

Leila got up from the table here. She disappeared for a few moments. When she came back, she had a cigar of her own in hand. A better one. Hand rolled. She removed her silver trimmer from its leather case. She took her time before lighting it, and more time before exhaling the smoke. Slowly, thoughtfully, in the opposite direction from where Carl Edgar was seated.

"Perhaps you'd like to spend more than just one night on the property before you commit to taking over my hotel," Leila told him. "I wouldn't want you to move too hastily on such an important decision."

That wouldn't be necessary, he told her. He'd seen as much as he needed. His team had already made a careful assessment of the negatives as well as the upside potential. "Given the condition of your current structure," he said, once again affecting a slightly pained demeanor, like a doctor delivering a cancer diagnosis, "we've based our price on the raw land," he said.

Leila placed her cigar to her lips and held it there a moment. A small, perfect ring of smoke floated out over the table.

"I should warn you, we do have a small problem with insect life here at the hotel," she said.

"We've got experts ready to deal with extermination issues," Carl Edgar told her. "You should see some of the places we've gone into. Crawling with bugs and whatnot. By the time we're done, you wouldn't find so much as a fruit fly on the property."

"Perhaps you aren't familiar with scorpions," Leila told him. "We've got a variety here that's impervious to any chemical known to man. You could construct a whole other building, ten stories high, and the scorpions would still find you. Then of course there are the snakes."

"I doubt the odd scorpion would be a deal breaker," Carl Edgar told her.

She laughed. "We've got odd scorpions, all right," she told him. "Very odd ones."

He told her he'd pass on dinner. He had picked up a snack at Pollo Campero in San Felipe. He had it in his briefcase. That would tide him over till morning. Given all the paperwork he had to take care of he'd eat in at the desk in the gallery. He had some calls to make to the head office.

"Too bad," Leila told him. "It's going to be such a clear night. The stars will be extraordinary."

"I'll catch them another time," Carl Edgar said.

At this point in her story, Leila took a long sip of her drink.

"I should give you some background," she told me. "As you may have noticed, the roof is in need of repairs at the moment. At the time Carl Edgar paid his visit, Luis and Elmer had been redoing a section of thatch on the hotel roof."

This was never an easy job, Leila explained, in large part because removing thatch always resulted in the mass exodus of large colonies of insect life that had taken up residence in the palm leaves over the years. Scorpions in particular. Whole nests of them. The men made sure to dispose of these far from the hotel. That afternoon, they'd just built an enormous pile of discarded thatch with the plan of burning it in the morning.

Leila had chosen to personally turn down the bed in Carl Edgar's room. This was generally Maria's job, but that night Leila told Maria she'd take care of it. After she finished the task she went to bed herself. That night she slept particularly well.

She was awakened—as were Maria and Luis, who came running— by the sound of surprisingly high-pitched screaming emanating from the Jaguar Room. Carl Edgar was in the hallway, in his pajamas.

"My bed's crawling with bugs," he told her. "They've got these nasty little pincers. They got me all over my body."

Leila had expressed regret, of course. "It's such a shame," she told him, shaking her head. "We've tried everything to get rid of them. The pesticide hasn't been invented that kills them off. Whatever we do, these darned scorpions always seem to find their way back."

"I don't know how you stay in business here," Carl Edgar said. "This place is impossible."

"I know," Leila said, adopting a demeanor of regret. "I just want to say, I'm so relieved that you have children already. It's an unfortunate aspect of the bites from this particular variety of scorpion that they frequently lead to sterility in men. A certain amount of erectile dysfunction also occurs following scorpion attacks, but it's hardly ever permanent."

Carl Edgar spent the rest of the night on the patio evidently, fully dressed, with the aloe leaf Maria had provided him to rub on his wounds. As soon as the sun came up, he was climbing the steps to the road, where his Land Rover was waiting for him.

Leila recounted all of this as we sat on the terrace, having a gin and tonic and watching the sunset. When we got to the part about the scorpion bites we had broken into laughter, a sound I barely recognized in myself anymore. Maria, off in the kitchen—though she claimed she spoke no English—had merely smiled.

But I recognized a deeper truth in Leila's story—the part that wasn't funny.

Carl Edgar's development company might not be making an offer, after all, to buy Leila's hotel. But her financial problems were grave. Her debt to the bank was large, with interest accruing daily. It was only a matter of time before someone would come along to demand payment. Sooner or later—and probably sooner—Leila would have little choice but to sign over the deed to La Llorona. If she was lucky she'd find a buyer readier than Carl Edgar had been, to preserve what she'd created here. It was difficult to imagine who such a person might be.

The night Leila told me the story of Carl Edgar's attempt to take over her place and destroy everything she'd built there, I lay awake in the Jaguar Room. The threat to Leila's hotel mattered more to me than I would have guessed it would. It came to me in the night, why.

It seemed to me that La Llorona was the closest Leila had to a child—a beautiful creation of her making to which she had devoted her life. She wanted the place to outlive her, but it was in danger. As I knew well, no woman wants to outlive her child.

26
Buying a pencil

I had been staying at the hotel for three weeks and I wasn't even all that sure of my room rate, but every time I spoke to Leila about paying my bill, she told me we'd work it out later. La Llorona wasn't the kind of place that posted this information on your door, but when I finally sat down to estimate how much I must owe my host by now, the figure approached what I had left from Roman's gift from his casino winnings. I knew I had to talk with Leila about this, but every time I brought up the issue of money—the cost of my room, my meals, those nightly glasses of wine we shared—she shrugged it away.

"It's not important," she told me. "It's all going to work out as it should."

I continued to be the only guest at the hotel, a fact which seemed not to surprise or trouble Leila. For me, it felt like a gift, having these evenings to talk on the patio. My hostess seemed to know without my telling her that what I needed at that moment was a safe haven, and with or without the presence of an occasional scorpion (whose bite, though unpleasant, carried none of the side effects she'd described to her recent guest, the real estate developer) there was no place I could imagine feeling safer, right now, than this one.

By great good fortune, I'd landed at a falling-down hotel sitting on the edge of a lake rimmed by volcanos in a country I'd barely known to exist until the Green Tortoise bus had deposited me here. The oddest thing had happened then. At La Llorona, a whole morning might go by in which I almost felt like a normal person. For the first time since the accident I took an interest in things—Leila's story, for one. The garden, another. Goings-on in the village. My talks with Walter. Maria's cooking. The birds. I decided I'd stay on at the hotel until my money ran out, whenever that turned out to be.

I could glimpse a future again, even if it was only a month or two ahead. I signed up for Spanish classes with a woman in the village and began tutoring Walter in math and giving him English lessons. At a time in my life when I thought I was no longer capable of opening my heart, I'd made a friend. Several of them, in fact.

The thought had come to me that I might like to draw something, so at a little shop in the village I'd bought a number two pencil and an eraser.

If part of being alive is caring about other people and what happens to them, I was coming back to life. More and more, now, I worried about Leila and the future of her hotel. In my bed at night in the Jaguar Room, I tried to think of how to save La Llorona.

27

A long-lost daughter. A paint box

That afternoon, as I wandered through Leila's gardens, my eyes fell on a particularly beautiful hummingbird, whose feathers were an iridescent violet, with a yellow breast. I wished I had my colored pencils.

"Just a moment," Leila said. She rose from the table. When she came back she was carrying a flat tin box in one hand and an assortment of brushes in the other. Very fine brushes, it turned out. Back in my old life in San Francisco I had admired brushes like these at art supply stores, but could never justify the expense.

It was a paint box. Fine English watercolors, a brand I recognized, though from the logo I could tell that these dated back at least a couple of decades and probably longer.

"I got these for my daughter," she said.

A dead child. My mind went there of course. I'd ask no more. But Leila volunteered.

"Her name is Charlotte," she said. "Her father was a guest at the hotel at the very beginning, back when we were still building the place and all we had was the one room. He was Spanish, an ornithologist. He came to the lake to study birds. It was a brief romance, nothing more."

I didn't speak. I just waited.

"I was very young," she said. "When I got pregnant, I didn't know what to do. By the time our daughter was born, the relationship with her father was over. I didn't think I'd know how to take care of her.

Javier told me he'd take Charlotte back home with him to Spain. His mother would raise her."

Within months Leila knew she'd made a mistake. She wrote to Javier. She should never have relinquished her child. It would have been enough just to see her sometimes. She'd move to Barcelona. The two of them could share the responsibility of caring for her.

"By then Javier had fallen in love with someone else," Leila said. "By Charlotte's first birthday they were married. She never knew any mother but Sofia."

Javier wrote to say that Charlotte was happy in Spain. She loved her grandmother, her uncles, their cat. There was a whole family who loved her, a baby brother on the way. "If you care about Charlotte's happiness, you'll let her go," he wrote.

What could she do?

Over the years, Leila begged Javier and Sofia to visit with the child they spoke of as theirs. Finally, when Charlotte was eight years old, they brought her to the lake.

"I promised I wouldn't tell her who I was," Leila said. "I was just this person who ran the hotel where they stayed. But she liked me. She wanted to be around me all the time. This made Sofia crazy."

Charlotte looked just like Leila. One night under the stars, Leila had taught the little girl to dance the way Noemi had taught her long ago, back in Nebraska. From the Folies Bergère. Sofia, seeing the two of them together, announced they were leaving earlier than planned. The next morning they left on the first boat.

After that visit, Leila wrote many letters—first to Javier, then to Charlotte herself, in care of Javier. Who knew if she saw any of them?

"Giving up my daughter is the great regret of my life," Leila told me. "I still wonder about her. Sometimes I dream she'll show up at the gate one day. She'd be nearing forty years old now.

"These were for Charlotte," Leila said, placing the paint box in my hands. "I never got a chance to give them to her.

And what happened to her daughter, I asked Leila. Did she never go to Spain, reach out again to Javier, try to find her?

"It's a closed book," she said, handing me the paints. "Use them in good health."

28

Six hundred and seventy two varieties of birds. Not to mention fireflies

By the start of my fourth week at La Llorona, I had developed something resembling a routine. I rose very early, with the birds, then headed out to the patio for breakfast, which Maria would have set out for me, every day on a different woven cloth and served on Leila's ceramic plates, decorated with birds more fanciful, even, than the real ones in her garden.

Leila never joined me at these times, though on occasion she left something out for me to read with my coffee—a book about Mayan ceremonies, or ancient instruments, a yellowed clipping concerning the visit, to La Esperanza, of a famous Spanish guitarist who'd composed a song about the lake.

For more serious study, she'd lent me a very fine book from the 1960s featuring hand-tinted photographs of birds of the area. According to the bird book Leila kept on the table in her living room at all times, 672 varieties made their homes in this part of the world. I registered an odd little shiver when I got to the news, on the back flap of the cracked but well-preserved book jacket, that the author of the book I held in my hands—Merle G. Finster—had succumbed to a rare tropical disease while completing the manuscript, which had been published posthumously.

The discovery of Merle G. Finster's book gave new shape to my days. I still took my hikes with Walter, and Leila and I still walked to town every afternoon to buy vegetables at the market. But every day now, when we returned from the village, I set up Charlotte's paint box on a small folding table Luis had provided for me, with a glass of water and the beautiful sable brushes. Sometimes I painted flowers from the garden. Sometimes insects. Most often, I painted birds, whose names I figured out from Merle Finster's book. *Spot-crowned woodcreeper. Slaty-tailed trogon. Purple-crowned fairy. Laughing falcon.*

We were sitting on the terrace with our coffee, finishing a dessert of passion fruit ice cream and macarons. From across the water—a nighttime church service, probably—I could make out the distant sound of bells, then singing. In front of us, lake water lapped against the rocks. Over the water, I observed something sparkling. First just a single flicker of light, then another. Then more.

"Oh good," Leila said. "I knew the day was approaching. I was hoping I'd get to see them again."

What was she talking about?

"It's the fireflies," she told me. "They come out every year around this time. They put on the most amazing show for one glorious night, then disappear. It's probably a good reminder: Nothing beautiful lasts forever. We need to take joy in what comes our way instead of mourning when it's over."

29

A fall

I had been staying at La Llorona for just over four weeks at this point. Leila and I were on our afternoon walk to town. Partway up the steps to the road, she had to sit down to catch her breath.

"It's nothing," she said. "Sometimes the afternoon sun makes me dizzy. Go on without me."

Late that afternoon—back from my solo excursion to the market with my basket of produce for Maria to transform into another amazing dinner—I set up my paints with the plan of recording a particularly astonishing sunset. Leila must have seen this too. Dressed in one of her long, flowing silk outfits, she walked over to me. The two of us stood there looking out across the water to the sky. I had never seen a more blazing sunset.

"You're not finished with love, you know," she said. "You don't know it yet, but these birds will heal your heart."

I didn't say anything, but I didn't have to. "There will be many chapters yet to come in your story," she said. "You won't replace whatever it is you lost. But you'll find something else. Something wonderful. I suspect it has to do with love."

At the time, I would have said love—the idea of having or pursuing it—no longer featured in my universe. An hour didn't go by that I didn't think about my son and his father. The idea of loving anyone else, ever again—the idea of opening myself to that much possibility of further loss—was unimaginable. Love of the sort I'd known once—for a man, and for a child—was like a meal I could no longer consume, a marvelous food to which I was allergic. Though it would occur to me later that I had already begun to rediscover what it was to open my heart to another person. I had done it with Walter, and with Maria. I had opened my heart to Leila.

That afternoon, the two of us looking out to the volcano as the last rays of sunlight disappeared, I let myself imagine Lenny's face, and the smell of his sweater as I buried my head on his shoulder.

"You just need the courage to risk it again," she added. "Never forget that." She looked me square in the eye.

"I think I have to go into the house now," she said. "I have a headache." The picture came to me of that parrot, descendant of the one who'd escaped from the exotic pet store back in southern California, that day he'd directed his sharp, piercing gaze through the glass of my apartment window from his perch on the sill outside. As if he understood everything. That's how Leila looked at me just then.

She was halfway across the garden, headed back to the house, when her legs seemed to give out from under her.

"Oh my," she said. Her voice sounded more surprised than alarmed. The way she'd crumpled reminded me of what happens to one of those odd, inflated figures they put outside certain kinds of shops, to attract business—pizza parlors, mattress stores—when they suddenly let the air out, and the whole thing crumples to the ground.

I knew from the moment she dropped onto the grass that she hadn't simply fainted. There was something different about how she had fallen, the way her elegant form lay there on the grass, her long white curls fanned out around her head like a halo. You would know to look at her that all life in her body had taken flight.

I was still holding the paintbrush, as a single pure white heron made her way across the late-afternoon sky and disappeared.

In the doorway, I saw the face of Maria, her hands pressed against her cheeks as she cried out for Luis and Elmer. From the clothesline, where she was hanging up the sheets, Mirabel came running, her beautiful face a mask of anguish. We must have all known this before any of us reached her.

Leila was dead.

30

Mourning, overdue

Luis and Elmer carried her body into the house. She had seemed to me like such a strong and powerful person that it was only now I realized how thin she was, how effortlessly the two of them lifted her.

They carried her into her bedroom, a room I'd never entered until now. Maria lit candles.

The five of us—Maria, Luis and Mirabel, Elmer, and I—sat in the living room for a while. Maria prayed. There was nobody to call. For me, this was a familiar experience.

It was dark when Luis carried her body back outside. In the moonlight, at the far end of the garden, Elmer had finished digging the hole. Where I had come from, there would have been paperwork to fill out, a medical examiner to call. Here in La Esperanza, people took care of their dead on their own.

Watching the body of a woman I had known for just a month being lowered into the ground, the thought came to me that I'd never had a chance to grieve my mother. More than twenty years earlier, when I'd lost her, there had been no body, no memorial service, no grave, and in all the years my grandmother had never spoken of her. Now I could finally weep.

I was the daughter of a woman who—from my brief time with her—had revealed herself as incapable of being without a partner for a space of time greater than forty-eight hours. You could say that it was my mother's incurable need to attach herself to a man that had put her in that basement on East Eighty-Fourth Street that day.

As for me: Until I met Lenny, I had taken care of myself for most of my life, but after he died, I no longer knew how to live on my own. It had been an unexpected gift, coming at the lowest moment in my life, to have met Leila—a woman who had made a life for herself in a whole new country about as far from Nebraska as a person might travel, in a whole new language, on her own. Spending time with her, as I had been fortunate to have done on our walks to the market and on all those nights on her terrace, as the sun went down and the stars came out, I began to imagine a life in which I might locate a similar brand of courage. Or simply, a life.

31
The last chapter, the first chapter

The next morning, Maria had breakfast prepared, as usual. But nothing was usual of course.

"What happens now?" I said. I had slept exactly twenty-eight nights in this house. At this point I might have packed up my bag, paid my bill, walked into town, taken a shuttle to the airport, and left forever.

"The lawyer is coming tomorrow," she said. "He wants to see you."

I spent the day in the garden. Even when something very sad happens, even when someone dies, the birds don't stop singing.

I was still learning who Leila was and suddenly she wasn't there anymore. It was as if you'd been reading the most wonderful book—a very long, very beautiful novel that had kept you up every night—and one day you couldn't find it, and though you searched everywhere, the unfinished book never showed up. But unlike *Charlotte's Web*, whose final chapters I had eventually managed to read, years after Daniel had carried it off that day he and my mother broke up, there was only one copy in existence of this particular story, the one Leila had been telling me. I'd never know how the story ended. I'd have to make it up on my own.

Sometime late that morning I took out the paint box. I set up a table under the jocote tree and laid out a piece of fine, thick paper from Leila's desk.

A particular flower had just come into bloom, a jade thunbergia. Not a single flower, actually, but a cascade of them that reached from high over my head clear to the ground, with a hundred brilliant turquoise blossoms bursting out from a single stem. Just below it Leila had built a bird bath. A small gray bird—not one of the more brilliantly colored varieties—perched on its edge.

I dipped my brush into the water, and by combining two shades in the paint box—blue, with a drop of yellow—made a pool of color in the bowl beside me.

A feeling came over me whenever I made a picture from life. I became eyes and hand, nothing else. Breath maybe, when the act of making certain lines—very fine ones, very straight, or impossibly tangled—made it necessary to keep a particularly steady hand.

I kept expecting the bird to take off, but she didn't. I must have sat there painting for a good three hours. I continued to work on my painting until I heard Maria's voice calling to me, that dinner was served, but that night all appetite abandoned me. I went to my room and climbed into bed, searching for sleep, and for a few hours I found it.

Sometime in the middle of that night—or maybe it was morning by now—I got out of bed. I wandered the rooms of the hotel in the semidarkness, studying everything, as if doing that would allow me to continue my conversation with Leila. I read the titles on every book on her shelves—the poems of Rumi and Elizabeth Bishop and Yeats—also Pablo Neruda, the notebooks of Leonardo da Vinci. There was a wonderful leather-bound edition of *Don Quixote* in Spanish, and *The Lover* by Marguerite Duras in French.

I ran my hand over the wood of every piece of furniture in the room. I moved down the long hall, that row of hand-carved doors, stopping at hers. I hesitated, considering whether a person in my position had any right to enter, but besides Maria, who else was there?

Leila's bed had been made. There were still flowers in the vase next to it and a book open on the table, alongside a pair of tortoiseshell glasses I'd never seen her wear.

I moved to the closet, her wonderful dresses and gowns, the linen palazzo pants and another pair, silk. I pressed my face into the fabric of the blouse she'd been wearing that last evening we spent together. I could still breathe in her scent.

The volume that lay open beside Leila's bed, open to a place close to the end, was Isak Dinesen, *Out of Africa*—a book I'd always meant to read. I started at the beginning.

"*I had a farm in Africa, at the foot of the Ngong hills.*"

32

A visit from the lawyer

Next morning as I drank my coffee, Maria appeared.

"The lawyer from the city is here," she said, gesturing in the direction of the stone path leading down from the road, the place I had first descended just a month earlier.

He was wearing a very fine suit in lightweight gray linen, shoes of a kind not well suited to walking on dirt roads. He carried a briefcase of fine leather, and his hair was groomed in the style adopted by a certain class of Latin man. Heavy on hair product. He smelled of good cologne.

"I'm Juan de la Vega," he said. "Leila was my client.

"It is highly unusual," he said—in heavily accented but perfect English—"for the details of an individual's last will and testament to be made available so soon following her passing. But my client was adamant about this point when we last spoke."

The conversation had taken place just days before, he told me. Leila had called him at his office in the city, asking that he revise the papers concerning her estate.

I asked Juan de la Vega if he'd been aware that Leila was sick, and if Leila had been aware of this herself.

"Perhaps you knew about the aneurysm," he said. "She used to say it was lying in wait for her. She always knew that at some point the blood clot was going to travel through her blood system and make its way to her brain."

"I never knew her until a few weeks ago," I told him. If this fact surprised him, he showed no evidence that it did.

Maria appeared, with a pot of coffee and hot milk, a bowl of sugar, small silver spoons, a plate of macarons. Long ago, Leila had taught her to make them.

"I suppose you wonder what I'm doing here," he said. "I confess, it's an unlikely mission."

I didn't wonder, actually. Nothing that happened at La Llorona surprised me anymore. I had learned by now that how life went in this place seldom resembled the way things went anyplace else.

"My client's sole asset was this property," he said. "But there is an interesting additional matter of relevance now. Years ago, Leila had purchased a life insurance policy, the proceeds of which amount to a substantial sum.

"She had no family," he said. "That is to say, none she claimed."

"Maria and Luis were very dear to her, as you might guess. She left instructions that their salaries be paid to them out of the funds in the policy for the duration of their days.

"My client worried greatly about the future of La Llorona," the lawyer continued. "Much as she loved her workers, they're old themselves, and not equipped to take on a place like this one. The insurance money was meant to ensure that the property could carry on after her passing."

It was ironic. While she was living, Leila had no money to repair the hotel. Now that she was dead this would be possible.

"That's good to hear," I said. I held the plate of macarons out to our guest. Why was any of what he was saying relevant to me?

Juan de la Vega laid a piece of thick, creamy vellum paper on the table. The words were in all in Spanish.

"In our final conversation Leila informed me of her desire to leave La Llorona to you," he said. "Because she had granted me power of attorney some years before, I was able to carry out her wishes on that point."

With a perfectly manicured hand, the attorney handed me the paper.

There at the bottom of the page was my name and my signature in the guest book the day I arrived. There was the date, handwritten, in deep blue ink. I studied the paper more closely, trying to take in what Juan de la Vega had just told me. It made no sense.

"I understand this must be something of a shock," the attorney commented. "News of an unexpected inheritance, however ultimately beneficial, often inspires a mix of emotions."

He was right about this, of course. My mind went to our last conversation in the garden. Though I had spoken many times to Leila about my admiration for what she'd created at La Llorona, never in all that time had I exhibited an extravagant display of emotion toward her or she toward me. She had taken my hand one time, but I had never so much as hugged her. One time, but one time only—when she asked me how I'd slept, the morning after my first night there—I'd said something to her about how much it had meant to me that for the first time in years I had not awakened once in the night.

"You must be very tired," she'd said. "And not just from your trip." She'd touched my shoulder then. Nothing more.

"I don't understand," I told the attorney. "She barely knew me. I don't know anything about running a hotel."

"In my many years of representing my client," he said, "I have come to recognize her supreme skills as a judge of character." She had a sense about people, he said. She was seldom wrong.

There were surprisingly few papers to sign. Tax documents, the title to the land, which measured five hectares, though if you'd asked me how much that represented, I would have had no clue. One by one, he turned the pages, pointing out the lines requiring my signature, I felt as though I were dreaming, but I signed.

"I believe we've taken care of everything," Juan de la Vega told me, finally. "But feel free to call," he told me, handing me a business card as thick and expensive-looking as the earlier document, with an address on the front from the city.

He'd driven three and a half hours to deliver this news, and because the boat that would deliver him to his car stopped running at sunset, he had to take his leave. He reached out his hand. Mine was still shaking from the shock of the news he'd delivered.

"You will have an interesting life here," he said.

33

Fixer-upper

"*Es tu casa ahora*," Walter said. It's your house now.

Only for a little while, I told him. "I don't know anything about running a hotel or tending a garden. I'm not a citizen of this country. I can't speak Spanish."

I said this in English, as usual. To this boy, and no one else, I could say what was true—protected by the absence of a common language between us, though there were times when it seemed to me he actually did understand what I was telling him.

"Everyone I've cared about the most ended up dying," I said.

Walter must have understood me.

"I'm still here," he answered.

There was nothing for me back in San Francisco—only the memory, every time I walked the streets of that city, of the worst day of my life, and another memory of standing on the Golden Gate Bridge, planning to end it. Though I had no place to go from here, staying on in La Esperanza seemed equally impossible.

Still, who would buy a property like this one—a falling-down hotel with a mountain of unpaid debts in a town accessible only by a scary flight, a long bus ride, and a bumpy ride on a boat with no life preservers on board? Who, besides some developer like Carl Edgar, would put money into a property that probably hadn't turned a profit in a decade, if ever?

I would do everything I could to keep La Llorona from falling into the hands of the Bigwig Corporation. The only thing for it, I told myself, was to fix the place up—use the money Leila had left to me to get La Llorona in the kind of shape that would attract a buyer willing to preserve its original owner's vision rather than tearing it down.

I'd accomplish this as swiftly as possible and sell the hotel. Then I'd get back on the boat and disappear.

34

A particularly fine tilapia,
a long list of repairs

Though he had spent no more than a half hour on the property, total, and less than five minutes in the kitchen with Maria and Luis before our meeting on the patio, Juan de la Vega had evidently explained to them the details of Leila's plan. If I supposed that, as Leila's loyal employees for over twenty years, they might have been resentful of my utterly unexpected ascent from hotel guest to owner, I would have been wrong. Maria, in the midst of dinner preparations, had always displayed warmth, but something had changed in her. We were partners now in the endeavor to run the hotel.

Pablito had come by that afternoon with a particularly fine tilapia he'd harpooned in the water just in front of the hotel. "After great loss, it's important to eat," he said. "Keep up your strength. You will need it."

There was so much to do. Rainy season was still a few months away, but if the roof weren't repaired by then, water would pour into every room. The dock was falling apart, and the ceramic tile on the patio was badly chipped, and the garden, though exploding with colors, was badly overgrown. These were the kinds of things a person might not notice when she first laid eyes on the place, but now, suddenly placed in charge of everything, signs of trouble presented themselves wherever I looked.

I couldn't think of looking for a good buyer for the hotel until we'd taken care of the areas most desperately in need of repairs. Even a potential buyer who loved the place and respected its heritage—the

146

kind of person Leila would have wanted running La Llorona—would never take on a property with as many issues of deferred maintenance as this one. I had no idea where to begin.

I asked Luis and Maria if we could talk.

"We want to help in any way we can," Maria said. "My husband will tend the garden with his whole heart. I will be honored to cook for you. Elmer is ready to work hard. Mirabel too."

I studied the faces of the two young people—shy, awkward Elmer, and beautiful Mirabel, both still in their teens. As devoted as they were to the hotel, it seemed unlikely I could rely on them to oversee the business. They all seemed to be counting on me to do that.

Leila had died on a Wednesday. Juan de la Vega had appeared with news of my surprising inheritance on Friday. At seven thirty on Saturday morning, just as I finished my coffee, Maria informed me, once again, that a man was waiting at the gate, hoping to see me. Should she let him in?

"His name is Gus," she told me, in Spanish. "He used to work for Leila. We haven't seen him around in a couple of years."

There was a look on her face. Whoever this person was, she appeared to have some doubts about him.

"What do you think about him?"

Maria shook her head. "It's not for me to say," she told me. "He used to work for the señora. Then he stopped coming around. We haven't seen him in a couple of years."

"He knows this property well and he works hard," said Luis. "We could use the help."

"Send him down," I told Maria.

35

The man for the job

Gus was not a tall person, or even a particularly large one, but he had the hands of a man familiar with hard physical work. He came from England—Blackburn, a town where nothing mattered more than the sport of football. From the look of him, he had a few years on me, though he had lived a harder life. Physically speaking, anyway.

"I've done a bit of brawlin' in the past," he told me. "But that ain't me no more. Four years back, I found myself a nice gal and settled down. Got ourselves a little place up in the valley and a kid, light of my life naturally, except when I want to smack him a good one. Number two's on the way."

Word had gotten around, evidently, that Leila had left her property to me. He offered his congratulations. "You could've knocked me over with a feather," he said. "But one thing about Leila, she always did things her way.

"I ain't the crying type," Gus told me, "but when I heard the old girl was a goner, it smacked me one right here, you know?" He pointed to his chest. "I said to my missus, 'Well, maybe that new lass that's taking over will want to put some life back into the old joint.'

"If so," he said, "I'm the man for the job.'

He had brought a notebook along, and compiled a list of what he called first, second, third, and fourth priorities. In addition to re-thatching the roof, these included serious attention to the foundation on the lake side of the house which he'd observed—even from a quick glance, times he rode past on the lancha boat—appeared to have seen better days. Then there was the dock, which was no longer usable, and the stone path from the road, where at least half the steps were seriously in need of repair.

"The water pump's living on borrowed time," he told me. He knew this much because the last time it broke down, he'd been the one they'd called to fix it. "I did the best I could, but the coupling's rotted out and the floater's shot," he said. "One thing you don't want is to find yourself with no water, smack bang in the middle of the dry season. Plants'll be knackered in two days."

He was the chatty type, Gus. But there was something refreshing about this, as he went on to discuss the issues of the electrical wiring at La Llorona ("you've got four breakers doing the work of eight," he said, as if I'd know what that meant) and the mold issue in all four of the hotel's bathrooms. Then there were my retaining walls to consider. He hadn't taken a gander at these yet. When he did, it wouldn't be a pretty picture.

But the big issue, he said—"hold on to your hat"—was my septic system.

"My better half, Dora, would know a more ladylike way to put this," he said. "But all I can do is tell it straight. It's a miracle the tank hasn't overflowed yet, but when it does, the stink will reach clear to the top of that volcano." He pointed across the lake to El Fuego, in case I'd forgotten where it stood.

With the exception of those early years in which my mother and Daniel and I had lived in motels and campgrounds, mostly, I'd been an apartment-dweller all my life. I knew nothing about septic systems.

"You got your loo," he said. "You got a pipe heading out, and a tank buried three feet under, maybe four. When it fills up, the crap's meant to leak out into the ground, which might work fine if you got a good ten feet of sand in all directions, 'round your stink pot. Even five feet might cut it. What you don't want is a septic tank buried next to a lake. A lake where people swim, if you get me."

I could almost feel myself getting dizzy, Gus's list was so long, of the work needed to get La Llorona back in shape. All of it urgent.

"Chin up, love," he said. "We'll get this place shining like a new penny." There was something comforting about this man, even as he delivered bad news about issues like dry rot or sketchy wiring. Whatever there was that needed doing, he was up for it.

One thing was clear. It was fortunate that Leila had left that insurance money. I would need every penny.

36

Honeymooners

In the month since my arrival, no other guest had appeared, and Maria had made no mention of any. But something inspired me to open the reservation book that morning. I was probably just wondering how often, if ever, people had come to stay here in recent months. Or years.

What do you know? A couple were arriving that afternoon.

The handwriting in the book was Leila's of course. That much I knew from those mornings when I'd come out to the patio for breakfast to find the note she'd left me, expressing her hope that I'd spent a good night and offering some interesting suggestion for how I might spend my morning, or part of it. (A particular flower had opened, in the garden next to the waterfall. Here was a poem by Neruda I might enjoy. Did I like flan?)

Now here came her voice, as if speaking from the grave, with her notes about a couple named Harriet and Sam Holloway. The Holloways made their home in New Hampshire. Flying in from Boston, they were due to check in sometime that afternoon.

Leila had written extensive notes about Harriet and Sam. "*Luna de miel*," she'd written. Honeymoon.

Below this, she'd made one final note. "Want to hike volcano."

They showed up at the gate shortly before sunset, same as I had, in the company of Walter, who carried a very large Samsonite suitcase on his head, in addition to a smaller bag in one hand and a duffel over his shoulder.

The Holloways looked very young—early twenties, if I had to guess. Even back in the United States, Sam Holloway would have qualified as a tall man, but here in this country where few adults stood above five foot two or three, he seemed like a giant, a beanpole. Harriet was only an inch or two shorter—still over six feet, I estimated. She looked at him with a gaze of total love.

"I can't believe we're really here," Sam said, as we stood on the landing of the long stone stairway leading to the house.

"You don't know how long he's dreamed of this moment," Harriet said.

It took longer than usual making our way down the steps, Harriet was so transported by the plant life along the path, and the birds, who always reappeared in great numbers at this time in the day. Every few steps, Harriet called out to Sam, remarking on some particularly amazing plant that caught her eye.

Sam didn't share the enthusiasm of his bride until we reached the foot of the long hill, and the lake stretched out before us. Standing on the terrace afforded the Holloways a clear view of the volcano, unlike what they'd encountered on that bumpy boat ride, holding on for dear life. Backlit by the sunset, the sight still took my breath away.

"El Fuego," Sam whispered, as a person might when entering the Vatican, or landing on the moon. "Eight thousand, two hundred forty-seven feet. Two thousand, five hundred fourteen meters, give or take a few centimeters."

In the small mill town where the two of them grew up, the main forms of work, farming and a manufacturing operation providing light bulbs for the automotive industry, Sam Holloway had developed, early, his unlikely passion for volcanos.

"He was always drawing them, even in third grade," Harriet said. The two of them had known each other all their lives.

"And you?" I asked her.

She laughed. "I was drawing his name in my notebooks. His and mine, with a heart."

Her observation seemed not to have registered with her husband. He was still overcome by the sight at the other side of the lake.

"I only ever saw a volcano in a picture," he said. "Until today."

This was the reason for Sam and Harriet's unconventional choice in a honeymoon destination. "Our parents wanted to send us to Disney," Harriet said. "But Sam——"

No explanation necessary.

I led them down the hallway to the room Leila had selected for the Holloways—with a door handle carved into the wood resembling an iguana.

"We'll be serving you dinner on the patio at seven," I said. "Let me know if you need anything.

"My name's Irene, by the way."

On my first night Leila had joined me for dinner, but for Sam and Harriet, touching down just two days after their wedding, Maria and I set a table for two, with a circle of rose petals surrounding them. Dinner was a stew made of freshwater crabs from the lake. I'd seen one of the fisherman paddle up to the dock that morning to sell them to Luis.

I had my dinner in the kitchen with Maria and Luis. We ate in silence, mostly, looking out from a respectful distance at the young lovers, staring into each other's eyes across the table. More accurately, Harriet stared into Sam's eyes. Sam stared out at the volcano.

They had made the plan to climb it a couple of days later. Elmer would accompany them: Five hours up, four hours down. But they were in good shape.

I had scheduled a follow-up meeting the next morning with Gus, who had promised to present me with a budget for the first phase of repairs on the property, hoping that the insurance money, less what I'd need to hold on to for Maria and Luis's salaries, would be sufficient.

When I got up, a little before seven, Harriet and Sam were already outside. Harriet, in a short pink dress that looked like something she'd bought specially for the trip, crouched over a rock, studying one of the small armies of ants that sometimes paraded across the lawn, carrying crumbs or bits of chewed-up leaf. Sam stood at the farthest edge of the property, motionless, facing out to the lake, holding a pair of binoculars focused squarely on El Fuego.

"All night Sam couldn't stop talking about El Fuego," Harriet told me.

It might not be the best news to hear from a new bride, that the man with whom she was spending her honeymoon, not to mention the rest of her life, had passed their first night in one of the more romantic destinations a couple might find themselves, discussing a volcano.

"My husband is in paradise," she added.

"And you?" I asked.

"The truth is, the whole volcano thing is Sam's dream, not mine," Harriet said, quietly, as if he might overhear, which he couldn't, from where he stood with the binoculars. "An eight-mile hike up a steep trail isn't actually my idea of a good time."

I might have pointed out that she could tell him this. But the two of them were in that young and endlessly hopeful stage of love I remembered, when all you want to do is make the person you love happy. In the case of Lenny and me, it had never been difficult accomplishing this.

37

A large check

After breakfast the two of them headed into the village to explore. On her way over from the boat the afternoon before, Harriet had seen a poncho she liked, and a storefront offering cranial sacral massage, and she wanted to bring a bag home for her grandmother.

Within minutes of Sam and Harriet's departure, Gus arrived. He had a tape measure with him and a notebook, and a calculator.

"Now I know cash can be a bit of a sore point," he said. "And I want to give you the best deal I can. I won't lie to you. I had a bit of a ding-dong with Dora about the bid being so low.

" 'You know as well as me,' she says. 'Any other guy in town would charge twice the price and end up tacking on another 10 percent before the job was done.'

"Don't get me wrong," Gus said, "Dora's a good gal. I'm betting once you two meet up, you'll be the best of friends and probably leave old Gus in the dust."

I was about to offer a comment, but Gus had more to say.

"I've got a feeling we'll make a cracking team, you and me," Gus said.

"Sounds like a plan," I said. I gestured in the direction of the coffee-pot. He indicated yes. I offered milk. Did I have cream perhaps?

For the foundation work, he said, we were looking at a crew of six men for roughly three weeks' duration. The septic, which could be carried off at the same time, would call for roughly equivalent numbers of men and days. In the notebook he'd brought, he'd scrawled a bunch of other numbers I couldn't fully decipher, having to do with bags of cement, lengths of rebar, deliveries of sand.

The total bill he projected, all things added up, and converted to numbers I could make sense of, came to somewhere a little north of ten thousand dollars. This would cover the most urgent priorities on the list. We'd get to the rest after.

"The good news is, if we do it all in one whack, you won't have so much downtime at the hotel. Sooner you're back in business, sooner you can start hauling in the cash."

This was optimistic. My examination of Leila's reservation book two days earlier had revealed that other than the weeklong stay of Sam and Harriet, there were no other guests booked for two months, and even then, only a lone Australian described, in Leila's notes, as "poor as a church mouse, but says he'll bring his didgeridoo."

I admired Gus's enthusiasm, his can-do approach. Already, he'd filled me in on the name of the man who sold the best chicken in town, and where to go to buy a special kind of rare green stone that would look wonderful in my front wall, when we got around to repairing that. He had a truck going to the city the following week. "Anything you need at the market, just say the word," he told me. "We can throw it in, on the house.

"Tell you what," he said, when he'd finished taking the measurements of yet another part of the property he'd pronounced in need of immediate attention. "Let Dora cook us all dinner over at our place tomorrow night. We'll get you set up right. Maybe I didn't mention, but she's a yoga teacher. Best in town. Tantric, but that's for another day."

Meanwhile I gave him the go-ahead on every one of the repair jobs he'd listed for me. What did I know about foundations and septic systems or fuse boxes and wiring? Thank God Gus did. I wrote him a large check.

38

A dinner party, a volcano

Sam and Harriet returned from town late that afternoon. Now it was Harriet's turn to be excited.

She was wearing her new poncho and carrying a woven bag. I didn't ask what she'd paid for them, but she volunteered anyway. "Everything's so incredibly cheap in the market here, I feel guilty," she said. "When the woman told me the price on the bag, I had to give her an extra few dollars."

"Not dollars," Sam corrected her, a habit I had now recognized in him. "*Garzas.*" It was the Spanish word for heron. This was a country that honored its birds.

They had lunch in this little tienda, and the woman had taken out her special collection of Mayan artifacts that her grandfather dug up. That was the impression Harriet got anyway, not speaking the language. When she heard Sam and Harriet were newlyweds on their honeymoon, the woman insisted on giving her one of the artifacts, after which Harriet had bought three more, at a ridiculously low price.

"You know that man in the little lean-to with all the dogs out front?" she asked me. This could have been many men. Many lean-tos. "The one with the sign in front that says Mayan Astrology?"

Andres. I remembered what Leila had told me about him: *Stay away.*

"He was outside, making these amazing drawings of Mayan symbols, and he had this shirt on, with all kinds of ribbons and beads hanging off of it. I told him *No habla español,* but he just shook his head, like that wasn't a problem, and pointed to his heart. I really wanted to go inside and get a reading, but Sammy said we needed to get back and rest up, if we were getting up at four to do the volcano hike."

Sam and Harriet took off for the volcano before I got up next morning. Maria had fixed them coffee and a picnic lunch. Elmer met them in front of the gate with a *tuk tuk* to bring them to the trailhead and from there, accompany them up the steep side of the volcano.

Gus and the crew of men he'd assembled showed up a little after seven. Sitting in the garden, drawing—a much-needed break from my long and confusing perusal of Leila's spotty records—I could hear their voices talking and laughing most of the day. Sometime around noon, a small group of women in the traditional *traje* of the village appeared and made their way down the steps to deliver baskets that evidently contained lunch for their husbands—small ceramic pots of beans and rice, and freshly made tortillas wrapped like presents in hand-woven cloth.

On the other side of the lake, I studied the looming form of the volcano, trying to imagine where Sam and Harriet might be at this point. At five o'clock they weren't back yet. I knew Maria needed no instructions concerning dinner preparations—only the reminder to leave the top gate unlocked. I headed to Gus and Dora's with a bottle of wine from Leila's collection.

Most houses in the village—those built by gringos—favored a rustic style, with thatch roofs and irregularly shaped adobe walls that met each other at unlikely angles, covered in white stucco, with twisted coffee wood verandas with vines spilling over the sides and wind chimes hanging from the trees. The house Gus and Dora had built bore no resemblance to these. Except for the stand of bamboo in the yard, and the hammock, the design and construction materials suggested a place in some small, anonymous working-class suburb, inhabited by solid nine-to-five types. As much as the place lacked, aesthetically, there was a certain reassuring solidity to the knowledge that this man built structures to last, and probably rebuilt them with a similar goal in mind.

As I made my way down the paved walkway to the front door, a small dark-haired child ran out to meet me—a boy around the age my son was when I lost him. I might have thought this would be difficult, but I felt no need to turn and run. The child, Luca, was followed by a largely pregnant woman who extended her hand. Dora was not the hugging type.

"I've heard so much about you," she said, though I wondered how, since my visits with Gus so far had involved a lot more listening than speaking.

She spoke with an accent—Dora had grown up in Chile—but her English was flawless, and suggested a background of a certain education, if not money. She wasn't beautiful, but she had the kind of face you were likely to remember—small, narrow but piercing eyes that took in everything, large teeth, whiter than seemed possible. I had the impression, meeting her, that she was sizing up every single thing about me—not just my appearance and my clothing, but more so, what I might be doing here, whether I was likely to stay around and if so, whether that was good news or bad.

Dora was one of those women who carried her pregnancy in one place only, like a basketball tucked under her shirt. Every part of her body besides her large and bountiful-looking belly appeared magnificently toned, a fact confirmed when we took our seats at the table, and she folded into a perfect lotus position.

It wasn't difficult to see that Dora was not the type to wear a bra or feel a need for one. Partly due to the imminent birth, no doubt (and, it turned out, to the fact that she was still nursing their son, who was just a little under three years old) she had extraordinary breasts—ripe and full. She carried her breasts the way a woman does who considers them a source of wonder, and they were.

"My husband says we're going to be best friends," she said, as their son Luca settled in under the folds of her blouse to nurse. "So, are we?"

Dinner was healthy—lentils and roasted vegetables, an Argentinian drink I'd never tasted before, yerba maté, that Dora instructed me to sip through a straw. To me, it tasted bitter, but I finished my glass of the stuff. After, Dora set a pudding on the table, made with carob and flaxseed.

If Dora seemed serious, and intense, Gus was the opposite—funny, playful, self-deprecating, and quick to praise others. Dora, number one.

Gus reserved his greatest outpouring of admiration for the guru at the ashram where the two of them had met in India, who'd changed his life.

"I'll level with you, mate," he said, as he passed me the joint he'd just finished rolling, made from his home-grown weed. Dora herself never touched the stuff.

"I was a real scallywag in my younger days," he said. "If I was delivering beer to a pub, and it seemed like nobody was watching, might just pinch a six-pack or three. I got into my fair share of bust-ups. You might say I was no stranger to incarceration. As many times I got put away, back in the day, I got to calling the old jailhouse the Lancashire County Hotel."

"What changed?" I asked him.

Dora had made him a new man. Though they never would have met if he hadn't high-tailed it to Goa, one time when they had a warrant out for him for a robbery at a fish and chips establishment. Some rat from Burnley tried to pin a heist on him—a chippie down the street from where he lived. "I was nowhere near the joint at the time," he told me. "But what's a boy to do when the one to provide his alibi for the night in question is his best friend's mum, with her husband out of town?"

A song from long ago came to mind, "Long Black Veil." For a moment, I could hear my mother's voice. Then Gus's again.

"I only showed up at the ashram for the free food," he said. "But I stayed for this one."

His eyes went to Dora again. Always to Dora. This was not the first time Dora had heard Gus tell his story. She leaned back on the pillows, the sleeping form of Luca still at her breast, and rolled her eyes.

"At first, she flicked me off like a fly on a cowpat," he said. "But I didn't give up. Once I set my mind on a task, you won't get rid of me."

When it turned out that Dora attended the sunrise meditation at the ashram, he was there to join her. Years of physical work had made him strong, but hardly limber. At the ashram, he practiced yoga with as much devotion as, in former days, he'd visited the Olde King Hank.

"I'd known his type," Dora observed. "Big-talking blowhard. Interested in one thing."

"But I showed you different, didn't I, love?" he said.

A couple had turned up at the ashram, who practiced acro-yoga, Gus explained. "We were out on the beach, watching them. Sunset, chanting. Candles. The two of them looking like a pair of frigging gods from, where is it, Mount Olympus?

"Ten or fifteen we were, standing there gawping at these two, and I'm telling you, not much causes me to shut my piehole, but the sight of the two of them, going at it with the yoga moves, brought out the romantic in me. Then the bloke turns to us, asks if there's someone who might like to volunteer to be the one to hold up a partner while she flew."

Gus had stepped out to the front. "I'll give it a whirl," he said.

Dora would not have volunteered, but the instructor picked her. "You look like you know what you're doing," the acro guy said to her. Seeing her as she was now, folded on a pile of cushions, holding their sleeping son, it was easy to understand why he might have chosen as he did. She had an air of focus and determination about her, and a low tolerance, if any, for failure.

"It takes a lot to rattle me," Gus said. "But lying on that mat, with my pegs in the air, and this woman I'd been dreaming about for a good two weeks by that point. The old ticker was thumping so hard it could've drowned out the chanting at a Rovers game."

The acro-yogi had instructed Dora to stand facing Gus, with her toes lined up against the fingers of his hands, one on either side of him, and the soles of Gus's bare feet pressed into her stomach—lower than that, actually, closer in to the pelvic bones. Just that—the feel of her amazing body against his toes—was enough to make Gus draw in his breath.

The woman acro-yoga teacher told her to lean forward now. *Take hold of his hands. Let go of the ground.*

He straightened his legs. Not so easy for a guy whose quadriceps had been largely employed, since he dropped out of school on his fifteenth birthday, in hauling wheelbarrows of cement and hoisting beams. "I sure wasn't what you'd call a flexible man. Physically speaking," he added.

"But I wanted to lift this little lady as high as I could. I wanted to make her dream come true." For once in his life, he didn't blow it.

Their wedding was held at the ashram—Dora in a beautiful white dress, Gus also in white. "If my old football mates back in Blackburn could have seen me, they would have said I was off my rocker," he said.

"But I was a sane man. For the first time in thirty-one years. I talked this woman into marrying me."

Talking people into things. This may have been the greatest of Gus's talents.

39
Honeymoon, interrupted

On the walk home I thought about Gus and Dora and the life they'd made in their little cinder block and adobe house with the vegetable garden out front and the chickens wandering the yard and the sweet-faced boy and the baby on the way. I'd gotten the unmistakable sense, over the course of our dinner together, that these were two people in possession of a powerful connection, more powerful even than love or sex—the common goal of making a family together, a home. Gus would do anything to make sure nothing got in the way.

They might have seemed like an unlikely pair—Gus with his warm, effusive, big-talking bluster, and Dora, who stayed on the sidelines with a certain cool-eyed detachment. Even that first night in her company I recognized her protectiveness of her husband. As he laid out his plans for helping me get the hotel back on its feet, I observed a wariness in Dora. No doubt she was well-acquainted with her husband's good humor and generosity. It was her job to make sure I didn't take advantage of him.

This didn't undermine my affection for Dora. I respected her for her attention to order and discipline, and above all her unshakeable loyalty to her family, Gus in particular. Though Gus had made it plain to me that first day he'd shown up at the property that I should never hesitate to call at any hour of day or night I needed him, that night at their house Dora had quietly reminded me never to call after five o'clock. This was her time.

I recognized in Dora a person accustomed to maintaining a businesslike distance, where Gus had announced himself, at that first

163

dinner we shared, as a man ready to be, for me, the brother I never had. Possessing three loaves of bread in a famine, he'd give two and a half away. If a hotel guest dropped her diamond ring in the composting toilet Gus wouldn't hesitate to dig into the muck and retrieve it. Dora would be the one who had to remind him to bill me for the job.

The stars were out, and because this place offered so little in the way of ambient light—no streetlights, no house lights on at this hour—I had seldom witnessed a clearer or more brilliant view of the constellations.

The thought came to me that I might give La Esperanza a year. It would probably take that long anyway, getting the hotel in shape. I thought about Gus's story, the life he'd led before, the choice he'd made to create a new one, bearing no resemblance to anything preceding it.

I unlocked the gate of the hotel. Making my way down the still-unfamiliar steps I spotted Harriet on a stone bench in the garden, crying. I wasn't sure if I should leave her alone, but she looked up.

"I'm sorry," she said. Harriet was one of those people who apologized a lot, even for things, like crying, that nobody should have to apologize for.

"That volcano hike is no walk in the park," I said. "I haven't tackled it myself, to be honest."

"Partway up I turned my ankle," she said. "Sam was trying to be sympathetic, but I knew how disappointed he'd be. So I told him he should go on up without me. I guess I didn't really think he'd leave me, but he did."

Elmer was required to accompany Sam to the top. Nobody could approach the crater except in the company of a guide.

"I told them I'd be fine, waiting," she said.

Half an hour after they'd continued up the volcano, an insect bit Harriet. "I was scared it might be something poisonous, but I guess it wasn't because after a while it didn't hurt so much anymore," she said. She had counted to three hundred in Spanish—for practice.

The place Harriet's husband had left her when he made his way to the top of the volcano had been above the tree line. When they first reached the spot, it was still morning, but by noon the sun was directly overhead, and Harriet had forgotten her hat. She was a fair-skinned person, and it turned out the sunscreen had been in his backpack, along with their backup water bottle. She was nearly finished with the first one.

Birds circled overhead. She wondered if they were vultures. To take her mind off this, she lay down for a nap. When she woke up, two men were standing there, holding machetes.

Maybe they'd only want money, but when they found out she didn't have any (that, too, was in the backpack with Sam), maybe they'd do something worse. She could feel her heart beating fast. She imagined one of the men holding her down.

She tried to remember things her brother had taught her when they wrestled in the basement—moves you could use even if your opponent was stronger than you, if not bigger.

This gave her an idea. Possibly her one chance. She stood up, allowing the men to take in the full sight of her six-foot-one-inch stature.

Her mother was always criticizing her for her bad posture, but this time, Harriet stood up very straight. She looked the men in the eye. She was a full head taller than they were.

The men took one last look. Then ran.

It had been almost six o'clock by the time Sam and Elmer returned to the spot where Harriet was waiting for them. She was sunburned now, and the insect bite still hurt, though not as badly as her ankle, which had begun to swell. Before she had a chance to tell her husband what happened, he was describing his day to her.

"I got to look inside the crater," Sam told her. "It was glowing. And there was steam coming out."

"Some scary men came," Harriet told him. "I made them go away."
Now was the moment he would put his arms around her, tell her he
should never have left, congratulate her on her bravery.

"That's my girl," he said. No further comment. On the way down,
he was talking about all the other volcanoes he hoped to climb now
that he'd made it to the top of this one.

Next morning Harriet stayed in their room. I found Sam over by the
bougainvillea. For once, he wasn't looking at the volcano. He was staring down at the dirt, poking it with a stick. I handed him a glass of
Maria's freshly squeezed orange juice.

"Even people who love each other a lot sometimes go through hard
times," I told him.

A picture came to me of Lenny, on a drive home after a Sunday visit
with his parents—his hands gripping the steering wheel. "I wish you'd
make a little more of an effort to get to know my parents," he'd said. "It
makes me sad, seeing you sitting on the couch not even trying to be
part of the conversation." A wave of regret passed over me. How little
it would have taken to make him happy that day.

"I wanted Harriet to share my passions," he said. "But all she wanted
to do was get back to the hotel. All of a sudden I felt like I didn't even
know her."

"She told me she was never even into the idea of coming here. She didn't
care about seeing the volcano. It was all an act, making this trip with me."

"I wouldn't call it an act."

I was trying to imagine what Leila might have said to him. "I'd call
it what a person does sometimes, to make someone they love happy.
Caring about the other person's desires more than your own."

"How can you expect to spend the rest of your life with a person that
doesn't even value the same things you do?" he said.

"She values *you*," I said. "She values your relationship." But my
voice carried none of the authority Leila's had.

"We had all these great plans," he told me. "Every year for our anniversary we were going to explore a different volcano."

"And when was it going to be her turn?"

"Her turn?" He sounded baffled.

Later that morning, I walked Harriet to the dock to catch a boat back to the mainland. Walter accompanied us, with her purple flowered bag on his head, her new, married initials monogrammed on the front.

"I wish you two could talk it out," I suggested one more time, as the lancha pulled up.

"I just want to get home," she said.

Sam stayed the rest of the week at La Llorona on his own, bent over books about volcanos from Leila's collection. When he moved out, he did not head back to the city and the airport, as Harriet had done. He rented a room in one of the very cheap hostels in the village. He had decided to stay on and take a course at the meditation center in town, Las Fuentes.

In the days that followed—days, then weeks—I saw him now and then, wearing the white pants and tunic of the meditation students. I tried to talk with him once on the path, but he shook his head and made a hand gesture over his mouth that evidently meant he couldn't speak. Then I remembered one of the practices at Las Fuentes, engaged in by the most serious followers of the center's guru, Andromeda. They observed a two-week period of silence, followed by a week in which they were given a walking stick and blindfolded and led around town by workers from the center—indigenous people from the community, who probably found the practice only slightly less baffling than all the other baffling behaviors of the gringo community there.

After that, I didn't see Sam Holloway for over a year. I know, because by the time I saw him again, the septic job at La Llorona had been completed, overseen by Gus, along with the dry rot replacement, and the rewiring of my electrical system, and the rebuilding of the stone steps from the gate to the front door of the hotel—jobs that occupied Gus and his workers for many months. His bill for all of this had come to double the original estimate, and there was more to be done, but I felt lucky to have him there, making sure everything got taken care of. The man was like a brother to me.

40

Just a traveler passing through

Two rainy seasons came and went. Thanks to the money from Leila's insurance policy, there was a new gate at the top now, with lights that actually worked illuminating the path, new floors in the kitchen, new counters, a refrigerator that didn't make a roaring noise. We were weeding the garden, cleaning out the fish pool, pruning the roses. The place was beginning to look, once again, as it must have in Leila's prime. A few bookings were coming in—and sometimes travelers who weren't even staying at the hotel, who'd heard about Maria's cooking, made reservations for dinner. We weren't raking in cash. But I was paying my bills, compensating my workers well, with something left over every month.

I would have thought I'd be gone from the lake by now, but every time one job neared completion, Gus had five ideas ready for our next project. In an odd way, this suited me. Though I still saw myself as someone just passing through this place until I could sell the hotel, the seemingly endless renovation projects allowed me to defer the next chapter of my life. The problem would come when it was finally time to move on, because I had no idea where I might go.

There remained, in the back of my mind, the memory of the man who'd paid a visit to my art teacher—an FBI agent, from the sound of things. As little as I had to offer in the way of the answers he'd been looking for, I wanted to steer clear of his questions.

I had walked into town to pick up a replacement part for Gus's sander, and there was the former honeymooner, Sam, sitting at a little folding table in one of the stalls alongside the path with a sign hanging in front, "English-Speaking Volcano Tours." Beside him was a very pretty, very young indigenous woman in a gorgeous blue huipil who appeared to be functioning as his assistant in the operation. His business appeared to be doing well, from the looks of how many backpackers could be seen hanging out there when I passed.

Walking back to the hotel that day from town, I thought about what it was that allowed this young man to do what I could not—start over in a whole new language, in a town three thousand miles from home. Sam wouldn't even put it that way, probably, if you asked him. La Esperanza was not, for him, a village three thousand miles away from home. La Esperanza *was* home, now.

It was possible, in this place, for a person to change his life almost overnight. One trip up a volcano might accomplish that.

For me, it didn't work that way. Wherever I went, whatever I did, I carried the old story inside me, of what happened before. I could stand at the edge of that impossibly blue lake, take in the beauty all around me—the birds, and the flowers, and the taste on my lips of the most perfect mango, its juice dripping down my chin—but I still felt like a traveler passing through.

I still told myself that at the rate work was going at La Llorona, I should be able to put the place on the market within another six months at most.

41

The question of family

One night after she'd cleaned up from dinner—the last of the dishes put away, the tablecloths cleared from the tables, new cloths set out for the morning, silverware wrapped—Maria had asked if we could sit down to talk.

"I hope you are happy here," she said to me. I no longer had difficulty understanding her Spanish, even when—as now—it was hard, to provide the response she deserved.

"I am a lucky woman," I told her. "You and Luis and Elmer do such a good job."

"I think it must be lonely for you," she said. "All alone in this big place."

"You're here every day. And Luis. And Elmer. Mirabel. Walter. Not to mention the hotel guests." We were booking rooms now. Not every room, every night, but more so than before.

"Hotel guests are not your family," she said.

I did not speak Spanish well enough to say all I might have on the subject of family.

"It's good you work so hard," Maria said. "But don't forget about love."

42

A folder of letters

There had been one drawer in Leila's desk I'd never ventured to explore. The first time I'd opened it, I'd been discouraged by the enormous pile of papers stuffed inside, in no particular order from the looks of them. There were envelopes addressed to the hotel but never opened, letters that appeared to have been read, but discarded. Then finally one day I took a closer look.

One folder contained nothing but love letters—with postmarks from Venezuela, Australia, Italy. A man named Jasper appeared to have been corresponding with Leila over the course of over a decade, his letters filled with reminiscences of their times together in Panama, Roatan, Oaxaca. He wrote about a time they'd swum with dolphins, a night they'd slept in the jungle and encountered a jaguar.

"Every night I dream about you," he had written, in a letter Leila had evidently never opened.

Then came the correspondence from potential guests—more than twenty years' worth of inquiries from travelers interested in offbeat vacation destinations, travel agents, even, who'd heard about the hotel and expressed interest in sending clients. From what I could tell, Leila had neglected virtually all of these.

A woman had written to Leila, back in the eighties, to say she conducted an annual conference on Mayan textiles, with participants from all over the world. Would Leila consider hosting a group of them at her hotel? A man wrote from a university archaeology department to say he wanted to bring down a group of students to explore the recently discovered ruins nearby. Like the others, the envelope containing that letter had never been opened.

It became clear, as I sifted through the contents of the drawer, why the hotel had not done well over the years. Leila was an artist in every sense—creator of spaces and meals, gardens, waterfalls, stained glass windows, mosaics. But as a businessperson, she was a disaster.

There was one ancient-looking folder. I found it in the bottom of the drawer. These letters had been opened before—opened and, from the looks of the paper, read more than once. Studied carefully many times over the years, perhaps. They concerned Leila's lost daughter, Charlotte.

The first couple of letters offered terse descriptions of a child's development. "She can walk now. She spoke her first word. She loves dogs. She appears to have a talent for dancing."

For a while there it appeared that Javier was sending updates a few times a year. Then every few years. Then no more. The last piece of correspondence in the folder contained a black-and-white photograph of a good-looking couple in their thirties standing alongside two very beautiful children—a boy who looked around ten years old and a girl around twelve. The single piece of paper contained in the envelope offered only two sentences. *"Sofia and I have no intention of showing your letters to our daughter. Please don't waste your time writing to her."*

Maybe Leila continued to write. If so, no further responses arrived from Spain.

The date on the final letter, February, 1979. Then nothing.

43

The queen of trash

Though La Esperanza and its environs possessed great natural beauty, the town had a big problem disposing of its trash. In the old days, before foreigners arrived, plastic had been unheard of. But when more stores opened up, suddenly products like orange soda and Coke started showing up, and bags of chips, and candy. People who had never eaten these foods before now viewed them as highly desirable, to the point where even the poorest people bought them when they could and gave them to their children.

By now I'd observed, more than once, the phenomenon of earnest, well-intentioned travelers, passing through, who—observing the amount of garbage littered along the path—had decided they'd do something about it. Invariably, this led to the construction of some new fancy-looking receptacle for collecting garbage in the center of town, with a polite sign posted alongside it reminding the people of the village of the importance of throwing away their bottles, cans, and food wrappers. Every time another traveler passing through embarked on a mission of this kind, the mayor would be enlisted to show up for the purpose of making a speech and dedicating the trash receptacle. People would nod and smile. The traveler would go away with the warm feeling, no doubt, of having made a valuable contribution to the community, and, in a small but meaningful way, to the planet as a whole.

A few days would go by. A week. Two. Trash would begin spilling out the top and sides of the fancy new receptacle. Pretty soon there'd be an enormous pile of trash surrounding the trash can, nearly

obliterating the sign. By the time a month had passed since its dedica-
tion, the new trash receptacle would be abandoned. People were back
to scattering their plastic soda bottles and chip bags.

What the do-gooders failed to understand was that once the recep-
tacles were filled, there was no truck coming along to empty them. If
there had been, there would be no place to bring the contents of the
truck. No place besides some other road, where it would all get dumped
out again.

Then Amalia came to town. She was a dramatic figure—tall, with
wild curly hair, dressed in outfits she appeared to have made herself,
with beads and fringe and bits of silk stitched along the hem. The
dresses she wore looked like what a person might construct, if every
piece of fabric on her clothesline had been ripped to shreds, and she'd
stitched them all together. The coat of many colors, with more scraps
of fabric than the one Dolly Parton herself sang about.

In the village now, they called her La Reina de Basura, the garbage
queen.

Amalia had been born into communist Germany. She was raised in
a very small village. "We were poor," she told me. "We played in the
forest and built houses in the trees. My brothers and I put on plays and
operas. My mother sewed my clothes, and taught me how to sew. That's
why it is that I know how to make beautiful treasures out of scraps.
Give me a pile of rags, I'll create a gown for a queen."

As early as her young teens she began working as an activist, as a
champion of human rights and freedom of speech. She was arrested
shortly before her twentieth birthday.

At the prison where they brought her, in East Berlin, she'd endured
a year of solitary confinement and torture that took the form of blaring
noise delivered through the walls of her cell every hour. She had served
two hard years in that prison, and another year after that, living in a
cave in the forest, because anywhere else would have been too loud,
with too many people, too much going on. For a long time—over a

year—she had needed a dark, quiet place to stay, and had found it in the woods not far from the village where she'd grown up.

When she was finally ready to go out into the world, she headed to the city. She got a job at the studio of a fashion designer, making patterns from the designs he'd drawn. Soon she was making patterns from her own designs, far more original than those of her employer. Clients of the designer started to notice her work, though he never told anyone it was Amalia who'd come up with these designs.

But her years in the prison had left Amalia unable to withstand loud noise. The city was way too loud for her. There were too many people, too many buses and cars. She had seen an article in a magazine once, about this lake, with the volcano—a place where men fished in wooden boats and nobody owned a television set. In the picture, there were many birds. So when she had enough money saved up, she bought a ticket to cross the ocean, and another that brought her here. In an odd way, it reminded her of her childhood in Germany—the small adobe houses, not so different from the one where she grew up in the forest with her parents and her brothers. The terraced hillsides planted with crops. The small barefoot children running alongside the highway. The dogs and chickens. The volcano was new.

Amalia was what people might have described as "a strong personality"—a woman with fierce opinions who appeared to fear just about nothing. She showed no sign of caring whether people liked her, and no doubt many did not.

The people in the village who found favor with Amalia were its indigenous citizens. Children in particular, even though she had none herself. She could generally be counted on to have a straggling band of children following behind her, none of whom looked older than six years old. Every child in the village knew Amalia, and every child adored her.

Observing, as we all had, the problem of trash in the village, Amalia had devised a building method she called "the eco-block"—in which a discarded plastic pop bottle would be stuffed with plastic wrappers from junk food like chips packages and gum wrappers, then sealed up with the original bottle cap.

Amalia employed a workforce of very young children—some no older than three—to stuff wrappers into pop bottles. For every eco-block a child created, she'd reward her or him with a pencil or an eraser. Ten eco-blocks earned a notebook. Fifty, a set of markers.

She stored the eco-blocks on her property, not far from the center of town. When she had a sufficient number assembled, she'd enlist the help of a local carpenter to build a plywood frame, into which the eco-blocks were lined up to give the frame not only stability, but insulation from wind, rain and cold. These formed walls Amalia would use for the construction of houses, tiendas. A classroom, even, and a health center for the distribution of prenatal vitamins.

She called her organization Pura Natura. In the early days, I gathered, nobody paid much attention to Amalia's crazy idea. Nobody but the children, at least. But by the time I came to town, she had been operating her one woman-many child recycling project long enough that over a dozen structures had been created around the village, built entirely from eco-blocks. Schools in the area had started inviting her to speak to their students now, not only about picking up trash and keeping the lake clean, but even more so, to teach about the underlying nutritional issues for a town in which people went undernourished, of eating junk food in the form of soda and chips. She'd written a bunch of simple Spanish songs about the benefits of eating vegetables and fruit—the kind of good wholesome nutrition the indigenous community of years before had practiced before packaged foods entered their world. Back when people in the village lived on rice and beans and corn and vegetables.

The November I'd first landed in La Esperanza, Amalia and her team of very small workers had just finished collecting enough trash and stuffing enough bottles for the creation of a preschool, the first ever in the village. Sometimes, on my trips to the market, I'd observe her striding down the path followed by a little parade of children, gathering plastic wrappers as they went. A dozen years since Amalia had overseen her first eco-blocks construction—long before I'd arrived at the lake—the streets were virtually free of trash.

44

The lizard men

When Leila was alive, she had walked into the village every after-noon to buy food for Maria to prepare for that night's dinner. I had accompanied her on those walks. Now I made the trip to the market on my own.

Every day, making my way down the path, I'd pass a table at Harold's occupied by three aging gringos.

Chuck, Vinnie, and John had renamed themselves Carlos, Vincente, and Juan. They had not known each other before they came to town, around fifteen years earlier, but they had met up soon after, and they must have recognized each other as kindred spirits. Soulmates, except from the first time I laid eyes on the three of them, it seemed clear to me that if there was one thing none of them possessed, it was a soul.

The houses where they lived were situated within a stone's throw of each other—large, cheaply constructed but showy structures, possibly inspired by Italian villas, or more accurately, by the kind of fake Italian villas featured in gated communities in certain parts of the Florida coast. Only here you could own one for a lot less money. They all had columns in the front and statuary that appeared to have been based on past Playboy bunnies, and a row of stiff, clipped cedars designed to block out any view of the locals, walking by with their loads of wood and cinder block, vegetables and children.

At some point, Carlos and Vincente and Juan must have had to engage in a certain amount of interaction with the community—hiring their gardener, and their maid, and furnishing their big houses with oversized leather sofas and king-sized mattresses and large-screen

TVs—but for as long as I'd lived in the town, virtually the sole activity of these three men was meeting up around the back table at Harold's café, where they'd spend the day drinking—coffee until noon, then they switched to beer.

There was always an ashtray on the table, filled with the butts from their hand-rolled cigarettes. They might have been in their forties when they arrived at the lake, but their panama hats had not saved them from the fate of major sun damage. They had the look of old reptiles, brown and scaly-skinned, sitting nearly motionless all day with their cigarettes and drinks, until closing time, when they'd lurch home to grill a steak and turn on CNN.

This much I knew from Maria, whose niece had worked briefly for Carlos, but quit when he'd put his hand on her breast one night.

Carlos—Chuck, in his former life—had retired early from his career as a pilot for TWA. Harold had told me he heard once (from Carlos himself, under the influence of multiple shots of whiskey) that the airline had let him go after he was caught drinking on a flight from Seattle to Dallas. The pension he'd received had been enough that Carlos had been able to build an Italianate mansion featuring a cement fountain at the entrance, in which the water spurted from the breasts of a naked woman.

Vincente had worked as a barber, in his Reno days, back when he was probably known as Vinnie. The third in the group was John, now Juan, who—in his previous life—had been employed as a probation officer in Florida.

They had a reputation for paying their workers poorly. "You know how to keep a girl around to cook and wash the dishes?" I'd heard Carlos say, one time when I'd stopped in at Harold's for my smoothie. "Marry her."

"I'd rather just use paper plates," Juan had said.

All day long, the Lizard Men eyed the girls of the village as they made their way up and down the path, to school in the mornings, home in the afternoons, then to their jobs if they had them, waiting on tables or selling fruit or tending the taco stand. Whenever a young girl of the town walked by, you could see the eyes of the three lizards following her. The ten- and eleven-year-olds didn't notice, but the thirteen-year-olds did. They hurried past Harold's, as if a bad smell emanated from the café. Their mothers, if they walked alongside their daughters, held on to them more firmly than normal, approaching the spot where the lizards were staked out.

The lizards had no use for the women their age, or even those, like me, younger by forty years than they were. They liked their meat rare, they said.

One day, when Vincente had put his hand on the breast of a young waitress at the café, Amalia—a woman who'd known torture in an East German prison—told the Lizard Men to get lost. They just laughed at her. They might crawl under a rock for a day. But everyone knew they'd be back tomorrow.

45
Paperwork

An envelope arrived from a government office in the city by special courier, containing a thick sheaf of papers having to do with Leila's estate. They were in Spanish of course, and though I managed to get the gist of much of what they contained, many of the fine points were lost on me.

Also enclosed was the title of the hotel—the *escritura*—that required my signature. The letter also addressed an issue I had not considered before, namely my ability, as a noncitizen of the country, to own property here.

This was not impossible, but I gathered, from my reading of the letter—my comprehension level somewhere around 50 percent at this point—that to successfully register ownership of La Llorona in the municipality required me to identify an individual—a *representante*, a person in possession of citizenship—to whom I would assign certain rights and powers of attorney. Evidently Leila, though she'd been a US citizen when she arrived in the country long ago, had relinquished the passport she'd brought with her, from the country of her birth, for the privilege of citizenship here.

It appeared that I, too, could embark on this process, but doing so these days was considerably more complicated than it had been in earlier times. I took in most but not all of the language in this document, which was not simply Spanish, but legal Spanish. Even back home, reading contracts and doing things like filing tax forms had never been a strong point of mine. Now, studying the document, the words swam in front of my eyes.

I called the office of Leila's lawyer, Juan de la Vega, but he was on holiday, his return three weeks away. So I brought the document over to Gus and Dora's house. Dora spoke a fine, elegant Spanish, and if memory served me right, her field of study at the university in Santiago, before she became a yogi, had been public affairs and prelaw.

She was finishing a prenatal yoga class in the garden when I arrived—presiding over a small, glowing group of round-bellied gringas in shavasana. Seeing me at the gate, she motioned for me to make myself at home in the kitchen.

After the women left, she fixed us a pot of yerba maté. I took out the contents of the envelope. She studied the papers for several minutes before looking up.

"The government here makes things very complicated," she said, shaking her head. "Any time they see an opportunity to bury you in paperwork, they're likely to take it."

"Here's a perfect example," she said, pointing to a paragraph in the document that I had skipped over entirely, because its meaning escaped me.

"They want you to initial this box, right?" she said. "And if you did that, you know what you would have just agreed to? Paying an extra five thousand *garza* tax for something called the foreign residency lake preservation fund."

Dora took a sip of her yerba maté, shaking her head and frowning.

"You need to remember, you're living in a country where the people in power are always ready to take advantage of everyone else. They count on foreigners not to see what they're up to. Americans who come here tend to take out their checkbooks any time they see a piece of paper with an official stamp and a bunch of big Spanish words on it.

"I'm not going to let them get away with this," she added.

"So what do I do?"

"You don't understand how things work here," Dora said. "There are very bad people who would like to take your property away. They see a single American woman whose Spanish isn't that great. They move in for the kill."

I put my head on the table.

"I guess I could make the trip for you," Dora said. "Go to the lawyer's office. As your legal representative."

I told her I'd pay for a private car. "You and Gus have been such good friends," I said. (*Like family*, I could have added. If I'd had a better idea of what family was like.) "I don't know what I'd do without you."

Dora set off for the city two days later, carrying a briefcase from her student days with the document we'd prepared and had notarized—also in Spanish—assigning Dora the rights to sign whatever paperwork was needed on my behalf.

She'd gotten back to the village sometime late in the night (her return, after dark, requiring a private boat I had been more than willing to pay for).

Next morning I brought Gus and Dora a carrot cake by way of thanks, and a drawing I'd made of Luca one time when they'd come over for dinner, in a handmade coffee wood frame.

Dora handed me back the envelope with the documents. I stuck them in the bottom drawer of Leila's desk with all the rest of the papers nobody had ever read.

46
Piece of heaven

These were days before internet connection had been established in the village. We didn't advertise. The hotel was listed in no guidebooks. Maybe this partly accounted for the continued low occupancy at La Llorona. If we were lucky, we might have two rooms filled, but almost never all four, and in the rainy season, with rare exceptions, the number generally stayed at zero.

Thanks to the contents of the bank account Leila had left to me, I managed to keep Maria and Luis employed, along with Mirabel and Elmer. But with all of the projects Gus had undertaken at the property, the money from Leila's insurance was running low, and there was more work still needed, he'd pointed out. It seemed as though every time his crew completed the original jobs on his priorities list, new items appeared. The bamboo railings on the stone steps were rotting. The stone risers were uneven.

"You don't want some geezer taking a dive and suing the pants off of you, mate," Gus reminded me. Which brought to mind another issue: the need for night lighting on the stairs. And once we were installing a new electrical box, why not install lights in the garden, and one in the jocote tree? Gus could see it now, the way the flowers would glow. I could have myself a regular Covent Garden, right in my back yard. Maybe he'd put in a red bulb, for extra effect. What about outdoor speakers?

The built-in garden lights and red light bulb in the tree had proved a little more garish than I'd bargained for. Left to my own devices, I preferred keeping the place sufficiently dark, when night fell, that the stars were visible in all their glory. But Gus loved that light so much I didn't have the heart to mention this. I just marveled at the red glow lighting up the garden, the first time he flipped the switch—making note, privately, to turn it on only on evenings when Gus and Dora came for dinner. We shared a meal at least once a week now—with their son Luca and their daughter Jade. Along with Maria and Luis, who had never warmed to Gus and Dora, they had become, for me, the closest thing I had to family.

Now when I walked to town, I'd stop by Casa Colibri to say hello— drop off a fresh coconut for Luca and Jade or ask Dora's help with some Spanish phrase I needed in my communication with the town office concerning property taxes, or the bank. Dora never exuded the easy warmth or humor Gus did but in an odd way, the fact that Dora displayed none of Gus's easy, affable, effusive style was, for me, another reason to respect her. Gus was easy to love. Dora was easier to believe.

Every Friday afternoon for over three years now, since Gus started working for me, the two of us sat down together, going over the hours his crew had put in and the costs of materials. His own fee was a pittance, he reminded me, but he couldn't help himself. He loved giving jobs to the local blokes, and they needed the cash more than he did. Not to mention (though he did, regularly) that he loved this property like it was his own. Given the low returns from bookings at this point, I recognized I was spending more than I should on improvements. But Gus's enthusiasm was contagious. I admired his imagination, and how hard he worked, and his devotion to the local men on his crew, who always looked so happy and grateful when payday came around.

"Piece of heaven you got yourself here, mate," he told me. "Or it will be."

We were a great team. Him with the brawn. Dora the brains, with the perfect Spanish that she was always ready to employ when I had to place a phone call to the city, or deal with a big order of materials or a bank. My role was the easiest. I wrote the checks.

47
An herb that makes babies possible

I received a letter from a woman in China, asking if I had room at the hotel for her the following month for a stay of unspecified duration. I wrote back immediately, of course. We'd fit her in.

Two weeks later Jun Lan arrived at my gate—accompanied by Walter, of course—with two large suitcases. "I may be here for a while," she explained.

Her flights from China had taken thirty-two hours. Still, she did not look particularly weary. If I were to describe her as she appeared that day, the first thing I'd mention would be her eyes, which seemed almost to glow. She had the look of a woman on a mission, though I had yet to learn what that mission might be.

"Your husband didn't come with you," I said—a statement, not a question.

"He works all the time," she said. "And anyway, my husband thinks I am a crazy person for coming here."

As I led Jun Lan down the long hallway to her room, we passed one of the few additions I'd made to the decor at La Llorona—a series of drawings I'd had framed of birds and plants I'd found in the garden around the property.

"Who did these?" Nobody ever asked about my artwork. Gus and Dora must have been at my house a hundred times and never gave the drawings a second glance.

"I used to be an illustrator," I said. "Medical books, mostly, but I love drawing from nature."

"You know plants then," she said. "That's very good."

She was the only hotel guest that night, and asked me to join her for dinner. "Perhaps I should explain what brought me here," she told me. "I may need your assistance."

In nearly perfect English, she told me her story—as much of it as had occurred, so far.

"This will help you to understand my mission," she said.

Jun Lan (the meaning of her name, Pretty Orchid) was born in the small rural village of Heng Shui in the early days of the Cultural Revolution.

Her parents had been educated people with good jobs, but they were among those who had been stripped of their property and money in the days of Mao Tse Tung, leaving the family to cultivate rice and potatoes on a piece of land so small that you had only to walk ten paces to reach the patch cultivated by your neighbor. The family shared a one-room hut.

When Jun Lan was five years old, her mother gave birth to a son, Jun Wei—*Wei*, the word for greatness. To their parents, this characterized the event. From that day, Jun Wei occupied all the attention and affection of their parents. He was the one on whom they had bestowed the gift of an education. It was he they brought to the city of Shi Jia Zhuang when they took jobs in a factory there to pay for Jun Wei's schooling.

Jun Lan stayed home in the care of her grandmother, Lao Lao. They spent their days together cultivating the little garden next to their tiny house. They spent most afternoons on the hills above the village. It was on those hills that Lao Lao taught Jun Lan to recognize the medicinal herbs and plants she'd learned about from her own grandmother, and the many generations of grandparents before her, as they had learned them from the great classic book that served as the bible of all Chinese medicine: *Ben Cao Gang Mu, The Compendium of Materia Medica* by the ancient teacher from the fifteenth century, Li Shi Zhen.

Though Lao Lao could never have afforded to buy the books that represented Li Shi Zhen's life work, which numbered over fifty, she had once brought Jun Lan to the house of a woman who owned several volumes. Together, they had spent hours studying the drawings of the plants Li Shi Zhen had identified as among the most medicinally powerful.

Over their many afternoons on the hillside together, Jun Lan and her grandmother searched for these plants. When they found one, Lao Lao brought it home and boiled it in water to make a bitter drink which she gave to Jun Lan to make her strong and brave and help her brain grow powerful.

On her one and only visit to see her parents and brother over the years that followed, Jun Lan had seen just enough of the city to recognize that this was the place for her.

Back home, she gathered herbs on the mountain with Lao Lao. A farmer in the village paid her to pick up stones in the fields to make them easier to cultivate. With the money she earned from this, Jun Lan bought a bicycle—a very old one-speed with an extremely rusty chain meant for a much larger person than she. Never mind. That bicycle was, for Jun Lan, the vehicle that would transport her to a new life. She was fourteen years old.

A hundred and twenty kilometers separated the village of Heng Shui from Shi Jia Zhuang. The roads were dirt, and very bumpy, with parts along the way where the incline was steep. After a full day of riding, Jun Lan was only partway to the city. She slept in some bushes by the road with her cotton jacket for a blanket, and sang herself to sleep with a song her grandmother had sung to her when she was small. She had wrapped a few dumplings in a handkerchief for the journey.

When Jun Lan reached the city, she did not present herself at the home of her parents. She knew they would not welcome this. She went to the largest hotel, the Shi Jia Zhuang Palace, where she offered her services, free of charge, as a tour guide for foreign visitors. She did not tell the concierge at the hotel, to whom she made this offer, that she had set foot in this city only once, and was more in need of taking a tour than giving one.

"Come back tomorrow," the concierge told her. "If we have any guests who'd like a tour, you can take them around."

That afternoon she found a small room to rent—a bed in a room, shared with another girl, a student at the university, which was Jun Lan's dream for herself someday. Early the next morning, the girl, Xi Liu, showed her around the city, enough so she could give a tour if called upon to do so.

For the next seven months, this was how Jun Lan spent her days—presenting herself at the Shi Jia Zhuang Palace every morning, waiting on the steps—sometimes all day—on the chance that someone would want to take her tour. Though she made herself available for any guest at the hotel who chose to avail himself or herself of her services, Jun Lan always hoped the travelers who chose to do this might be Americans, or British at least. Her goal: to learn English.

At night, she studied the books of Xi Liu, and when she could, she crept into the back of the classrooms to hear the lectures of the professors at her roommate's college. When she felt ready, she passed the exam and was admitted to study there herself. Four years later, having distinguished herself with top honors, she enrolled at medical school.

It was there that Jun Lan met Lei Kai Wen, one year ahead of her in his studies. Lei Kai Wen (his name translated: *Thunder. Triumph. Education*) came from a prominent professional family that had managed, even during these years of cultural revolution, to maintain a standard of living very different from anything Jun Lan had known. Lei Kai Wen was very serious about his studies. He recognized that even in a college filled with ambitious and highly disciplined students, Jun Lan stood out as a person whose passion for the study of medicine matched his own.

After a year of courtship—the year Jun Lan earned her medical degree—they married. On their wedding night, Lei Kai Wen's mother had placed the traditional gift of peanuts, seeds, and dates under the pillows where the couple slept. *Zao Sheng*, they called it. Tokens to ensure fertility.

Two years after the marriage, no child had appeared. In silent shame, Jun Lan considered the reasons. She knew—though her husband had not appeared to notice this—that in all these months, and the many preceding her marriage, dating back to her young days as a tour guide in the city, she had never known the monthly bleeding of other young women. Something was wrong with her. Secretly, she visited a doctor at the hospital where she and Lei Kai Wen both worked.

Up until now, Jun Lan had delivered the facts of her history with quiet thoughtfulness and a surprising, almost clinical precision. But when she reached this part of her story, tears came to her eyes.

"You will never be blessed with a child," the doctor told her. "You are a sterile woman."

"My husband buried himself in his work," she said. "He came home later and later, saying little when he did." But for Jun Lan, the doctor's dismissal of all hope of her conceiving a child was more than she could bear. Though she had spent the last eight years in the study of Western medicine—emerging first in her class, once again—now she returned to the wisdom of her childhood, the Chinese medicine as she remembered it from those days long ago on the hillsides of Heng Shui, gathering herbs with her grandmother.

She told her husband she needed to see Lao Lao. This time she made the trip on a bus, not a bicycle.

Until now she had told no one about the doctor's words to her, but now, drinking tea with her grandmother, she did.

"I am so ashamed," she told Lao Lao. "My husband calls me *Shi nu*." Stone Girl.

"No shame," Lao Lao said. "This same problem you speak of afflicted me once. I cured it with herbs. Then I gave birth to your mother."

But when they set out up the hillside to find the plant Lao Lao was looking for, it had disappeared, along with so many others from their long-ago days. Only then did Lao Lao weep.

"The pesticides," Lao Lao explained to Jun Lan. "They have killed off the most precious of our herbs. There's nothing left here but weeds."

Lao Lao was old by now, and Jun Lan knew it was unlikely she'd see her again. Before she left for the bus that would bring her back to her husband in the city, she asked Lao Lao a question.

"All these years," Jun Lan said, "I have never known your real name. You were always Lao Lao."

"Oh, well," Lao Lao told her. "It doesn't matter. It's not much of a name that they gave me."

In those times she was born, a female child was of so little value to her family that few parents troubled themselves with girls' names. "They called me Ya Tou," Lao Lao said. Same name as almost every other girl in the village. *Girl.*

Five days later the news reached the apartment Jun Lan shared with her husband, Lei Kai Wen. Lao Lao was found dead on her cotton mat in the small bamboo house of Jun Lan's childhood. That afternoon, Jun Lan went to the library at the university where she worked. She took from the shelves many volumes of *Ben Cao Gang Mu.* She was looking for a drawing of the herb she and Lao Lao had set out to find on the hillside that day—the precious herb that might grant her fertility, if she could only find it again.

Bent over the book with a magnifying glass provided by the library, Jun Lan read Li Shi Zhen's description of the herb she sought. The Chinese name might no longer serve her in her search, but she read about the climate and terrain on which the herb might thrive, the kind of soil, the angle of the sun required, for it to grow.

She set out to find a place, somewhere on the planet, where these conditions might be found. One location stood out above all others as the place where a person like Jun Lan might locate the magic medicinal herb that would make possible her dream to have a child.

"This herb I seek is most likely to be found on a high mountain by a lake, in a region where pesticides remain blessedly absent," she told me. "It favors soil rich from volcanic ash."

The place she described was La Esperanza. The mountains behind my hotel.

So Jun Lan bought a plane ticket. Now here she was, eight thousand miles from home, in her quest for the magic herb that might allow her to become a mother.

48

Rubber boots on the mountain

Jun Lan was already having her tea when I came out to the patio just after sunrise. "Maybe you'd like to rest up for a day before Elmer takes you up on the mountain," I suggested. She shook her head.

It was the rainy season, but Jun Lan didn't care. I lent her my high rubber boots and a long yellow raincoat, a walking stick for places on the trail where the mud would be thick so she wouldn't lose her footing. A layer of mist and a deep chill hung in the air.

The two of them were gone for many hours. Early that afternoon, Gus showed up with samples of a kind of tile he recommended we lay down in the kitchen, to replace the old and partly cracked ceramic tiles—blue, hand-painted, but chipped—that Leila had laid there decades earlier. The replacement tiles were made from some synthetic material I disliked. For once, I told Gus I preferred to keep things as they were.

"You won't need to replace these babies for another forty years," Gus told me, stroking the smooth synthetic surface with the touch of a lover.

"And that's the bad news," I told him. "Because I'd want to."

Gus and I had the kind of relationship by this time where banter came easily between us. He didn't give up lightly.

"Back to the drawing board, luv," he said. "If this style don't suit your fancy, I'll find you one that does."

"Or not," I said. Really, I didn't feel a need to change the kitchen floor. This would have been true even if the money Leila had left me to cover renovations were not nearly used up.

Gus had noticed unfamiliar shoes in the hall—Jun Lan's, that she'd taken off when I gave her my boots to wear.

"Who's the new guest?" he asked.

"A young doctor from China," I told him. "She came here in search of a medicinal herb."

"Must be a damned special herb," Gus said. "A gal doesn't hop on a plane and fly halfway across the world to pick a bunch of dandelions, now does she?"

"Evidently the plant's extinct in China," I told him. "It's a unique herb."

"So what's this plant she's so keen on digging up?" he said.

It was not for me to tell him her story. "Research," I told him. "She's interested in botany."

"I thought you said she's a doctor."

"A person can have hobbies," I said. I had seldom seen Gus this tenacious.

Jun Lan and Elmer returned from the mountain just before sunset. Even with my boots and rain slicker to protect her, Jun Lan was soaked. They had spent hours looking for the herb to match the drawing in the Chinese medical text, but came home empty-handed.

Next morning they returned to the mountain, and again the morning after that. Evenings back at the hotel, after their hours of searching the muddy slopes, we fixed tea for our guest, and every night at seven Maria set a plate in front of her. Except for a few forkfuls of rice, Jun Lan ate almost nothing.

I was having a late-afternoon beer in the garden with Gus, hearing him out on a new plan he had for the property—a waterfront jacuzzi that would allow my guests to look out to the volcano while soaking in bubbling waters. Solar heated. I could run the thing for pennies.

Over his shoulder, I caught sight of Elmer and Jun Lan, returned once more from their daily search on the mountain. One look at Jun Lan's face and I knew. They'd found her magic herb.

"There was this grove of banana trees," she said, when she reached the spot in the garden where Gus and I were engaged in our daily discussion of building projects—I with my drawing pad at my side, he with his ever-present calculator. "It would have been so easy to miss. The plants grow lower to the ground than I'd imagined. The leaves are so delicate."

I had not filled Gus in on the reasons for Jun Lan's quest to find the herb. But he had only to see her and listen to the breathless, almost euphoric tone in which she described her discovery, to understand the significance of this herb. Whatever its health benefits, they must be substantial.

"Good on you, mate," he said, taking a long swig on his beer. "My wife's something of a horticulturist herself. No doubt she'd take keen interest in this herb of yours. Can't say it looks like much, on the face of things, but looks can be deceiving, am I right?"

Back in the kitchen—Gus having said his goodbyes—we showed the clump of leaves Jun Lan had gathered to Maria, who set a pot of water on to boil.

"Li Shi Zhen instructs us to soak the herb for one hundred minutes," she told me. "It's important to drink the whole thing, all at once if possible, then lie in a prone position for two hours."

A woman desirous of benefiting from the effects of the herb should repeat this process every day without fail, Jun Lan explained— information I conveyed to Maria, to whom all of this made total sense. The ways of ancient Chinese medicine differed less than one might think from those of her culture.

Once the pot of brewing leaves had been prepared, Jun Lan disappeared to her room. We did not see her again for the rest of the evening.

In the days that followed, Jun Lan did not venture again from the property, preferring to spend her time stretched out on a lawn chair, reading or writing in her journal. From the moment she'd returned with the herb, something had changed about her. There was an air of serenity in Jun Lan, and a kind of quiet dignity that even a person like Gus seemed to recognize.

"I get the feeling our girl wants to be left to herself," he observed.

"She needs to rest," I said.

It was never easy for Gus, accepting the idea that anybody would choose not to have a chat with him. "This business with the herb," he said. "What's that about?"

"It's nobody's business but Jun Lan's," I told him.

Jun Lan had been staying at La Llorona almost three weeks at this point. Money appeared to be no particular concern for her. Neither did the notion of contacting her husband, Lei Kai Wen, back in China. "He's working," she said, the one time I inquired about him. "He does not think of me at such times."

Then one morning she appeared on the patio looking so radiant it was as if a sunbeam had broken through the clouds in such a way as to hit only one spot, her face.

"When I woke this morning, there was blood on the sheet," she told me. She did not deliver this news by way of apology or concern over the question of the stain, which Mirabel would easily enough remove with cold water and hard scrubbing. This was joyous news. Proof that the herb had done its work.

She was on the phone within the hour, arranging her flights home to China. By three o'clock her bag was packed. Walter met her at the gate to walk her to the boat.

"Your friend took off a bit sudden, I'd say," Gus observed, when he showed up next day. "You two have a spat?"

"She was ready to go," I told him. Her business here was finished.

Six weeks later came the letter in a thin blue envelope, with so many stamps they covered most of the front. Inside, the news.

Jun Lan was pregnant.

49

Fancy sneakers and a bag of basketballs

A couple came from Portland, Oregon, who worked for Nike—a return visit for the two of them. On an earlier trip to La Esperanza the year before, they had been troubled by the way girls in the village were excluded from participating in the sport of football. At the same time, these two had been moved by the passion with which young girls in the village embraced the game of basketball. The problem was, they'd had no instruction in the game.

Claudia and Rick had been serious college basketball players. He'd played professional ball briefly in Europe. This time when they came to the lake they brought four oversize suitcases along, containing sneakers and shorts with the *Just Do It* logo on the front and a bag of regulation basketballs. They tacked up a few flyers around town, announcing that they'd be hosting a basketball clinic. This was all it took.

Rick and Claudia became the instant celebrities of the village. It didn't matter that neither Claudia nor her husband spoke more than a few words of Spanish. They spoke the language of basketball.

In the seven days of the couple's time at the lake, the two of them spent virtually all their time on the court in the center of town teaching fancy moves to the girls. The young men of the village stood on the sidelines as the two of them demonstrated the crossover dribble, up and under, and posting, unknown to even the best young male players in the town. I had supposed that once Rick and Claudia witnessed the longing of the male players to learn the new moves, they'd invite them to join in, but they stood firm. This week, at least, basketball belonged to the girls.

They played their hearts out. In the past, when I'd seen girls on the court, they'd been wearing the molded plastic pumps women bought at the market. Now every girl on the team sported pink Ultraflights, though except for Claudia, they wore them with their traditional long skirts, tied with a woven belt and an embroidered huipil.

I had never seen more determined play. In the market and on the street, most girls giggled and hid their faces when boys spoke to them, and in the past, I'd seen the way they cleared off the court whenever the male players wanted to start up a game. That week it was the boys who sat and waited as the girls tore up and down the court.

As I stood on the sidelines taking in the final game of Rick and Claudia's week with the basketball girls, I spotted a familiar face. Mirabel. As she always did, she stood out among the others, in her woven skirt and the special beaded belt she'd been working on all year wrapped tightly around her waist, her braid flying behind her as she raced up the court to intercept a pass. When she made a three-point shot from mid-court that day she dropped to her knees to make the sign of the cross.

It seemed as though the whole village turned out that day to watch the final game—the older women who'd never set foot on a basketball court themselves and likely never would, the boys and men, seated alongside me, looking on in amazement and a certain envy—more accustomed to seeing girls making tortillas than foul shots.

Two years from now, half of them might be holding babies in their arms, but that day, they knew no greater love than basketball. The star of them all, Elmer's beloved Mirabel.

50

An unlikely proposal. (Two of them.)

Over the months and now years I'd spent overseeing the endless list of projects at La Llorona, I retained, with scrupulous consistency, the ritual of taking out my watercolors every afternoon and making a painting—sometimes of flowers or trees, sometimes birds. So long as I was studying an image from nature and trying to capture it on the page, I could forget my grief. I was never happier than when I was painting.

At some point, realizing that I had made a few hundred images, I mounted a show of them in Rosella's restaurant in the village. The prices were reasonable—twenty-five or thirty dollars apiece. The point was never to make money.

A man showed up at my gate. "I saw the art you make," he said. "I've come to make you an offer.

"I know this sounds crazy," he told me. "But I feel it's destiny that I found you. There's this extraordinary tenderness to the way you paint. Even when your subject is nothing more than a leaf or the bud of a flower.

"I want you to make a book with me," he said. "It's about birds."

Nobody, meeting Jerome Sapirstein, would have called him a handsome man. He had narrow shoulders and the complexion of a person who doesn't get out much. He wore khaki shorts that came down to his knees and high white tube socks with sandals and a hat well suited to a safari, with a chin strap and a brim so broad it covered half his face. But there was this sweetness to him that I recognized the minute we met. Also enthusiasm. "You can't imagine how thrilled I am to meet you," he said. I could not imagine why. Around his neck: a pair of what appeared to be extremely expensive binoculars.

Jerome Sapirstein owned a publishing company in New York City. He was also an amateur—though passionate—birdwatcher. He'd come to Lago La Paz having heard that more varieties of birds made their homes around the lake than in any other part of the world.

His single goal in making his pilgrimage to La Llorona had been to take in birdlife and add as many new varieties of birds to his lifetime count as possible. For the past ten days, he'd tromped along trails with a guide he'd hired to accompany him, making side trips to the jungle and the Pacific coast. Though he had yet to catch sight of the bird that represented, for a birdwatcher like himself, the ultimate—the rare and elusive quetzal—he'd managed to study more varieties of exotic birds in his time at the lake than he had in the last two decades of weekend birding expeditions back home.

But when Jerome Sapirstein had seen my watercolor paintings of birds at Rosella's restaurant the night before, an idea had come to him to commission a book featuring amazing stories of birdlife from around the globe, accompanied by my artwork.

"Naturally I'd want to include some of the gorgeous images you've created of birds around the lake," he said. "But we'd also include paintings of birds in other parts of the globe. Bolivia for flamingos, maybe. Antarctica, for penguins."

The list went on: The swallows of Capistrano . . . the ravens at the Tower of London . . .

"Can you imagine anything more thrilling than to watch a pair of fluffy-backed-tit-babblers in their native habitat in Indonesia?" he said.

I could, actually. But I kept this to myself.

The piece of work Jerome Sapirstein had in mind would be what was known in the world of publishing as a coffee-table book—oversized, with full-color illustrations, high quality printing stock. No expense spared. "I believe we can create a masterpiece," he said. Budget for the project was no concern.

To say this idea arrived unexpectedly would be an understatement. Ten minutes earlier, I'd been in the back of my hotel with Gus and Luis, in discussion over issues concerning the hotel septic system. My plans for the day also included a visit to a plant nursery to look at roses, a flea bath for our dog, Cuzmi, a visit with Josephina, a local weaver, about pillow coverings, and responding to a couple of inquiries from prospective hotel guests asking the perpetual question: Was it safe to drink the water? How worried should they be about banditos and kidnappers? (*Water—filtered. Banditos and kidnappers—not an issue.*)

Within the space of a few minutes, I was contemplating trips to London and Antarctica. More surprising than that, even, I was picturing the possibility of reentering the kind of career I had imagined for myself back in my San Francisco days. I'd closed that door five years earlier. Now here came Jerome Sapirstein with his binoculars and his safari hat, flinging it open.

Sitting on my patio together, drinking one of Mirabel's juice concoctions, he laid out his vision.

"There's so much more to tell you," he said, adding to please call him Jerome. "I can tell, this will be the start of an amazing adventure for the two of us."

Jerome's interest in having me illustrate a book had brought me back to a time in my life I thought about less and less often—not just my work as a medical illustrator but my life with Lenny and Arlo— the three of us hiking in Point Reyes, with Arlo in the backpack, Lenny making up crazy songs and stopping to examine interesting things we spotted on the trail—a patch of moss to lie on, a fungus growing from a tree, the shell of a horseshoe crab on the beach. Then back home on Vallejo Street, studying the conures outside our window. And drawing them.

When pictures of those times came to mind now it was as if I were watching a movie of someone else's life. Except for that little show of work at Rosella's restaurant, the only people who ever saw my paintings were guests at the hotel. Now here came this man reminding me of a part of myself I'd nearly lost track of.

I thought I was done with all that. Years past the date by which I'd planned to sell the hotel and move on, I remained deeply immersed in construction projects and renovations, my days filled with paying bills for wood and cement and meetings with Gus. Just that morning he'd stopped by with the plan for a massage pavilion he thought we should construct by the water. It was a simple enough structure—four bamboo posts, from which he proposed he'd hang white cotton curtains Dora could whip up in no time, with some kind of altar to hold candles and flowers and maybe (until we installed that sound system he was itching to put in for me) a tape player and speakers. If it was anyone else, he said, he'd charge them a pretty penny for a job like this, but for me, he'd keep the price down to practically nothing. This had become a familiar speech.

"Just don't let the missus know," he told me. "She'd have my hide for asking so little." This was the line Gus invariably delivered when bidding a job. I chose to see it as part of his charm.

Now another man—a very different type—sat with me on the patio. Talking about birds, and art, and listening to every word I spoke with rapt attention.

We talked for hours, and as evening approached, Jerome had asked if I'd have dinner with him in the village. "I know this is highly unusual," he said. "But I was thinking I could take you into town for a meal. You might like a change."

There was only one spot in La Esperanza where a person could get a meal that came anywhere close to the ones Maria created at the hotel—Rosella's place, Il Piacere.

We could have taken a *tuk tuk* into the village, but Jerome suggested we walk. It was that time of day I loved best, when the sun was sinking behind the volcano and the sky changing color every few seconds—rose color giving way to peach, giving way to violet, a golden glow on the hillside, and the birds swooping low over the water.

Because of my responsibilities at La Llorona, at least two years had passed since I'd had a meal at Rosella's restaurant. The last time we'd met on the path—each of us with our maguey bags of vegetables—we'd exchanged a quick hug and hurried on our way, back to tend our respective businesses.

The last time I'd seen Rosella, I'd noted that she'd been holding hands with Wade, the onetime Chicago attorney-turned-owner of the rabbit restaurant. She was now barely recognizable.

"I never thought I'd get pregnant again at this age," she said, when I greeted her. "It's twins."

"You and Wade?" I asked her.

"After all these years," she said. "Can you believe it?"

I was still thinking about Rosella's pregnancy as Jerome and I took our places at a table. The voice of Maria Callas filled the garden—*O mio babbino caro*. Puccini. Jerome ordered us a bottle of wine—the best in the house, not that this said much.

"To our collaboration," he said.

Jerome and I had probably spent the better part of eight hours that day in the most animated conversation, but amazingly, to me, we had not run out of things to talk about—the kinds of subjects (art, books, travel) that were unlikely to come up in my conversations with Dora and Gus. It felt good, talking about a project totally unrelated to the hotel. At ten o'clock, when Rosella was closing up, we were still deep in conversation.

"I think I should tell you, I have ulterior motives," Jerome said. "Not that I didn't mean everything I said about your talent as an artist. But I was wondering why there's no man in your life. I guess I wanted to ask if the position might be available."

I studied his face. Those kind gray eyes, his hair sticking out in all directions. He'd changed his shirt for our dinner together to another, equally uncool.

"I think I could make a great partner for you," he said.

What was he talking about? We'd met less than twelve hours earlier. I knew virtually nothing about this man. About me, he knew less. I pointed this out to him.

"Look," he said. "I don't go to bars, and even if I did, I'm not the type to strike up a conversation with women. A person reaches a certain age and they ask themselves, what really matters in life? Falling in wild, passionate love is probably a fairy tale constructed for the very young. To me, a marriage is like a good collaboration. At this point, I want to spend the rest of my life with a woman I respect who cares about some of the things I care about. Someone I can talk to the way we seem able to do."

I couldn't think of a response. To tell the truth, I liked the idea of falling in mad, passionate love. I'd never viewed what I had with Lenny as a good collaboration. Start to finish, it had been a love affair.

"Haven't you ever wanted children?" he said.

It was not a subject I allowed myself to explore anymore—not with Jerome, or even in my own head. Though I could not pretend that the sight of Rosella, pregnant at forty-five, had not given me pause.

"Because I do," he said. "I just need to find the woman to raise them with. Maybe I just did."

We had planned to work again the following day on the outline for our bird book, but when we met up the next morning on the patio he had another suggestion.

"I've been studying that volcano," he said. "You ever climb it?"

In all my time at the lake, I never had.

"I'll make you a proposition," he said. "Spend the day with me. We'll get to know each other. If you don't hate me by the time we get down off the volcano, maybe you'll marry me."

It was such a crazy idea I actually said okay.

51

Thinking about babies

Normally I would have enlisted Elmer to be our guide, but Luis needed his help on a building project so we decided to go alone up the volcano. Maria packed us a lunch—also, knowing how long this was likely to take, she included a bag of macadamia nuts and chocolate for extra energy.

Nothing about Jerome Sapirstein's appearance suggested he was the athletic type. Not that he was overweight in any way, he just looked like a man who had spent most of his life sitting at a desk. I had actually guessed that we'd probably give the volcano hike no more than an hour or two before turning back. But after four hours, Jerome showed no sign of giving up.

It turned out that he spent almost every spring and fall weekend hiking in Harriman State Park, and in summer, camped in the Adirondacks. The previous summer he and his brother, Elliot, had done five nights in the White Mountains of New Hampshire.

"The worst part was Mount Adams," he said. "There wasn't even a trail. Just one enormous rock pile. Six hours of nonstop trudging uphill over a pile of rocks.

"Any time one of us—my brother or I—has an experience that feels really hard," Jerome told me, "we just point to each other and say 'At least we're not on Mount Adams.'"

I surprised myself that afternoon. In my years at the lake, nearly all my focus had gone to my property. For much of that time, this had been therapeutic. I didn't want to think about my life. Apart from a few excursions to the city for supplies, I'd barely seen the rest of the country, or even the landscape around the lake, except from my spot on the patio with my coffee. A central fact of my life over all this time: that there was no space in my life, or interest, in a relationship. Now, for the first time in years, I allowed myself to imagine the possibility that I might have one with this man.

It was a little after three when we reached the top of the volcano. The weather was on our side, with clear views for miles and no wind. From where we stood a safe distance from the crater, we could still see into its depths, the red-hot glowing lava, the smell of smoke and molten rock. Jerome had brought along a box of expensive-looking chocolates that must have come from New York, and a bottle of wine. I could tell how hard he was trying to make this a really great day.

As much as he loved birds, Jerome Sapirstein was not an outdoorsman. Insects worried him. Many things did. But I also recognized, as we made our way up the trail, what a good man he was. He had brought along sunscreen, and reminded me more than once of the importance of reapplying it regularly—also three bottles of water and hiking poles and bug spray and calamine lotion in case we encountered poison ivy (not native to these parts).

"I hope you don't mind," he said. "I just feel this overwhelming desire to take care of you."

I can't pretend Jerome's words didn't move me. With the exception of Lenny, for that brief, wonderful period that lasted just over three years—and Daniel, long ago, when he was with my mother—I had taken care of myself for much of my life. The idea that there might ever be, again, a man to look out for me was not entirely unwelcome.

But something else played on my mind when I considered Jerome Sapirstein's proposal.

Ever since Arlo's death, I'd told myself I'd never have a child again. But my years at the lake had changed me. I was learning what it was to be happy again, and hopeful for the future. The sight of Rosella the night before—pregnant—had a powerful effect.

I was thirty-six years old. There was still time. But not endless amounts of it.

Now here was this very good, kind man who seemed ready to step in and make a family with me. Maybe it wasn't such a crazy idea.

For a few brief hours as we climbed the volcano together, I allowed myself to imagine how it would go with Jerome. I saw myself holding a baby again, placing her against my breast, singing to her, as I had to my son, the songs my mother used to sing to me. (In my fantasies, the baby was always a girl. In my mind there could only be one son, ever. The one I lost.)

A girl then. I saw us playing on the grass, coloring together, taking out paints, walking down the road (what road? Where?) holding hands as she skipped. It probably said something about this fantasy that the pictures which came to mind seemed to be largely of the two of us. The father of this fantasy child of mine remained a hazy figure, outside of view.

It was at just this moment that Jerome Sapirstein tripped on a tree root and fell to the ground. He tried to look as if it was nothing serious, but when he stood up, he winced.

"I think I might have sprained my ankle," he said. "To be honest, I have no idea how I'm going to get back down."

52

The kiss

There was nothing for it then but to spend the night on the volcano. We still had the tortillas Maria had packed for us along with a few pieces of cheese and a bag of nuts. That morning we had stuffed hooded sweatshirts in our packs in anticipation of a late-afternoon chill, though I doubted they'd be enough to keep us warm through the night.

We found a flat spot, sheltered from the wind by a rock outcropping.

Jerome laid out a piece of fabric Maria had sent along as a picnic cloth. He was the type of man who, even when sleeping under the stars, lined up his shoes, side by side, with his hat next to them. He kept his socks on.

"I've been thinking about our book," he said. Not the most romantic line for a man to deliver to a woman under the stars—but you had to give him credit for sincerity.

"Have you heard of the exotic conures that escaped from a pet store somewhere in California years ago and settled in San Francisco?" he said. "There's a whole flock of them now, living on Telegraph Hill. We could go there together. You'd paint them."

For a moment then, I pictured returning to San Francisco with Jerome, and how it would be to go to my old neighborhood with this man. "I've seen those conures," I told him. "A long time ago."

We lay on our backs, facing the stars. "Would it be all right if I put my arm around you?" Jerome asked.

He recited a poem for me—a favorite of his, "The Lake Isle of Innisfree." I must have read it in school at some point, but until now, I hadn't realized what Yeats was talking about—the urge the poet had felt to make his escape to a small cabin by a lake, where he might find some peace. For me, that place was La Llorona.

Not intending to stay out overnight, neither one of us had brought along a toothbrush, but it turned out that Jerome had thought to pack mints. "Could I kiss you?" he asked.

Much has been said in literature and song about the power of a single kiss, the way this seemingly small event may incite feelings of love and passion, and the realization that the person whose lips just pressed against your own is someone with whom you might want to spend the rest of your life. It is equally true—though less well-documented—that a kiss can serve the opposite function.

How does a person describe the shortcomings of another person's kiss? (Lips too tight, too dry, too stiff? Tongue too aggressive? Teeth in the way?) I knew the moment Jerome Sapirstein kissed me that as good a man as he was—good, kind, interesting, respectful of my artwork—I could never make a life with him. The truth was, the very thing he'd dismissed as a fantasy reserved for the foolish young (passion and love, head-over-heels) was the only thing that made it all make sense to me.

"I'll rent you a studio where you can paint," he said. Money was no object. "Our bird book will be just the beginning.

"I'd love to have a baby with you," he said. "Two, if we can.

"I know it sounds a little crazy to be saying this to a woman I've only known two days, but I think I could make you happy, Irene. I can see it so plainly—the life we could have together. I want you to come back to New York with me."

We had been lying on the picnic cloth, but now I sat up. I needed to face him squarely when I said this. The hardest words.

"I can't live with you in New York," I said. The idea of having a child in my life, someone for whom I might feel love, someone who might love me back, even—though who knew about that part?—had terrified me. But the problem with marrying Jerome Sapirstein had nothing to do with that fear. The problem was Jerome.

"I want to spend my life with you," Jerome said. "You're the most perfect woman I ever met. Not perfect, okay? Just perfect for me."

Something was happening to me as he spoke. It was like clouds rolling in, with a terrible swiftness. Like the slow, ominous rumbling in the distance that happens in rainy season, just before the storm hits.

"Call me crazy," he said. "But I think I could picture the whole thing, the moment I laid eyes on you. I just wanted to take care of you. I'm good at taking care of people."

He probably was. But what might I offer him in return? And where was love in this picture Jerome had painted for us? He hadn't spoken the word.

Maybe he loved me, or (more likely) maybe he thought he did.

The problem was, I didn't love him back.

We spent a sad, chaste night together, side by side on the picnic blanket, looking up at the stars. In the morning, Jerome's ankle was sufficiently healed that he could make it down the volcano, though not without pain. We did not speak of what had changed between us, but we both knew.

Later that day, Jerome Sapirstein and I climbed slowly up the steps of La Llorona—he with his wheelless suitcase in one hand, the safari hat in the other. Maybe there seemed no point anymore, trying to impress me with its jauntiness, if that had been his intent in wearing it, before.

I kissed him goodbye on the cheek.

"I hope you find an artist to illustrate your book," I told him.

"That book only mattered because I'd be making it with you," he said. He placed the funny, uncool hat on his head and picked up his suitcase. "At least it wasn't Mount Adams," he said before his lean, loping figure disappeared down the road and out of sight.

53

A daughter and two mothers

A reservation request arrived. This time it was from a family, Helen and Jeff Boggs, from Minneapolis, and their daughter, Sandra. It was unusual for a family to choose La Llorona as a trip destination, not that I would have inquired as to their reasons. But Helen volunteered them.

The Boggs had adopted Sandra five and a half years ago, when she was eighteen months old, from an orphanage in the city. Since bringing Sandra home to the United States they had not returned, until now.

"We want to show our daughter where she came from," Helen told me. "Give her a sense of her roots." Though adoption was not uncommon in this country, it was a rare choice among adoptive parents, I suspected, to bring their child back to the country of her origins. I told Helen Boggs I admired the decision she and her husband had made and would do everything I could to make their trip a meaningful one.

"I should probably tell you," she said. "A year ago, we hired a man known as a searcher. We paid him a sum of money to try and find Sandy's birth mother. We didn't have a lot of information, but we wanted to try."

Three weeks before, they'd gotten the news that the searcher, Santos, had located the woman who'd given up the baby now known as Sandra Boggs. Seven years before, she'd left her baby on the steps of a tiny hospital in a town fifteen kilometers from La Llorona, a place where she still lived. This was the reason the Boggs family was making their trip.

I was just finishing my morning coffee when I received Helen Boggs's call. After, I set myself to preparing a room for the Boggs family—the Monkey Room, with a double bed and a smaller single, with carvings of monkeys along the bedposts and a swinging chair on the small private veranda out the French doors. The little girl would like that.

Three weeks later they arrived at the gate.

Helen Boggs was a pleasant-looking woman, around my age. Her husband, Jeff, was a true redhead, she strawberry blonde.

The child looked nothing like her parents. She was small, solidly built. The person here who could have passed as a member of her family was Walter. Same coffee-colored skin and ink-black hair. That same timeless profile that you could find any day on a dozen different women selling vegetables in the market or, with equal ease, on an ancient stone carving at the ruins recently uncovered in the jungle up north.

The sight of a child—in all this time, the first child I'd ever welcomed as a guest at the hotel—caught me up short. She was carrying an American Girl doll, dark-skinned like herself. But the part that got to me was the balloon. Her parents must have bought it for her in the village and wound the string around her wrist to keep it from floating away.

"You must be Sandra," I said.

She loved the Monkey Room. She didn't want to wash her face because to do so would have meant unfolding the towel Mirabel had left on her bed, folded into the shape of a swan. I told her I'd get her another.

. The Boggses were the only guests at the hotel that night, and they asked me to join them, something I did now and then on slow nights, though this time I hesitated. I was still getting over the balloon.

"I should probably check on the arrangements for tomorrow," I told them. "I'll make sure Maria packs you a good meal for the trip."

The plan was for the Boggs family to take the boat over to Santa Clara the next morning to meet the searcher, and from there, travel into the hills to meet Sandra's birth mother. I knew from Helen that she'd been told they were coming, and wanted to see them, though out of sight of the people in her village. To have given up a baby as the woman had done was a source of terrible shame.

More than the parents, it was the child, Sandra, who insisted I sit with them that night.

"You know I'm adopted, right?" she said, twirling her straw in the mango drink Mirabel had set in front of her.

"Your mom explained," I said. "This is a pretty big deal for you, probably. This trip."

"I have two moms," she told me. "I came out of the other mom's stomach. But my real mom is my mom." She indicated Helen.

"You probably only have one mom," Sandra said.

"My mom died a long time ago," I told her. "I had a grandma though."

"The mom that had me in her stomach couldn't take care of me," Sandra said. "She didn't have any money for food."

My eyes met Helen's. I had just made the acquaintance of these people, and didn't want to overstep. No doubt they'd spent hours planning how to approach this event. They probably talked with a therapist about it. Who was I to weigh in? But Helen and Jeff Boggs seemed to take it in stride that their daughter had included me in the conversation, even about a subject as crucial as this one.

"I bet it was really hard for her to let you go," I told Sandra. "She must have loved you a lot."

"That's just what we told our daughter," Jeff said.

"You have kids?" Sandra asked me.

"No kids," I told her.

"Not *yet*," Sandra offered. "You never know what's in your future, right?"

"You have to excuse our daughter," Helen said. "Sandy never met a stranger."

Dessert was chocolate mousse with whipped cream and strawberries. It wasn't anybody's birthday, but I'd instructed Maria to put a sparkler in Sandra's.

"Are you busy tomorrow?" she asked.

"Just the usual, I guess," I said.

"Then you should come with us," Sandra said. "You speak Spanish, right? All my mom and dad can say is '*hola*' and '*buenos dias*.'"

"I think this should be a private family time for the three of you," I told her. "You and your parents and your birth mom probably want to be by yourselves."

"The truth is, Jeff and I might like that too," Helen said. "We never met the searcher before. I mean, we never met you either until today, but I get the feeling you understand."

"I'm with Helen," Jeff said. "We're kind of flying blind here. We actually talked about this, when we were out in the garden. That it would feel good, having you with us."

"My Spanish is a lot better than it used to be when I first came here," I said. "But it's a long way from perfect."

"You can talk better than these guys," Sandra said. She pointed her straw in the direction of her parents. Just then she caught sight of Cuzmi, the hotel dog she'd been trying to get to retrieve sticks all afternoon, and took off after him.

With Sandra gone, I raised my concerns once again to Helen and Jeff. "Are you sure having me with you wouldn't feel strange?"

"Listen, the whole thing is a little strange, right?" Helen said. "We've come all this way to introduce the child we love more than anything in the world to the woman who gave birth to her. You think there isn't a part of me that's thinking we should just forget the whole thing and spend tomorrow shopping for beaded bracelets and worry dolls in the market? Only there's this other part of me that knows, someday our daughter's going to have a lot of questions for us. Whatever we can offer to help her understand her story, she deserves to get that."

I'd meet them on the patio after breakfast, I told them. I knew some things myself about what it meant to be a person who never fully knew where she came from. If your mother blows herself up when you're six years old, odds are you'll end up with some unanswered questions.

54
Worry dolls

The four of us—Jeff, Helen, Sandra, and I—made our way to the boat next morning, and from there to the mainland where they'd arranged to meet up with the searcher. Sandra skipped ahead along the narrow cobbled street, pointing out items for sale in the stalls she wanted to go back and check out later—a skirt that looked like her size, embroidered with quetzal birds, a necklace strung with tiny ceramic girls with faces not unlike her own, a cloth bag filled with worry dolls. "The idea is, you put one of these dolls under your pillow any time something's worrying you," I told her. "In the morning, the worry's supposed to be gone."

The Boggses had made an arrangement to meet Santos, the searcher, at a café across from the market. At first, when we got there, I assumed he must simply not have arrived yet, but as we made our way to our table, a young man—I'll call him what he was, a boy—got up to join us.

If this boy was sixteen, I was twenty. From all I could tell, he didn't shave, and when he opened his mouth to greet us, he spoke in a register that indicated he had yet to go through puberty.

He had ordered the Plato Tipico—huevos rancheros, with frijoles, queso, platanos, and crema, also orange juice, with a side order of pancakes. At the moment we met him, he was bent over his meal, mopping up the last of his beans with a tortilla. His shirt—procured at the used clothing market, no doubt—said Kiss me, I'm Irish.

I was baffled, of course, at how this boy had managed to enlist clients in Minneapolis. Even more remarkable, I wondered how, out of all the tens of thousands of indigenous women in this country who'd given birth, alone probably, in small rural villages where nobody ever wrote down their name—he had apparently succeeded in locating, for Jeff and Helen Boggs, the woman who'd borne their beloved child. Maybe some older person in the family—an uncle or aunt, if not a parent— had done the real work of tracking down Sandra's birth mother, and merely sent Santos along to accompany their clients for the meeting as a translator. It became apparent swiftly that even this role was beyond Santos's reach. While his command of Spanish was hardly in doubt, his English appeared limited to a few words only. "Cool," "Got it," and— oddly—"groovy" serving as the mainstays. He was also adept at pointing out the cost of things.

"Bus ride here, fifteen *garza*," were his opening words to Jeff, delivered as he held out his palm. "Got a car. Air condition," he said. Two hundred *garza* for the day.

Helen and Jeff were eager to get on their way, as was Sandra. "Do you think my birth mom will be pretty?" she said. "I'm bringing her a picture I made of a unicorn.

"Maybe she's got other kids," Sandra continued. "Then I'd have sisters and brothers. Maybe they've got a dog."

"She probably lives in a very small house," Helen said. "She doesn't have things like a kitchen and a TV, like at our house. She might be hungry."

"Let's bring her our toast." Sandra reached for the untouched slices our waitress had set on the table and slathered them generously with jam before wrapping them in a napkin that she stuffed into her backpack. She had also brought along her report card from first grade, she told me, and another picture she'd made—this one of Celine Dion, which might have been the best picture she ever drew, she told me. "I'm going to give her this," Sandra said. "Maybe she'll hang it on her wall."

"It's probably a good idea if we don't get our hopes up too much," Jeff said, gentle as ever. "Even though Maria knows we're coming, this experience will probably be a little overwhelming for her."

"Me too," Sandra said. "This is like Christmas only bigger."

"I don't know about anybody else here," Jeff said. "But I'm ready." He paid the bill and we headed out onto the street, where the car Santos had arranged for us was waiting. You might have thought, for the money the Boggs had laid out, it would have been a Chevrolet, at minimum, but our ride turned out to be a very old pickup.

The cab of the truck had room for one passenger in the front on account of the bags of onions on the seat, along with some cabbages. The rest of us—Jeff, Sandra, Santos, and me—climbed into the back and held on to the roll bar for the hourlong journey up the mountain. Now and then our driver made the choice to pass some slower vehicle up ahead, leaving us in the lane of oncoming traffic without a lot of acceleration capacity. Times like these, Jeff banged wildly on the window, gesturing to our driver to slip back into our assigned lane, but this never had any effect.

It was a little before noon—the sun burning down with an intensity that must have been particularly worrisome to the redheads in our midst. Wherever we looked, there were coffee beans laid out on rooftops. They gave off an odd, rancid smell nothing like coffee, once roasted.

Suddenly the truck lurched to a stop and Santos hopped out the back, holding out a hand to help me. Then came Jeff, who lifted Sandra out and set her down as tenderly as an egg.

"Where do we go now?" she said. "Which one is my other mom's house?"

Not counting the church, there were four small structures in this village—a lean-to tienda with a sign out front advertising Fanta and three even smaller lean-tos surrounded by dirt in which a few straggly chickens wandered around, searching for bugs. Santos led us to the open front door of the smallest of these. Jeff came next, followed by Helen, holding Sandra's hand. She had stopped bouncing now, her manner suddenly subdued. I walked in last.

A woman sat on the couch. Not a couch so much as a cot, covered in an old bedsheet that might once have had flowers on it. There was a picture of the Virgin Mary on the wall, and another of the Pope, though not the current one, if memory served me. Other than this, the only furnishing was a wooden crate with a television propped on top, with a cord draped from the ceiling to the doorframe and leading to what appeared to be the only plug in the house, turned on to one of those shows featuring a Mexican soap opera.

"This is Maria," Santos said, gesturing toward the woman on the couch. She was wearing a shapeless, bag-like dress—not one of the beautiful hand-embroidered huipiles of the women in my village—and her feet were bare. A bandana covered her hair. If I'd been asked to make a guess I would have estimated Maria's age at sixty-five. It was hard to imagine how she could have given birth to the seven-year-old child who now stood, utterly still, facing her, looking shell-shocked.

I waited for Santos to say more, but it appeared he viewed his job as having been completed. He had stepped outside, onto what a person might refer to as the porch, if that person had never seen a porch until now. He lit something that smelled like a joint.

"This is Helen Boggs," I began in Spanish. "And her husband, Jeff. And this is Sandra."

Maria glanced at the three of them—Jeff first, then Helen, and finally the little girl. She turned her gaze back to her television program.

"They came from the United States to meet you," I said.

I looked at Helen now for guidance. No doubt she and her husband had spent long hours imagining this moment, and what they'd want to say, what they'd ask, the things they'd tell Sandra's birth mother about their child, the pictures they'd planned to show her, of Sandra's first steps, her first day at preschool, her birthday party at the ice rink the winter before: Sandra, pushing a plastic penguin to keep her upright, then—gloriously—setting it to the side and taking off across the ice all by herself on her small brown skates.

We had been at Maria's house all of four minutes at this point, but already this entire expedition seemed meaningless. Though she had bounced into the room as a person might, who expected nothing but good in the world and none but friendly faces to greet her, Sandra leaned against her mother now, one hand twisted into Helen's skirt, three fingers of the other in her mouth.

"Maybe Santos got the details wrong," Jeff said to me. "Maybe you could ask her to clarify. She could be the grandmother. Or a family friend."

"We came here to meet the woman who gave birth to this child," I said. I was looking hard at Maria, though searching, too, for some other room, beyond this one, where a woman might be found, younger by thirty years, with kinder eyes—someone who might actually reach out a hand now to Sandra and her parents.

"I dreamed of this day," she'd tell them. *"Do you still have that heart-shaped birthmark on your leg? Do you know that the first thing you did, when you slipped out of my body, was open your eyes and smile?"*

She did put out her hand, in fact. Not in the direction of Sandra, but Jeff.

"I need money," she said.

I didn't need to translate this part. Jeff reached into his wallet and took out a hundred-*garza* bill. He placed it in the hand of the old woman.

"We need to go now," Helen said.

On the short walk to the truck, which had been parked a hundred yards down the dusty street, Helen reached for her daughter's hand, but Sandra chose not to take it. She held tight to the straps of her backpack with the report card and the pictures inside of Celine Dion and the unicorn. Her steps were slower now.

Back in the town where we'd catch the boat, Helen suggested that we check out a few stalls at the market, since we were here. She bought a shawl for herself, a panama hat for Jeff, who was badly sunburned. "I'd call this locking the barn door after the horses got out," he said, as he set the hat on his thinning red hair, the skin below bright pink now, like his face. They pointed out a number of items that might interest Sandra, but though she picked out several as gifts for her friends back home (a turtle made from a shell, with a bobbing head and tail, a ceramic bird), she chose only one thing for herself—a small cloth bag of worry dolls.

Next morning they were on the boat, headed home to Minnesota. Leila's words to me, long ago, came back to me. "You may not find what you're looking for when you come to this lake," she'd told me. "But you'll probably find what you need."

55

Mysterious disappearances

Back in my early days at La Llorona—in the months after Leila's death—I began noticing the disappearance of small but significant objects at the hotel—a very beautiful kaleidoscope Leila had kept on her desk, a silver flask designed to hold whiskey, a wooden case with inlaid mother-of-pearl containing a set of real ivory dominos, a bottle of very good aged port, and the Walkman I'd picked up on a rare visit to the city.

At first when things started disappearing, I'd told myself that I was just absent-mindedly mislaying them, though in the case of the port, it occurred to me that perhaps someone staying at La Llorona had taken off with it for a romantic evening back in the room.

When Gus came by, I'd told him about the missing objects.

"Don't look at me," he said. "I ain't lifted so much as a bag of crisps since I met the little lady back in India. I'm a reformed man."

"You were never a suspect, Gus," I told him. Just the thought made me laugh. "I've already trusted you with pretty much every aspect of my life."

"You can count on me, luv," he said. "You're like the sister I never had, you know."

That afternoon, as Elmer was carrying in a new jug of purified water for my guests—bending low over the ceramic dispenser we kept in the kitchen—something fell out of his pocket. My Walkman.

"I think you have something that doesn't belong to you," I told Elmer. "We need to talk."

At the time, Elmer was sixteen years old. He was so mortified he could barely speak.

"I don't expect you to forgive me," he said. "There is no excuse for what I did. I brought your things to a man in Santa Clara. He gave me money."

"I trusted you," I said.

"I lost my mind," Elmer said. "All I could think about was Mirabel."

Mirabel? What did Mirabel have to do with this?

That day on the patio, his voice barely above a whisper, Elmer had explained to me what led him to commit his crime. There was no excuse for his actions, he agreed. But love had made him lose his mind. Love of Mirabel, of course.

He wanted to buy a piece of land—a goal that would have seemed impossible to most boys his age. He had been saving his money since he was twelve. All the extra *garza* that other boys spent on sneakers or tacos or soda, Elmer had kept in a box under his bed. Even his parents didn't know about this. It was his secret dream that one day, when the money in the box was sufficient to purchase a small plot—just big enough for a little house and a garden—he would come to Mirabel with the title to the land that had his name on it—his name and hers. Then he would ask Mirabel to marry him.

Four years since Elmer had started saving up, he was still far from his goal, but he knew he would get there. Then a terrible thing had happened: The box under his bed was empty. No telling who'd stolen the money. It could have been any small-time thief in the village.

"I went crazy," he said. "All I could think about was the time I'd lost. What if Mirabel chose someone else while I was still working to earn that piece of land?"

That was the day he'd taken my letter opener and brought it to the man in Santa Clara who paid cash for stolen goods. "Bring me more things like this," the man had told him. "I'll give you lots of money." From then on, he'd made weekly trips to Santa Clara. One time he brought the antique ivory domino set. Another time it had been a string of Leila's pearls.

Elmer was sixteen years old when I confronted him, but at that moment, he looked very young. He stood up straight as he faced me, as if he were approaching the gallows.

"It has been my honor to work for you," he said. "I don't expect to keep my job. It is the greatest shame of my life. If my mother knew what I'd done, it would kill her."

I sat there for a moment, taking in what Elmer had done. As much disappointment as I felt over his betrayal of my trust, this event would not define him in my eyes. He had been a young man who mattered greatly to me. He was still that person.

"This will be our secret," I said. "I know you'll never steal from me again. You can keep your job."

But Elmer believed he needed to do some kind of penance for his deeds. As difficult as this had been, he had taken it upon himself to confess his crime to Mirabel—believing, as he did so, that she would see his actions, misguided as they had been, as further proof of his devotion. But after he told her she had refused to speak to him. This proved a more devastating consequence than any he might have imagined. Elmer was dead to Mirabel now.

From that moment on, his one mission in life was to earn back Mirabel's respect. I never again found reason to question his loyalty to me. But Mirabel could not forgive his crimes. When Elmer passed through the kitchen now she looked through him as if he was made of air. He looked back at her with eyes of undying love.

56

A rival

After I'd caught him stealing that day, Elmer had turned his life around. From that day on he had chosen to live in the simplest way possible. No fried chicken from the cart in town. No new sneakers or backpack, no football jersey with the name of his favorite team. When his friends had invited him to join them at the annual *feria*, he shook his head. After working long hours at La Llorona, he walked many kilometers in the dark every night to stand guard at Wade's restaurant, El Buffo. When the sun came up, he returned to La Llorona to work, again, for me. All this he had done to once again accumulate sufficient money for the purchase of a plot of land—the only thing he could imagine that might melt the heart of his beloved.

A year after he delivered his confession to Mirabel, the event Elmer most dreaded had taken place. Another boy in the village—Herman—had started hanging around the basketball court to watch Mirabel play. Elmer had seen him walking her home. One morning at church they were seated next to each other, and there was a look in Herman's eyes as he beheld Mirabel that Elmer understood well—feeling it himself, only more so. Nobody could love Mirabel as much as he did. But that day in church, observing Herman alongside the woman he loved, it was not simply Herman's attentiveness to Mirabel that Elmer recognized. It was Mirabel's, for Herman. When his beloved smiled at his rival it was as if a knife pierced Elmer's heart. He knew that if Mirabel chose Herman, he would never love anyone else ever again.

Late one night in the kitchen, Elmer confided in me about his heartbreak. He could not pray for bad luck to befall Herman, he explained to me. God would not take kindly to such a prayer. Still, he kept hoping the other boy would do something to prove himself unworthy of Mirabel. Maybe he'd buy a bottle of Quetzalteca and get drunk. Maybe he'd be drawn to another young woman in the village—though the idea of any woman ever distracting a man who had won the affection of Mirabel seemed, to Elmer, unimaginable.

Then an amazing thing happened—an event he could never have dreamed. Herman's mother had become very ill with a fever, a malady for which no doctor seemed able to find a cure. At the height of his despair, Herman had visited the church late in the night, to speak to God. "If you will spare my mother," Herman said, "I will dedicate my life to serving you."

The next morning the fever was gone. Herman's mother got up from the bed. "I want to make tortillas," she said. Remembering his promise to God the night before, he told his mother he was going to become a priest.

All of this was history. Elmer was twenty-two now, Mirabel twenty-one. Herman had kept his vow to join the priesthood, but Mirabel had still not forgiven Elmer. Apart from the most basic exchanges—a request that he carry in a tank of propane for the stove or bring a sack of dog food for Cuzmi down from the bodega—she had not spoken to him since the day he offered his confession. The crime he had committed in the hope of winning Mirabel's hand in marriage had the effect of turning her heart to stone. In the years that had passed since that terrible day, she showed no sign of reconsidering.

Still, he had not given up. He had continued to save his money. Now, finally, he had enough to pay for a small plot of land owned by his uncle. With Herman no longer a contender for the affection of the woman he loved, Elmer wanted me to know—me, before his parents even—that he was ready to go to Mirabel and declare himself. He had spoken with his uncle, who had agreed to sign the title over to him. That day, Elmer told me, he would show Mirabel the title and ask her to marry him.

He had given this a lot of thought. Years' worth, in fact. He had waited all this time until he had something of substance to lay at her feet: the promise of a home, a secure future, for herself and the children he hoped the two of them might have, if God were willing.

"The work my mother does here, in the kitchen, is not so difficult for her," he said. "But my father is old. He deserves to rest. It is my dream that as the years pass, Mirabel and I can take care of my parents, and her father."

"I think you would make a wonderful husband for Mirabel," I told him. "Of course, the choice is hers."

"Today I will ask her," he said. "Today our life together begins."

57

Sweeping stone

She said no. Nobody needed to tell me. I saw it on Elmer's face when he arrived at work the next morning. He always started the day carrying the giant jug of purified water on his back that he set on the stand in the kitchen. Normally it was nothing for him, carrying in the water jug, but that day he moved as if there were a boulder on his back. Or a cross.

When Mirabel arrived for work an hour later, she busied herself with the laundry, then fresh sheets for the Quetzal room, the swan-shaped towels laid out on the beds, the little bars of cardamom-scented soap, extra candles. She looked beautiful as ever. Nobody, studying her face that day, could have guessed that only hours before, she'd broken a young man's heart.

If Maria knew any of this, she didn't let on. She set to work making a stew of fresh tilapia and crab. The dessert that night would be orange soufflés, served in the hollowed-out skins of the orange.

Elmer was sweeping the steps just beyond the patio as Mirabel set the perfectly risen soufflés in front of our guests. On the sound system Gus had recently installed for me, a singer I loved, Rosanna, was singing "Si Tu No Estas Aqui." Possibly the most heartbreaking song on the whole tape. *If you aren't here, I don't want to breathe.*

I looked out at Elmer, standing with his broom, going over the same one patch of stone. I remembered that feeling of loss. I was there once.

58
Death of another mother

Gus came by to deliver terrible news. Rosella had gone into labor the night before. Wade brought her by boat to the hospital.

It turned out that Rosella had been suffering from an undiagnosed condition of pregnancy known as preeclampsia—extreme high blood pressure causing a poisoning of the blood and, when not discovered soon enough, irreversible damage to the vital organs. In the final stage of delivery, she had suffered a massive stroke and died in the delivery room. The twins, a boy and a girl, had survived.

"She was too old, was the thing," Gus said, shaking his head and taking another swig on his beer. "There's a time for having kids, and a time for hanging it up. She should have quit while she was ahead."

I pictured the two motherless babies. I tried to imagine Wade, tending bar in among the rabbit cages, trying to care for them. A disbarred Chicago lawyer-turned-rabbit-farming-restaurateur did not seem a likely candidate for single parenthood of a couple of newborns.

59

Some people say only boys get to be doctors

That afternoon I walked into the village, still thinking of Rosella and Wade's newborn twins. I found Amalia in her garden, sewing. She was in the company of one of her favorite little girls in the village, Clarinda—the youngest of seven children of a woman in the town, Veronica, who could be found, most mornings, lying by the side of the road, passed out with a bottle of Quetzalteca at her side. (The label featured a pretty woman in traditional indigenous garb—her hair tied with ribbons, a belt around her trim waist, holding up a bottle. Nobody I'd ever observed, drinking the stuff—as so many in this village did, given its low price—bore any resemblance to the woman on the label. Certainly not Clarinda's mother.) Not surprisingly, Clarinda spent more time at Amalia's little one-room house, and in the garden there, than she ever did in the adobe hut of her mother and her older siblings. Her father had died years before, from alcohol poisoning.

That day she and Amalia were busy sewing hats for the new twins, with the plan of delivering them to Wade's house in the valley later that day.

"What's he going to do with two babies?" I asked.

"He'll hire a girl to take care of them, of course," Amalia said. "Two, maybe. If the price of childcare gets too much for him, he can always marry one of them."

"I love babies," Clarinda said. She was not yet ten years old, but already her services had been enlisted by her two older sisters, both of whom had given birth before their sixteenth birthdays and were pregnant again. I knew from my conversations with Amalia on the subject of Clarinda that her goal was to keep this little girl—a favorite of us both—in school, and away from boys for as long as possible.

"We all love babies," Amalia said. "That doesn't mean you need to have them anytime soon. You're going to the university."

I had no idea how Amalia thought this would happen, but I figured she could probably find a way. As little money as she had for herself, she was surprisingly good at scaring up funds for the projects she organized. I would help too.

I asked Clarinda what she'd like to study. When I'd stopped by to see Amalia, I had imagined the two of us talking about Rosella's awful and unnecessary death, the fate of the twins. It was a relief to find myself in the company of this particularly bright, lively child, who had managed somehow, despite the hardships of her life, to maintain an attitude of optimism and joy.

"I'm going to be a doctor," she said.

"You'll need to work hard on science," I told her. "But I bet you'll do it."

When she was very small, her brother had gotten some kind of sickness, she told me. All day long she sat by the bed, taking care of him. His skin was burning up. She kept cool cloths on his forehead and when there was money, brought Popsicles to place on his lips.

"I kept wishing I knew how to make him better," she said. Something better than Popsicles.

She was six when Byron died. The last few days, he had been unable to eat anything. She put drops of water in his mouth—one drop at a time, like a bird—but he didn't open his eyes anymore. She slept on the floor next to him.

When she woke up in the night, she had put her ear to his chest, listening for the beating of his heart, but heard nothing.

Men came to carry his body away. He was so thin, she could have almost have carried him herself.

"I want to know how people's bodies work," she said. "I want to learn how to make sick people better.

"Some people say only boys get to be doctors," she told us.

"You can be anything you want," Amalia said. "Look at me. I said I would fly across the ocean and build my home in a beautiful place by a volcano, and I did. I said we could build a school out of trash. And turn scraps of old dresses into beautiful princess costumes. And we did that."

"You know some people say she's crazy," Clarinda said to me, pointing her embroidery needle in the direction of Amalia. She was laughing.

"Call me crazy if you want," Amalia told her. "But tell me how many empty soda bottles you saw as you came down the path to visit me today."

Not even one.

60

A visit with the Mayan astrologer

A young couple showed up. Not honeymooners, but the way they looked at each other, they might as well have been. This was one of those nights when I instructed Maria to scatter rose petals around the table at dinner and put on a tape of Andrea Bocelli. Candles, naturally. Champagne.

There was no way I would have intruded on Bud and Victoria Albertson's evening, but the next morning, when I set the coffeepot on their table, Victoria had invited me to sit with them.

"We're looking to buy a piece of property here," Bud said, still barely taking his eyes off of his wife's face even as he addressed me. "We're hoping you can give us some advice."

I asked how they'd come up with this idea, naturally. It seemed an unlikely choice for a car salesman from Arkansas and his wife, a piano teacher. But they were ready to change their lives.

"After we got married, we bought a little house outside of Little Rock," Bud said. "I had a good job down at the Subaru dealership. Vic had a waiting list of parents wanting her to teach their kids piano. Both sets of our parents lived within a few blocks. All these great friends that we went out with every weekend. Church every Sunday. We were happy."

One night, changing the channels, they'd come upon a National Geographic special about volcanos that featured El Fuego and Lago La Paz.

"The next morning we woke up and looked at each other," Victoria explained, "and we both said it at almost the same time. 'Is this all there is?' Like maybe it was all too comfortable, this life we'd made for our-selves, where the biggest adventure we ever had was our senior trip to Washington and our honeymoon at Disney World."

"We're ready to simplify our lives," Bud said. "Get back to the basics. Make a difference."

"We knew what we wanted to do. Sell everything. Move down here. Once we pick up Spanish, Vic can teach music someplace and I'll do volunteer work. We've got enough from the sale of our house so we can take it slow, assess the situation."

"You might want to try this out for a while," I suggested. "Rent a place for a month, see how it feels."

"I can see how you'd think that," Bud said. "Our parents and our pastor told us the same thing. But sometimes a person has to jump in with both feet. We know it's going to be a big adjustment. That's part of what we're looking for. If we wanted to do something easy, we could've stayed home."

"There's a whole lot of beauty in this village," I told them. "Obviously, I wouldn't be living here myself if I didn't think it was a wonderful place to live. But it's complicated." I remembered Leila's words to me when I'd first arrived at the lake. "You remember the story of the Garden of Eden?" she'd said. "Every paradise has its serpents."

"We know it won't be easy," Victoria said, stroking her husband's hand. "The thing is, we've always got each other. Our love's strong enough that we can handle anything."

I suggested they speak with Gus and Dora. Gus knew everyone in town, and if anyone were selling property, he'd be the first to know.

They took off right after breakfast the next day to meet Gus, and by noon he had lined up a piece of land to show them where he could build them a nice little casita, he said, for a price so low his missus would skin him alive if she found out.

The piece of land Gus showed them first hadn't proven right for the Albertsons. As beautiful as the spot had been, there'd been a deep ravine running through the center of the land that made Victoria and Bud nervous. "I'd always be worrying about someone falling in and never getting out," Bud had told Gus. "One wrong step and it would all be over."

After they returned from looking at the property Victoria and Bud had headed off for lunch in town. They wanted to visit the market. Bud, who had admired the machete Luis used to trim brush on my property, wanted one for himself. Victoria wanted to buy a bag.

I learned the rest later. On their way back to the hotel from the market, Victoria had been drawn, as many foreign visitors before her had been, to the stall of Andres, the young man with the shingle out front that read MAYAN ASTROLOGY. Wanting to expand her sights beyond the Presbyterian church and Bible study group she'd attended most of her life, she'd struck up a conversation with the man out front. He seemed to possess a curious power.

Andres had lived in the United States when he was younger, so his English was nearly fluent, and he spoke with virtually no accent. He was, without question, an unusually handsome man, with a shock of thick black hair that fell over his eyes in a way that only made you want even more to look into them. And when you did, here was the strange thing. Unlike virtually every other indigenous person in the village— whose eyes were brown, almost black—his were blue. Pale blue in fact, like the eyes on an Alaskan malamute. Remembering Leila's words to me about Andres, when I'd first arrived in the village, I'd chosen never to speak to him.

Except for times when he was with a client—almost invariably, a woman—Andres sat on a little stool outside his stall for much of the day, his shirt open low enough to reveal, on the smooth brown skin of his chest, a piece of coconut shell carved into a form that no doubt bore significance, if I'd known more about Mayan symbols.

When tourists passed, he was always ready to engage them in conversation. They'd start out speaking their bad to virtually nonexistent

Spanish to him, and at times he'd go along with this, never revealing his own near-fluency in English.

On several occasions that I could remember, a guest at La Llorona had set out to have a reading with Andres. Each of the young women who'd gone for a reading had returned to the hotel strangely silent about the experience. One, a very beautiful young kindergarten teacher visiting from Seattle, had left abruptly on the afternoon of her reading. She never said anything that connected her departure to her experience with Andres, but I had wondered about it enough that when guests asked me for recommendations among the many massage therapists and body workers and self-proclaimed healers in town, one I never recommended was Andres.

That afternoon, when Bud and Victoria returned to the hotel, I knew right away that something was wrong. I had seen how the two of them made their way down the steps to the hotel—Bud with both arms around Victoria and she, leaning onto him as if she'd tip over otherwise. When they reached the entrance they had walked past Maria and me without speaking, heading directly for their room and shutting the door.

Gus showed up a few minutes later. He reported that while in town he'd run into the young guests—now his real estate clients—sitting by the side of the road shortly before their return to the hotel, but when Gus had greeted them with the news that he'd come up with another house for them to check out, Victoria had seemed not even to recognize him.

"I know when a gal's just on her delicate time of the month," Gus told me. "With this one, it was more than that. From the look on her face, you would have thought the woman had stared into the eyes of Margaret Thatcher. That or my dead grandmother."

That night, it all came out. Bud had wanted to accompany Victoria into the small back room behind the Mayan astrology storefront for her session, but Andres had explained to him that for Victoria to accomplish the work she needed, she had to be alone with him, undisturbed by the vibrational field of anyone else, even someone like Bud who loved her. Bud had accepted this. He waited on the stool outside for his wife.

Her session with Andres had seemed normal enough at first. (What did either of these two know about what a normal Mayan astrology session might look like? Apart from one time they'd visited the Ohio State fair and, just for fun, checked out the booth of a fortune teller, neither one of them had ever engaged in anything like this.)

He asked her birthday. Month and year, both, which allowed him to know her sign was obsidian. Animal guardians, Toucan.

He asked next for her husband's information. Animal guardian, Crocodile. Energy location, rivers and seas. Stone, turquoise. Compatibility with Toucan: The worst.

"You and this man you married," he said. "He is not your destiny. You will leave him."

At first, Victoria told Bud after, she had laughed this off, or tried to. But Andres just kept nodding. "I know," he said. "This is hard to hear. Toucan wants to make a life with this man, this Crocodile. You want to reject my words. But you cannot reject your destiny."

"I love Bud," Victoria told Andres. "I trust him more than anybody in the world. Everyone in my family loves Bud. My mother adores him."

Andres kept nodding. Nodding and humming. "Take this drink," he said. "It will help you."

He handed her a cup of some kind of thick, almost muddy brew. She took a sip.

"More," he told her. "Leave nothing in the cup.

"Toucan is very loyal," he said. "Loyal, even when it may do her harm. She wants so much to believe. She would rather stay blind to the truth than face its harsh glare."

There was something in his eyes when he spoke to her. As if there were laser beams coming out of his pupils, pointed directly into Victoria's brain.

What was he saying? The room started to spin.

"You are afraid of your sexuality, aren't you, Toucan," Andres said. "You chose a safe man. A good man, but one for whom you feel no passion."

"I love my husband," she told him.

Of course you do. If you have a dog, you probably love your dog too.

"It's not like that."

Finish your drink.

"Bud's a wonderful person."

Of course he is. But do you respect him? Do you hunger for his body?

Pictures came to her then, times she'd forgotten, flooding back now. A Friday night, out with their friends at Applebee's, Bud—on his third beer—telling about the time he'd met Bill Clinton at a fair in Little Rock.

"Hello, Mr. President," Bud had said, shaking his hand.

"Call me Bill," he'd responded. That was the whole story. Victoria must have heard it a hundred times. She remembered her embarrassment, in front of their friends, when her husband had repeated it. How foolish Bud had looked at that moment, presenting himself as someone on a first-name basis with the president.

And other times. Things Bud did that she had chosen to put out of her mind, only now they were whirling around in her brain. The stupid shirt he wore, that said I'M INTO FITNESS. FITNESS BEER INTO MY BELLY. And in fact, he had been putting on weight lately. She had pretended otherwise, but this bothered her.

"Your husband may be a good friend to you," the astrologer told her. "But he does not move you as a lover."

She thought about the way Bud left his Kleenex next to the TV and didn't even bother to crumple it up to conceal the boogers. The necklace he'd given her for Valentine's Day, in the shape of the state of Arkansas. Did he actually believe that was a romantic gift? It seemed never to have occurred to her husband that there might be other ways to make love besides climbing on top of her.

"You married this man to make your parents happy, didn't you?" Andres said.

"It's not like that," she told him.

Or was it? The words of the Mayan astrologer had opened up this door inside her brain and now all these horrible pictures started pouring in. And horrible ideas: the part about how she hadn't really been so sure about marrying Bud after all, that she'd done it to please her mother.

"Maybe there was someone else, another man," the astrologer, Andres, was saying now. "Someone for whom you felt that passion you long for now. You knew you should have been with this other man but you didn't let yourself. It was too much, too strong. The man you brought home to the house of your parents should not give off the smell of sex."

She thought about her college boyfriend Alex. Sophomore year. They'd slept together, something she'd never told Bud. For one semester, the two of them barely got out of bed. To this day, her husband believed she was a virgin on their wedding night.

One time, when she had sex with Bud, she pretended it was Alex she was doing it with. Sometimes when she played the piano—if it was Chopin—she summoned an image of him.

By this point in her astrology reading, Victoria was crying. "I love my husband," she said to Andres. "I mean everything to him. He's such a good person. I don't want a divorce."

"You wanted to get away from your parents," he said. His voice, that had been close to yelling before, had suddenly turned to a whisper. At some point another button had come undone on Andres's shirt, that had already been unbuttoned halfway down his chest. Bud's chest had a great deal of hair on it, as did his back. Andres's skin was smooth as a baby's. Those ice-blue Alaskan malamute eyes bore into hers. He was whispering, softer than ever, directly into her ear.

"You thought you could escape all of this by selling your house and moving to another country far away from all of that, where you could start over, didn't you?"

"Yes," Victoria told Andres. She was whispering now too. "I did think that." The idea of moving to this place—quitting his job, giving up his place in the bowling league, selling the '71 Plymouth GS 455 that he'd rebuilt with his dad, having to learn another whole language—these were all things Bud had gone along with for one reason only. He loved Victoria that much. He would do anything to make her happy. And he could see she wasn't happy. Not really. She was bored. All this time she'd only been pretending, just as Andres had said.

More than anything, Bud wanted to make his wife's dreams come true. When the truth was that if Victoria's dreams actually did come true, he would not be part of them.

All of this had come to Victoria while she lay on the table in the back room of Andres's Mayan astrology center. Her whole body was trembling by now and she was weeping. She didn't know what to believe anymore. She could no longer speak, but Andres did.

"There's poison in your brain," he told her. "Bad spirits. Dark energy."

Maybe the astrologer was right. Maybe she was never supposed to marry Bud after all. Maybe her whole life was a lie.

"Would you like me to help you?" he said. "Would you like me to take these demons out of your body?"

This was when he told her to take off her clothes. Not just down to her underwear. Everything. "We need to bring you back to the beginning of everything," he said. "When you were a baby. Newborn."

For that one moment, it had sounded like a good idea, this nakedness. Even after she'd set her bra and underpants on the chair ("and your watch," he said. "Don't forget that. And your wedding ring") she still felt this would be good for her. Like medicine that tastes terrible, but it helps you get better.

"Close your eyes, little Toucan," he said to her, his voice tender and low. "You are under the waterfall. Mountain streams are cascading over your head."

It took her a moment to realize what was happening. His hand was resting against her inner thigh. Then his hand was moving up her leg to the place only two men, ever, had touched. Bud, and the other one, Alex—the first man she ever slept with, whom she still thought about in the dark, whose name she had not spoken since the day she'd broken up with him, eight years ago, until today.

The Mayan astrologer's fingers were on her then, moving inside, parting her lips, entering. She made a sound like a puppy hit by a car.

"Hush," he said. Then no words at all. His fingers moved deeper in and he was humming again.

"I'm taking the bad spirits out of you now," he said. "It won't hurt so much if you breathe."

What was he taking out? What was in there?

"It's the poisonous Crocodile energy," he said. "We need to pull it out of you. You will feel different after."

Victoria did feel different, after. Not in a good way. She felt sick, and ashamed. She felt dirty.

She sat up on the table; Andres had disappeared. She stepped back into her underpants and fastened her bra. She pulled her blouse over her head. Zipped up her skirt, buckled her sandals. Andres had told her she could leave the money on the chair. Two hundred *garza*.

Bud was outside waiting, the sun hitting his face. He was munching on chips. "How'd it go?" he said. "Did he reveal the mysteries of the universe?"

"It was okay," she told him. Her voice had gone flat.

"I was thinking I'd take my gal out for a smoothie at that little café down the path," he said.

"I think I'd rather go back to the hotel," she said. "I'm a little tired."

Walking down the road in the direction of La Llorona, her husband had studied her face. "You sure you're okay?" he asked.

They were most of the way back when she felt it coming on—dizziness so great she would have dropped to the ground if Bud hadn't caught her. Then the vomit rising up her throat. She could taste it. She bent over and threw up in the dirt.

The English guy, Gus—the one who'd taken them to see that property on the mountain that morning—passed by on the road, headed in the direction they were, and greeted them. He was saying something about a house for sale. He could take them there. Now, if they were interested.

Bud shook his head. "Not a good time, man," he said. Victoria threw up some more.

"Oh, honey," Bud said, placing a hand on her belly. "Maybe we're pregnant." *We.* For Bud, it was inconceivable that anything taking place would not equally concern them both.

She shook her head.

Then she told him the story. All of it. Leaving out nothing. One thing about Bud: He might not be the lover of her dreams. But he was definitely her best friend.

Later that evening—Victoria asleep in the room—Bud had come downstairs to find me on the patio.

"I know I shouldn't bother you with this," he said. He didn't know what else to do. He wanted to talk.

This was Bud Albertson for you. The part that tormented him about his wife's story had not been the admission that she'd slept with another man before they were married, and the harder truth that she still thought about that man. It had been difficult, hearing her list the many ways in which his behavior had irritated and offended her over the years. He could even take it, hearing that she'd questioned whether she really loved him, or married him just to please her mother. Victoria had not left out the part about her lack of sexual passion for her husband, or the fact that sometimes, when they made love, she thought about her To Do list for the next day.

All of this had been hard for Bud but he could take it. He loved Victoria that much. "I read one time that in every couple there's usually one person that's more in love than the other," he told me. "I don't mind being the more-in-love person. I feel lucky to be that person. I feel fortunate, loving Victoria as much as I do. It makes me a better man, just wanting to be good for her."

The part that tormented Bud—and there was no other word for it— was the way Andres had abused and violated Victoria's body. The part he was finding hard to bear—so much so, that he'd felt compelled to walk out onto the patio that night, as his wife lie on their bed, asleep at last—was the idea that the woman he adored had been . . . it was hard for Bud Albertson to speak the word . . . that she'd been raped. Andres, the so-called Mayan astrologer had taken something from Bud's beloved wife. Something precious and irretrievable.

There was one other part of the story that made it impossible for Bud Albertson to find sleep that night. It was the knowledge that Victoria had not been Andres's first victim, and unless someone took a stand she would not be the last.

"Someone has to stop him," Bud told me.

Bud was right, of course, that Andres had evidently managed to carry on his abuse of women for many years, free of consequences. Hearing what had happened to Victoria that day, I thought back to other guests who'd availed themselves of Andres's services, and the looks on their faces, after.

I also understood why none of the women I'd known who must have experienced some version of Andres's unspeakable violation of their

bodies and their minds had felt able to report him to the local authorities. There were police officers in the village of La Esperanza, and a
mayor who maintained offices in a large white cinder block structure
up on the hill known as The Muni. But for all we knew, Andres might
be the mayor's second cousin. Even if he had no powerful connections
at all, and had never bribed anyone, this was also a town where the
accusations of an American woman, or any foreigner, against a local
man would have been easily enough dismissed.

I poured Bud a glass of my best rum. In a sisterly way, I put my hand
on his arm and reminded him again of the words Leila had spoken to
me, years before, in this same spot. "Every paradise has its serpents."

61

A very deep ravine

The next morning, Bud was up early, looking a little better, though I doubted he'd slept. He told me not to expect Victoria to come down for breakfast. No problem. Maria would bring her a tray.

He wanted to go see Gus, he said, without elaborating. I told him how to get there. He was gone a few hours. I couldn't say he looked the same, when he returned, as he'd appeared, four days earlier, when he first showed up at the hotel, full of plans for his new life here with the woman he adored. But the heaviness I'd seen on the shoulders of Bud Albertson, weighing on him hard the night before, seemed to have lifted. He was even hungry, so we fixed him a sandwich and a bowl of soup. When he took off up the steps, carrying his new machete, there was a purpose to his step. His shoulders no longer seemed sloped.

He and Victoria left the next day for the airport. They were heading back to Little Rock. No further mention was made of buying real estate, signing up for Spanish lessons, locating a piano, though Bud did ask me, as he paid his bill, whether I had an opinion on *The Joy of Sex*. He was thinking about picking up a copy. "I just want to make my wife happy," he told me.

"Buy it," I told him.

As they said goodbye to me, Victoria held tight to her husband's arm.

After they left, Maria came to me. "The American left his new machete," she said. This surprised her because he'd been so excited when he'd bought it. I told her she should give the machete to Luis for yard work. He had one of course—every man in the village did—but the one Bud had purchased had a much sharper blade.

It was three days later before I had reason to walk into the village again. When I did, I was met with a curious sight in front of the Mayan Astrology stall.

The sign was gone. The door was shuttered. The bench where Andres could usually be found, reading his well-worn copy of *The Alchemist* or making his pictures of Mayan symbols, sat vacant.

At Harold's, where I stopped for a smoothie, I noticed that the lizard men—Vincente, Juan and Carlos—seemed more animated than usual. A police officer had come by a few minutes earlier, evidently. He was questioning everyone as to whether they'd seen Andres in the last forty-eight hours. His mother had reported him missing.

"I told them I didn't know anything," Harold said as he peeled the mango for my smoothie. "But we all knew that guy was bad news."

After, I paid a visit to Dora and Gus. Dora was in the garden with the children. Gus was mixing cement for the new addition they were planning.

"I guess you gathered, Victoria and Bud had a change of plans," I told him. "They had a run-in with Andres. Now he's disappeared."

"You believe in karma?" Gus asked me.

"It's like 'what goes around comes around,' basically," I said.

"That astrologer had a serious karmic debt on his tab." Gus's tone as he spoke sounded uncharacteristically somber.

"You think something bad happened to him? Like God, striking him down or something?"

"Sometimes God needs a little help from us mere mortals," Gus said. "Not that I know anything more than the rest of us." He dumped a shovelful of wet cement on the ground.

"You know the problem with that property I showed those two, up in the valley?" he said. "It was that damn ravine.

"They say it's a good half-mile deep," Gus told me. "The wife, Victoria, took one look at that pit and said she'd never live there on account of if someone fell in—like a kid—they'd be a goner, for sure. No one would even hear you call for help."

Warm as it was that day, a chill came over me. "Hardly anyone ever goes there," I said. "It's not like you could bring a person to that spot against their will."

"Unless they had a machete pressed against their ribs." Gus dug his shovel into the cement again.

"Shame about the astrologer fella," he said.

62
Swimming lessons

A person might suppose that a woman who had chosen to live on the side of one of the more spectacularly beautiful bodies of water on the planet would dive into it regularly if not daily. But I did not. Ever since my mother's boyfriend, Indigo, had thrown me into a pool when I was three years old, I'd had a fear of water. I'd never learned to swim.

Many times over the years, some helpful person or other, hearing this, had volunteered to teach me. The first was Daniel. He'd made many attempts, all that long summer we made our way from California to New York headed to Woodstock, by what had to be one of the most circuitous routes of all time. Of all the places we passed through over the roughly three months that constituted our odyssey, it was my swimming lessons with Daniel—sometimes conducted in a motel or campground pool, sometimes a swimming hole, and now and then an actual lake—that I remember best. New Orleans was in there, but so was Lake Superior; the Rocky Mountains and the Smoky Mountains, and Texas, and the outer banks of Maryland, and, on one crazy detour, the battlefield at Gettysburg.

But it was the swimming, not the history lessons or geography, or the diner breakfasts, or the paper umbrellas I collected from drinks at our rare special-occasion stops for my birthday or my mother's, that stayed with me most. Every time we crossed into another state on our trip, my mother would read out loud from the almanac, announcing the state bird, the state flower, the state nickname (Oklahoma, the Sooner State; Utah, the Beehive State; Pennsylvania, the Gem State, New Hampshire, Granite). Then Daniel would announce the closest place to take a dip.

Diana knew how to swim, but seldom ventured into the water, unless we were at a hot spring where she could be naked. For Daniel, swimming was as essential as breathing, or close, and he had the plan of instilling his love of the water in me. He never succeeded.

I had not forgotten how it felt, standing at the edge of some body of water or other, shivering in my too-big polka dot suit from Goodwill, Daniel at my side, or in the water, urging me to jump into his waiting arms—the terror in the pit of my stomach, a feeling that never left me even when he held me close to his chest, or buckled me into a life jacket, even when the water came up no higher than my waist.

"You're fine," Daniel told me. "I won't leave you." Only he had. Not by choice, but one day he was there. The next he wasn't.

I was just getting past my fear—had progressed to frog kick—the day Daniel took off down the highway, and for the rest of my childhood after that, the only person who ever took me into a pool was my grandmother, in her embarrassing pink swim cap with the flowers glued all over, and her varicose veins. She brought me to a city pool in Flushing on Saturdays in summer with those inflatable pillows over my arms.

By junior high and high school everyone assumed I could swim; it was too late to learn. In art school, I got invited to the summer house of a girl in my printmaking class, on a weekend her parents weren't around, and we got high and played this one Jefferson Airplane album over and over, and everybody took off their clothes and jumped in the pool except me. They all thought I was just shy about getting naked, but it wasn't that.

Nobody tried harder than Lenny to teach me to swim. One weekend we went to a hotel in Calistoga with a heated pool. "By the time we come home, you'll be a fish," he said. And though this wasn't quite true, it had been the first time since way back with Daniel when I felt safe with someone in the water. All that first day, he had me holding on to the noodle, but on the second day he said, "Leave it on the side of the pool. You don't need that thing anymore.

"I'll never leave you," he said. Not his fault either, but he was gone now too.

Six months after the loss of my husband and son I'd landed at the lake. Every morning for almost seven years now, I'd walked to the edge of the water carrying my coffee cup to watch the herons and the fisher- men, out in their small wooden boats scooping crabs out of their nets. I watched my guests as they dove off the dock. In all that time I never went in the water.

Then something happened. I have no idea why it was the thought had come to me on that day, out of all the others. But when I reached the gate of La Llorona, and after, when I got to the bottom of the steps—with the sun just going down over the water and a pelican just coming in for a landing in search of dinner—I knew it was time I got over my fear of the water. Maybe I felt in need of some kind of baptism. Maybe I just wanted to cool off.

Pablito, the fisherman who brought us whatever he'd caught that day, three times a week, had just pulled up at the dock, as I arrived, with a five-pound tilapia on a string, and a smaller fish—a black bass—in his other hand.

Of all the people in the village from whom I bought food for the hotel, Pablito was my favorite. We never spoke more than a few words, but over the years I'd come to look forward to his deliveries of fish, and the brief exchanges we'd have after his small boat pulled up to my dock when I invited him into the kitchen to clean that day's catch for me.

He worked on that fish like a surgeon—slicing the freshly har- pooned fish along one side, opening it like a book, then loosening the skeleton to separate the whole thing from the body with a single expert twist of his wrist. He'd draw his knife over the silvery scales, then wash it clean before returning it to its sheath.

As he worked he'd tell me the story of where he'd located this par- ticular fish, what part of the lake, how deep. I had learned from Maria that harpooning fish in the way Pablito did it—the old way of *los ancianos*—was a dangerous occupation. A man could get tangled in another fisherman's net or stuck between a pair of rocks or become so absorbed in his struggle with a fish he might miscalculate the amount of air left in his lungs and fail to reach the surface of the water in time. If he stayed down longer than he'd bargained on, he might lose consciousness and fail to make it back to the surface before the oxygen remaining gave out.

At one point, Maria said, Elmer had dreamed of becoming a harpoon fisherman, but she and Luis had begged him to choose another way to earn his living. Wielding a harpoon well was the best way to get your fish, but making a mistake with your harpoon or staying down too long in search of a fish was the surest route to breaking a mother's heart.

Pablito didn't make mistakes. He was well known in the village as the best of all the fishermen. People said he knew every meter of the lake, the parts where the fish lived anyway. He could dive deeper than anyone, stay under longer, locate the largest fish. He was not a young man anymore—late thirties, maybe forty—but his body, as he emerged from the water, was as lean and perfectly defined as that of any boy in the village. Broad shoulders, narrow hips, strong legs, even stronger arms. His smile came easily—particularly when setting a freshly harpooned fish on my counter.

That day he'd brought me two particularly fine fish. His smile seemed to light up my kitchen.

He leaned his harpoon against the counter, a single dot of bright red blood still evident at the tip from where it had entered the belly of the fish.

"I've been wanting to ask you a question," I said, placing the money I owed him in his palm. "Would you teach me to swim?"

63

One thing about having an operator for a friend

"Next thing you know, our girl's going to be swimming the Channel," Gus said, when I announced that I was taking swimming lessons from Pablito.

The three of us—Gus, Dora, and I, along with their children Luca and Jade, naturally—were having our weekly Friday-night dinner at their place—a healthy vegan meal followed by a football match Gus had recorded earlier that day. Even though the game would be long finished by the time we gathered around Gus and Dora's large-screen television to watch, Gus never allowed himself to find out the final score in advance. "Spoils all the fun," he said. "When Dora was in the family way, I didn't want to know if she was popping out a girl or a boy neither," he added. "Suspense. Keeps life interesting."

Dora and I had never discussed our feeling about football night, but I sensed a mutual understanding. This was Gus's passion, not Dora's or mine—and possibly not even Luca's, though at age nine now, he was diligent about putting on his Blackburn Rovers shirt before we sat down for the kickoff. At age six, Jade preferred playing with her dolls.

Dora had no choice but to watch the game. She was married to a Blackburn fan. But what was it in me that compelled me to show up every Friday night to join in the ritual? Not love of football, certainly. It was love of Gus and Dora. Along with Maria and Luis, they were the closest I had to family.

"You're like the sister I never had," Gus said to me. (He'd said this before of course. It was his refrain.) I might have said, in response, that he was like a brother.

And as would be true of a brother—or how I imagined it would be if I had a brother—I could recognize his flaws and failings, the corners he cut (even in his work at the hotel for me), his tendency to inflate his prowess at carpentry or electrical wiring, the ease with which he could bend the truth, when telling a story about his old days back in London, or his adventures in India, his caginess in outwitting the cops or any other body of authority, if it served his interest to do so.

"It's a dog-eat-dog world, luv," Gus said to me, when he'd demonstrated for me his expertise at turning back the electric meter outside his house (and mine) to keep the bills low. Gus was an operator, and I recognized this early on. The fact this was so never caused me to withdraw my affection. Almost the opposite.

I could see, with Dora, that Gus's big-talking manner got on her nerves sometimes. He'd be telling a story we'd heard before, and she'd roll her eyes.

I never minded when he got that way. Gus was like one of those little boys you went to school with long ago, who made up stories—that his father used to play for the Yankees, that he lived in a mansion, he single-handedly rescued a drowning man, he got cast in a movie but his mother said he couldn't take the job. He was like a puppy—not yet trained, if he ever would be. Knocking things over, making a mess sometimes, but ceaselessly enthusiastic, and—this mattered most—perpetually happy to see you.

I never showed up at Gus and Dora's house without Gus locking me in a bear hug before I was even in the door. Over his shoulder, I'd observe Dora; she loved him all right, but she was no longer charmed by him, if she ever had been. Maybe that's what accounted for Gus's total admiration and respect for his wife. She was the one woman—the one person maybe—who didn't fall for his lines.

I might know he was selling me a bill of goods, but I bought it anyway, as a sister might, the misbehavior of a lovable if feckless brother. Gus's bragging inspired in me something like tender, sisterly affection. He was an operator. But he was *my* operator. And here was the great thing about having an operator as your friend (never mind having him for your brother): So long as the two of you were on the same side, he was going to be operating on your behalf.

64
An unlikely mother

The day after the death of Rosella and the birth of her twins, Alicia and Mateo, a traveler came to town from somewhere in northern California. She called herself Raya Sunshine. Raya had started out in life as Susan, but this was the name on her passport now, and it fit. With the exception of my husband Lenny, I may never have encountered a more ceaselessly cheerful person.

Raya had a few teeth, but not the ones in front. When she smiled, as she did often and easily, there was a large open space where teeth used to be. As little as she had in the way of teeth, she had less in the way of money.

Unlike the majority of travelers passing through the village, Raya was not young. She might have appeared less wrinkled if she weren't also very skinny, but as it was, she looked a little like a witch, though a friendly one. I had seen her the day she got off the boat in town, with a single backpack and a shoulder bag full of yarn she told me later she intended to make into bikini tops, which had been big sellers for her at various other stops on her travels. There were many balls of yarn in her bag, which she'd procured, she also explained, by buying very cheap sweaters in the market and unravelling them for the wool.

Raya was not someone who'd be checking into La Llorona. When I met her on the path, she was looking for a hostel, and asked me which one was the cheapest. I pointed her in the direction of Iguana Perdida, up in the valley.

She had a very old backpack. Nothing more. Raya traveled light.

That day the whole town was talking about the death of Rosella and the birth of the twins. Under normal circumstances, when a mother died in childbirth here, the family would step in to care for the baby, but in the case of Mateo and Alicia, there were no grandparents around, no relatives at all other than Wade, naturally, and Rosella's other children, all three grown and gone.

Patrizia, the cook at El Buffo, the rabbit restaurant, was nursing a baby of her own at the time and volunteered to help. Given that she was already nursing one infant, Patrizia had told Wade she could only manage the care and feeding of one more. She chose Mateo. This left the question of what to do about Alicia.

The hostel where Raya was staying—in a tiny room behind the kitchen that shared bathroom facilities with the occupants of five other rooms—sat just up the hill from El Buffo. The morning after her arrival, Raya had stopped in there, to inquire as to whether she might trade some kind of services for food at the restaurant.

"Know anything about skinning rabbits?" Wade had asked her. A vegan for over twenty years, Raya shook her head.

Still, she had stopped in at the restaurant every day, on the long hike up the hill to the hostel. She liked visiting the rabbits, though it also made her sad of course. She figured she'd do her best to help them have a good life, for whatever short time they had left.

It was on one of these stops at El Buffo to see the rabbits that Raya learned about the twins. Patrizia had Mateo at her breast. Alicia had been placed in a box that looked suspiciously like an old rabbit cage turned on its side. Workers at the restaurant, and occasionally even guests, took turns picking her up and feeding her from a bottle of formula, though on at least one occasion, when she'd been crying particularly loudly, someone had dripped crème de menthe into the bottle, to see if it might calm her down. She'd been out cold three minutes later.

Raya had observed all of this. At the time of the crème de menthe incident, she had been cuddling a bunny. It seemed like a pretty natural choice to suggest she switch over to the three-day-old baby girl.

At closing time, she asked who was going to take Alicia for the night. Patrizia said they'd move her box into the kitchen, where it was warmer. "I could take her back to the hostel with me," Raya said.

Wade, over at the bar, mixing one last El Buffo cocktail—this one for himself—said "OK by me." Patrizia handed her a box of formula and a bottle.

On her way out the door, Raya asked what he was using for diapers. Wade handed her a stack of cleaning rags and a couple of safety pins.

The next morning, Raya brought Alicia back to El Buffo, but nobody seemed particularly interested. She spent the morning holding the baby while the restaurant staff ran around cutting up vegetables for salad and rolling silverware into napkins. Somewhere out back, she was aware, a boy was slitting the throats of that night's rabbits and parting them from their skins. She didn't want to see that part and didn't think it was a good thing for a baby to be around that kind of thing either.

"Mind if I take her back to my room?" Raya asked Patrizia, who had Mateo on one breast at the time, and her ten-month-old, Silvia, on the other. Wade was nowhere around, so she seemed like the authority figure. Knowing no Spanish, she asked her question in English, but Patrizia seemed to get the point. She shrugged and handed her another stack of cleaning rags.

This went on for a couple of weeks. At first, Raya mostly cared for Alicia in her room, but after a while it occurred to her that it would be a lot nicer not only for herself but for the baby to be out in the world, hearing the birds and taking in the life of the village. They spent a lot of their time sitting on the dock, looking out at the volcano—though her favorite sight was simply Alicia's face. She had it memorized: her brown button eyes, the single tuft of almost-black hair, the distinctive cleft in her chin that seemed, to Raya, the only thing about the baby remotely resembling her father, which was fine with her.

Someone must have told Raya that Alicia's mother was Italian, and in honor of this, she sang her the one song she knew that had any Italian in it, "That's Amore," that she could remember dancing to with her high school boyfriend back in Lompoc. It was mostly in English, but it had a certain Italian feeling, and of course there was the amore part.

When she sang "Bells will ring, ting a ling a ling, and you'll sing vita bella," she'd wiggle Alicia's toes one at a time, and even though Raya sounded nothing like Dean Martin, Alicia smiled when she did this. People said babies this young never smiled, but they didn't know this one.

One thing that was difficult for Raya about caring for the baby, as much as she loved doing it, was earning money. Even when Alicia wasn't taking her bottle, she liked to be held. The only time she ever cried, in fact, was when Raya set her down, so she could get a little crocheting done. This hardly ever worked.

Raya was running down to her last *garzas*. She had to think of something. Around this time, she met Clarinda on the path—Amalia's particular favorite, who took a great interest in Alicia. She asked Clarinda if she'd like to hold the baby for a while, and Clarinda did. This was how she managed to get to work crocheting bikini tops, which proved to be good sellers in this town full of young hippie women who favored the bare-midriff look. On a good day, she might sell five of these tops. One day she sold eight.

Raya would never have guessed, when she landed in this town two weeks earlier, that she would find herself with a newborn baby to care for. In the absence of money to pay Clarinda, she crocheted her a bag for her schoolbooks, and a skirt after that, and then a hat. Clarinda spoke almost as little English as Patrizia, but one thing they both understood, perfectly, was babies.

After close to a month of this, it seemed to Raya that she should have a serious conversation about the baby with Alicia's father, Wade. A good week had passed in which she hadn't felt a need to stop by El

Buffo. The only reason for doing so—picking up a new stack of cleaning rags—had been eliminated since she'd purchased a pile of cloth diapers from a woman in the market.

It was mid-afternoon when she arrived at the restaurant with Alicia. She had also bought herself a shawl of the sort that the indigenous women in the village used for carrying their babies, and now Alicia lay sound asleep, snoring faintly against Raya's chest as she watched the workers at the restaurant going about their business, mopping the floor, setting out the tablecloths, carrying rabbits out back. Off in the kitchen, she could hear the sound of Mateo, crying. Alicia hardly ever cried like that. Why would she? Raya virtually never set her down, and now that she had her shawl, and Clarinda as backup, Alicia lived her life in one pair of loving arms or another. No wonder she smiled.

Finally Wade showed up.

"Looks like you two really hit it off," Wade said, observing Raya in her seat at a table alongside the wall of rabbits, with Alicia in her arms.

"Whenever I come in to check him out, the boy's always howling," Wade said. "What's your trick?"

She might have told him that she had learned to place Alicia on the left side of her chest, inside the shawl, so she could hear the steady beat of Raya's heart. But this information seemed too private to share with a man like Wade, too intimate. Something told her not to let him know how much the outcome of this conversation meant to her.

"She's an easy baby," Raya told him. "Hardly any trouble at all."

"You have kids of your own?" he asked. Up until now, nobody here had displayed the slightest interest in Raya's story, which was fine by her.

"Never did."

"I guess you're a little old for that now, huh?" Wade said, taking a swig on his beer.

"If you were up for it, I could keep taking care of her," Raya told him. "I was thinking I'd stay put around here. Things are pretty good for me in this town."

She had a check coming from the states. As soon as she got it, she'd be renting a little casita in town.

"I could keep Alicia there, if you wanted," she said. "It would be no trouble at all."

She hoped she didn't sound too eager.

"You really want to do something like that?" he said. "The diapers, the crying?"

"No trouble at all," she said, holding her breath.

"Fine by me," he said. "To be honest, it's a relief. One kid is hard enough. Two? Forget about it."

He opened his wallet and counted out some bills.

"Just a little something to help out," he said.

She studied the bills on the table. A pile of hundred-*garza* notes, as many as ten of them. All week, she'd been rationing out peanut butter. Three crackers a night was dinner.

"That's very thoughtful," she said. "But we'll be fine. My crocheting business is taking off.

"Use the money for her brother," Raya added. Not that it was a shortage of money for food that made Mateo cry. A shortage of attention, more likely. This would not be Alicia's problem.

65

Raising a baby on macramé

Raya had found a house. It was very small, but so was Alicia, and the two of them shared the one bed.

"I was thinking about all those months she spent in her mom's belly," Raya told me. "She always had her brother curled up with her. It must feel lonely not having him there anymore."

But Alicia was a happy baby. Every time I saw the two of them in the village—Raya with her display of bikini tops strung out on the fence, Alicia wrapped in her shawl (and later, on a straw mat Raya set up for her, with blocks she'd made out of wood scraps she'd sanded so Alicia wouldn't get splinters), the little girl was nearly always smiling.

There was no shortage of babies in the village, and even among the sellers who set up their wares here—the single narrow path that led from the dock to the twin places of worship here, the basketball court and the Catholic church (the soccer field, a little farther out)—Raya was far from the only one who had a child in tow. The woman selling ponchos had three children with her, most days, none of them older than five, and the banana bread woman had two. In nearly every tienda, there'd be a box under the counter with a baby inside, or an older child, pulling himself up on a crate of onions or carrots, gnawing on a tortilla.

Two things set Raya and Alicia apart. One was Raya's age. Except for the ones now nursing their sixth or seventh child, most of the mothers in town looked to be in their teens or twenties. When their baby got hungry or tired, they placed him or her against a breast and carried on with their work. In Raya's case, of course, the only choice was a bottle.

All the other babies had the black hair and brown skin of the indigenous community. Alicia—though she lived a life closer to that of the indigenous children—was a gringo baby. Her mother had listened to Maria Callas arias. Her older sister studied at the university in the city. Somewhere, far back in his past, her father had evidently passed the Illinois state bar exam.

Alicia's world bore no resemblance to theirs. Raya spoke English to her, but she wanted Alicia to learn Spanish, so she had bought a book of Spanish phrases, and even before Ali turned one year old, she incorporated them into her conversation with the baby whenever possible. "*Por favor*" and "*De nada*" and "*gracias,*" mainly. Some tourists had left a Spanish edition of *Goodnight Moon—Buenas Noches, Luna*—in their room at Iguana Perdida, and Israel, the owner, had thought to give it to Raya, who read it out loud to Alicia many times a day. "En la gran sala verde, habia un telefono y un globo rojo y una pintura de una vaca saltando sobre la luna . . ."

Her accent was pretty bad, but Alicia always looked happy when Raya read to her. And most other times, too. Watching them together, times I stopped by Raya's bikini-top stand—it struck me that at this particular moment, anyway, for this particular child and the woman who cared for her, life worked well. Life worked better for them than it did in many families, actually, even those who may have owned houses and swing sets and toys, people with cars and bank accounts and computers.

At the moment, all Alicia needed was Raya, and all Raya seemed to need was Alicia. They wanted for nothing.

66

A fish without a bicycle

Sometimes, to make a little money for her family (her father long dead, her mother drunk most of the time), Clarinda sold the bags she made with Amalia to tourists. These were unusual bags, different from any others sold along the path. Under the guidance of Amalia, Clarinda had stitched gemstones onto the straps, and the bags were lined with silk from ripped-up scraps of flea market clothes, with secret pockets inside, into which she would have tucked an interesting stone or shell or an old button, also retrieved from Amalia's store of flea market treasures.

"Don't give these away," Amalia told Clarinda, the first time she set out down the path with a half dozen of the special bags over her arm. Never let anyone sell you small." She meant "sell you short" but Amalia sometimes got her expressions wrong. Another of her favorites, that she'd read in an article about Gloria Steinem from a magazine someone left at Harold's café, was "A woman without a man is like a fish without a bicycle." Only she'd forgotten the last part.

"*Una mujer sin hombre es como un pez,*" she told Clarinda, who had nodded solemnly, hearing the news. A woman without a man is like a fish.

Clarinda liked fish. She wouldn't mind being one so long as she steered clear of Pablito's harpoon.

It was November, those gorgeous days after the end of rainy season when everything was its greenest and the air moist and clear. I had walked into town to pick up supplies—some mangoes for a salsa Maria would make to accompany that night's meal of fish.

Entering Harold's smoothie bar, I saw the lizard men at their customary table, the ashtray at its center filled with the day's butts, though there would be more before the day was over. Carlos and Vincente were nursing beers. Juan had moved on to rum and coke.

The part that disturbed me was the sight of the small person standing next to their table, engaged in what appeared to be animated conversation. It was Clarinda. She was trying to sell them one of her bags. Something about this scene—as commonplace as it appeared—left a bad taste in my mouth, as if I'd bit into a piece of fruit that turned out to be rotten.

Among the children of the town, Clarinda was a particular favorite of mine, as she was of Amalia. She had a quick wit, and a playful way of talking that might have seemed flirtatious in a woman, but at her age was just a game.

"*Veinte garza,*" she was telling the men, holding out one of her bags. "*Muy bonito. Muy linda.*" She kept her Spanish simple for their benefit, knowing that these three, though they'd made this town their home far longer than she'd been alive, had never taken it upon themselves to learn the language. The price she quoted for her handiwork, twenty *garza*, amounted to a couple of dollars.

"Five," Carlos told her. "It's my final offer."

"I'll give you five fifty," Vincente told her. The difference in price between his bid and that of his friend amounting to roughly three cents.

Clarinda put her hand on her hip and giggled.

"*Es arte fino,*" she said. Amalia had taught her this. *Don't sell yourself short. You are an artist, not a beggar. Remember this.*

"OK Four," Carlos told her. Among other things, he was drunk. Clarinda held firm.

"Twenty," she said, tossing her ponytail. Hand on her hip. These were Amalia's moves, when she'd stood in front of the mayor, telling him why the town needed to stop handing out free samples of strawberry-flavored powder sent by the Nestle company to encourage mothers to switch from breastfeeding.

"You're cute, you know that?" Vincente told her. "How old are you anyway?"

No joking now. She was nine.

"Her mother's a whore," Carlos said. He was speaking to the men, but it was easy enough for Clarinda to hear him. He spoke in English. She knew these men's language far better than they knew hers.

"I'm giving her five," Carlos said, slapping a bill on the table.

"I'm raising you ten," Juan announced.

Now Vincente had got his hands on Clarinda's bag, with the coconut shell fastener and Amalia's special amethyst that she'd found in Mexico tucked into the pocket.

"I'm raising you a hundred," he said, tossing a pile of coins and bills on the table, some of which ended up on the ground. Clarinda looked down at them, confused.

All this time, I'd been leaning on the counter, waiting for my smoothie. I tried hard to steer clear of this bunch, but it was no longer possible.

"Leave her alone, for God's sake," I said. I told Clarinda I was buying her bag.

"Well, *buenos dias*, Mary Poppins," Carlos said.

The blender was still going, but all I wanted was to get out of there.

"Bitch couldn't get a man if she was the last chick on earth." Carlos again.

"*Una mujer sin hombre es como un pez*," Clarinda whispered, as we left.

Two fishes who'd escaped the hook. Off we swam.

67

Five-star rating

It had taken seven years—six years longer than I'd bargained on, and every penny of the insurance money Leila had left to me, and then some—but the hotel was looking good. Better than good. Spectacular.

In addition to the new ceramic tile roof, replacing the old thatch that had provided a home to so many happy families of scorpions, and the new septic system, the new run of stone steps from the road to the front entrance of La Llorona, and the upgraded wiring, the new lighting fixtures, Gus and his crew of local men had laid down a whole new floor in the kitchen, with new countertops replacing the old, cracked concrete. They'd built a beautiful new dock and replaced every window in the hotel with huge panes of double-thickness glass, hung new doors, expanded the patio to provide more dining space for the customers I prayed would come.

Paying Gus's bills as general contractor along with those of the other workers we'd brought in to do the actual labor (work that Gus himself appeared less and less inclined to perform) had emptied every *garza* in the fund Leila had left me. Money had gotten so tight in the final months of the renovation that I'd taken on the job of painting and staining the walls myself—work that might have been hard to accomplish if we'd had more guests. In all the years I'd run the hotel, we seldom operated at more than 50 percent occupancy, and often less.

This was a worry. One question a potential buyer would ask would have to do with the revenues of the hotel in recent years. They'd want to see my books, and when they did, the numbers wouldn't look good.

Then came a piece of great good fortune. That January, when the rains ended, a woman showed up at the hotel who introduced herself as a travel writer doing a story on off-the-beaten-path destinations south of the border. These were still the early days of the internet, when the concept of blogging had yet to enter the vocabulary, but she published a weekly online letter to travel-oriented readers. She told me she'd like to feature La Llorona. Assuming I'd waive the usual room fee, of course.

With occupancy at its usual low, I agreed to Caroline Timmons's proposal, instructing Maria and Luis to take particularly good care of our guest, not that they ever did less. We gave her the Jaguar Room, and Mirabel took pains to fold her towel into the shape of a penguin—a skill she'd recently learned from an article I'd cut out of a five-year-old *Martha Stewart Living* magazine left by a former hotel guest. The night of Caroline Timmons's arrival, Maria served her special crab-stuffed, tempura-battered squash blossoms with a Cobán chile mango mojo followed by hibiscus flan with pomegranate syrup.

She stayed at the hotel only a single night, and made no comment about the hotel during her visit except to let me know that there had been problems with the hot water in her shower, and she'd found a spider on the bathroom mirror and an iguana in the sink. After, I worried that she'd give us a bad write-up. If we were lucky, I figured, she'd simply bypass the whole experience in her writings.

Ten days after Caroline Timmons's departure, the phone started ringing. Five reservations in one day. Seven, the next. When I asked my usual question, "How did you learn about us?" in every case the answer was the same. "After that amazing review from Caroline Timmons's *Footloose*," they told me, "we couldn't stay away."

I looked up the review. Maria's meals, she wrote, were "a revelation"—"a perfect blend of traditional cooking using the freshest locally sourced ingredients, augmented by the unexpected addition of a European sensibility." She specifically singled out the macarons we served—my homage to Leila—as "better than anything you can find in the best Parisian pâtisserie."

Caroline Timmons had given us her top rating, five stars.

Within twenty-four hours of the publication of that write-up, we had over a dozen reservation requests. A week later, the hotel was fully booked two months out.

I hired another worker to help out in the kitchen, and a week later another. We had to create two separate seatings for dinner, one for the six o'clock crowd, a second at eight.

"What did I tell you, mate?" Gus said, on one of his near-daily check-ins. "Dora told me way back when we were working on the septic, you'd be raking the shekels in soon as we got this place up to snuff for you."

Speaking of which: He had an idea for a Japanese meditation pavilion. He could whip it up in two shakes. Dora would have his hide if she knew how little he'd charge me for this. But we were family.

68

A buyer shows up

The word must have gotten around. In the middle of the flurry of bookings came a call from a man named Gerry Harwich, owner of a chain of what he called "one-of-a-kind luxury boutique vacation experiences." Gerry Harwich wanted to know, was I interested in selling La Llorona? If so, he and his business partners had a strong interest in acquiring the property. Here at last came the moment I'd been waiting for all these years: the buyers who would make it possible for me to move on with my life, if I could just figure out, move on to what?

"We've been studying trends in the tourist industry," Gerry Harwich went on. "There's a new airline adding service to San Felipe, and a company of modern shuttle buses ready to transport guests.

"If you're motivated," he said, "we can move fast."

Three days later, Gerry Harwich arrived at La Llorona along with his team—an accountant and marketing specialist and his interior design consultant. From the moment they appeared at the gate Gerry and his partners started raving about the place. (*Oh my God. Can you believe these turquoise flowers? This waterfall? Check out the tree full of orchids! The carved stone egg. Guests will go nuts!*)

The five of us shared a dinner of pistachio-crusted tilapia on the terrace. At one point near the end of the meal a flock of white-collared manakins landed in the tree below us. After, Maria came out with her fabulous orange soufflé paired with a plate of macarons. The evening could not have been more of a success.

I had not forgotten Leila's story about the visit to La Llorona of Carl Edgar, the man who wanted to turn her property into a gated community of luxury condos. It was a relief to hear that though Gerry Harwich acknowledged a need for expanding the hotel to make it possible for more than four guests at a time to stay here, he appeared respectful of maintaining the integrity of the hotel as Leila had envisioned it.

The next morning when we met for breakfast, Gerry's team had an offer waiting for me. The price they quoted was more money than I had ever imagined. I told them my chief condition for the sale—that Luis and Maria's jobs, as well as Elmer's and Mirabel's, be secured for as long as they chose to stay on. "No problem," Gerry said. "Just so long as Maria keeps cooking the fish that way and baking those macarons."

By noon, I'd signed the papers. As soon as the money was deposited in my bank, the hotel would no longer belong to me.

69
God must be angry

That night it began to rain. First just a gentle sprinkling, but by midnight I could hear it pounding on the tile roof, and when I woke up, sheets of water were pouring down in front of the windows. It was raining so hard you couldn't see the lake, let alone the volcano. The fishermen were long gone.

I'd lived through seven rainy seasons by this point, but I'd never seen a storm like this one—water pouring down the hillside, cutting through the gardens, washing over my ceramic animals in such a way that it looked as if they were swimming. The sound of the water was so loud I had to yell for Maria to hear me. Luis was outside already, bringing in the furniture. Elmer had taken down the silk banderas Amalia had made to decorate the patio. Now he was asking my permission to go to the village. He didn't have to tell me why. I watched as he battled his way up the steps through the sheets of water, his shirt already soaked and clinging to his body. He was heading for the house of Mirabel.

Then came the wind, with such force that a branch of my precious jocote tree landed on the roof of my garden casita. A storm of rose petals swirled over the patio.

The lights went out. From where I sat in the darkness, looking out across the lake in the direction of the larger town of Santa Clara, not a single light still glowed. The entire lake had gone dark.

We were never without candles at the hotel. I lit every one. Maria defrosted what was left in the freezer, making us soup over the gas flame of the stove as, outside, the pitch dark of the sky suddenly lit up from a bolt of lightning behind the volcano.

Just opening the door against the wind was a struggle, but Luis ventured out. Maria didn't want him to leave the safety of the kitchen, but he had reached for his shovel, with the plan of creating pathways for the water to flow to keep it from washing away a wide swath of hillside.

It rained all that day, and into the night—sheets of water, howling wind. With no electricity, Maria and Luis and I lit a fire. Maria made a pot of rice over the stove. Cuzmi stayed close. At some point, long past midnight probably, though I had lost all sense of time, Elmer made it back from town somehow. When he'd reached Mirabel's house her father sent him away.

On the second day—with the power still out—the storm reached new levels of ferocity, though I would not have believed it possible. The wind blew in from a new direction, causing the rain to hit the windows sideways. The sky darkened to the point of turning close to black. The water was coming down so hard that I wondered whether the tiles on my roof might be knocked off, but there was no going outdoors to check. The wind would knock me down if I tried.

I'd become accustomed to the nonstop sound of rain on the roof, wind battering the walls and windows of the hotel, the sound of water running down the hillside. But that night I woke to a new sound unlike anything I'd ever heard.

Not quite true. I'd heard this sound, but only on the runway at an airport, as a plane was taking off. A roaring so loud that if there had been anyone else in the room, and I'd wanted to say something, I would have had to shout to be heard.

When I reached the kitchen Maria and Luis were already there in their nightclothes. Luis was holding a candle, and his machete. Elmer stood behind them.

A river was pouring down the hillside. Not a stream. A river, that had not existed twenty-four hours before, or even one. Come from nowhere, headed toward the house. In its churning waters were branches and whole trees, and, from the bodega by the gate where Luis stored his tools, a propane tank set loose and tumbling down the steps, along with a rubber hose and a shower of Luis and Elmer's building supplies. (Nails, drill, hand saw, bags of cement even.)

We always stored the ten-gallon jugs of purified water in the bodega at the top of the steps. Every few days, Luis or Elmer hoisted one on his back and carried it down the stone steps to the house for guests. Now a dozen large plastic ten-gallon bottles plummeted down the hillside—bobbing and spinning crazily, like flotsam going over Niagara Falls.

"The rock!" Luis called out, over the roaring of the water. I looked up just in time to see a giant boulder tumbling down the hill, shattering a wall of windows. Another six inches and it would have crushed Maria.

Luis and Elmer headed outside to check on the retaining walls that held back the lake. If they gave way, the water would take the hotel.

"It's like in the Bible," Maria said. She was praying now. "God must be angry," she told me.

Out the window, we watched as Luis and Elmer piled cement blocks alongside the back of the house while the water pounded down. We watched as a boulder the size of a refrigerator crashed down from somewhere at the top, landing within a few feet of Luis.

In the past, when problems arose at the hotel, I'd called Gus. More often, I didn't even have to call, he'd just come. That night I understood he and Dora had struggles of their own going on. This time we were on our own.

70
The birds sang louder

The men worked all night. Maria and I huddled in what was left of the kitchen, unable to move. In the morning, the sun came up—the sky bluer than we'd seen in days—and we were able at last to look around. A bomb might have landed here and created less damage.

Wherever we looked lay debris from the storm, some of it recognizable (tools, rebar, a cast-off toilet, a coffeepot). Some of what showed up must have been carried to my property from some whole other part of town—a roll of chicken wire, a soccer ball, three unmatched sneakers, a bathtub, origins unknown.

But mostly what now surrounded us was mud. Mud and rock, tree branches, entire trees. Falling rock had shattered the ceramic tile on the hotel roof, and the tile of the terrace too. Inside the hotel, six inches of mud, at least, covered Leila's oriental rugs. Her bookcases had been knocked over, books strewn everywhere. The painting I loved, depicting a range of potential disasters, had somehow been spared, but not the desk or the wonderful antique textiles. Downstairs, we studied the smashed-in wall, and the boulder that stood now in the middle of the patio. Broken glass everywhere. Leila's precious blue dishes. Oranges rolling on the floor.

The hardest part was what lay beyond the hotel. What I still thought of as Leila's gardens had been ravaged—plants uprooted, shrubs stripped of blooms. Fruit trees, bougainvillea, a couple of rose arbors, the stand of black bamboo—all flattened.

Later that day I walked into the village to see for myself. It was a miracle, everyone agreed, that only one person had been killed in the storm—a very old man, one of the last of those who still knew and still practiced the art of making maguey bags like the one I used to carry potatoes home from the market. Bartolomeo had been asleep in his little adobe home on the mountain when the storm hit, full force. His wife said, after, that he'd ventured out into the raging night to retrieve the skeins of twisted maguey he'd laid out in his little yard. He must have been gathering these when the river took him. His body had been found a half mile down the mountain, leaned against a tree as if he were sleeping.

Apart from this, the rest of the damage, though great, had been only to property, not human life. A great number of the tiendas were demolished, the school windows shattered, Rosella's beautiful oasis, Il Piacere, torn apart. The statue she'd rescued years before from the ruins of a crumbling cathedral in the city had shown up, facedown in the mud, a half mile away, outside Roberto's blues club. Her woodstove lay in the lake by the dock. Three of the small pyramid structures Andromeda employed to house students at her retreat center now bobbed in the lake. The basketball court where Rick and Claudia had taught the girls of the village trick shots and dribbling moves was buried in mud.

The town's dogs appeared to have all survived *il tormento*, as did its pigs and chickens, for the most part. The birds seemed only to sing louder, after the storm.

Among the buildings most badly damaged was the Catholic church. The rains had brought a river that never existed before crashing through the center of town—the church, its heart. Now ten feet of mud covered the wooden benches where the people came every morning to pray, and the altar at the front with the statue of the Virgin and another larger one of Jesus on the cross.

One sight and one sight only warmed my heart. The floodwaters from the storm must have crashed into Wade's restaurant, El Buffo. All over the village now, rabbits could be seen, hopping freely among the wreckage.

The next day, when the power came back on and internet service returned, I found a letter waiting in my inbox from Gerry Harwich, chief executive office of the luxury boutique hotel consortium I'd met with just three days earlier.

In light of the recent hurricane and associated damage to the area, he wrote, he regretted to inform me that he would be withdrawing his offer to purchase La Llorona. He wished me well and trusted that we'd "bounce back"—hard to picture that part—as swiftly as possible.

Reading his words, I registered a surprising emotion. Relief.

We had to cancel all of that month's bookings of course, and when it became clear, in the first few weeks after the storm, how serious the damage was that the hotel had incurred, we canceled what was left of the reservations for the remainder of that year. With virtually no money left in the bank and no prospect of income ahead, I figured it was all I could do to cover the pay of Maria and Luis and Mirabel. There was no way I could afford Gus anymore, and, strangely, he hadn't come around as I'd expected. I figured he must be caught up in repairs at his own house. Fair enough.

I had no funds to replace the shattered roof tiles, so we opted for the cheaper solution, thatch. Elmer took on that job while Luis worked to repair the damaged kitchen wall and the shattered windows and rescued what he could of the garden. Maria and I shoveled mud out of the upstairs rooms and scrubbed the dirt.

The day after the storm, Walter showed up with a bouquet of calla lilies from the mountain. Then he picked up a shovel too.

71

A tortilla saleswoman in the road

To bring the property back to where it had been would require replanting of at least a dozen fruit trees, and easily a hundred smaller plants. I could start cuttings of those, of course, but it would take a good six months before things at La Llorona started to look as they had, and years for trees to grow back. So I made the decision—an odd one, probably, for a woman with as little money left as I had—to spend the last of what I had on flowers and trees. More than the hotel itself, or the restaurant, this place was about the garden. The only way I'd ever restore La Llorona would be with flowers.

As soon as the roads opened, I hired a driver with a truck, Miguel, to bring me to the city. I spent most of what I had left on plants that day. We filled the truck.

On the long ride back, I thought about what the hurricane had done to the garden. Partly, of course, my choice to travel the hundred kilometers to the city to buy plants might have been described as a business decision: A hotel that prides itself on offering its guests the experience of staying in the midst of a beautiful garden had better deliver on the promise. But there was more to it.

It was about Leila. She'd been dead for seven years, but she still presided over this piece of land and the buildings on it. In the brief time I'd known her, I'd come not only to understand her passion, but to share it. I felt an obligation to maintain what she'd built here. A garden was a living thing. You had to tend it every day.

"Nothing stays the same forever," Leila had told me one day as we made our way along the paths on the property, stopping to study certain favorite plants. "Not gardens, or love affairs. Not joy, or sorrow either. Animals die. Children grow up. The thing you have to learn is to accept the changes when they come. Welcome them if you can. See what they bring to your life that wasn't there before."

It was difficult to see the landslide as a good thing. But that day in the giant vivero greenhouse in the capital, filling my cart, I felt a kind of thrill my younger self would have found in an art supply store, picking out colored pencils or flipping through a bin of old vinyl records.

By three o'clock I'd paid for my purchases. Miguel and I were back out on the road, headed to La Esperanza—the overland route a lot more rugged than the approach by boat.

A half hour from home, with darkness setting in, our journey was interrupted by the presence of a woman selling tortillas in the middle of the road. There was no way of getting around her.

Miguel got out of the truck to ask her to move. She shook her head. "We have to wait," he said. "She won't move until she's sold all her tortillas."

"I'll buy all her tortillas," I said, handing over some coins and a few bills. In a minute he was back again, shaking his head.

"She doesn't want to sell them to you," he said.

It was nine o'clock when the last tortilla was sold and the woman folded up her table , allowing us to make our way through the village for home. By the time we reached La Esperanza and the gate of the hotel, the lights were dark down below. Luis and Maria and Elmer had gone to bed. They'd all worked so hard in the days since the storm I didn't have the heart to wake them.

Miguel had to return the rented vehicle to its owner, but first we needed to unload the plants—a truckload of trees and flowers—easily a couple hundred containers, all needing to be carried down the long steps to my stone-and-mud-filled garden.

I looked at Miguel. He was young and strong, but this was too big a job for the two of us.

A woman was walking past on the road, with a young child, and another woman, probably her mother, alongside her. "Do you want a job?" I asked her.

"Round up some people in the village to help me unload this truck," I said. No need to say more. For a woman in this town, the prospect of any employment other than an occasional job cleaning the house of a gringo was rare.

Josefa was back in ten minutes, this time in the company of a dozen of her friends.

I didn't have to explain what to do. The women positioned themselves at intervals all the way down the stone steps, a few of the strongest among them in the truck bed. One by one, they passed each plant down from the truck into the hands of the first woman, the second, all the way to the bottom, where the last of the women set each plant in its plastic container on the grass, to be set into the garden the next day, or the day after that. A bucket brigade.

As they worked, they talked and laughed. These were women accustomed to seeing each other at church or in the market, but never in circumstances like these, doing the kind of work more typically assigned to their husbands. It was funny to them, and exciting. For once they'd get paid for their labors.

It was past ten o'clock when the last of the plants had been unloaded and I could send Miguel off to return the truck. Reaching into the pocket of my jeans I pulled out the last of my money. I put a fifty-*garza* note in the hands of each of the women before saying goodnight. I could hear them still talking and laughing all the way down the road.

A strange thing happened over the weeks that followed. All this time I'd seen myself as a person passing through this place. It had taken me years longer than I'd supposed, getting La Llorona back in shape, but I'd accomplished what I'd set out to do. I'd even—briefly—found my buyer—the goal I'd named as my objective all along.

Then the storm hit, and instead of defeating me or inspiring me to throw up my hands and disappear, as I'd done when I got on that bus in San Francisco, for the first time ever I felt that I belonged here. As the weeks passed, spent laying tile and hammering boards, repainting plaster, replanting garden beds—first weeks, then months—it came to me that I wasn't going anywhere else after all. I was already home.

72

A school made from soda bottles

It was a full six months before the village got back to normal, or close, but things were different too. A river, a good ten feet wide, now divided one side of town from the other, requiring the construction of a bridge. More than that, a canal had to be built to contain the water. Nearly every able-bodied man—shovels in hand, and picks—contributed to this effort. By Christmas the canal was finished.

It was one of the things I had come to recognize about this town: the extremes it brought out—in its weather, its topography, and people— the range of human behavior that ran the gamut from worst to best, ugly to beautiful.

Within days of the storm, word spread of certain individuals in the village—gringos, not locals—who'd hoarded precious supplies of rice and beans, flour and peanut butter—to get through the period of shortages. One of the wealthier foreigners had made a trip to the city in his Land Rover, returning the next day with a carful of fried chicken and chips that he was selling at a 50 percent markup, along with some kind of powdered protein drink that (according to him) contained every vitamin a baby needed, far superior to what they'd get from breast milk.

Some women in the village ignored this claim. Others spent their precious *garzas* to purchase the magic powder.

The high winds created by the hurricane had left the streets of town overflowing with debris. As soon as the sun came out after the storm had passed, Amalia—the Queen of Trash—put out a call to the children. Her little army was ready. They knew the words to all her songs, and sang them as they gathered up the mountains of trash—more litter now than ever before—and stuffed them into the plastic bottles. By New Year's, they were out in the schoolyard setting into place the trash-filled eco-block walls for three new elementary school classrooms.

Every day when I passed Amalia's house over the weeks that followed, the pile of eco-blocks had grown taller. Within weeks Amalia and her little crew had enough trash-filled blocks to rebuild the school. This was how things went in the village of La Esperanza. Tragedy struck—often, and with ferocity sometimes, as depicted in the painting that hung on the wall of La Llorona. But after it was over, people got on with their lives. They were always ready to work hard.

Except for the river that flowed through town now, in the new canal the men had dug to contain the floodwaters unleashed by the storm, by the time of the annual town *feria* you wouldn't have known there'd ever been a hurricane.

73

Must be some herb

Gus was back. On his way down the steps to lay out his latest idea he'd picked up my mail. Now he handed me a letter. Chinese stamps on the envelope, familiar handwriting.

Inside was a photograph of a smiling Asian woman with a newborn baby in her arms and another child, a couple of years old, at her side, along with a serious-looking man, his hand on her shoulder.

I guess the sight must have made me appear more emotional than usual. There may even have been tears in my eyes.

"What's with the waterworks, mate?" he said. "I haven't seen a mug like that since the Rovers lost the tournament in '96."

"It's good news, actually," I told him. "Remember Jun Lan, the woman from China, who stayed here a few years back?"

"The plant-lover," he said. "Who could forget? That girl was tromping up the side of the mountain in the middle of rainy season, all so she could find, what was it, some kind of herb?"

Gus took a long, slow sip on his beer, reflecting on Jun Lan and her quest. "I had my days of loving the weed, mate," he said, "and I won't say I don't still take a puff of the stuff on occasion. But the plant's not been invented that would get me out on a muddy hillside in the middle of rainy season, just to dig up a root or two or collect a handful of some seeds."

"It wasn't a drug, exactly," I told him. Back when Jun Lan had been trying to get pregnant, I had regarded her quest as private, but now that she'd had her baby—and another after that, as her letter to me had just revealed—I felt able to share the information with Gus.

"There's this plant she knew about from her grandmother," I said. "She'd been told she could never have a baby, so she came here to find it. She just wrote to tell me she gave birth to her second son."

"That must be some herb," Gus said. "You happen to know what they call this miracle herb?"

I didn't.

"Or you could just show me where they grow," he continued. Gus had never before displayed such an interest in botany.

"If you really want to know, I can show you a picture I made," I told him. I went upstairs to retrieve one of the journals I'd filled with drawings and watercolors of plant life around La Llorona. I showed Gus the drawing I'd made in my notebook of Jun Lan's herb, with its strange, feathery leaves. "See those berries," I told him. "Maria crushed them and steeped them in boiling water to make a special tea for Jun Lan. Ten months later she gave birth to her son."

"I'll be jiggered," Gus said, studying my drawing with the kind of focus he normally reserved for the football scores. "You wouldn't know where a bloke might find himself one of these, would you mate?"

I shook my head. For all the days Jun Lan and Elmer had made their way over the mountain, in search of the plant, I'd never accompanied them. "All I know is that according to Jun Lan, the herb responsible for curing her infertility only grows in one spot," I told him.

"An herb that gets gals in the family way when they've lost all hope," Gus mused. "Now there's a million-dollar idea."

74

An unexpected art lover

My swimming lessons with Pablito were going well. Some days he was too occupied with his harpoon-fishing to make it over to La Llorona, but at least three days a week he'd stop by on his way back from whatever spot he'd chosen to dive to accompany me into the water. The first few times I wore a life jacket, but by the second week I was getting pretty good at the frog kick. Putting my face in the water no longer frightened me.

One time during our lesson the clip I'd been wearing to keep my hair out of my eyes had fallen out in the water. Like a dolphin, Pablito lifted his body just enough to create sufficient momentum, then plunged straight to the bottom, like an arrow. A few moments later he surfaced, holding my clip over his head. He had the most perfect teeth, the broadest smile. "*El tresor!*" he called out. The treasure.

I had progressed to learning the crawl stroke now, though staying close to shore still—Pablito at my side—the day Dora stopped by. I could not remember the last time she'd come to the hotel by herself. Gus was a regular, almost daily visitor, but except for dinners at the hotel on nights when we were between guests Dora hardly ever put in appearance at La Llorona.

I'd been so occupied by the swimming I didn't see her arrive. Then, just as I came up for air, there she was standing on the dock, wearing a pair of the floaty cotton linen pants she favored and a very small top that showed off her impressive abdominal muscles. Delivering two babies had done nothing to alter her great figure.

"Five more minutes and I'll make us a cup of tea," I told her.

To pass the time, she folded herself into one of her more ambitious yoga poses. It had always seemed odd to me, watching Dora practice yoga—something she did a lot, at odd moments—that however beautiful and meditative the pose, her expression, while engaged in it, often appeared anxious, even scowling. The easy-going, devil-may-care style of her husband had not rubbed off on her.

After emerging from the water and waving goodbye to Pablito—who'd taken off in his cayuco—I wrapped a towel around my waist and headed into the kitchen. Dora was waiting for me.

"I was thinking about that Asian woman who stayed here a few years back," Dora said. She was never one for small talk. If there was something Dora wanted, she got to the point.

"That herb she got on the mountain, that helped her get pregnant. Gus said you had a drawing of what it looks like?"

I looked up from fixing the tea. Hibiscus, from the garden.

"Are you two trying for a third?" I asked her.

"Oh God no," she said. "I was just wondering. For a friend."

Never before, in all the time I'd known Dora and Gus, had either of them expressed an interest in my artwork. Now she studied my drawing a long time.

"You're really talented," she said. "Would you mind giving me one of these?"

I ripped the page out my notebook and handed it to her. A rare event followed. Dora smiled.

75

A no-hands game

A call came from Dora. She was at the hospital in San Felipe. There'd been an accident. Could I go pick her children up from school?

I said yes, of course. Then came the story.

In the middle of the night, Gus had been awakened by a rustling sound in his yard, and the clucking of his chickens. When he went out to investigate, he'd found a man from the village, Samuel, in the act of stealing the family's laundry off the line. Two towels, a sheet, a few diapers, one of Dora's brassieres.

No stranger to fighting—he was a Blackburn man—Gus tackled Samuel. The two were unevenly matched, not only because Gus was unusually strong, but also because, unlike Samuel, he was sober. But just as Gus had succeeded in pinning Samuel to the ground, the miserable drunk had retaliated in the only manner that remained. He sank his teeth into Gus's hand.

The shock, not to mention the pain, caused Gus to recoil, just long enough for Samuel to make a run for it. Gus lay in the dirt for a moment, surrounded by laundry, then headed back into the house to pour himself a glass of stout and nurse his wounds.

This was when he saw it. Not just the deep wound in the palm of his right hand, but dead center, at the juncture of his life line, sticking out of the skin: a tooth that until recently had belonged to his attacker.

His wound hurt even worse once he pulled the tooth out. This must have been the moment Dora woke up. She fixed him an herbal remedy and boiled water to sterilize the place where he'd been bitten.

In the morning, Gus's hand had swollen to the size of a baseball mitt. By nightfall, it was the size of a football. His arm was throbbing and he had a fever. "We need to see a doctor," Dora told him.

"I'll be okay," he told her. "I'm betting by tomorrow morning the old paw will be right as rain."

It wasn't. By nine o'clock Gus and Dora were on the boat headed for San Luis. It was a little after noon when Dora called me. A massive infection had set in.

"The doctor said if we'd waited one a few more hours he would have lost his arm," she said. "They're telling me they want to amputate his hand."

It was possible, the doctors agreed, that the antibiotics they'd shot into him might arrest the infection, but if they didn't, there was no telling how fast it could travel. They'd seen a case not unlike this one a few years back where a man refused to let them take his leg, and the next morning he was dead.

There was no consulting Gus on this one. The fever had so over-taken Gus that he was now delirious, talking about his mother and football, a girl named Pamela and a teacher back in second form who'd accused him of stealing erasers.

"I don't know what to do," Dora said. She was calling from the hallway outside his room. I'd never before heard her sound anything other than strong and confident, but at that moment there was terror in Dora's voice. The doctors needed a decision, fast, if they were going to operate.

"It's not for me to say," I told her.

"It's his right hand," Dora said. "What if he never forgives me?"

At that moment I thought of my mother. Suppose instead of dying that day at the house on East Eighty-Fourth Street, my mother had only lost her hand. I would have grown up with a mother. Suppose, in the accident that killed him, that Lenny had only lost a limb?

"If it was me," I said, "I'd choose a husband with one hand over the possibility of no husband at all."

Gus came home three days later. You couldn't tell right away that his hand was gone, on account of all the bandaging. They'd put him on very strong painkillers, which had made him subdued, which had made him unrecognizable.

That night I stopped over with food—a vegan casserole and brownies, a bottle of wine. Gus was stretched out in the recliner chair he always chose for watching football matches, and the television was on, though there was no game. In his left hand, he held a joint. He looked ten years older than the last time I'd seen him.

"Bum luck, eh?" he said to me, as I set the casserole on the counter. "All the other guy lost was a tooth."

"I'm not going to say a bunch of cheerful things at the moment," I told him. "I know how irritating that is at a time like this."

"The doctors said they have these amazing prosthetics now," Dora said. "As soon as Gus heals, we'll go to the city so he can get fitted and start learning how they work."

Gus took a long drag on the joint.

"If anyone can handle something like this, it's you, Gus," I told him. "Remember after the hurricane? How you had to practically rebuild your whole house from the ground up? And you ended up making it even nicer than before."

"One small difference," he said. "At the time, I had my two hands to work with. "

"I'm sorry," I said. No more attempts at upbeat observations.

"There's one good thing, anyway," he pointed out. "Football's a no-hands game."

76

I'm a fish

I didn't see Gus or Dora for almost two weeks after that, and except for a couple of times when I sent Walter over to the house to deliver a meal, I left them alone. This would be a hard time for their family.

At the hotel, we carried on. Thanks to Caroline Timmins' article on the internet—a form of advertising that had barely existed when I first took on the task of running La Llorona—all four rooms were booked solid for most of the month. I had never been more grateful to be occupied with work.

I wasn't the only one dealing with sadness. Elmer still arrived on time every morning, putting in his usual long hours. More so than ever, with Gus no longer coming by to assist with the more demanding projects. His face, as he worked, bore a look of pained acceptance. Herman had made the choice to become a priest, but it struck me, observing Elmer as he was in the aftermath of Mirabel's rejection, that Elmer, too, might as well have joined a religious order. The more rigid and self-denying, the better.

Now that I no longer stopped by to visit with Dora, the main person I visited in town was Amalia. I didn't even stop by Harold's café anymore and hadn't done so since that day I'd observed the lizard men bargaining with Clarinda for her handmade silk-lined purse. I had described the event to Amalia, who was not surprised by their behavior.

"Pigs," she said, handing me a piece of starfruit on a small, perfect, though cracked plate.

"I told Clarinda to stay away from those men," I said. "I don't think she'll try to sell them any of her bags again."

"I want her to attend a better school," Amalia told me. You had only to walk past the elementary school in the village to know it offered little to a child as bright as Clarinda. Every time I walked through the village I could hear the teacher, calling out the words of that day's lesson, and the children, in unison, chanting back the accepted response. English lessons were the worst.

"Good morning," the teacher called out, in heavily accented English. "How are you today?"

"*Good morning,*" they answered, all together, "*I am very fine thank you.*"

"How much does it cost to send a child to the school in San Luis?" I asked her. Attending the better school would mean riding on the boat every day, but a number of children in the village did this. Gringo children.

I told Amalia I'd come up with the money for Clarinda's tuition.

A week later, Clarinda enrolled at the Academy of Life in Santa Clara. Amalia had ridden over on the boat with her a few days earlier to buy supplies. We bought her a backpack too, and pencils, and notebooks, a slide rule, and a dictionary. Also new shoes and three pairs of white socks with bows on the cuffs, and a pack of barrettes and a navy blue school uniform with a pleated skirt. I had suggested we get her two of those, but Clarinda explained that if she washed her uniform out every afternoon when she got home it would be dry by morning. One was enough.

At the school Clarinda had attended in the village, every child got a bowl of rice and beans for lunch, but students attending the Academy had to bring their own meal. Amalia and I both understood that Veronica, Clarinda's mother, was unlikely to provide her with food to get her through the day.

"Maria and I can pack her something to bring with her on the boat," I said. "She walks past the hotel on the way to the dock. I'll bring it up to the top of the gate."

That first day, Amalia and I accompanied Clarinda to the boat. We were there at the dock around four that afternoon to greet her. We wanted to hear all about her first day of course. As many people as lived in Clarinda's mother's little two-room hut, it was unlikely that anybody there would think to inquire about her studies.

There we stood as the boat pulled in—two childless women, awaiting a nearly motherless child. Our girl was the last one off the boat—having waited for all the old women with their baskets of verduras, the old man with the crowing rooster, the young girl—no more than three years older than Clarinda, from the looks of her—with that small bump inside her shawl that indicated the presence of a baby.

Clarinda practically skipped down the dock to greet us—her pigtails, laced with ribbons, bouncing. She was carrying a bean plant—an experiment for science class, she told us—and a drawing she'd made, in art, of a jocote tree, its branches filled with birds.

"I told my teacher I'm going to be a doctor," she said. "One of the boys in my class said 'you mean a nurse.' I said 'no, doctor.'"

On our way up the path from the dock, we passed Harold's café. The three lizard men were outside, as usual. By this hour in the afternoon, I knew, they'd all be half-seas over, same as Clarinda's mother would be when she got back home.

I held her hand tightly as we walked past.

"They can't hurt you," I whispered.

"Soy un pez," she laughed. *I'm a fish.*

77

King Bass

I had gotten so busy with my guests that a few weeks went by in which I'd told Pablito I had no time for my swimming lesson. Then one day he showed up with the most beautiful black bass he'd ever brought us.

"I've been trying to catch this one for three years," he told me. "But he was too smart. Every time I'd point my harpoon at his belly, he'd slip away."

"How did you finally get him?" I asked.

"There is a special place at the bottom of the lake my father showed me many years ago, when he first taught me to dive," Pablito said. "A cave. I hid there, waiting for him. Finally he came."

I knew from our earlier conversations, sitting by the side of the water after my swimming lessons, that Pablito could hold his breath underwater longer than any other harpoon fisherman at the lake. He had spent many years building the power of his lungs, increasing the time he could survive at the bottom before coming up. Now he could stay down for nine and a half minutes, allowing the last twenty seconds for his return to the surface.

"My father spent thirty years searching for this cave," Pablito told me. "We had heard the legend that somewhere at the bottom of the lake an ancient Mayan village had existed once. Many divers traveled to the lake over the years, in search of this place. It was my father, Pablo, who discovered where it was. When I was ten years old, he brought me there.

"All these years I had a picture in my head of this spot," Pablito told me. "I remembered what it felt like, swimming along the bottom of the lake with my father just ahead of me, watching his flippers as he moved through the water. All around us, there were these giant round carvings with characters on them from the Mayan language. I could read some of them."

Back when he and his father had swum together at the bottom of the lake, in among the stone carvings of the ancient village, the two of them had only been able to stay underwater for seven minutes. Pablito was younger then but he remembered those few minutes as if they'd taken place yesterday: A temple with a long staircase. Ceramic pots lying on their sides. Something that looked like the pila sinks still used by women in the village to wash the clothes. Carved heads depicting warriors and gods.

Later, Pablito told me—after they had returned to the village—his father contacted a man at the university in San Felipe. They sent out a team of archaeologists who knew how to dive. Not free-divers like Pablo and Pablito. The divers who came from the university had tanks on their backs.

"They told us the ruins we found were more than three thousand years old," Pablito said. It was a mystery how they came to be underwater, but the archaeologists had guessed that there must have been a volcanic eruption that changed the water level of the entire lake.

Later, more experts came to study the site, this time from the United States and Europe. A magazine published an article about the discovery. Though Pablito could not read English, it was plain, looking at the words on the page, that his father's role in the discovery was not a part of the story, only the studies conducted by the experts. "These represent some of the most important finds in the Mayan world in the last hundred years," one of them had said. This much Pablito had understood.

But the location of the ruins had been kept a secret, to protect them from the pillaging of amateurs. Not long after Pablo and Pablito had come upon the ruins that day, and the cave that had been part of them,

Pablito's father, Pablo, had died in an accident. "He was diving off a very high cliff," Pablito told me. "My father thought he knew every boulder on our side of the lake, but not the one that killed him," he said.

In all the years since, Pablito had searched for those ruins. He had a general idea of the area, but the lake was so large—100 square kilometers—and deeper than anyone knew, that finding the spot again had proven impossible. Until today.

"This morning, I brought my boat to a spot I'd never dived before," he told me. There it was, the ancient submerged city. And in among the ruins he made another discovery: The giant bass he'd been chasing since before the birth of his own son—Pablo, like his father and grandfather.

He knew when he spotted the fish that this was his moment. He'd been hiding in that cave close to four minutes—his time running out—when the bass swam past, in range of Pablito's harpoon. One strike and Pablito had the fish.

He wanted me to have his prize. I'd been a good customer—his best. But it was more than this, he told me, refusing my offer of payment.

"I brought you the fish to honor how you have worked, learning to swim," he said. "Many people might give up, but you did not."

He gutted the fish for me and scaled it. Then he returned to his boat.

"This is the biggest bass I ever saw," I told him.

"Well, there was one even bigger," Pablito said. "Swimming alongside. I missed that one, but now that I know where to go, I'll go back and get him. Then I'll feast with my family."

That night Maria cooked the Queen Bass—our name for the second-biggest fish in the lake. She made slits on each side, into which she stuffed a mixture of parsley, cilantro, garlic, chives, tarragon, and *chipilin*. She opened a bottle of beer and poured most of it down his mouth, then set him in a warm bath to steam. She made chimichurri to accompany the fish, along with coconut rice. Everyone said it was the best meal of fish they'd ever tasted. The best meal, period, perhaps.

Three days after this, I entered the kitchen to find Maria standing over the sink, where Luis had hung the skeleton of the giant fish so we could all admire it.

"Pablito's gone," she said.

His wife had come to her with the story. Pablito had returned to the place he'd harpooned the Queen Bass, she told me—the place in the lake where the ruins of the underwater city lay, a hundred meters down. With his harpoon in hand, he dived down in search of the fish he'd spotted on his earlier dive. The King.

As he'd done before, Pablito hid in the cave of the ruined city. We all knew Pablito could stay underwater for a long time. He must have been hoping that at some point over the course of those precious minutes, the king of all bass would swim past.

Something must have happened to Pablito's belt as he hovered there at the bottom of the lake, holding the weights he used to keep himself from floating up to the top. It got caught, probably. He must have tried to take it off. Maybe his fingers were numb from the cold. Maybe his brain had lost function when his lungs were nearing the end of their capacity to go without air.

He never made it back up. A group of other harpoon fishermen from the village of La Esperanza, and others from Santa Clara, had set out to look for him. They knew where to look when they'd spotted his little cayuco boat.

The men dove down many times before discovering the body of Pablito. He was wedged between two Mayan stelae, leaned against each other. His harpoon was at his feet, its blade plunged deep into the belly of the King Bass. They must have perished together.

The men had presented Pablito's harpoon to his wife. "I will keep it until my son Pablo is ready," she'd told Maria.

Ready?

"To become a harpoon fisherman."

78

In appreciation for services rendered

Five weeks passed in which I still hadn't seen or heard from Gus and Dora. People in town who knew them—as everyone did—mentioned seeing Dora now and then, on rare occasions when she'd come to the market. Nobody had laid eyes on Gus.

"Poor guy must be having a hard time," Harold said. "It's not like he's some philosophy professor or a banker. Everything Gus does is about using his hands. He's a handyman, for God's sake."

Was.

A lawyer came to my gate. Not Juan de la Vega this time. It was an *abrogado* from San Felipe—a crude-looking man in need of a shave who wore sunglasses and smelled of cheap cologne. He was here to deliver papers, he said, on behalf of his clients, Gus and Dora Gulden. A summons to appear in court, to answer to the charge of unauthorized occupancy of property legally registered in their names.

The hotel.

"There's been a mistake," I said. "This is my property. I inherited it from the previous owner eight years ago. Gus and Dora are my friends. Like family."

The lawyer took a document from his briefcase. "You must have a copy of this," he said.

I remembered it of course. At the time this document had been executed I'd been buried in all the paperwork left unfinished by Leila. I could barely read Spanish—the reason I'd turned to Dora for help, rather than consulting Leila's attorney as it was now clear I should have done.

The lawyer pointed to the second paragraph on the first page. My Spanish had improved enough over the years since I'd signed my name on the last page that I could understand what I'd agreed to that day, in my haste to get the documents taken care of.

"The undersigned hereby assigns to Dora Gulden the rights, in perpetuity, to the entirety of her legal property, land and buildings known as 'La Llorona' in gratitude for services rendered as her legal representative."

The attorney turned to the last page of the document. He pointed to the signature. Mine.

My property was not my property after all. My friends were not my friends. La Llorona belonged to Gus and Dora now.

79

The wall

I consulted a lawyer of my own, naturally. I got Mayra's name from Amalia, who steered clear of attorneys and all other official types, but had met her at a demonstration in the city, protesting the government's distribution of processed baby formula to nursing mothers around the lake. Mayra Asuncion had an office in Santa Clara. This time I did not hesitate to go there, personally.

Mayra took a long time studying the documents I'd brought with me. I watched her face as she read through the pages. When she was finished reading, she looked up and shook her head.

"Whoever drew this up knew quite a lot about the practice of law. The practice of law in this country, anyway," she said. "They've pinned you down pretty well with the language they came up with here.

"We could make the argument that you didn't know what you were signing," she added. "We could point out that Spanish is not your native language. Unfortunately, you also signed this other document"—she held out the form I'd had notarized, prior to Dora's visit to the city that day—"in which you specifically assert that you have studied these documents, and that that you chose to name Dora as your legal representative.

"This doesn't leave you with much of a case," she said. "If any."

"What do you recommend?" I asked.

"I'd try to negotiate. Strike a deal. A compromise."

"Strike a deal with two people who cheated me out of my property?"

"The best thing you have on your side right now is the fact that you physically occupy the property, and they do not," she told me. "It wouldn't be the easiest task, removing you from your place of business. The place where you live."

"And this could save me? This might keep them from taking La Llorona?"

Again the lawyer shook her head. "These two aren't likely to walk away."

There was this one glimmer of hope, Mayra told me. Not a solution to my problem, but there was a clause in the wording of the deed on the property that Leila had transferred to me concerning her longtime workers. She'd put language into the paperwork that protected, in perpetuity, the salaries of Luis and Maria Navichoc as well as their son Elmer for the duration of their lives. Who ever it was who assumed ownership of La Llorona also assumed responsibility for paying out a sum of money, twice a month, to the Navichoc family.

When the hotel did well, this wasn't a problem. But when occupancy went down—as it did in rainy season, and again after the hurricane, and as it could at any point in the future—Dora and Gus would find themselves legally obligated to come up with the money for Luis, Maria, Elmer, and Mirabel, whether or not the hotel was bringing any money in. I knew from personal experience how difficult it was, at times, meeting this responsibility.

"The Navichoc clause gives you some leverage," Mayra told me. "Not that I see a way for you to keep your property. But you might hold on to control of the hotel as a long-term tenant."

A tenant on my own property. I laid my head on Mayra's desk.

"Offer to rent back half of the property from Dora and Gus," Mayra said. "The part with the hotel on it. Assume responsibility for your workers' salaries. You get to keep running the hotel and living there. You won't own it anymore, but at least you can carry on with your life, and your employees will be protected."

So there it was. My best and only hope lay in slicing off half of the land Leila had planted and cared for all those years. I thought about certain flowers and plants I'd particularly loved. My jade thunbergia. The pelican vine. The jocote tree.

I thought about the waterfall we'd built, and the grove of papayas and jasmine where I liked to draw. My herb garden. The tree trunk Elmer had carried down from the mountain, covered with the orchids.

"Just half," she said. She studied the plot map that had been part of the other attorney's packet. "Luckily, even if you cut off half, you'll still have a nice little parcel left for your hotel guests."

The picture came to me of Gus as I'd seen him that last time we met up in the village, with bandages covering the stump where his hand used to be. This, too, felt like a kind of amputation.

"The best I can hope for is cutting my property in half and paying rent to the same people who cheated me?"

"I'm not saying this is a great solution to your problem," Mayra told me. "But it's better than nothing."

I could feel my chest tightening, blood draining from my face. The one good thing: Luis and Maria and Elmer would be okay.

"My strong suggestion is to make our counteroffer swiftly, before these two start coming up with more demands," she said. "I could get a surveyor over next week to draw up a line for the portion of the property you get to rent back from those two crooks."

The line was drawn in such a way that the stone steps remained on the portion of land I'd still get to use and the little reflecting pool Elmer had stocked with tiny fish from the lake with the waterlilies and the arch we'd formed out of bougainvillea vines. Among the parts of the property hardest to forfeit was a stand of black bamboo we'd planted shortly after I took on the hotel and a little path we'd built, with a special variety of green stone and hand-painted bird tiles inlaid along the edges, and a mosaic of the volcano made out of pieces of plates from Talavera, Mexico. Every time another dish broke, Leila had added them to her mosaic. And there was no way around this part: Dora and Gus got my jocote tree.

Hearing the news, Elmer, the most loyal of men, wanted to chop the tree down rather than allow Gus and Dora to enjoy its fruits. I told him no.

The day after the surveyor finished his work—leaving a slash of Day-Glo orange paint along what was now the new perimeter of the property I'd be renting from now on—we got to work transplanting flowers. In addition to Luis and Maria, I called Walter to help. Because it was a Sunday and she was off school, Clarinda joined us. Elmer was there with his shovel, though the presence of Mirabel, digging up a bed of white roses, left him too distracted to do much.

Amalia came by to help, as did Raya, who brought Alicia along.

"I never really trusted those two," Amalia observed, referring to Gus and Dora. "The wife always reminded me of a guard I knew back in prison who used to come wake me up in the middle of the night, banging a spoon against the bars just to drive me crazy."

Raya took a more accepting approach. "The way I look at it, nobody really owns anything anyway," she said. "We're all just temporary residents of the planet. Gus and Dora may think a piece of paper gives them some kind of power. But at the end of the day, we're all headed to the same place."

She picked up a handful of soil, nearly black from years of Luis's care. "What those two did is superbad, karmically speaking," she said. "But you're going to be fine."

"I'll go to his house in the night and beat him up," Walter offered.

"Revenge is never a good idea," Raya told him. "Look at me. I never thought I'd get to be anyone's mother, and then Alicia came into my life. I don't have any legal paperwork that says she belongs to me. No person belongs to anybody else, any more than a piece of land does, or a sunrise."

Alicia, sitting on a blanket playing in the dirt, had looked up and smiled.

"If Wade wanted to," Raya added, "he could probably take this precious girl away from me tomorrow. But in the meantime, I'm going to focus on this day we get to be together. You never know when it could all disappear. All you can do is be grateful for what you get for as long as you have it."

I set my shovel down for a moment. There they were, the two of them—an exquisite three-year-old child and the fifty-seven-year-old woman she called Mama, bent over an earthworm. For a moment, I let myself imagine what Alicia's dead mother, Rosella, might make of the scene. There was Alicia, the brown-eyed daughter of an Italian opera lover and a disbarred attorney turned rabbit-farming restaurateur. If things had turned out differently, and Rosella had lived, Raya would be back in California right now, trimming marijuana plants. Alicia would have been spending every August at Rosella's parents' vineyard in Tuscany. As it was, she lived in a one-room adobe hut with an aging and basically penniless seller of crocheted bikini tops. Life took surprising turns.

For a while there—for no reason other than the fact that I'd wanted to kill myself and ran away one day on a green bus bound for Central America—I'd gotten to be the owner of the most beautiful hotel on the shores of the most beautiful lake, surrounded by the most beautiful garden, looking out to the most magnificent volcano. Now the garden would be only half the size it had been. Now the hotel belonged to someone else. You could call that a big tragedy. Or, simply, life.

One thing to remember, Raya reminded me: Nobody had died here. Life would go on. Until it didn't. That was okay too.

Partway through the long afternoon of work, the group of us shared a pitcher of *rosa de Jamaica* iced tea on the patio, with a plate of Maria's macarons. Alicia chose a pink one. I brought out my bag of colored pencils, and we all made pictures—of the ceramic animals, the hummingbird drinking nectar from the center of a *thunbergia* blossom, the clouds over the volcano.

By the time my friends left, we'd located new homes for dozens of plants in what remained of my garden. Roses. Gardenia. Jasmine.

Eucalyptus. Baby's tears, birds of paradise. There was a very special plant for which I'd created a spot in part of the land that now belonged to Dora and Gus—a variety of orchid known as *Doce Apostoles*, the twelve apostles. The bulb was so delicate I'd dug it up with my fingers, then smoothed over the soil where it had grown to make its absence less noticeable. With Alicia's little shovel, Raya made a hole for it next to the waterfall.

"Beautiful things, placed closer together, are just as beautiful," Maria said, when she'd come out from the kitchen at the end of our long day of work to inspect the transformation. "It's a little like making a *caldo*. You can pour three liters of water in the pot, or one, but what gives it flavor is the crab. The less water, the more flavor from the fish."

A few days later, a small army of workers hired by Gus and Dora showed up on the property. All morning they carried bags of cement down the hillside to build a wall. I had hoped they might use bamboo to mark the dividing line of the property, but my former friends had chosen to construct their wall out of ugly gray cinder block, as they had done when building their house.

As I watched the workers pile the blocks, one on top of the other, slapping on the cement, it felt as though I were watching a prison under construction. The wall stood ten feet high at least, running from the road clear to the water, with a row of broken glass bottles along the top that might have reminded certain people in the town—those who'd made the long journey through Mexico and tried to cross the border into Texas and failed—of some men's efforts to keep others out. No one was getting over that wall.

Amalia, when she'd stopped by a few days later to inspect the damage, appeared undaunted by the sight. She was a woman who'd grown up on the wrong side of a wall in Germany. She'd also seen it fall. For her, too, no situation was hopeless.

"First we lay stucco over the whole thing," she said. "Then we paint a mural."

That night, after she was done clearing away the dishes from dinner—a slow night with only two guests—I asked Maria if she had a few minutes to spare.

Though she'd known, of course, about the division of the land, I had chosen not to share with the Navichoc family the details of what Gus and Dora had done, with the title to the property. As far as they knew, Gus and Dora had simply annexed off a part of the land to build a house. For some unfathomable reason, I'd allowed this.

Over a pot of tea on the terrace, with the guests returned to their rooms, I had a question for Maria.

"I was wondering how Leila felt about Gus, back when he used to work here," I said. "And about Dora. Would you say they were friends?"

A look came over Maria's face, followed by a long thoughtful pause, as if she were choosing her words carefully. It was not Maria's style to speak ill of anyone, except for one guest, long ago, who'd smoked a cigar in his room and spilled red wine on the good linen bedspread.

"He used to come here a lot," she said. "Then they didn't come over anymore."

"Why not?"

"The señora never told Luis and me, but we saw what happened," Maria said. "She found out he was cheating her."

Gus had billed Leila for some very beautiful marble. He said he was going to make her a table. Then one day she had stopped by their house, unannounced, with a gift for their son's birthday. That's when she'd seen the marble. And an antique silver tea service she'd shipped from France. Also a crystal wine decanter that had been missing for over a year.

"When she found out, she was so sad," Maria said. "She really liked those two. She thought they were friends. If Dora and Gus had asked for some of the marble, she would have given it to them.

"Then it turned out they'd taken a lot more," Maria said. "They'd bought all this cinder block and lumber to build their house and charged it to her account."

"I don't know what she said to the Englishman and his wife about that," Maria said. "But he never came back to the property after that. Until you hired him."

It made sense now, why Maria and Luis had kept their distance from Gus all those years, when he came to work for me. With everyone else, they were unceasingly friendly.

"The señora loved La Llorona so much," Maria told me. "She worried about what would happen to it after she was gone. She talked to my husband and me. But we are old. It takes a lot of work, running this place, as you know."

Then I'd shown up.

"Didn't it seem strange to you, Leila leaving me the hotel?" I asked her.

Not really, Maria told me. "She told me the day after you arrived, 'I like that girl.'"

She had been wrong about Gus and Dora. But Leila never stopped trusting her instincts. In those last weeks before she died she'd shared her plan with Luis and Maria.

"We knew you would take good care," Maria said.

Then look what happened. I'd failed. I'd let Leila's beloved home fall into the hands of the very people who'd cheated her.

"When I started hiring Gus to do all those jobs around the hotel, didn't you want to say anything about it?" I asked her.

"It wasn't our place," she said. "You were in charge."

80

A red light-bulb

As the months passed, it got easier to put away my sadness over the loss of my property, the diminished gardens. In addition to the mural Amalia had made to cover the stucco—assisted by Clarinda, who proved to be a wonderful artist, and a small team of younger children from her Pura Natura trash project—Elmer planted a new row of bougainvillea in a shade of purple I'd never seen before. The plants grew thick and strong, so even by the end of that first year blooms appeared, and by the next year they were climbing over the top of the wall.

In the end, the hardest part of the event I called the Dora and Gus Heist—the hardest, apart from the knowledge of my friends' betrayal—was what they did to the land we had tended so lovingly all those years—as Leila had, so many years before. When we'd first moved all those plants, I'd worried that Dora and Gus might go back to the lawyer with a new round of demands, but my former friends were not the type who paid much attention to flowers. They'd probably never noticed I'd taken any.

As much as I could tell, looking down from the road, the house the two of them put up on the other side of the wall was almost identical to the one they'd built in town—now rented out to tourists. Like the first house, and the wall, the new house was made from cinder block. No effort had been made to conceal the dull gray, pockmarked material or the cement oozing between the blocks. The roof was plastic lamina. The windows—though they looked out over a view of staggering beauty—were small and spaced far apart.

From what I could tell looking down on the property on my rare walks past, Dora and Gus had virtually stripped the soil of vegetation. A group of men had been hired to create terraces, for some future crop, evidently. Maybe coffee, I speculated.

Then there was this. Gus and Dora had installed a light in the jocote tree, bright enough to illuminate a football field, and for reasons unknown they kept it on all night. On a clear night, I could still make out the constellations, but nowhere near as sharply as I'd done before, thanks to the presence of the all-night lighting.

The bulb was red.

81

Always the volcano

I'd known periods in my life when time seemed almost to stand still, and the prospect of getting through a single day felt insurmountable. Summers with my grandmother in Poughkeepsie were like that—the television on nonstop (*Let's Make a Deal, Hollywood Squares, Jeopardy!*. And then the soaps). The way children who went on family vacations, or to camp in New Hampshire, counted the days until school got out, I'd counted the days until it started again. Worse was that stretch of months after Arlo and Lenny died, when I'd holed up in our apartment on Vallejo Street, and all I wanted was to fall asleep and not wake up for ten years.

After I moved to La Esperanza, time moved differently. I never wore a watch and except for times I'd enter a new booking into the ledger, I never looked at a calendar or knew what day of the week it was. In my first months at the lake, I'd followed the news of what went on in other parts of the world—though most of it reached me days or weeks late. But after a while this, too, faded. I could tell you the name of the president of the United States, and during all the years of my friendship with Gus I'd maintained a surprising command of what football teams were doing best in the league. Other than that, you might have said my world had shrunk to the confines of a single beautiful lake—a single village, even, and the comings and goings of its citizenry along a single path.

In another way, harder to explain, my world had expanded.

Every day I heard half a dozen languages, heard the songs of a few dozen varieties of birds. Babies were born. Old people died. Men planted crops and harvested them. Women slapped masa dough between their hands, forming tortillas, and moved their shuttles through the threads of the cloth they wove. They embroidered birds onto their huipiles. Harold peeled mangoes to place in the blender. Raya crocheted bikini tops. Elmer swept the stone steps and chopped off the tops of coconuts. How many thousands in a lifetime?

Boats dropped off passengers and picked them up again. Hippie travelers passed through, adopting puppies and abandoning them three weeks later when they left for the next Rainbow Gathering. Every season, flyers stapled to the trees announced some new and amazing new age healing technique—a workshop on the way water droplets responded to classical music compared to how they responded to heavy metal, a workshop in "The Power of the Mushroom" presented at the Fungus Academy, a month of silence, timed to coincide precisely with the cycles of the moon. Federico the Cacao Shaman still offered his ceremonies to travelers, though he maintained a website now, and a blog, and marketed his transformational cacao to online customers around the world. A couple passed through who had spent the winter gathering a rare and magical substance from the backs of a variety of frog found only in the jungles of Mexico which, when ingested, promised to separate a person from her ego, remove all blocks to her emotional well-being, and make her one with the universe.

In the indigenous community, the stakes were different. Women gathered wood for the fire. Men planted corn. Children went to school as long as the family could afford to send them. Then they worked, just as their parents had done. Pablito's son, young Pablo—no more than fourteen years old now—dove into the lake with his harpoon in search of black bass and tilapia.

In some ways, everything kept changing here; in others, it remained as unchanged as the outline of the volcano against the sky. I might not be the owner of La Llorona anymore, but if you took a measure of my life by how the days went, life was good. Guests still checked into the hotel. Guests checked out. Couples held hands on my patio, surrounded by rose petals, deciding to get married. Other couples broke up. Now and then the ones who got engaged at my hotel came back to celebrate anniversaries or bring their children. A widow returned alone to honor the memory of the man with whom she'd spent her honeymoon in the Jaguar Room.

The birds sang just the same as they ever did. Even on the sunniest days, when the sky was its bluest, that same one cloud still hung over the top of El Fuego.

Every morning, still, Maria set out the huevos, platanos, beans, cheese—*el plato típico de desayuno*. Every morning she squeezed the oranges for juice. Luis, too old now to wield the machete, swept the steps. Elmer silently emptied the water from a *garafon* into the water dispenser. The sadness of Mirabel's refusal of his offer of marriage never left his eyes. Cuzmi, very old now, lay in the sun. Veronica, in the dirt, lay passed out on the previous night's bottle of Quetzalteca. Her daughter, Clarinda, boarded the boat for school. In another couple of months she'd be graduating.

Walter, the first child I'd met when I arrived in town, was well into his teens now, no longer hanging out on the dock to carry the suitcases of the travelers getting off the boat, though except for times I hired him to help out at the restaurant when we got very busy, he had not found regular employment in the village. The three lizard men still occupied the same table at Harold's café. Just down the path, Raya still sold her bikini tops—except for Octobers, when she headed to Northern California for six weeks to trim the marijuana crop, at which point Alicia stayed with Patrizia and her twin brother, Mateo.

Somewhere over the course of her years as the closest thing Alicia had to a mother, Raya had grown not simply older, but old. I could see it in the way she moved along the path to the little stand where she sold her bikini tops, the difficulty with which she wielded her crochet hook, her fingers twisted by arthritis. Not just her fingers, but her whole body looked weary. I worried about her future.

"I think Alicia might want to leave me soon," Raya had told me, the last time she took off for California. "I don't know what I'll do without her. But she needs to follow her own path."

Mirabel was twenty-six years old now (old, for a woman in this town to be unmarried and childless). She remained beautiful, though lately I had noticed a change in her, on mornings she came to work at the hotel. Her easy, radiant smile seemed to have disappeared. There was a hard set to her mouth, as if she were sucking on some piece of sour fruit but couldn't spit it out. She no longer played basketball, and just recently, I'd noticed, her waist—always the tiniest in the village—had begun to thicken.

Amalia was still La Reina de Basura, though her little band of trash gatherers turned over every few years. Some of the children who followed her down the path, gathering chips packets to stuff into bottles, had children of their own now.

Now and then I saw Gus and Dora's children, Luca and Jade, hanging out at the basketball court or outside the school, but when they saw me they turned away. As for Dora and Gus—they never seemed to leave their property.

One winter, a group of archaeologists arrived, booking the entire hotel, with a camera crew and a team of scuba divers, to film a documentary about the underwater Mayan ruins at the lake. The team of archaeologists explained to me that the lake level had once stood fifty meters lower than its current level. One of their group identified himself as the man responsible for having discovered the ruins at the far end of the lake. No mention was made of the harpoon fisherman who'd come upon it first, submerged more than three hundred feet under the turquoise waters of Lago La Paz.

The lake might go up. The lake might go down. But it was always there. And always there would be the volcano. That was the one thing that never changed.

82

The deep heart's core

Suddenly, there I was, thirty-nine years old, soon to be forty. Somehow it happened that ten years had passed since I first arrived in La Esperanza.

A letter arrived from Jerome Sapirstein. "I thought a long time about whether it was a good idea to send this," he'd written. "But I felt you should know.

"I got married a while back," he wrote. "Her name is Jenny. She's an editor at the publishing house. Last year we had a baby. A girl. Except for the part about never getting more than four hours of sleep in a row, I wouldn't change anything."

Their anniversary had come up recently. To surprise Jerome, Jenny had booked a vacation. Knowing his love of birds, she'd googled where, in all of Central America, a person might find the most diverse range of birdlife. Knowing nothing of that brief time, years before, when he had announced his intention to spend his life with me—that one night we'd lain side by side together on the volcano—she'd booked five nights at La Llorona.

"I probably shouldn't say this next part," he wrote. "But it took a long time, getting over you."

So he was canceling the reservation. He just wanted me to know he still thought of me sometimes and wished me well.

"I wonder if you remember the poem I recited to you that time," he wrote. "That line 'I shall have some peace there, for peace comes dropping slow.' I hope you've found that. Peace, I mean."

Jerome had written more, then crossed it out. A few more lines followed at the bottom of the page.

He'd written out "Lake Isle of Innisfree" in its entirety. Not that I had ever been a big memorizer of poetry, but I had never forgotten that night he recited the poem on the volcano when I told Jerome Sapirstein I couldn't make a life with him.

After all this time, I could still recite the part about the "the bee-loud glade" and "evening full of the linnet's wings."

Most of all, what got to me had been the way the poem ended. *"I hear lake water lapping, with low sounds by the shore."* And the last line. *I hear it in the deep heart's core.*

I hadn't even known this, but in a certain way I must have been looking for this lake all my life.

83
Looking out for the family

In all the time that had passed since Gus and Dora took control of my land—what used to be my land—I had never once run into them on the road or the path through town, or at the market. I had set things up with my bank in San Felipe so the rent money I paid to the two of them for the use of the property that used to be mine came directly out of my account for deposit into theirs. That way at least I was spared the experience of handing money over, on a monthly basis, to the people who'd defrauded me.

In those first months after I lost ownership of La Llorona, I'd wake up in the middle of the night and look out my window at that awful red spotlight aimed directly into my bedroom. But the rage I'd felt over what happened had mostly departed now. It was like an old ache from a bone you broke a long time ago that only became bothersome when it rained. I'd survived greater losses than this one.

I'd often wondered, though, what I'd do if I saw Gus and Dora in town. From all I could tell, the two of them kept to themselves now at their cinder block bunker. Even when the day of the annual town fair rolled around, even when there was a basketball tournament or a concert in the center of town—even football—Gus and Dora remained notably absent.

Then one day there they were, walking up the path from the dock. They must have been coming back from a trip to Santa Clara or San Felipe. Dora—lithe as ever, just older now—was carrying a couple of large shopping bags. Gus had a backpack and a large box containing a microwave oven. Dora as I'd known her, before, would never have let one of those into their house. Gus must have prevailed, maybe because operating a microwave was easier than cooking on a stove with one hand.

My eyes went to the place his right hand used to be.

I had supposed, when I imagined this scene, that I'd behave as if the two of them didn't exist. But as they approached me on the path, I looked Gus straight in the eye in the manner of my old friend from Vallejo Street, the conure.

Dora stiffened. She had been holding on to her husband's arm. Now she held tighter, leaning in close as if confiding some wonderful, intimate piece of news. She was smiling—not the usual expression for Dora but her expression gave the appearance of being a performance, not a particularly successful one. I drew in my breath and stopped dead, planting myself directly in front of the two of them.

"It's been a long time," I said. The way I'd positioned myself on the path, it would not have been easy to pass me by.

"How's it going, love?" Gus said. He sounded almost like the old Gus. "Keeping yourself busy, eh? You're looking well."

All those nights, lying awake staring out my window at the red light shining in from next door, I'd constructed things I wanted to say to these two and imagined the questions I'd ask them. How did they live with themselves, knowing what they'd done to a woman who'd believed herself to be their friend? Was it worth it, to have that piece of paper confirming ownership of what had once been my property, knowing what it had taken from their souls to acquire it?

Now, standing in front of my former friends, I said none of this. But one question had been on my mind ever since the day the lawyer turned up at my door to let me know La Llorona was no longer mine.

"I've been wondering something," I said.

"Those papers Dora got me to sign, where I agreed to give ownership to the two of you. All that time you pretended to be my friends you must have known that I'd signed away my property. So what took you so long? If you were going to take away my land, why didn't you do it way back when I first put my name on the papers?"

"What kind of a fool signs a legal document without reading what it says?" Dora said. Her smile had vanished now. She had actually adopted an attitude of something passing for righteous indignation.

"A person who isn't good at reading Spanish, probably," I said. "A person who trusts her friends."

"You were always so busy with your projects," Gus said. "Gardens and whatnot. Making those pictures of birds and posies you were always so keen on. Building this, building that. Always after good old Gus to come to your rescue."

I got it then—the reason they'd waited as long as they did before lowering the boom. I had supposed the timing of Gus and Dora's property heist had to do with Gus losing his hand, and their sudden need to come up with a new source of income. But they'd devised the timing for the takeover long before the fight that lost Gus his hand.

If Gus and Dora had taken over ownership of my property sooner, they would have been left to undertake all those costly renovations and upgrades themselves. They would have been stuck with the bills for the new roof, the new stairs, the new dock, the retaining walls, the kitchen remodel, the yoga platform. Gus would have been deprived of his best and most high-paying customer.

"So . . . First you made sure I got La Llorona in really great shape," I said. "Then once I did, you took it out from under me."

"It's a dog-eat-dog world, luv," Gus said. The brother I'd never had.

"You never should have owned that property in the first place," Dora said. "Who do you think worked for Leila all those years, helping with the place, before you breezed in to cash in on everything?"

"Leila would never have left La Llorona to you," I said. Leila, the wisest, most perceptive person I ever met. I hadn't seen through these two. But Leila would have.

A terrible smile came over the face of my former friend then. His mouth twisted into a grin.

"If it wasn't for you she'd have left us the hotel," Gus said. "Dora and me, and that old dame? We were like this." He held up two fingers of his remaining hand.

"Seems to me Leila had some issues with you a while back," I reminded him. "A piece of marble that didn't belong to you? Among other things."

"We had a little dustup," he said. "But it was nothing. A little mix-up about some bills, nothing more. I never had the least doubt that the old girl still had it in her plans to hand the hotel over to us when the time came.

"Then you got in good with her. When the wife and me heard the news that Leila left the place to you, you could have knocked me over with a feather. The place should've been ours from the get-go."

"We were just taking back what was our due," Dora said.

"Looking out for the family," Gus said. "The kids and all. You wouldn't know about that. Family.

"Speaking of which," he said. "We'd best get home to ours."

84

A monkey, unchained

Mirabel came to me after she'd finished changing the sheets for the new guests and hanging out the laundry. She wanted to know if I had time to talk.

I fixed us a cup of hibiscus tea and set out a plate of Maria's Mexican cookies. In all the years she'd worked for me, Mirabel had never before asked to sit down with me this way.

"I am so ashamed," she said. "I have done a terrible thing. I have ruined my life and the life of my family. I have committed a sin."

I didn't ask her to explain. She would tell me when she was ready.

"There's a baby," she said. Her hand went to her belly. "It will come sometime in the spring."

"Oh, Mirabel." I put my hand on hers. "Can you tell me the name of the father?"

She shook her head and looked down at her lap.

"Whoever he is, he needs to know. You may not want to be with this man, but he has a responsibility to help you."

She shook her head. "He's a bad person," she said. "I knew I should never go to his house but he offered me a lot of money. My father was sick. I needed to buy medicine. It's all my fault."

"It's not your fault," I told her. "But you could have asked me for help."

She shook her head. "I thought I'd take care of it myself.

"He hired me to cook dinner for him and his friends," she said. "I thought I'd be all right, because the others were there too. I thought that would keep me safe. Since there were three of them."

The Lizard Men.

"The tall one with the hat asked me to come to his house. I brought chicken and fresh herbs to cook the meal, but when I got there the three of them laughed. They didn't care about the food I made. There was liquor on the table. 'Have a drink of this', they said. But I didn't."

"They told me to dance for them. I said no. They said 'okay, show us how you throw a basketball. We used to see you out on the court with the other girls. You were the best.'"

"'I will cook the chicken for you,' I told them. 'All I need is a pan and a knife to chop the herbs.'"

"'We aren't hungry for chicken,' they said. 'We want something else.'"

"Can you believe this girl?" the fat one said. "She speaks good English."

"I bet you had an American boyfriend one time, am I right?" said the tall one. "I bet her American boyfriend taught her a whole lot of things."

"I have no boyfriend," Mirabel told the men. "Please don't touch me."

There was a very large television screen in this house, Mirabel told me. Women on the screen with no clothes covering them. One of the men put on a hat. Another man lit a cigar and handed it to her.

"I don't smoke," she told him.

They had a pet monkey with a collar—a real live monkey one of them had brought back from the coast. The monkey's collar was attached to a chain that was wrapped around a tree outside the house. It was a very short chain, so short the monkey couldn't sit down.

"Show us some of those fancy moves from the basketball court," one of them said.

"I don't have a ball."

"She needs a ball," another one said. The first one threw her an egg. She wasn't expecting this. It landed on the hard tile floor.

"Now you made a mess," said the man with the hat. "Clean it up."

She did.

Then there were more eggs. The men were all throwing eggs at her. She tried to catch a couple but most of them broke. There were eggs and egg shells all over the floor. She was down on her knees trying to mop it up but nobody gave her a towel, so she used her skirt. More eggs kept coming at her.

"Now your clothes are all dirty," the one said, with the cigar. "Look at her skirt," he told his friends. "She got eggs all over it."

"I always wondered how those skirts work that they wear," Hat Man said. "How they wrap them around their stomach, like it's toilet paper on the roll or some damn thing."

"I think the trick is the belt," the fat one said. "Once you untie her belt there's nothing holding her skirt up."

His hands were on her waist then, on the beaded belt she'd spent one whole year working on, with the calla lilies and the birds. Most of the girls chose a simpler design, but Mirabel had wanted hers to be the most beautiful and it was.

The beaded belt fell to the floor. He'd pulled so hard, he broke the threads. There were beads all over the floor. One of the men had the fabric of her skirt in his hand.

"Turn around," he said. "Pretend you're a ballerina. Keep turning."

With some girls, if they're a little chubby, the fabric of their skirt might only wind around two times. If they were pregnant, maybe just one. For Mirabel, the fabric of her skirt woven by her grandmother, wrapped three times around her waist. Standing there smoking his cigar as the others watched, Hat Man made her turn around three times before her body was uncovered. She stood there in her underpants as the fabric dropped to the floor.

"I can't say what happened after that," she told me. "I'm too ashamed."

"We're going to the police," I said. This was different from what had happened that day Bud and Victoria, fresh off the plane from Little Rock, had visited the stall of Andres, the so-called Mayan astrologer.

This time, the person who'd been messed with—*raped*—was a daughter of the village, a girl everyone had known since she was a baby. They'd sat behind her at church. They'd watched her on the basketball court. They remembered the year she'd been crowned *La Princessa de La Esperanza*, the year she was seven, when she'd danced on the stage in the center of the park while a band of local musicians played a tune on the marimba and guitar. Mirabel did, in fact, know how to dance. She just hadn't wanted to dance for the three old Americans that day.

"I am so ashamed," she said again, so softly I could barely hear.

"You did nothing wrong," I told her. It wouldn't matter how many times I or anyone else told her this. She would always believe she had committed a sin.

If Mirabel had a mother, this would have been a moment she was needed. But Mirabel's mother was dead.

She asked if I would come with her to speak to the police.

At the municipal building, the two of us sat on a wooden bench outside the office of the police chief. There was a man ahead of us who said his neighbor had poisoned his dog for barking in the night and a woman who told us her husband had sex with her sister, a man who said his neighbor had stolen a pound of beans.

After an hour of waiting we were let into the office of the chief. He sat in a straight wooden chair at a desk with a very old typewriter. There was a calendar on the wall, a picture of the Virgin Mary, and a single metal file cabinet. He pushed a paper in my direction and gave an identical form to Mirabel.

After we'd turned in the paperwork, the police chief asked Mirabel to tell him what happened. She started, but broke down part way through, so I finished the story. Each time I offered a piece of the story, the chief looked at Mirabel. Each time, she nodded.

"Do you know the names of these men?" he asked. "Never mind. I knew where to find them."

Slowly, we followed the officers down the path. I held tight to Mirabel's arm. Her whole body was shaking.

The three of them were sitting at their usual table, a couple of empty bottles beside them. The ashtray, as always, was filled with cigarette butts, the air thick with smoke from Vincente's cigar. It took the Lizard Men no more than a few seconds to register what was going on.

"Are these the ones?" the police chief asked Mirabel. She nodded.

Already, Carlos was shifting gears. He spoke in the voice and manner he must have adopted, years ago, back when he flew those jets, the voice of a pilot, letting his passengers know there might be a little turbulence coming up, but nothing to worry about.

"What's going here, officer?" he said. Airline pilot grin. "*Que pasa?*"

Within a minute, the three men were in handcuffs. In the absence of a vehicle to transport them, the police escorted the men up the path, on foot, back to the station as people of the village stood watching.

"You can take her home," the chief told me. "We'll need her to come back to testify later, but we know enough to lock them up for now."

By the time I got back to the hotel with Mirabel the whole town must have known what happened. Three gringo men in handcuffs walking down the street to the municipal building was not a sight to go unnoticed. By nightfall, a crowd had gathered outside the *muni*—a hundred people, at least, holding torches and chanting.

Send them out to us. We know what to do with these pigs.

If the lizard men had walked free then, the people of La Esperanza would have hung them from the ceiba tree.

The police held on to them. This was as much luck as the lizard men were going to find that night or ever again. First thing in the morning, they were transported by police van to the prison in the mountains to await their trial. As the criminal justice system worked in this country, that could take a long time, the outcome of the proceedings in little doubt.

This I learned the next morning, when Maria came to work and reported the news. Elmer's face, as he carried a load of cement down the step to repair a broken retaining wall, could have been that of a Mayan warrior, for all it betrayed of grief or horror. Stone.

The morning after we went to the police, Mirabel appeared at my house one more time.

"I have to leave my job," she said. "I'm going to stay with my grandmother across the lake at the foot of the volcano."

No need to explain why. Or to try and talk her out of this.

That night, a picture came to me of the monkey. The big fancy Italianate villa Carlos had built with his severance pay from the airline would be abandoned now. The pet monkey would be there still with that thick chain around his neck, attached to the tree.

I woke Elmer and told him to get the metal cutters. He knew where to find Carlos's house.

When I saw him in the morning, a rare smile crossed his face.

The monkey was free.

85

A death in California

That spring brought bad news and good.

The bad news came from Humboldt County, epicenter of the marijuana trade that supplied a substantial portion of income for the gringo residents of La Esperanza—old hippies who made the trip north every late September to trim weed and returned in early November, after the rains ended, with enough cash in their pockets to make it through the year, after a fashion.

Among those who had traveled north to California that fall, and every fall, since Alicia was two years old, was Raya. A week or two after she'd arrived at the farm to begin her stint of eighteen-hour days, picking seeds off the stems of marijuana plants (transported, as always, with a bag over her head, as was true for every trimmer in the group, to avoid her ever saying where she'd been, or how she'd gotten there) Raya had been overcome by a pain in her belly so severe she had to be carried off by two coworkers to the cot in the dormitory they'd set up for the workers on the marijuana ranch.

The doctor who'd examined her later that day found a tumor the size of a grapefruit in her stomach and more cancer all over her body. There was no possibility that Raya could make it back home to the lake to see Alicia one more time. She called, but the connection had been terrible, and Alicia hadn't understood very well what was going on except that Raya was on a bed somewhere, and it was hard to hear what she was saying—only that the word love was in there. Love, and more love. *You were the best part of my life.*

She died two days later. When news reached Patrizia, she said she'd take Alicia in. Wade would help out with money. And the truth was, for a while now, Alicia had been staying over at her house, out behind El Buffo, at least as often as she did in the tiny hut of Raya, surrounded by half-finished bikini tops and wool from unraveled sweaters.

Alicia was six years old, and already she'd lost two mothers—the one who gave birth to her, and the one who had been so reluctant to ever set her down that she carried Alicia around in a shawl from dawn to dusk. Now Alicia would live with Patrizia, who was not her mother either. But she had her twin brother.

After hearing the news, I stopped by Amalia's. She was sewing a dress—made, as always, from fabric salvaged from some flea market purchase, but this one looked more conservative than her usual wild creations.

"It's for Clarinda's graduation," she said. "She's receiving an award for the top student in science and mathematics."

Word had come that week. Clarinda had earned a full scholarship to the university in the city. She'd begin in the fall.

"What will you do without her?" I asked. Though, I might have asked the same thing of myself. Every weekday morning for nine years, the day had begun with Clarinda's stop at the top of my steps to pick up the brown paper sack containing the lunch Maria made her. Maria, or me. Sometimes I liked to put a chocolate in it, or a poem in Spanish—Lorca or Neruda, or—because it always seemed like a good idea to show her the work of an accomplished woman—Lucía Sánchez Saornil, Rosalía de Castro.

They say that the plants do not speak, nor the springs, nor the birds, nor the waves with their rumors, nor with their brightness the stars; they say it, but it is not true, because always when I pass they murmur and exclaim: There goes the crazy woman . . .

The day of Clarinda's graduation, the three of us made the trip together to San Luis on the boat. Clarinda had invited her mother to come too, and Veronica had said at one point that she would, but the morning of the graduation she was drunk again. You might have thought, after all those years, that Clarinda would have given up looking for the mother she never had, but she never abandoned hope that one day her mother might get up off the dirt, toss away the Quetzalteca, and tell her daughter she was proud of her. It was a feeling that never left her—a feeling I understood.

That winter also marked a surprising return of a hotel guest from long ago, one of my favorites. She arrived at the gate unannounced, without a reservation (no doubt remembering how things had been, last time she stayed at La Llorona, when the hotel was nearly empty, most of the time). This time she arrived with a son around six years old, and a second boy a couple of years younger. It took me a moment to recognize her. Jun Lan.

She still lived in the city of Shi Jia Zhuang with her physician husband, but she had given up her medical practice in favor of practicing traditional Chinese medicine. Over our dinner on the patio that night with her sons, Jun Lan told me that it had been that trip to the lake, long ago—those days she'd spent trudging up and down the mountain in search of the precious herb that might offer the gift of fertility—that had convinced her to abandon Western medicine and return to the study of the herbs her grandmother had first taught her about in the village of her childhood. People came from all over China now to consult with her. Her specialty, assisting women who had been unable to have a child. It was not easy, locating the plants. She grew them when she could but mostly she procured the dried leaves on the internet. They were very costly of course, but people desperate to have a child would pay anything.

"I'm so glad the herb worked for you," I told her. "And that you've been able to help so many others."

We sat quietly with our tea, taking in the sound of the water. The fireflies were out that night—their annual visitation. Jun Lan's boys ran through the garden trying to catch some in a jar.

"You have made this place so beautiful," she told me, as we dipped our spoons into Maria's orange soufflé. "But I remember this property as being larger. There used to be a garden at the far end, with a very special tree."

"You're not wrong," I said. "There was . . . a problem with the neighbors. But it's not important anymore."

The day after Jun Lan's arrival at the lake she set out on a hike with her two sons to show them the countryside. When she returned, she had a surprising piece of news to report.

"Someone's growing it here," she said. She spoke its name in Mandarin first. "The Baby-Giving herb," Jun Lan called it. That's what we'd named it when she'd found it on the mountain after her many days of searching, the herb that Maria had prepared for her in that special tea, day after day, until it had done its work.

"Someone is growing the herb on a farm—rows and rows of plants. Hundreds of them, all up and down the hillside. Right next to your hotel."

No need to say more. Dora had always been a talented gardener. And an even better businesswoman.

86
One good man

I had no time to ponder this development. That afternoon Elmer came to me to say there was another guest at the gate. For years it had been Walter who brought most of my guests to the hotel, but this one had found me on his own.

In all my days of running La Llorona, we'd welcomed many different kinds of travelers. Most tended to fit into one profile or another: romantic couples, spiritual searchers, students of Mayan culture, people dreaming of making a new life for themselves, those on the run from their old one. Tom Martinez seemed to fall into none of these categories.

He looked a few years older than I was at that point—early forties, probably. Dark complexion, jet-black hair. Though he was dressed in loose cotton pants, a Yankees T-shirt, sneakers, he gave the impression of someone not generally accustomed to casual attire. Not a tall man, he had the build of a wrestler—broad-shouldered, barrel chested. No one would call him heavy, but the word "burly" applied.

"I flew in yesterday from New York," he said. "I was hoping you had a vacancy."

After he'd settled into his room, we met on the patio for a drink. Though only two other guests were staying at La Llorona that day, they'd taken a day trip to a market town on the other side of the lake, so it was just the two of us for dinner that night.

"You probably wonder why someone would come here alone," he said, reaching for the beer Maria had set in front of him. "I'm guessing you cater more to couples here."

"Almost ten years ago, I came here by myself," I told him. "I understand."

"My work is pretty stressful," he said. "I had a lot of vacation days saved up. I needed to get away."

As a person who spoke almost nothing about her own history, I had made it my practice not to inquire much about people's lives back home. So I did not ask, as some might, what kind of work Tom did. But he had questions for me.

"You live on your own?" he asked. "What brought you here?"

In all my years of welcoming travelers to the hotel, I'd never said this much before, but something about this man inspired my trust. Maybe I was just getting tired of carrying around secrets.

"I had . . . a big loss," I told him. "Someone I loved. Two people actually."

"Parents?"

I shook my head. It had happened years before, I told him, in a tone meant to shut down further inquiry. "I never knew my father," I said. "My mother died when I was six."

Tom Martinez didn't offer words of sympathy, but his face, as I said this, conveyed kindness.

"I lost a parent young myself," he said. "My dad. More than thirty years ago but sometimes it still feels like yesterday."

I might have said I understood but I didn't.

Over the next few days, Tom and I spent a surprising amount of time together. This was different from occasions in the past when I'd suggested activities for guests, or—in my role as host—joined a group of travelers for dinner on the patio. For reasons I had a hard time understanding, myself, I felt a kind of attraction that I had not known since that day Lenny walked into the art gallery. I found myself looking forward to seeing him when he showed up for breakfast. I liked being around him. Nights we met up for dinner on the patio—which was every night now—I took particular care to look good.

He lived in Queens, not far from where I'd briefly made my home with my grandmother before we changed our names and everything else. He told me he worked in government. No point discussing the particulars. (Never married. He had a cat back home, currently in the care of his neighbors, and there was a group of guys from work with whom he played poker, Tuesday nights. He loved to read.)

On Tom's second day at the hotel he asked if I'd like to go hiking with him. He told me about spending his summers with his grandmother in Puerto Rico and a year he spent there after her death, building a house with his cousins. He wasn't what you'd call an expert carpenter, but he liked to work with his hands. The stone walls on my property fascinated him—the thought and care that had gone into the placement of every rock.

"I'd love to work alongside the men here and learn how they do it," he said. Of all the guests who'd ever spent time at La Llorona, no one else had ever expressed such a desire. "In my next life, I think I'll be a stonemason," he said. He talked about his two nieces, Carmen and Flora—his sister's children, back in New York. Every Sunday afternoon, back home, he took them to the Museum of Natural History. It was the great regret of his life, he said, that he had no children of his own.

"Losing my dad young the way I did, and knowing what it did to our family," he said, "I think I always carried this fear of not being there for my family. Maybe I figured it was better not to have anybody counting on me that much in the first place. Crazy, right?"

"When you've had a big loss, the idea of ever loving anybody again can feel terrifying," I told him. I'd never shared such an observation with anyone. Not even my own self.

It became our afternoon tradition, heading out on some trail or other—to the waterfall, to an old church in the next village over, to an overlook for a picnic of wine and cheese. Tom had a quiet, self-deprecating wit and a big, easy laugh. When children came up to us on the road, he talked with them in fluent Spanish. One time we found a puppy lying in a ditch, close to death from malnutrition. Tom carried her all the way back to the village in his arms, bought her medicine and food, stayed up all night to keep an eye on her progress. We named her Celia, after a singer he loved, Celia Cruz.

One day he asked me about my mother—how she died, if she'd been sick for a long time. "It was an accident," I told him. You might say I was telling the truth, as I'd known it for most of my life—some part of that truth, anyway.

He was an early riser. Even before I got out of bed I could hear the splash that indicated Tom had made his dive into the lake, just after sunrise. He was a strong swimmer, spending an hour in the water before returning to shore. He'd disappear into his room then, just long enough to shower and change into one of the three Cuban shirts he'd brought with him. I came to know his wardrobe, and a surprising number of other things about him, though he was also such a good listener that I found myself saying more than I ever had in the past.

We started having breakfast together every day. He liked cream in his coffee and lots of sugar. I liked the respectful way he spoke to Maria when she poured his refill. When Elmer was having trouble moving a boulder, Tom stepped in to lend a hand. Watching the two of them working side by side with the lever moving the enormous stone, I took note of how strong he was.

He spent a lot of time studying the property. If a new flower came into bloom on the perimeter of the patio, he noticed and bent to take in its scent. Sometimes I'd see him kneeling by a wall, studying the placement of the stones. He was a man who paid attention.

"You'd make a great detective," I told him once. "You don't miss a thing." When I said this, he'd looked briefly surprised. Then laughed.

After breakfast—during the hours I went over menus with Maria and met with Elmer and Luis to discuss building projects and repairs—Tom took a walk into town. When he returned, he'd stretch out in the hammock with a copy of *Love in the Time of Cholera* that looked so worn I figured this was not the first time he'd read it. I could see him from my desk, as I went over the accounts of the property, sorting through bills and placing orders. Sometimes, reaching a particular passage in the novel, he'd stop and look out to the water for a while. I wondered if he was thinking about the García Márquez character Florentino Ariza—a man who dedicates his whole life to the love of a woman. The most romantic character in a novel ever, perhaps.

You could probably say I was obsessed, in a way I could not remember since I was fourteen or fifteen, living with my grandmother after we moved to Poughkeepsie, and I'd discovered Leonard Cohen, and went to sleep every night with his first album on my cassette player at a volume so low it was almost as if his voice was whispering in my ear. And again years later when I met Lenny.

From her post in the kitchen, Maria noticed that I was taking an abnormal interest in the activities of my guest. "That one's a good man," she told me. "He has a kind face. I see how he looks at you. Like a man with an open heart."

"I've been thinking about climbing the volcano," Tom told me one morning at breakfast. "Would you recommend the experience?"

"It's likely to take a lot out of you," I told him. "But judging by your swimming, I'd guess you've got the lung power."

After I said this, I regretted it. Now he knew I watched him. Maybe I wanted him to know this.

The thought came to me: Did Tom study my activities as closely as I followed his? If so, he would have noted that, unlike him, I never swam. There had been that brief, exciting period in which Pablito had taken me into the water and taught me the breast stroke, but I hadn't been back in the lake since his death.

And of course, Tom had noticed this about me too, same as he seemed to notice everything.

"One day maybe we'll swim together," he said.

There seemed no point in explaining that I didn't swim in the lake, or anywhere else. "Who knows?" I told Tom, and left it at that.

87

I've waited a long time for this

Every winter, the gringo population of the village put on the annual Spiritual Awareness Festival, an event that typically drew younger travelers not only from other towns around the lake, but even well beyond. For many years I steered clear of the event. I could only take so much drumming and ecstatic dance. My friend Amalia shared my view, as a rule. But that year she had written and directed a presentation about nutrition featuring a song and dance by the children of the village, each of whom she'd dressed in a costume representing a fruit or vegetable. Harold had been tapped to play the role of a fat cat from the city, trying to banish the dancing vegetables and replace them with packaged goods, played by a band of older children—alumni of Amalia's projects from past years. A good fairy arrived on the scene just in the nick of time to save the fruits and vegetables and (somewhat off-topic) to deliver a speech about the miraculous properties of chia seeds. This role was played by Amalia, naturally.

Though Amalia had been unsuccessful in convincing me to play the chia fairy, I decided to put in an appearance at the festival—just long enough to catch her part of it. I knew a number of the children in the cast: Mateo and Alicia, in the role of a Fanta bottle and a Snickers bar, Clarinda's littlest brother in the role of a dancing papaya. Pablo, the son of Pablito, the harpoon fisherman, was Brussels sprouts. I was curious to see how Amalia would have pulled off that costume, though I had no doubt she'd have produced something extraordinary. In truth, I had been so distracted by Tom's presence at the hotel that I hadn't been to town since his arrival.

"I'd like to go with you," he told me. But he was expecting a call from back home.

"I won't be gone long," I told him.

The festival was held on the grounds of Andromeda's meditation center, with the main entertainment taking place in the space typically reserved as the yoga temple. When I arrived at the festival a concert was under way featuring an assortment of musicians—all but one of them English speakers singing in rudimentary Spanish, addressing issues of climate change and the environment.

One aspect of these gringo-generated events that had intrigued and touched me over the years was the willingness of the indigenous community to join in, at least so long as no expenditure of *garza* was required of them, which it generally wasn't. Whatever the people who'd been born here thought about the phenomenon of blindfolded Americans stumbling around their village with walking sticks for the purpose of reaching higher consciousness, or chocolate ceremonies led by some redheaded Californian, and volcano tours directed by a man from New Hampshire, they appeared to take all of it with good-natured grace and a certain earnest curiosity.

So long as our activities in no way threatened the women and children of the town—and nothing in our concerts and drumming circles, yoga classes, and crystal ceremonies appeared to endanger anyone—they welcomed us, and even found us mildly entertaining, probably. Not to mention the gringo population had become crucial to the economy of La Esperanza.

So the crowd that day was a mix, as usual, of tall, tanned Americans and Europeans, with a small but enthusiastic assemblage of locals who'd camped out to take in the show.

Up on stage when I arrived, Katerina—La Esperanza's Number One Local Protest singer—was singing an original composition about the dangers of chemical fertilizers. "When you put chemicals into the soil, you put tears in my eyes," came the words, as nearly as I could make them out over the scratchy sound system. A row of local women in their *traje* nodded encouragingly.

After Katerina finished her set another woman stepped onto the stage. She had that look Wade had described once, referring to Raya Sunshine—"rode hard and put up wet."

Her name was Dawn. She had recently arrived in town. You wouldn't think it to look at her, but when she'd gotten up to sing at an open mic the night before, Amalia told me, she'd blown everyone away.

There were no more than thirty or thirty-five people sitting on the grass at this point, most of whom seemed more interested in checking out the crystals for sale and the pot brownies making the rounds than they were in the music on the stage.

A little unsteadily—like a person who'd lost track of where she was or what she was doing there—Dawn stepped up to the microphone.

She had no guitar. It was just her up there on the yoga platform in an old green dress, her long gray hair falling well below her shoulders, her hands hanging at her sides. She was wearing bright yellow Keds that probably came from the used clothing market. She was very skinny. As she took the microphone, she cocked her head to one side, as if trying to pick up a voice from someone who wasn't actually there—a voice that resided only in her head, maybe.

Whatever else might be wrong with this woman, from the moment she started to sing she was transformed. She looked utterly at home up on that platform.

The song she had chosen was one I knew, though more than thirty years had passed since the last time I heard it.

This one didn't come from Joan Baez or Bob Dylan or Pete Seeger. It bore no resemblance to the anthems everyone used to join in on at all those marches and sit-ins we'd attended when I was too small to see over anyone's head, unless Daniel lifted me onto his shoulders. I knew all those songs, but this one was different. It wasn't about some political issue. The skinny gray-haired woman up on the stage didn't seem to care about getting people all fired up about doing anything in particular today. It was plain she just loved to sing, and her voice was magic.

I was probably the only person on the grass that day, and possibly the only one anywhere along the shores of this entire lake, who would have known that this song was written back in the 1930s by the Carter Family. Long ago in our tent, strumming her autoharp, my mother used to sing it to me. The song this woman had chosen was about going away, promising to return, but never making it back.

I'm going away to leave you, love
I'm going away for a while
But I'll return to you someday
If I go ten thousand miles.

Sitting there on the grass at the meditation center—the air filled with the smell of marijuana and burning sage and frying chicken—the memory came to me of a night in upstate New York or maybe Vermont, as Diana taught me the words to the refrain and the harmony part.

The storms are on the ocean,
The heavens may cease to be
This world may lose its motion, love
If I prove false to thee.

Her voice was as beautiful as ever. After all these years, still unmistakable.

When the song ended she stepped down off the platform. I didn't walk over to her right away. I watched her return to her seat on the blanket next to Katerina, who handed her a piece of food. From the looks of her, she didn't eat all that often.

On the stage now, a man I didn't recognize was giving a speech about the importance of spaying your pet. After him came a woman offering details about an upcoming festival at the Mushroom Academy, details of a workshop in aerial yoga, and another woman discussing the transformational benefits to be obtained from the use of kambo, a secretion from the Giant Monkey Frog found in the jungles of Mexico, applied to wounds created by burning one's skin and injecting the frog secretion.

Then Amalia stepped up to the microphone to talk about the importance of good nutrition in the form of natural food rather than processed food. Then she introduced the dancing vegetables. Normally I'd be moving closer to get a better view, but I couldn't move.

At some point, the gray-haired singer got up off the picnic blanket. I could see from how she raised herself off the ground that this was not easy for her. Arthritis, maybe. Or just age. She drifted toward the gate, a very well-used backpack over one shoulder.

I had no idea what I'd say when I caught up with her, but I started to run. What if I lost her again?

But there she was on the path, stopping to light a hand-rolled cigarette. Her fingers were very thin but something about them was also familiar.

"Are you my mother?" I asked her.

She whirled around to look at me. Something about her eyes, and the way her hands fluttered as she spoke—like one of those birds that sometimes flew into the kitchen at La Llorona when we'd leave the windows open, and couldn't find their way out—suggested pure, bone-deep terror.

"I've waited a long time for this day," she said.

88
Vinyl records

"I call myself Dawn now," she said. "But my real name is Diana."

She had met Charlie, the man who made the bomb, at a rest stop on the New York Thruway the day after saying goodbye to Daniel. She was putting oil in our VW Bug (something we had to do on a daily basis, which may have partly accounted for the willingness of that guy we met at the Dead show to give us the car).

The two of them got to talking. In the space it took to pour a couple of quarts of Pennzoil into the tank, Charlie had written in Magic Marker on Diana's hand the address of the house where he and his friends were going to be staying on the Upper East Side, and invited her to join him.

"You can bring the kid," he said. Meaning me.

The house belonged to the family of a girl named Chris whose father had made a whole lot of money in some kind of manufacturing business. He'd invented cardboard. Something like that.

Chris and Charlie met up at a festival and he told her he was looking for a place a group of his friends could crash to organize some kind of protest against the war. "My parents are in Europe," she'd told him. "The house is empty."

Jamal came from Oakland. He'd split with the Black Panthers over ideological differences concerning the use of violence versus civil disobedience. He was more into civil disobedience, but the first day he arrived in New York, a policeman had stopped him on the street and brought him into the station to be part of a lineup. Someone with an Afro had robbed a liquor store on Fourteenth Street, and

Jamal had the same kind of hair. That was all it took to bring a young Black man in for a lineup. Later that night, when he met Chris and Charlie at Washington Square Park and they told him they were planning an action to protest police brutality against antiwar activists, he said he was down.

Diana had never been into this kind of thing, herself. She'd grown up working out the chords of Joan Baez songs on the guitar—old English ballads, her favorites. A boy she went to high school with got drafted the year of the Tet offensive and came home without a leg and messed up in his head, which turned out to be worse than losing his leg.

There at the rest stop, Charlie had given my mother the address of the house on East Eighty-Fourth Street. The next day we showed up there. The furniture was fancy, but the floor was littered with pizza boxes, and there were cigarette butts all over the place. My mother had her record albums in the trunk, and she brought them in. Nobody was that interested in Joan Baez and Judy Collins, but they played Jefferson Airplane over and over, and Jimi Hendrix, *Are You Experienced?*, which had been Daniel's, that he forgot to take. Maybe he left it with Diana on purpose, to remember him by, though I think the person who remembered him best—remembered, and missed him—had been me.

We'd been at the house one or two days when Charlie came back with all the nails. Diana had thought they were for a carpentry project. This was when Charlie explained about the basement, the bombs.

The next day Diana brought me to my grandmother's. "I'll be back soon," she told me.

I'm going away to leave you now. I'm going away for a while.

"I don't want you to go," I told her. I'd only met my grandmother two times, ever, and both times she'd cut my bangs way too short. She smelled of Noxzema and watched TV all the time.

"I'll be back," my mother said.

If I go ten thousand miles.

There had been five people in the basement of the house on East Eighty-Fourth Street that afternoon. Charlie, Chris, Jamal, Carol, and Diana, my mother. Charlie was the one who supposedly knew how to build bombs. Carol had contributed the nails and explosives. Chris's contribution was the use of her parents' townhouse.

This part I knew. I'd gone over it a million times in my head. Watching our orange VW disappear down the street in Flushing, my grandmother fixing us Chef Boyardee, after. Me, asking the question, "When is she coming back?"

Now, at the back table in Harold's café where I sat with Dawn, too stunned to order my usual smoothie (I'd asked if she wanted anything; she didn't), I heard the rest of the story.

"Charlie was one of those people who acted like he knew a lot more than he really did," she said. "He had this set of plans someone drew for him, with drawings of where to attach the wires and how to insert the explosives. The part that actually flipped me out the worst was the nails.

"I asked him if they were meant to conduct electricity or something. I thought maybe they were meant to serve as weights. He just laughed."

The plan was to bring the bomb to an army recruiting center in Brooklyn. ("On a train, could you believe it?" she said. "They were planning to transport this thing on the L train.")

Then Charlie was going to walk in and act like he was enlisting in the Army. Carol had suggested it might be a good idea to cut his hair before doing this, since the way he was wearing it at the time didn't give the impression that he'd be the type to sign up for Vietnam. But Charlie had resisted this idea. No way was he going to cut his hair. It took him four years to get it this long.

Once he got into the place where the recruiters were he'd plant the bomb—but in a spot where the poor suckers who were signing up wouldn't be so likely to get hit. Diana never really understood how it was that Charlie actually thought his bomb might only injure or kill the army guys, and not the inductees, but he had seemed confident on this point.

As soon as he managed to place the bomb under the desk—concealed in an innocuous-looking brown paper bag—he'd be hightailing it, naturally. Jamal, just outside, would take care of the detonator.

"When this baby blows," he told Diana, "nails are going to be flying all over that death house. By the next morning, all those young guys across America who were planning on enlisting will be rethinking their plans."

"What about the ones that get drafted?" Diana had asked him. "Isn't that the main issue we're trying to address? The draft? And all the Black kids the government's calling up, because the rich ones buy their way out of it."

"You wouldn't understand," he told her, though Jamal had been on her side. "Trust me, Chris and I have spent hours working out the details of our strategy here. I was a poli-sci major."

It was at this point that my mother had made the decision to leave the house on East Eighty-Fourth Street. She was sufficiently upset about the plan that she thought long and hard, debating whether to go to the authorities to report what was going on at the house. What kept her from doing this was the sense she'd gotten that Charlie and the rest of them, with the possible exception of Jamal, were too inept to actually pull off a bombing. She figured they were probably just using the whole thing as an excuse to hang out at a fancy house and order a bunch of pizza on Chris's father's tab and get high.

The next morning she threw her clothes in her duffel bag, planning to return to Queens and pick me up. She was thinking Maine might be a good place to go. She'd look for a waitress job.

She was halfway down the block when she remembered her records were back at the house—the precious vinyl LPs. She did a U-turn. (This was possible in a VW Bug.)

She had just stepped in the door, headed for the living room, where they'd set up the turntable, when the explosion hit. Suddenly, there was no floor under her feet anymore, and the ceiling was coming down. From the kitchen, she saw Carol, covered in blood, with a nail in her hand and another one in her chest. The force of the explosion must have propelled it hard and deep. When Diana had run toward her she saw the nail was embedded clear to the head, and there were more nails too, in her face.

There was no point going to the basement to see what had happened to Charlie. There was no basement anymore. No Charlie.

Jamal raced past her. There was blood all over him too, but from what Diana could tell, no nails. Carol was worse. There was blood pouring out of her side. She was holding on to one of Chris's parents' velvet pillows, but this, too, was filling with blood.

Diana herself was untouched, except for where a piece of broken window had scraped her arm.

"I did something very odd then," she told me. "I could say I was in shock, and maybe that was it. I could see Carol was dead, and I knew Charlie must be too, and I knew the others would be making a run for it, though it didn't seem likely they'd get very far."

She had walked over to the turntable, still spinning from whatever album had been playing before. Neil Young, she thought.

She lifted the record from the turntable and slipped it into its sleeve. She bent to pick up the others in her box and stuffed them into her duffel bag.

Fitting them in had required her to dump out everything else, but she'd done it. You might think this had been some elaborate strategy to confuse the police and the FBI, who would be crawling all over the place in a matter of minutes. (Already, she could hear the sirens.)

But it wasn't that. It wasn't even the realization that her passport and drivers' license would be useless to her now, and for the rest of her life.

She just wanted those records. The one remnant of her old life.

There was another, of course. Me. Off in Flushing with my grandmother—Diana's mother, with whom she'd never gotten along.

Nobody took any notice when she'd walked out the back door through the small garden Carol's mother had cultivated with rosebushes—the only part of the property seemingly undisturbed.

Diana walked down the street carrying the duffel. Two blocks down was a post office where, a few months later, the photographs of her onetime collaborators, Jamal and Chris, would be posted on the wall, as they would be for years to come, among the FBI's "Ten Most Wanted." Her name would never appear on that wall, for the simple reason that—having left her clothes, and her passport, and her license, not to mention the orange VW back on East Eighty-Fourth Street—everyone thought she was dead.

Carol's body had been easily identified. But in the case of Charlie, there was nothing left of him. The investigators must have imagined the same was true of Diana. Pulverized. Later, they'd turned up the tip of a woman's finger lying in the street. Everyone figured it was hers.

At the post office, she bought a box. She placed the record albums she'd loved inside the box. On the outside of the box she wrote my name along with her mother's address in Queens.

Recounting her story, my mother (Diana? Dawn?) conveyed a kind of lucidity I would not have expected, from the look of her. The moment we were having now was one she'd been playing out in her head for a few decades.

"I figured if they thought to check it out, it would look like I just wanted my daughter to have my albums before I did this crazy thing that was probably going to kill me. If some detective had been really smart, maybe he or she would have noticed the time stamp on the box was a good forty-five minutes after the blast. But nobody ever seemed to follow up on that. They were all so sure I was dead, I guess there didn't seem to be a point."

The next part I did remember. The arrival of the box. Because my grandmother didn't own a record player, it was years before I got to play any of the albums my mother had mailed to me that day—my sole inheritance. But I memorized all the covers. The first Joni Mitchell album, with a drawing by Joni on the cover, of a woman in profile with wild hair flowing down her back, and in the distance behind her, the sun setting over a lake or an ocean, and birds taking flight, and a boat. James Taylor in his blue work shirt, Donovan, Steeleye Span, Joan Baez of course—every single album, though my favorite, because I knew this was my mother's favorite, was Volume 2, the one where she sang "Barbara Allen."

So many record albums. She had *Yesterday and Today* featuring the original bloody baby album cover. When she'd taken it out to show it to me (I would have been five), she'd explained to me that someday this copy of the record would be worth a lot of money, on account of how the record company had pasted a different, less shocking picture over the original one. She'd steamed the album, to peel off the newer, pasted-on cover, but when she did this, she'd made one mistake: She left the vinyl album in the cover when she did so, which had warped it badly, rendering the record unplayable. She'd kept it anyway, for the record jacket.

I'd never forgotten her telling me that. When you have only a few years' worth of stories, every single one becomes precious.

Only now it turned out the story of my mother and me didn't end there after all. All these years later, here she was sitting across from me at a little coffee-wood table at Harold's café, telling me a day hadn't gone by she hadn't thought of me.

But she hadn't gone looking for me.

"At first I was just terrified," she said. "Also ashamed. I knew if I came to get you they'd arrest me, and I wouldn't get to be with you anyway. I didn't want you growing up, having to visit your mother in prison."

At least I would have known she was alive. I would have had a mother.

"Time passed. It didn't get easier to go back. Just the opposite."

She had created a new name. No Social Security number, no history. She flew under the radar, picking up jobs that didn't require background information. She cleaned houses and later cleaned up trash by the side of a highway in Oregon for a couple of years. She picked apples and strawberries on a farm.

The family with the farm had a severely disabled son. The two of them got along. The family hired my mother to care for him—a job she stayed with for almost fifteen years, until the heart of the boy, Ricky, started giving out. When he died—going on five years now— she went back out on the road.

A couple of years back her travels had taken her to Humboldt County, where she worked on a pot farm trimming marijuana buds. They worked you hard in those places—sixteen, eighteen hours a day, bent over long tables of weed, separating the seeds from the leaves and stems—but the money was good, especially for someone like Dawn with no work papers.

"They bring you there in the back of a truck with a bag over your head so you can't tell anyone where the place is or find it again, after," she said. "Kind of like hauling cattle to the slaughterhouse, except the cattle was us. They put the trimmers up in this big dormitory thing. Metal army surplus Quonset hut, hot as the dickens. You're living in a tin can, basically."

Most of the pickers were young people, she told me, but there were always a few old-timers like herself. They tended to stick together.

"All those hours of handling pot leaves, it makes your head a little funny," she told me. "Not stoned like you'd be from smoking the stuff. More like you aren't all there. Which for me was not so much of a problem."

One of the things Dawn had learned over her many years of living on the run, she told me, was to avoid making friends. Not close ones, anyway. (*Oh yes*, I could have said. *I know all about that*.) If you got too close to a person, you'd feel like telling them your story, and in Dawn's case, this wasn't a good idea. The good thing about all those years she spent taking care of the boy, Ricky, was that he couldn't ask her any questions. She never had to lie to him.

Like me, with Walter, I thought.

But at the pot farm she'd met this woman around her age who came north from Central America for four weeks every October to work on the pot farm. In one month of trimming weed she'd earn enough to live on the rest of the year in the village she'd settled in. She told Dawn she'd adopted a little girl that she left with relatives.

Dawn never asked the details. All she knew was this: Raya was nuts about that child. From the day she arrived on the farm, all she could talk about was getting home to the little girl she considered her daughter, Alicia. No doubt this story hit home with Dawn.

For three years they'd trimmed side by side, Dawn and Raya. Dawn let Raya do most of the talking. Somewhere along the line in all those hours the two of them spent at the trimming table, Raya had mentioned this woman she knew who ran a hotel in the village where she lived.

"It's funny," she told Dawn. "Irene's the spitting image of you." Not the spitting image of Dawn, as she was now. But what she must have looked like, twenty years earlier.

"Even though your name was different, I knew it was you," Dawn told me. "I used to have these dreams about you where you were living next to a lake. When Raya told me how you made pictures all the time with colored pencils, it was like she was telling me something I already knew. Even when you were little, you made the most beautiful colored pencil drawings."

That was the October Raya had doubled over in pain in the middle of the trimming day. Dawn was there when the doctor gave her the news about the stomach cancer. She was sitting next to Raya's bed when she died.

After, she knew what she'd do. For all these years she'd been too afraid to track me down, but now she'd lost two people who mattered to her—the only two, when you got down to it. Maybe it was knowing Raya and hearing about her life with Alicia that opened something up in Dawn. Whatever the cause, something had changed in her.

Dawn and Raya were around the same age, and one thing about gray-haired women in their sixties who've lost a few teeth and weigh around ninety-five pounds—they don't look all that different from each other. When Dawn presented Raya's passport at the border—she, a woman whose face would once have been plastered on Post Office walls across the country, if the FBI had known she was alive—the border agent hadn't given her a second look.

Six days later (it was a long bus ride, as I well knew, and another bus, and then the boat) she'd landed on the dock in La Esperanza.

Dawn was planning to do two things when she got to the village: First she'd go see Alicia and give her a letter Raya had written for her before she died, along with her earnings from the eleven days of trimming she'd managed to complete before she went to the hospital—all her money in the world—and a silver peace sign necklace that was about the only possession Dawn had found in Raya's duffel bag worth passing on, unless you counted her crochet hook.

It had not been difficult for Dawn to find the child. More difficult was explaining to a seven-year-old how it was she'd come to be there. It had not escaped Dawn's mind that she too had left a daughter motherless. Facing Alicia as she had done, the day before—placing the necklace in Alicia's hand—had made her think as she had never allowed herself before of how it must have been for me, long ago, hearing the same news about her.

"Your mother is dead."

The other important part of Dawn's reason for coming to La Esperanza was seeing me. This would be more difficult. She would not have any problem tracking me down, of course, but she had to get up her courage first. That's what she was doing that day at the Spiritual Awareness Festival when Katerina, who'd heard her sing the night before, had called her up onto the stage. She had not been nervous about singing. That always came naturally. The hard part was this.

"You want to know something funny?" she said. "Kathy and I were at Berkeley the same years."

There was a long silence then. When she reached out to touch my hand I felt the roughness of hers. She'd had a hard life.

"You have children?" she asked me. "I was hoping I might find out I was a grandmother."

No such luck, I told her. I kept the rest to myself.

89

I want to know about your life

So after all those years of believing my mother to be dead, I had her back. I wasn't even looking for her. Then there she was. I should have been happy but it wasn't that simple.

I thought about my son Arlo. (When was this not the case?) I tried to imagine a situation in which I would ever have disappeared from his life as my mother had disappeared from mine. As much as she'd explained her reasons, I couldn't get beyond the core truth that she'd abandoned me. Now here she was, showing up thirty-two years later, wanting to be a part of my life again.

Where had she been all those years up until now? She could have known my husband, my son, could have said goodbye to my grand-mother—the woman who raised me as well as raising her and spent ten years, from the day the bomb went off to the moment of her death, quietly grieving the loss of her daughter.

"I want to get to know you," she told me. "I hope it's not too late."

"I want to know about your life," she said. In her days with Raya up in Humboldt County, she'd heard about La Llorona. "I want you to show me your hotel," she said. Mostly she just wanted to see me.

I told her I'd invite her over—my voice sounding strangely stiff and cool, even to myself. "I just need a little time," I said. "This was a shock."

Her face seemed to fall in on itself as I said the words. You could see she'd been a beautiful woman once, but she looked like a person whose life had not gone well. She was playing with her napkin. Her hands were trembling. Her nails were bitten past the quick.

"I get it," she told me.

In the meantime, she'd found a job waiting tables at Harold's bar. "You know where to find me," she said.

I told her I'd be in touch.

90

The most beautiful voice

For years now, I'd dedicated a part of every afternoon to drawing—the one aspect of my day that never altered. Sometimes I'd focus on a particular plant or flower, sometimes a bird, though these were more challenging because they were constantly in motion. It was, for me, a kind of meditation, and especially when a wave of grief came over me about my husband and son—as happened, still—or when I was overcome by stress or anxiety, as I had been after learning the news about Gus and Dora's appropriation of my land. At times like these, taking out my water-colors and painting was the one thing most likely to bring me back to a peaceful state of mind. More recently, I'd found solace in my painting as I worked my way through my feelings about rediscovering my mother.

My mother. It had been hard to connect the woman I'd met at the Festival of Consciousness just days before with the beautiful young woman with hair down to her waist singing old folk ballads to me in our tent. Now there was this real person—a skinny, gray-haired, Keds-wearing stranger smoking hand-rolled cigarettes. The story she'd told me about what had happened all those years ago—the one that explained why she hadn't died that day after all—was a harder one to reconcile than the story of her death had been.

It's one thing to know your mother died in a tragic accident. (That she'd been misguided. Stupid even. But young.) It was a lot harder to understand how she could have carried on with her life, after—picking up beer cans along the side of a highway for two cents apiece, caring for somebody else's child during the very years when I most longed for her. Not once in all those years had she gone looking for me.

Who she was to me, now—this woman who called herself Dawn—was a sad reminder of everything I'd lost as a child, everything I'd done without. I knew she was still staying in town. Amalia had reported this. She'd rented a bunk at the hostel (a bunk, not a room) and put money down for a month in advance—the kind of thing a person does, I'd observed, when she's worried that if she doesn't come up with rent money now, she might not have it later.

I told myself I should be happy that Dawn was alive. But now that she'd reappeared in my life, a new kind of feeling had emerged, concerning my mother. Anger. At odd moments of the day, I'd find myself returning to the story she'd told me when we met up at the festival. I'd talk to her in my head.

Where did you go, after you left the post office that day? When you'd see a seven-year-old girl on the street—or a ten-year-old, a sixteen-year-old—did you think about me?

I thought about you every single day, I'd tell her. *First all day long, then only a few dozen times. Later, it was mostly when something bad happened, or something terrible, the kind of moment a person wants her mother. Prime example: That day in San Francisco when the ambulance came for my husband and son.*

I wanted you then.

I think of you when I look at the stars, I would tell her. *Because we used to do that, all those nights, camping out.*

I think of you when I hear certain kinds of music. Whatever else might be true, you always had the most beautiful voice.

Days passed, and I didn't invite Diana (or Dawn?) to La Llorona as I'd said I would. All I had to do to see her was pay a visit to Harold's bar, but I stayed away. I didn't know what I wanted to say to her, if anything. As much as I had missed her all those years, now that she'd returned, I wanted her gone. Or thought I did anyway. It was easier to think about the man with whom I was sharing breakfast and dinner on the patio every night. No words had been spoken between us suggesting that what we had was anything more than a friendship. But a different kind of feeling that had been growing in me, toward Tom—one I had not experienced for many years.

Though he had no idea she was living just down the road, in the village, the two of us did talk about my mother. As a person who'd also lost a parent young, Tom said, he wanted to know how I'd learned to deal with the experience. "I wonder where you and your mother would have ended up if she hadn't died," he said. "Were there any other relatives? Someone besides your grandmother?"

No.

For a moment I thought he might put his arms around me. I could see him wanting to. But he didn't.

91

The Gabriel García Márquez version

Two more weeks went by. I still hadn't reached out to Dawn with an invitation to get together at the hotel. Partly this had to do with my conflicted feelings toward her. But more and more, I was also distracted. Tom remained at the hotel, staying in Monkey Room. It began to occur to me that I might be falling in love with him.

In all that time, our routine—his, and mine—hardly changed. First he'd swim, followed by breakfast, a walk into the village, reading in the hammock, a late-afternoon walk with me.

Somewhere along the line I started telling Tom more about myself, things I'd never told anyone over all these years, with the exception of Walter, whom I could confide in because he wouldn't understand.

Tom would. "My mother left with me with my grandmother. We heard about her death on television.

"I used to be married," I said. "My husband and son were killed in a car accident."

He didn't put his arms around me then either, but he reached for my hand. "I don't know what to say," he told me.

"There was a time when I wanted to kill myself." I told him that.

His face, when I said this, had a look of sorrow but no judgment. I didn't say more. He never pushed me to do so.

I was clearing off the table on the patio, blowing out the candles from the evening I'd spent talking with Tom. Suddenly there was a flickering in the darkness over the water. The fireflies were back.

Tom had been halfway up the steps to bed when the fireflies came out. In all that time, I'd never said anything more than goodnight to him when he headed to his room. Not that I hadn't thought about it.

That night I had called him back.

"You might want to see this," I said. "It's one of my favorite nights of the year," I told him.

"Hold on," he said. "I think we need a glass of good rum. I happen to have some in my room."

He returned a minute later with the bottle and two glasses. Except for the glittering of the fireflies over the lake the night was still. Tiny sparkles surrounded us.

"You know what would happen now if this were a book by a great writer of romantic fiction?" he said.

I didn't know what to say so I took a sip of the rum.

"The hero would put his arms around the woman and look into her eyes. The stars would hang directly over the couple's heads. Which is pretty much the case at the moment. Or would be if you moved a few inches closer."

"I could do that."

He touched my hair. Earlier in the evening—preparing for our nightly dinner together—I'd pinned it up, but most of the bobby pins had come out by this point.

"I've been wondering if it would be all right to put my arms around you," he said. Then he did.

"What would happen next in the novel?" I asked him.

"You really never read García Márquez?" he said.

"The man would place his hand on the woman's cheek. He might say something like 'I've wanted to do this for a long time.' Then he'd kiss her."

At this point the conversation stopped. The fireflies probably stayed out for a while, as did the stars no doubt, but our attention was no longer focused on the sky.

92
A night in the Monkey Room

In all my years of running the hotel, I'd never spent a night in the Monkey Room. I had never experienced the sensation of lying naked on those six-hundred-thread-count sheets. Now I sat on the bed as Tom lit the candles and faced me in the moonlight. He displayed a surprising modesty as he unbuttoned his shirt.

He had a nice body. A real one, not the body of a man who spent his days at the gym. He had the body of a man who spent a few hours every day reading. Solid, but real.

"It's been a long time since I did this," I told him. "I think I gave up believing in love."

"We can discuss that later," he said. "And we will. At the moment I'd prefer not to talk."

The same intensity of focus I'd seen in him, reading *Love in the Time of Cholera*—and on all those evenings sitting alone on the dock, studying the lake or the volcano, or a particular bird or flower—was evident now in how he studied my body, and how he touched me. Much later (I had no sense of time, but the doves had begun their song, which meant the sun would be coming up soon), we fell asleep. I considered for a moment how it would be if Maria, letting herself into the kitchen to begin the preparations for breakfast, noticed my sandals on the kitchen floor, or the shawl I'd been wearing that night, draped over a chair. Many times over the years, she'd told me that she prayed for me to find love. That night I believed that I had.

Sometime a little after sunrise—with Tom asleep beside me, his arm around my naked body—I got up from the bed, slipped my dress over my head, and made my way down the hallway to my own bedroom.

When I showed up on the patio, later than my usual seven o'clock, Tom was already back from his swim and in his spot, sipping his coffee. Maria was pouring the orange juice. She eyed me knowingly. I detected a smile.

"I want you to know," I said. "I will consider what happened last night as this one amazing thing. It's not something I'm expecting to . . . replicate."

"Sort of like the annual arrival of the fireflies?" he said. "Once a year? And once they go, everyone gets back to hoeing the corn or gathering the firewood or whatever they do? In your case, applying yourself to those lovely watercolors of yours."

"I wouldn't want you to think I had . . . expectations."

He would go back to New York, to his job, whatever it was. I'd go back to being a thirty-nine-year-old woman who ran a hotel.

"Maybe I want to have expectations," he said.

"We have totally different lives. We don't know each other. We just had this—"

Tom finished my sentence. "—perfect night."

He reached for my hand. "I know more than you think, actually," he told me. "This place is sort of like the museum of you. I know you're someone who considers every plant in this garden, and what music to put on as Maria lays out dinner, and places an edible flower in my salad every night. I know you're someone who shares my belief that there's no such thing as too many candles. I know you're a person who had a carving of a monkey placed in the headboard of my bed even though the pillows cover it up."

"That wasn't me," I told him. "It was the woman who built this place, Leila."

"You know what I think?" he said. "You are a woman who grew up without a home. Your artwork has been creating one."

In the end, we did not pretend we were anything other than crazy about each other. If Maria and Luis and Elmer had a problem with that, it was their problem, not ours. From that day on, Tom and I were barely out of each other's sight. Sometimes we spent the night in the Monkey Room, and sometimes in mine, but always in each other's arms.

I gather that some people, meeting and falling in love at the stage in their lives when we did, feel a need to fill each other in on everything that happened before, as if they were picking up a book a few hundred pages in.

With Tom I never felt the impulse to explain everything that had happened. He knew I'd lost my mother when I was six. (The part about having discovered, just three weeks earlier, that she was still alive, I kept to myself.) He knew there'd been an accident, and that my husband and child had died, and that I chose not to speak of it. None of the rest felt significant—my grandmother, art school, my medical illustrations, the parrot on my windowsill, the image that had haunted me all those years, of my mother's fingertip. Only I knew now that the fingertip they'd found in the street that day had not belonged to my mother after all. Gus, Dora, the way my so-called friends had swindled me out of half my land. . . . At another moment in time, these were the things that would have occupied me. Now all I could think of was this good man, our days together, our nights.

After Lenny, I had never believed I could feel again, about another person, the way I felt now about Tom—the happiness I experienced waking up with him every morning, the ease with which we talked, and equally, the ease with which we were able to spend time in each other's company without saying a word. When the two of us took off our clothes and climbed into whichever bed we'd chosen that night, the world went away. That bed was the world.

We were sitting on the dock together one night, as we often did now. My head rested on Tom's shoulder. His strong arms encircled me. At that moment it felt as though nothing bad could ever happen again.

"There's something I should tell you," I said. "I've never been able to tell you the truth about who I am. What happened to me. You deserve that."

"You could tell me anything," he said. "It wouldn't change how I feel about you."

"When you love a person, you shouldn't keep a secret from them," I said. "I did that once, with my husband. I've always regretted it."

"There's more I could tell you too," Tom said. "Something . . . difficult."

"It's about my mother. How she died. I never told you the whole story," I said.

He did an odd thing then. He shook his head, almost as if he were afraid of hearing what I had to tell him. Or maybe this was it—afraid that if I told him, it might change something between us. That maybe later I'd wish I hadn't. Maybe he was aware that if I shared a painful secret, he'd have to do the same. He didn't want to risk losing me.

"Why don't we hold off on the difficult things," he said. "It doesn't matter what happened before. Tonight I just want to think about where we are right now."

So I didn't tell him—about starting out my life as Joan, or about my mother's boyfriends, the orange Volkswagen, the house on East Eighty-Fourth Street, and what came after. I couldn't get my grandmother's voice out of my head. *Never tell our secret. Take it to the grave.*

After that night I kept waiting for a good moment to talk about it, but the moment didn't come. I forgot all about the other part of what happened on the dock that night—Tom telling me he had a secret to share too.

We were just so happy, I think. Things were perfect as they were. If only nothing ever changed.

93
One piece of paper

Amalia came by the hotel. "I was over at Harold's," she said. "Dawn wanted me to give you this."

She handed me a piece of paper, folded up.

"I don't blame you for feeling I let you down," she had written, her handwriting a barely legible scrawl. "But I want so much to talk with you. Even if it's just one time."

I sent a note back to Dawn, in care of Amalia. "Come to the hotel tomorrow afternoon."

94

A wallet goes missing

The next morning at breakfast Tom looked troubled.

"I don't want you to worry about this," he said. "But my wallet's disappeared."

One time, years before, when my possessions had shown up missing, it had turned out to be Elmer who'd taken them. Now I called him to my office. Since Mirabel's refusal of his proposal of marriage, followed by her departure some months before this, to wait out her pregnancy at the home of her grandmother, Elmer had been a shell of his former self.

"Our guest, Tom, is missing his wallet," I said. "I don't believe you did this. But I need to ask if you have any idea what might have happened."

Elmer looked terrified. "I swear on my mother's life I didn't do anything," he said. "But I'm going to find the person who took it."

Two hours later he came to me, accompanied by Walter, the child I had cared for above all others in the village, now age sixteen. The look on his face reminded me of Elmer, the day I'd confronted him about a similar theft. He wasn't crying but he looked as though he wanted the earth to swallow him up.

"I took the wallet of the American man," he said. His voice was a whisper.

"You were out walking with him," he said. "I came to the hotel with some coconuts for Maria and the beans she wanted me to get for her from the market. The door of Monkey Room was open. I saw the wallet on the dresser. All I could think about was the money.

"I'm so sorry," he said.

"You broke my trust," I told him. "It's not the first time that has happened. But I also know that making a very bad choice does not make you a bad person."

Tom's wallet sat on the table. Walter was trembling. "You have been like my mother," he said. Only we both knew, he didn't have one. He didn't cry but he looked as though he might.

"And you have been like a son to me," I said. I told him I was terribly disappointed, but I also knew he would never do such a thing again.

"You need to apologize to my guest," I told him.

I reached for Tom's wallet. I opened it, only to see that the money was there, as it was of course. This was when I saw what else was contained in that wallet.

The badge of a New York City police officer.

Where do I begin describing the levels of betrayal that hit me in that moment? What Walter had done in stealing Tom's wallet now seemed like the least of these. The real shock—the devastation—was what the discovery of the policeman's badge revealed to me about Tom.

For the first time ever, I'd trusted a man with the truth of my story, when all the time he'd just been fishing for information. I'd loved him and I believed he loved me. Now it appeared that everything he'd been doing all these weeks was motivated by the single goal of gathering evidence about the bombing. He'd been looking for me all this time. But not the way a woman wants a man to be looking for her. The way a police officer looks for a person to solve his case.

All this time, I'd believed in Tom's interest in me. Now it was clear, all he ever cared about was locating my mother.

The memory of my art teacher's visit from the man asking questions about my mother and me, back in San Francisco, came back to me now, and the magazine show I'd watched with Lenny about breakthroughs in tracking criminals through DNA. The realization sickened me: The man I'd trusted with my heart had never loved me. He was just doing his job.

Tom must know my mother hadn't died that day. He'd tracked me down (through my art teacher, Marcy? My birth father, Ray? Lenny's parents, to whom I'd written that letter? A travel writer's review of the hotel that mentioned me?) in the hopes that I might help him locate Diana. What he did not know (at least, I prayed he did not know this) was that she had recently arrived in this very place. At this very moment, while he lay outside in the garden reading his book (that part was probably a sham too; had he ever read *Love in the Time of Cholera?*), the woman Tom had been searching for all these years was probably on her way over to see me. And as much as that sad old woman had failed me, what I felt now was a desperate need to protect her from the man who—only minutes before—I thought I loved.

I ripped a piece of paper from the pad on my desk and scribbled a note, then handed it to Walter.

"We'll talk about what you did with the wallet later," I told him. "Right now you need to do something for me.

"You know that gray-haired woman who works at Harold's bar? Bring her this. Right away."

Once Diana/Dawn read what I'd written, she would not be coming over to La Llorona. She'd be on the next boat out of town. Odds were I'd never see her again. Later—after the truth about Tom sank in—I'd register the sadness in the fact that after finally rediscovering my mother, I'd lost her again. This time forever, probably. But as much anger as I'd felt for how she'd left me the first time, I didn't think an old and broken woman deserved to be hauled back to the United States to be put on trial for events that had taken place more than half her lifetime before.

Walter understood none of this of course. But he did not question my request. He was already sprinting up the steps to the road as I called out to him. *Run fast.*

Now I watched as the man I had loved up until moments before headed into the house, unaware of what had just taken place with the return of his stolen wallet. Both of us having abandoned the pretense of being anything other than who we had been over those days—a pair of lovers who were crazy about each other—he slipped his arm over my shoulder. Uncharacteristically for him, he'd chosen to dive back into the lake after his reading session in the hammock. His hair was wet. He wore a thick terry cloth bathrobe I'd given him. For a moment, I felt the familiar warmth that always came over me at the sight of him, the yearning for his touch as he bent to kiss me.

Even if I hadn't turned my cheek away, he would have registered the change in my demeanor toward him. "What happened?" he said.

Whatever bad news I'd just received, Tom would not have imagined it had to do with him.

"Elmer got your wallet back." I pointed to the place on the table where I'd set it after seeing what it contained, other than money.

It took him only a moment to realize. "The badge," he said. "I need to tell you about it."

"Don't."

"It's not what you think. I'm not who you think."

"You're right about that part. I thought you were a man who'd fallen in love with me. I thought you were a man I loved. Not a law enforcement officer come to spy on me."

"I do love you," he said. "That's real. It's a long story."

"Spare me."

"Whatever it was I thought I was doing when I came here, that's not how it ended up."

"Here's how it ends up," I told him. "It ends up that you pack your bags and get out of here. I never want to see your face again."

"I don't blame you for being angry," he said. "I can explain."

"No explanation needed. You lied to me."

"There's something you don't know."

"Nothing you tell me now could make any difference."

"I never loved a woman the way I love you."

Just go.

Ten minutes later he stood outside the door with his suitcase. He looked at me and headed toward the steps to the road, then turned around one more time.

"You're not wrong that I came here to find out what happened to your mother," he said. "But after I met you everything changed."

It was that fingertip that started him on his quest, he told me. The one they'd believed to be that of my mother, Diana Landers. When the FBI tested the DNA of that fingertip—when such tests came into existence—it turned out to match that of someone else who'd been on the street that day of the explosion—a completely different missing person who had nothing to do with the group in the house that day, except that she'd been unlucky enough to be walking down East Eighty-Fourth Street that day.

"I was obsessed with tracking down the woman who'd gotten away," Tom said. "I had a reason for needing to find out where she was. But once I saw you—once I knew you—everything changed. It wasn't about finding Diana Landers anymore and bringing her to justice. The only person who matters to me now is you."

I could hear his words, but I'd turned my back. I headed into the house, where Maria was washing dishes. She said nothing but her face displayed her sorrow.

Walter must have reached Diana in time. She never showed up—not that night, or the next day. When I made it into town later that afternoon, Amalia told me she was gone. Who knows, she might have taken the same boat out as Tom. Ironically, though she was the one he'd been looking for all the time, he wouldn't have recognized her.

I did what I'd always done then. I got on with my life.

I gave my workers the day off. I wanted to be alone. I stripped the sheets off Tom's bed and washed them. I hung them on the line to dry.

Tom had left his copy of *Love in the Time of Cholera*, a book I'd never gotten around to reading. I picked it up.

It was still morning when I started reading—in my chair by the lake where, just a day before, I'd sat with Tom. I was still there as the sun set, turning the pages slowly. Sometimes a passage in the book would so move me I had to stop and read it out loud three times over. When I reached a line that spoke to me most acutely, I underlined it.

"*It was the time,*" García Márquez had written, "*when they loved each other best, without hurry or excess, when both were most conscious of and grateful for their incredible victories over adversity. Life would still present them with other mortal trials, of course, but that no longer mattered: they were on the other shore.*"

The other shore. With Tom, I'd thought I had reached it.

"*Think of love as a state of grace,*" García Márquez wrote. "*Not as a means to anything, but an end in itself.*"

A state of grace. For a few weeks there, it seemed we had inhabited one.

"*She felt the abyss of disenchantment.*"

Oh yes, I knew about the abyss.

After the last light was gone, I moved into the house. It was after midnight when I finished the novel.

I set the book next to my bed and went downstairs. I had left the sheets on the line, and now, in the darkness, I took them down, folded and smoothed them and placed them in the very back of the linen closet.

Done.

A few weeks after Tom's departure from La Llorona, a letter arrived with a New York City return address. Knowing how long it took mail to travel here, I guessed Tom must have written it on the plane.

I placed it in the bottom drawer of Leila's desk. Three days later, another letter, and the next week another. On the outside of the next

envelope that arrived were the words: *GIVE ME A CHANCE.*
PLEASE READ THIS.

The letters kept coming. I opened none of them.

95

The dream of America

Walter came to see me.

"I'm leaving," he said. "I came to say goodbye."

He was going to America. Meaning North America. He was heading out the next day.

My heart caught in my throat. As much as he'd disappointed me by taking the wallet, I loved this boy—a young man now, not so many years older than my son would be. He felt to me like a member of my family. He'd let me down, but even family members did that sometimes. (My mother certainly had. So did my grandmother. Even Lenny, in a way. He'd let me down by dying.)

"Is this because you took the wallet?" I asked him. "Because I can forgive you for that. I already have."

He shook his head. "I can't forgive myself. I need to become a better man," he said. "There's nothing for me here."

Walter didn't have papers of course. He had nobody waiting on the other side to help him if he made it over the border. He'd been saving his money for this since he was ten, but the recent stretch in which he'd been unable to find employment had left him with no more than a few hundred *garza* for food along the way.

For Walter, no doubt, the decision to go north had been prompted by his disgrace. But the choice of a young person in the village to seek out opportunities in the United States was not an unfamiliar story. For as long as I'd made my home here, I'd watched hopeful young men setting out with the same dream. Nobody had the money to pay, up front, the fees of the man who promised to get them over the border—the going price to hire a *coyote*: eight thousand dollars. What they did was to sign a promissory note to pay the fee back, with high interest, from the wages they imagined they'd be earning once they made it across.

Some succeeded. Many did not. I knew of at least a half a dozen boys from the village who'd died trying, locked in the back of a panel truck with twenty others or drowned in the Rio Grande. Or they'd died of heat stroke trying to make it over the desert. At least half had been rounded up and sent home. Either way, they carried the debt to the *coyote*. No money-back guarantees.

The danger of the trip never seemed to discourage them. Neither did the fact that almost none of them spoke English, or had any family in whatever place it was—Arizona, Texas, California—where they hoped to find the work that would make it possible for them to pay back their debt, send money home, and someday—far in the future— return home themselves, with enough to buy a piece of land, build a house, provide a good life for their children.

I should have anticipated that Walter might be drawn to making the trip north. Walter, a boy who'd been greeting American guests at the hotel since before I got there and observing up close, as he did, the wealth and privilege of their lives, so different from his own. Here was the boy who, at age seven, had inquired of me whether, in my travels around America, I'd ever run into Spider-Man.

I tried to give him money, but he wouldn't take it. All he wanted was my blessing. It was difficult giving him this, knowing what I did of what lay ahead for him. In the past, when some young man in the village had spoken to me about the idea of making the trip north, I'd tried to discourage him, or at least to paint a more accurate picture. People in my country would pay them the lowest wages they could get away with, I said—many dollars less than what an American with papers might receive. It would be hard, finding work without a vehicle, or tools, or a command of the language.

And then there was this, the hardest part of the story, or at least the one most difficult to convey to one who'd spent his entire life in this one small village. "You are used to having your family and friends all around. Your culture. Your language, the beauty of the natural world all around you," I told the boys—whatever boy it was, that month, dreaming of California. "Imagine a life without a lake, without birds singing every morning, without a volcano?"

Here in La Esperanza, they knew everyone. When somebody got sick, the women of the village all showed up with food. If a hurricane took your house, your neighbors showed up with their shovels and helped rebuild it.

Imagine a life so far from your family you only got to talk with them on your cell phone every Sunday.

"I used to see men from places like this lined up outside Home Depot on Sunday mornings, looking for work," I said. "And standing alongside the highway. For every job, there were fifty men waiting."

"I don't mind working hard," Walter told me. "I want to work. That's the problem here. No work."

I wished I had a phone number to give him, of someone to call when he made it over the border. But it had been so long now since I'd lived in the country of my birth, I didn't know anyone there anymore. The irony did not escape me that the place Walter wanted so desperately to get to was one I had so desperately needed to leave.

"I'll be back someday," he told me. "One day, I will be the one getting off the boat and walking out onto the dock with my suitcase."

After he left, I sat on the stone steps. I had told myself, long ago, on those hikes Walter and I used to take together, when he served as my guide and protector (never mind that he was seven years old at the time) that I would not let myself love another child ever again. I was not going to love this boy. But I had.

96

Five million dollars

Hank and Martha Purcell checked into La Llorona that afternoon, having flown in from Connecticut with a surprising amount of luggage, considering they'd only planned a two-night stay. At first I was baffled at what they were doing at a place like mine. They had the look of people accustomed to staying in four-star establishments run by some big hotel chain—the kind of people who might have appreciated the vision that man, Carl Edgar, had presented to Leila when he attempted to buy the hotel out from under her years before. We weren't even halfway down the steps before Martha had started asking if there was an easier way to get to the hotel. An outdoor elevator, maybe? A funicular?

"Are there spiders?" she said.

"Definitely," I told her. "But only nice ones."

This was a business trip, it turned out. Hank was an executive with a large pharmaceutical company in Connecticut that invested in developing new drugs for the marketplace and underwriting the testing necessary to gain FDA approval. As unlikely as it might seem, he had come to check out the possibility of acquiring a small farming operation he'd heard about here in La Esperanza.

At this point, Martha shushed him, or started to. "Isn't it a little early to be talking about this, honey?" she said. "You know how gossip spreads."

"I'm not worried," he told her. "We've already sewed up the option to acquire 100 percent ownership of the operation. For a tidy figure, I might add. I'm just down here to tie up the loose ends before the current stockholders sign off on things."

Current stockholders. I was trying to imagine who, in the village, fit the description of a stockholder.

"We've been getting reports about this herbal product being marketed on the internet to address infertility issues," he told me. "Right now, they're a two-bit operation, but if this herb tests out, the growth potential could be through the roof.

"I'll be meeting with this couple tomorrow," he said. "If all goes well, Martha and I will be back in Darien by Friday with a signed contract for the rights to sell a multimillion-dollar natural herb that could offer millions of women struggling with infertility the opportunity to become mothers. We're calling it YouBeMama."

No big mystery who the couple was Hank referred to. *The stockholders.* They would not have far to travel for their business meeting, I told him.

"They live next door." I pointed to the red light, illuminated day and night. "On the other side of the wall."

97

End of the world. Almost

I ask myself now whether my memories of the next morning are real or whether I constructed them, after, in light of what happened that day, and my need to preserve everything I could of how it all was, or used to be. Before.

It had started out a beautiful morning, but of course nearly all of them were. The birds. The lake. The smell of the fresh-brewed coffee Maria set before my place on the patio, the vase of roses on the table. Roses I'd bought in my San Francisco days almost never had a scent, but the ones I grew in my garden at La Llorona always did. As I sat there drinking my coffee, I remembered how it had felt when Tom came in from his morning swim. When he did, he'd put his arms around me.

"I should dry off first."

"No need."

The couple from Connecticut had not yet arisen. I was grateful I could have my breakfast alone, without having to endure more of Martha's complaints.

A wind came up. The birds were restless. I remember that part—the doves, first, clucking much more loudly than normal, and the way a whole flock of swallows had appeared, easily five times as many as on a normal day, not landing on their usual tree, but circling the lake as if they couldn't decide what to do next. Had the insects always buzzed this way? Had the black-billed cuckoo always shrieked in the high-pitched fashion he did now?

Out on the lake, the fishermen sat in their cayuco boats as always, barely moving, waiting for a sign that a crab or two might have made his way into their nets. From one of the rental houses nearby, someone was playing the accordion, and from another, I could make out the sound of drumming.

Suddenly, from the village, came the sound of an explosion, but there seemed nothing so unusual about this. The men of La Esperanza loved fireworks. Only this sounded louder than any I remembered, ever.

Then came more. Not a single explosion this time, but a low rumbling, growing louder by the minute. The memory of the hurricane and the landslide that followed was not so distant that I'd forgotten the sound of those boulders tumbling down the hillside toward the hotel—like a plane coming in for a landing, I'd thought at the time, though I'd known of course that this was impossible. But the sound that enveloped me now was even louder.

Now I could see the fishermen looking up from their nets. Maria ran from the kitchen holding her Bible, then Luis, then Elmer, who had grabbed his machete, as men here tended to do, first thing, whenever a sign of danger appeared.

They were looking in the direction of the volcano. And for a moment you might have thought nothing was different from how it had been for the last few hundred years—the steep sides, grooved by hundreds of years' worth of rains and erosion, the place where the trees thinned out—the spot Sam Holloway had once abandoned his bride, Harriet, on their honeymoon, leaving her without hat or sunscreen so he could see the crater at the top, as he'd always dreamed. The place their marriage had ended. The place where I spent the night once with Jerome Sapirstein.

For as long as I'd lived here—as many thousands of times as I'd taken in the sight of El Fuego—the crater had been nothing but a dark and empty bowl. I had watched the sun disappear behind the volcano a few thousand times over my ten years living at the lake. I'd seen it illuminated in the darkness, as if by a giant strobe, when lightning filled the sky in rainy season. Sometimes, too, it had been covered in so much mist the top of the volcano was obscured completely.

Now it was plainly visible. But utterly transformed. The volcano glowed bright orange. Smoke was pouring out from the top.

The fishermen were forming a circle with their boats, speaking to each other over the growing rumble from across the water.

"*Está en erupción*," Maria cried out. *It's erupting.* She dropped to her knees.

Years earlier, when the hurricane hit, Luis had raced out into the night to protect the property—and Elmer, to find the woman he loved. This time, Luis just stood there and crossed himself.

Not Elmer. Elmer already had his backpack on his shoulders. "I have to go," he said, racing to the door.

One word only on his lips. "*Mirabel.*"

For five months now, none of us had laid eyes on her, but we knew where she was: staying with her grandmother while she awaited the birth of her baby. She was living in shame at the foot of the volcano.

Elmer disappeared out the door. Maria and Luis and I stood outside on the patio looking out to the volcano. Our eyes stayed locked on the glowing lava making its way down the sides of the massive peak. The rumbling grew even louder, if that was possible, as if the earth itself was breaking apart. The smoke was thicker now, though not so thick as to obscure the orange flames shooting up from the crater. A few thousand years of mounting pressure from deep in the core of the volcano was suddenly releasing itself.

For all the years I'd lived in this village, there had remained one image, above all others, that everyone carried with them. Ask a local child to make a picture and it would invariably feature the same thing, a tall green triangle, rising up over a vast blue lake. It was always a benign image, friendly even—a comforting constant, like the framed photograph of the Pope on the wall of every villager who was not an Evangelical or the beatific smile of the Virgin Mary.

Now the old familiar form seemed to be rising up out of the water like a sea serpent lurching furiously toward us.

The volcano wasn't going anywhere, of course. Only the lava was. As we stood, immobile, we watched streams of it pouring from the crater. At first just a single glowing river, then more. From every direction, molten lava was making its way down the sides of the volcano.

If I had imagined this scene, which I never had, I might have supposed the lava would move slowly, creeping down the sides of the volcano—oozing, like some weird excretion of a rare poisonous jungle frog. But this lava was pouring out fast—a great, burning mass of liquid minerals and gases racing down the mountainside faster than a man could run, or even a car possibly—making its way to the base of the volcano and beyond to the place where the houses of the people in my village stood, and the farms, the church, the school.

Directly in its path: the home of Mirabel's grandmother.

At some point, the couple from Connecticut arrived on the patio. Martha had heard the explosion of course. "I don't know how the people here stand living in such a noisy place," she said.

One look at the three of us—Maria, Luis, and me—and she stopped talking.

"Oh my God," she said. "I knew we should never have come here."

I never climbed the hundred steps between the hotel and the road that led to town faster than I did that day. No point bringing anything with me. No passport, no keys, no cell phone.

Outside on the dirt road that led to town I watched the people of the village as they ran past. Women in their *traje*, babies wrapped in their shawls and older children clutching their skirts. Men calling out to each other. "It's coming this way!"

Hardly anybody in La Esperanza owned a car. There were a few trucks, now loaded with as many people as you could fit in the back of a pickup, and another twenty more. A man missing a leg. A woman known to be crazy. The old people. The mayor.

In among the fleeing villagers came the travelers—the young women in their crochet tops and trailing skirts, the young men in their yoga pants. Barefoot, in many cases. Stoned, in a few. Someone carried a drum. Someone carried a dog and three newborn puppies. One woman—a local—was pulling a pig on a rope, but when he wouldn't budge, at the urging of her children, she abandoned the pig.

There were *tuk tuks* and a couple of bicycles, and some gringos (Alejandro, Roberto, Wade) on motorcycles. An elderly French woman on her pink Vespa. Andromeda, in her white robes. Just behind her I spotted Amalia, her wild hair flying even more wildly than normal, her gypsy dress swirling around her, a tribe of three and four-year-olds who must have misplaced their parents following behind. Overhead, I spotted the single-engine plane belonging to Federico, the shaman of cacao. He must have just taken off from the hangar at the edge of the soccer field.

The smoky air stung my eyes and made it hard to see, but I could make out the river of lava moving relentlessly toward us. At certain points, the lava flow seemed to switch course for no apparent reason and pour over someone's cornfield or tienda, obliterating them when it did. Those who dared to look back in the direction of the village could see whole houses crushed by the flowing lava. I heard someone call out over the crowd that the basketball court was gone, the school, buried, though by the time the lava hit there, the teachers had managed to get all the children out.

I did not run. Maybe it was the fact that Maria and Luis remained motionless at the top of the steps—watching but going nowhere—that left me unable to join the growing mob of fleeing villagers. It seemed to me as if the ground under my feet was moving, but maybe it was only that with all the people racing past, dirt and small rocks were flying everywhere now.

"Elmer," Maria was calling out to the friends who passed. "Have you seen my son?"

I spotted Alicia, the child raised for her first six years of life by Raya, with her twin brother Mateo at her side. Clarinda's mother, Veronica—her daughter off at university, thank God—looked dazed as she stumbled alongside her children, who led the way, bottle of Quetzalteca in her hands. Harold from the café was carrying his precious Italian espresso machine.

I watched them all as they ran past, shouting and crying. Beside me, Maria still searched the fleeing mob for the sight of her son.

Then there he was, so covered in ash he looked like a ghost. He moved more slowly than the others, but for good reason. He was carrying someone in his arms. Mirabel. One arm hung limp at her side, her long black braid swinging.

"We need to bring her down to the house," he said. "There's a lot of blood. She can't go any farther."

What was I thinking, as I made my way back down the steps to the hotel, even as everyone around us fled the village? What possessed me to stay put?

I know why, of course. At that point, it didn't seem to matter whether it might be a lava flow that took me or a tsunami off the lake or smoke inhalation or crashing boulders—or a minivan rounding a San Francisco street corner too fast, racing home to catch a ballgame.

I just wanted to be there at La Llorona with people I loved around me. If the world was ending, let it end there.

To my surprise the picture that came to me at that moment was of Tom—his kind face, the safety I'd felt when he put his arms around me. In spite of everything, I wished he was there.

The volcano was still pouring out smoke and lava as the five of us—Maria, Luis and me, Elmer, with Mirabel in his arms—made our way back down the stone steps to the hotel. After taking in the scene at the road—the exodus of virtually the entire population of La Esperanza, fleeing for their lives—the hotel felt strangely tranquil. We laid Mirabel out on a bed. Only then did I remember.

"Where's the baby?" I asked.

"When I got to her grandmother's, the house was gone," Elmer said. "The old woman's body was in the yard. A tree must have crushed her when the lava flowed through."

One look at Mirabel's grandmother and Elmer had known she was past rescuing. At first he thought Mirabel must be dead too.

He found her lying under the *pila*, not making any sense, but breathing. She'd crawled there to protect herself from the falling cement, the falling roof, the flowing lava, the smoke and ash. All this had happened before Elmer reached her, he said. At the point he had found her, Mirabel's whole body was covered in ashes. Ashes and blood.

She had given birth there.

At the point when Elmer arrived, Mirabel could talk only in a whisper. She was probably delirious at this point. She had spent the last twenty-four hours in labor, attended only by her grandmother, and then, after the tree fell down, alone.

Elmer had carried her up the steep hillside to the road then. It was a good two miles from there to the village and another half mile to the hotel. Only one explanation existed for how he'd accomplished this. Love.

The four of us gathered around Mirabel's bed in the Quetzal room. Her voice was barely audible.

"I thought I was dying," she said. "All I could think was that I didn't want my baby to be buried there with me, under the *pila*."

Her grandfather's cayuco had been sitting by the edge of the water. "It looked so peaceful there," she whispered. "Everything else was on fire."

She had managed to crawl down to the water somehow with her son—less than an hour old—in her arms. She had kissed him one last time, then placed him in the boat and set it loose from its moorings. Maybe she hoped one of the fishermen out on the lake would see him and bring him safely to shore. She lay there—dying, she believed—as she watched the boat float away, out to the middle of the only place that wasn't on fire. The lake.

Elmer found her there. Alive after all, but with her baby gone, as I knew well, she wanted to be dead.

It seemed impossible that any trace might remain of Mirabel's grandfather's cayuco with its lone precious passenger. But something compelled me to walk out onto the dock. I looked out onto the water.

The fishermen had disappeared. So had the birds. No lanchas in sight, naturally. Tourists in their kayaks long gone.

At first it appeared that the lake was deserted. Then I spotted something—a lone wooden boat, drifting a few hundred feet from shore. No passenger visible.

For as long as I could remember, I'd been afraid of the water. The picture of my mother's stoned boyfriend throwing my three-year-old self into a motel pool remained alive in my memory. I never forgot the sound of his laughter, or my relief when I felt Diana's hands around me, pulling me up from the bottom.

Later, at another motel pool, a kinder man—Daniel—had fastened inflatable rubber floats on my arms and told me he'd stay beside me in the water. But even then, terror held me in its grip. I remembered the time with Lenny in Calistoga. Just the two of us, with all the time in the world. "Let go," he said. "I won't let anything happen to you." Even with Lenny, I never could trust that was so.

Now here I stood at the edge of a vast lake in the middle of a volcanic eruption, looking out to the once-turquoise water at a single bobbing wooden boat containing a baby a few hours old. The only times I'd ever entered the lake and swum there the harpoon fisherman had remained at my side. We'd never swum out far.

I thought about Lenny, flinging his body into the street that day to save our son. The picture came to me of Tom—his strong, steady stroke as he made his way back to the dock every morning to have his coffee with me.

I dove in.

I made my way out into the lake—nothing but water in all directions, a hundred square kilometers of lake. My body took over. My legs kicked hard. I was doing the crawl stroke that Pablito had taught me.

"*Soy un pez*"—the words Clarinda used to say to remind herself how strong she was. *I am a fish.*

I kept swimming, my stroke surprisingly strong. Off in the distance, the volcano was still spewing smoke and fire, lava pouring down its sides. I had almost reached the bobbing cayuco.

What if the boat was empty? What if the baby had fallen out, or if the whole story had been part of Mirabel's delirium—the part about placing her newborn son in the cayuco boat, pushing it out from the reeds along the shore. What if Mirabel had imagined the whole thing, and somewhere, back at the home of her dead grandmother, a newborn baby boy lay trapped under the remains of a tiny cinderblock hut, or washed away in a river of molten lava?

Reaching the cayuco at last, I had just enough strength remaining to pull myself up on its wooden side and peer into the spot where, in easier times, Mirabel's grandfather had paddled across the water in search of crabs.

Inside lay what looked like a small package, not much bigger than a loaf of bread, wrapped in a piece of fabric. But it was moving. As tightly as his mother had wrapped him in the fabric, a small hand reached out from the bundle. A tuft of black hair.

I pulled myself up into the little boat, taking care not to tip it. There was no paddle so I had to use my hands to bring us back to shore.

They were all waiting for me as I stepped out on the dock holding the baby. Maria. Luis. Elmer. Mirabel.

She wanted to call him Elmer, after the man who'd saved her life, but Elmer had shaken his head. They named him Moses.

98

Saved by a wall

Maria said it was the hand of God at work that day that had saved the baby. It was God, she said, who had brought Elmer safely to where Mirabel lay, bleeding, and God who brought the two of them back to La Llorona. She had no doubt it had been the hands of God that carried me across the water to the place where the baby lay, whom she would come to call her *nieto*, her grandchild. It no longer mattered who had fathered him. It would be Elmer—Elmer and Mirabel—who raised him.

God had spared La Llorona, even as so many of the houses and tiendas in the village had been destroyed in the eruption.

The river of lava and ash had bypassed the hotel. My gardens—the half still occupied by me after the other half was appropriated by my former friends—remained untouched. This was particularly remarkable considering what had taken place on the piece of land directly adjoining mine—my former garden, turned herb farm, and the cinder block home of Gus and Dora. By the time the lava flow had finished its work there was nothing left of the herbs they'd cultivated. Judging from what I observed on their piece of land, after, the lava had flowed over just about everything on the property. It was that wall they'd built—the wall whose construction I so mourned—that had spared my gardens and my hotel.

The day after the eruption, news reached my hotel guests, the Purcells—huddling in their room, consuming the last of Martha Purcell's Xanax—that the pharmaceutical company for which Hank Purcell served as CEO had abandoned its plan to pursue the acquisition of rights to the miraculous fertility herb that had been cultivated next door. The value of Gus and Dora's enterprise had just gone from five million dollars to zero. As soon as the road opened again, Hank and Martha beat a hasty retreat back to Connecticut, never to be heard from again.

Not long after this, Gus and Dora and their children moved to someplace in Uruguay where, according to Harold, they launched a pyramid scheme involving the sale of paintball franchises. Eventually— the statute of limitations for his former crimes having expired—they moved back to Gus's home town of Blackburn, where Dora set up a small yoga practice while Gus tended bar.

99
Unopened letters

One of the many good things about life in a village like La Esperanza —a place where most people have very little in the way of material possessions or wealth—is that they get very good at surviving on little, or even less. People here were resilient, and unafraid of hard work. They were unlikely ever to ask "Why me?" or to reflect on the unfairness of life. Whatever happened was all God's will. What mattered was that you'd end up in heaven when it was over.

Though the months that followed the eruption of El Fuego proved harsh, the people of the village helped each other to rebuild. Andromeda held a fundraiser. The designer from New York City who'd made it to the pages of *Vogue* with her huipil-inspired line of fashions sent a check. A donation arrived from Rick and Claudia, the couple who'd created the first-ever girls' basketball team in La Esperanza, and an even larger donation from Jun Lan and her husband, who'd seen a report of the eruption on television in China.

With Amalia in charge of the reconstruction effort, dozens of structures were created by the one-year anniversary of the disaster. By the time the children of the village had collected enough plastic bottles and trash to fill the fifty thousand eco-blocks needed to complete the project, a visitor to the town would have been hard-pressed to locate, anywhere within its borders, a single discarded chips packet or empty Fanta bottle, or any other piece of trash for that matter. The president of the country herself came to town to present a medal to Amalia and her team of exceedingly young workers in recognition of their outstanding service to their fellow citizens and to the planet. For the ceremony to welcome the president, the children chose to wear their vegetable costumes—carrot, cauliflower, eggplant, broccoli—and serenaded her with their song about the importance of good nutrition.

A year after the volcanic eruption, a letter arrived from Clarinda letting us know she'd been accepted at medical school. With her mother dead from alcohol poisoning and her siblings scattered, she had no particular need to return to the village, though she wrote that one day she'd come back and start a clinic.

More letters arrived from the New York address. I continued to place them in the bottom drawer, unopened. I could not bring myself to read his words. I must have known the effect they'd have on me. I didn't trust myself not to open my heart again. The cost was too great.

Eventually the letters tapered down to once a year, always around the date of the fireflies' annual return to the lake. Sometime around five years after the day I'd sent Tom away, I realized six months had gone by without the arrival of a new letter from him. Then a year passed without word from him, then two.

It seemed clear to me that whatever Tom Martinez might have offered by way of professions to his undying love, all that was over now. He'd moved on but I couldn't help it. I still thought about him.

Sometimes I thought about my mother too. When I looked back on the brief time we'd spent together that day after I heard her sing, the old bitterness and anger that welled up in me then had melted away. What came to me now was the memory of how thin she'd looked, how unwell. I could still see her hands as she tried to roll her cigarette, the trembling of her fingers, and hear the pure, clear sound of her voice as she sang.

100

One more letter

I was forty-six years old. Sixteen years had passed since that day I first showed up at La Llorona. If my son were alive, he'd be past high school now. Past college even, heading out into the world.

By now the internet had entered our lives. Now people could read about La Llorona on websites featuring unique, romantic vacation destinations. We had a five-star rating. "The most magical hotel I've ever visited," one woman wrote, who turned out to be a travel blogger with a few hundred thousand followers. All four rooms were booked months in advance. Though the suggestion had often been made that I expand, I had no interest in making the place bigger. I liked my life as it was: Coffee on the patio, a walk into town, my afternoons in the garden painting flowers and birds.

I swam a mile every morning now. All fear gone.

On the hillside where the jocote tree stood, that had been Leila's once, and then mine, and then the property of my former friends, Gus and Dora—the layer of volcanic ash that had destroyed their crop of the magic fertility herb (YouBeMama) had dissipated, leaving the soil richer than ever.

Given the reputation they'd made for themselves for a variety of scams, it seemed unlikely that Gus and Dora would return to the village. People still talked now and then about what happened to the faux-Mayan astrologer, Andres. It had not escaped notice that the last time anyone laid eyes on Andres, he had been in the company of Gus, heading up the mountain to that exceedingly deep and treacherous ravine.

An idea came to me one day, while swimming. I paid a visit to the law-yer in the village who'd represented Gus and Dora back when they'd laid claim to my property. I asked him to reach out to his clients in England.

The sum of money I offered to buy the land back from them was enough that Gus and Dora agreed to it. I in turn signed the deed over to a group of young indigenous families. These were the younger genera-tion in the village whose parents and grandparents had been persuaded to sell off their own land to gringos. At the time the land had been sold to the gringos, the fee the local people had been paid seemed like a for-tune, but twenty years later, the children of the original landowners had been left with no space to raise crops. That piece of hillside provided, for them, a place to grow what they needed to feed their families. Now corn grew on the hillside again, and beans, and broccoli. The new generation built an irrigation system and a garden where they cultivated flowers to sell in the market. The presence of flowers brought many birds.

Sometimes now, working in my own garden on the other side of the wall, I could hear the voices of the farmers pumping water from the lake, hoeing up weeds, laughing and calling out to their children as they played among the rows. Now and then one of them stopped over with a basket of jocotes for me from my old tree.

Mirabel and Elmer's son Moses was seven years old by this point, a star player on the football team at his school in the village. He and his parents and little sister, Estrella, had moved into the casita in back of the hotel with Maria and Luis. We'd added on a couple of rooms for them. Mirabel still whipped up her amazing nonalcoholic concoctions of fruits and herbs and fresh coconut milk. "If you could just bottle this," my guests always told her, "you'd make a fortune." When they said this she just smiled.

I kept waiting to hear from Walter—that he'd made it to California or some other warm place where he'd managed to find work. No word came. He'd bought into the dream of paradise in America—McDonald's and Disneyland, but no volcano, and no volcanic eruptions. Who was I to say what was better—to be a poor man in a place of great natural richness and beauty, or a man with money in the bank who has lost his home?

Walter would be in his mid-twenties now, younger by only a few years from how old I'd been when I first stepped off the boat—the day he'd announced he'd take care of me. Even now, every time I saw a lancha boat pull up to the dock, on days I came into town to shop, I'd study the most recent assortment of travelers to town—the girls with their bare feet and dreadlocks, the young men with their drums and guitars, the ones with gray hair who probably remembered their own young days. They came, they meditated, they went, and now and then a few of them fell in love with the dream of the simple, magical life they might build here on the proceeds from the sale of crystals or macramé tops or kombucha or on a budget dictated by a modest Social Security check. It was a familiar story by now.

In among the faces of the new arrivals, I kept looking for Walter's. Every time the buzzer rang and I climbed to the top of my property to open the door, a scrap of hope remained that the person on the other side of the gate would be him.

More than ten years after Tom's departure from La Esperanza—and my mother's, and the volcanic eruption that followed—another letter arrived. The New York return address was familiar. This time I ripped the envelope open.

"A day hasn't passed since the last time we saw each other that I haven't thought about you," he'd written. "I know I betrayed your trust. I deserve your anger. There's not a reason in the world you should forgive me for deceiving you as I did. Though it is you who taught me about forgiveness, believe it or not. It was meeting you, and falling in love with you, that allowed me to lay down the bitterness that had poisoned my life all those years until then."

I was sitting on the patio as I read the letter—the place Tom and I used to have our coffee every morning during that brief happy time before I'd learned the secret contained in his wallet.

"I hesitated a long time before writing this, for fear of opening an old wound," he wrote. "I would do nothing to hurt you further. But for reasons I'm about to explain, I decided to reach out to you one last time. You've made it plain by your silence up until now that you don't want to hear from me. I'm writing now with no expectation of a response.

"You will remember, I think, that on the day we met, you told me that you'd lost your mother when you were very young. I knew this about you already, but I concealed it from you. I told you nothing more than that I had lost my father when I was young, too.

"In those letters I sent to you over the years, I wrote of how I longed to see you again. I wanted to tell you face-to-face what it was that drove me to track you down as I did. I needed to explain to you the root of my obsession with locating your mother. Before my other obsession took hold. My love for you.

"Since I no longer expect to see you ever again, I want to tell you here, in this letter, the rest of my story that I should have explained the day we met."

Here it was. Until now, I could not have taken the words in, but I was ready at last.

"Perhaps you will remember this name," he wrote. "Jose Aurelio Martinez—the police officer who lost his life on the day of the explosion at that house in New York City where that group of young people were making bombs. Officer Martinez was not on duty that day. He was heading home from work. He had plans to go to Yankee stadium that night to bring his ten-year-old son to a ballgame. That boy was me. Tomas."

Officer Martinez had been one of the first men of Puerto Rican descent to be recruited for the NYPD. Born in San Jose, he'd come to America in 1963, inspired, in part, by watching *West Side Story*.

"Except for Rita Moreno, there was hardly a single actor of Puerto Rican descent in the movie," Tom wrote. "But even though the story was a hard one, my father fell in love with the dream of coming to New York. He had this belief that if there were more people on the police force who looked like him, maybe there would be less gang violence. He graduated in the top of his class at the police academy.

"I know just where I was when my dad's partner showed up at our door to tell my mother my dad had been killed," Tom wrote. "I had my Yankee jacket on and my glove sitting on the kitchen table. I was hoping to catch a fly ball that night. My mother was cooking dinner. After we got the news nobody remembered to turn off the stove. I can still smell the *tostones* burning."

His mother never got over the death of her husband. None of them did—though like me he had been cared for by his grandmother.

Eventually, Tom had enrolled in the police academy himself, to honor his father, but he had never been a street cop. "I work in homicide," he said.

"You may remember that long ago you told me I'd make a good detective," he wrote. "Well, I am one."

All his life Tom had held on to bitterness over the crime that robbed him of his father, but for a long time there seemed nothing more to be done about it. The perpetrators had been killed. It appeared that the ones who fled the scene had all been captured and prosecuted.

Then came a breakthrough in the field of DNA as a tool in identifying criminals. With this new tool, old cases were suddenly reopened. This was when Tom learned the FBI had undertaken DNA testing of the woman's fingertip found on the street in front of the house on East Eighty-Fourth Street that day. This was when he learned that the fingertip believed to have been that of Diana Landers was not hers after all—meaning that Diana Landers might still be alive. If so, the best way of locating her would be to find her daughter.

Though federal agents were no doubt on the case, it had been Tom—working on his own on nights and weekends—who'd tracked me down. He remembered an old episode of *Columbo* he'd seen as a kid (the same one that had inspired my grandmother, no doubt) in which a woman on the lam applies for a copy of the birth certificate of someone she knew, around her age, who'd died.

Hundreds of women around the age of my grandmother had died in Queens around the time of the explosion. But it had occurred to Tom that the number of recorded deaths there for children around the age of Diana Landers's daughter would have been low. When he investigated this, he'd come up with only three names. Two had been boys. One, a girl—six years old, same as Diana's daughter would be—had been named Irene.

The trail took Tom to San Francisco, where my name came up again—the name I had gone by for twenty years. He tracked me down from a notice about an art show being held where a person with my name was showing her work. He'd made a trip to the art school, but hit a dead end. Then, not long after, my name had come up again, this time in the obituary of my husband and son. This led him to Lenny's parents in El Cerrito. He'd paid them a visit.

"Those two loved you," he said. "If they had believed that by telling me where you were, they'd bring you any harm, they would never have said anything. But I lied. I sat on the couch in their living room, surrounded by pictures of their son and their grandson—and you— and told them I was an old friend from art school, trying to track you down to offer my condolences and lend support. They had received a letter from you, a few years before. Then nothing. They were worried about you. So they showed me the stamp on the envelope. It wasn't much to go on, but enough that I took a bunch of vacation days and got on a plane."

At a bar in San Felipe, Tom had asked around about where a person might be likely to go in this country if she were an American wanting to disappear. An old expat with a gray beard and a Grateful Dead shirt had told him, "La Esperanza. No question."

When Tom got off the boat—with no idea still if this was the right place, or where I might be living even if it were—he'd met up with a man missing one hand who asked him if he was looking for anything. He'd shown my photograph to Gus. Ten minutes later he was standing at the top of my gate, ringing the bell.

"My plan was to get you to tell me about your mother, of course," Tom wrote. "I figured she might even be living with you, hiding out. Even if she wasn't, it seemed like a good bet you'd know where to find her. The man I was then had been carrying around this anger for thirty years. It sat like a stone on my heart. I was bound and determined to find the woman I blamed for my father's death.

"I wasn't bargaining on the next part," he said. "I started to fall for you. It got to mean more to me, being with you, than bringing Diana Landers to justice."

He wrote that he had wanted to tell me the truth. "Do you remember that night on your dock, when you said you wanted to tell me something?" he wrote. "I said I had something to tell you too. Only I never did. I was so afraid of losing you."

"That badge you saw in my wallet," he said. "It wasn't mine. It belonged to my father. Ever since he died, I've kept it with me."

After he returned to New York, Tom might have contacted the FBI with news about the case he'd been following for nearly thirty years now. He hadn't located Diana Landers, but they would have been interested to know he'd found her daughter.

"I didn't tell anyone about you," he went on. "I decided to leave the whole thing. I hadn't laid down my anger over my father's death, but I couldn't bring you any more grief. I quit the force the following spring. I teach criminal justice at a small college now. I'm done being a cop.

"I'm not expecting you to write back," he wrote. "I just wanted you to know two things.

"Number one, my love for you was real. I would hate for you to think I was lying to you about that. I used to believe the kind of love Gabriel García Márquez wrote about in his novel was a fantasy. It was falling in love with you that taught me it could be real. Now I understand a man like Florentino Ariza, who holds onto an unrequited love for fifty years. I am such a man. Or will be."

A song came to me then, one my mother used to sing. Sweet William on his death bed, for love of Barbara Allen.

Tom needed to tell me one more thing. This would be hard news. He wished he could be there to put his arms around me when I read the words.

The year before, a woman had shown up at his door—frail-looking, with long gray hair in a too-thin coat. "You'll recognize my name," she'd told him. "I'm one of the people responsible for the death of your father."

It was my mother, Diana.

All her life, she told him, she'd carried the guilt for her part in the explosion that killed Jose Martinez. She'd spent the last thirty years running and hiding. She couldn't do that anymore.

She told him she was dying. Lung cancer. He could turn her in to the FBI if he chose. It didn't matter. The only thing that did: coming to see him as she was doing now. Admitting her guilt. It was too late to seek forgiveness from her own mother or the daughter she'd abandoned. Here she was, asking this of him. "I don't actually expect it," she'd told Tom. "I just need to tell you how sorry I am."

This could have been the moment when Tom Martinez picked up his phone and placed a call to the FBI. Instead, he fixed her a bowl of *sancocho*, his mother's recipe. The two of them sat together in his kitchen. They spoke for many hours. She told him about her life on the run, he told her about his quest to find her. Then he recounted how he had met and fallen in love with her daughter.

Tom had told my mother the thing that may have mattered most to her, the one thing I could remember of my complicated childhood that had been nothing but beautiful. He'd told her that I remembered her singing to me.

Tom asked Diana if she knew any songs in Spanish. Only one—"Guantanamera." There in his kitchen in Queens, she sang it for him.

"I forgive you," he said. He had not known, until he spoke the words, what a burden it had been, holding on to so much bitterness for so long.

Who could have imagined this: that it would be the son of the policeman who'd died that day who paid weekly visits to my long-lost mother?

"After all those years of searching," Tom wrote, "it wasn't I who found your mother. It was your mother, who found me."

At the point she came to see him, Diana was living under her own name at a women's shelter in the Bronx. Tom took to visiting her on Sundays. When the cancer progressed to the point where she could no longer stay there, he paid visits to her in hospice. He had begged her to let him contact me. Diana wouldn't have it.

"She's made her own good life now, away from me," she told him. "Let her be." But my mother made him promise her: After her death, he'd write to me. Perhaps she held out some small hope that she might actually bring about a reconciliation between the two people still living who carried the wounds of that day. Maybe—though he'd told her this was impossible—we'd actually find our way back to each other.

"Your mother died last week," Tom wrote. He had taken care of the arrangements. By writing this letter he was fulfilling his promise. There was no happy ending to this story, but it was over at last. "I expect nothing from you," he wrote. "I just wanted you to know."

101

The return of the fireflies

How do you grieve the loss of a mother you barely knew? That night I would play a very old Joan Baez album and light some candles. I wished I could have called Daniel up, but I had no idea where to find him. It's a terrible thing, losing track of people who matter to you. I'd lost a few. I'd been such a person myself for a few people. Lenny's parents, top of the list.

So many years had passed by this point. I could even say I was happy now, or happy enough. (García Márquez had words to offer on that as well. "One could be happy not only without love but despite it." That was me, now.)

From the top of the steps, I could hear the buzzer ringing, and from the kitchen, the sound of Maria chopping vegetables. I set Tom's letter on my desk and climbed the steps to the gate. A woman stood there.

"I don't have a reservation," she said. She had no suitcase. She wore a velvet jacket that perfectly picked up the blue in her eyes. She looked to be in her late fifties, but had that kind of beauty that does not depend on youth. I had known another such woman once. Leila. To whom she bore an uncanny resemblance.

"You're Irene," she said, her English fluent, but with the accent of a person who makes her home in Spain. "I've heard about you in the village. I know you run the hotel now. I don't need to stay but I wonder if I could just see the place again."

Her name was Charlotte. Her mother, Leila.

We sat on the patio as the sun went down, having one of Mirabel's amazing drinks.

For all her life, Charlotte told me, she had believed her mother to be a woman named Sofia, married to her father, Javier. They had made their home in Barcelona, though later Charlotte had moved to Paris to pursue her studies of ballet. She'd danced there for many years.

"Your mother would have loved that," I told her. "Before she fell in love with this place her favorite city in the world was Paris."

It was only the month before, when her father died—her mother having predeceased him years before—that she discovered the folder of Leila's letters to Javier, begging him to let her visit and be part of her daughter's life. "They were wonderful parents to me, so I have to forgive the two of them," Charlotte said. "But it's hard knowing what I missed."

I showed her everything then, the gardens her mother had built, the stone carvings, the arbors, the handmade avocado chair where Leila had presided over meals. "Do you remember coming here when you were eight years old?" I asked her.

"I want to remember," she said. "I think we danced on the grass. Leila gave me a paint box, but my parents took me away before we got to make any pictures."

When we got to the path where Leila had hidden ceramic animals in among the plantings, Charlotte let out a small cry. "I remember this," she said. "My mother made a game for me, seeing how many animals I could find in among the plants of this garden. There was a rabbit, and a camel, and a frog, and this funny stone egg."

There it was.

All these years I'd kept Leila's silver bangles in a box on my dresser, unable to wear them. Before Charlotte left, I gave them to her.

That night the fireflies came out. It wasn't the season for their return, but sometimes, I've learned, things happen for which no explanation exists. The next morning before the sun was up I packed a bag with only a very few items. As Leila had taught me years before, three good dresses were enough. I would not be gone long.

The boat brought me to San Felipe, where I boarded a small plane. This brought me to a larger plane, that brought me to JFK airport, where I hailed a cab. I reached my destination—Queens—just before nightfall.

The man who opened the door looked considerably older, as I did, but his face was familiar.

"We're too old to wait fifty years, like characters in some novel," I said.

I had recently turned forty-six years old. Tom would be closing in on fifty by now. His hair was starting to turn gray.

One more thing. On her last visit to La Llorona—recently renamed *The Bird Hotel*—Jun Lan had left me a packet of her magic herbs.

"I'm way too old for babies," I said.

"You never know," she told me.

They worked.

Acknowledgments

Ten years ago, or even five, it's highly unlikely that any issue would have arisen over the idea that a Caucasian writer (myself) might write a novel set in a Central American country. But times have changed. In the fall of 2021, when I first sent the manuscript of this novel out into the world, I was told again and again that it would be viewed as "appropriative" for a non-indigenous, non LatinX writer like myself to write about the world in which this story takes place. Though at no point in the book do I set forward the point of view of anyone other than my North American, expat central character, the mere fact of my having chosen to locate my story in a country not of my birth was deemed by many as unacceptable.

I won't hold forth here on all the reasons why this new brand of cultural correctness strikes me as narrow-minded and wrong-headed— or cite the dozens (hundreds) of examples of literary works that would not exist, had such prohibitions been levied against their authors. (Can a man no longer write from a woman's point of view? Must a Black writer populate her work only with characters who are Black? Must I be transgender to include in a work of fiction—as I did, in my last novel before this one—a character who transitions?)

To me, this trend does not simply relegate a writer to the narrow box of her own cultural background and heritage, but—more egregiously—it limits the very qualities that stand at the center of good fiction: imagination, invention, curiosity about the world beyond one's own. I am deeply grateful to Mark Gompertz and the editorial team at Skyhorse Publishing for their rejection of this new brand of gatekeeping.

My deep appreciation and thanks go also to my agent, Laurie Fox, who championed this book relentlessly, as she continues to do in all of our work together. I want also to express my particular appreciation and deepest respect for my French publisher, Phillipe Rey, for being the first to accept that a non-Latin, non-indigenous writer might still create a work of fiction set in a country and culture other than the one into which she was born. As much as I embrace the importance of honoring the territory of artists of color to claim their own unique narrative, it would be a sad day if a writer—whatever her cultural heritage—were required to limit her storytelling to the world she inhabited. Let us never forget it is the job of a writer to imagine lives beyond her own. The challenge of each of us is to do it believably and well, and in a manner that respects the heritage of all.

It is a reality in the world of publishing today that for a writer to reach her audience, she'd better maintain a strong presence on social media. But how is a writer to accomplish this and still give her undivided attention to writing books? I owe a debt to Judith Swankoski, who supports my presence in social media with so much talent and inventiveness and an uncanny ability to post what I would have said on Instagram, if only I'd said it.

Quietly and without fanfare or drama, my treasured assistant and friend, Jenny Rein, has kept the coast clear for me to keep telling my stories by taking care of so many of the other tasks that keep a writer from her work. I long ago lost count of all the times Jenny put out fires on my behalf, and allowed me to keep doing what I love best. Every writer should have someone like Jenny in her life, but there is probably only one of her.

Finally ... the people in my life to whom I owe the greatest debt at the moment of completing this book are the men and women of the small Mayan indigenous community of San Marcos la Laguna, Guatemala, where I have made a part-time home for over twenty years. I am a foreigner in their world, and will always remain so. But the warmth and kindness and support I have come to know in that place has instilled in me the greatest respect and devotion. More than this: love.

Book Review Questions

Set 1

1. For over twenty years, the author has had a house on Lake Atitlan in Guatemala where she goes to write as well as offer writing workshops. The country depicted in *The Bird Hotel* is fictional, but her actual home has both a lake and a volcano. What do you think inspired her to draw on this location for *The Bird Hotel*?

2. *The Bird Hotel*'s opening line "I was twenty-seven years old when I decided to jump off the Golden Gate Bridge" is gripping. Did you have any initial perceptions of what direction the book would take after reading this line? Were you surprised at the direction the book took after this revelation by the narrator?

3. Following a devastating tragedy, the main character, Irene (formerly known as Joan) is transported to the La Llorona (The Bird Hotel), a run-down but beautiful hotel that is located on a lake at the foot of a volcano in Central America. She initially intends to simply fix up the decaying hotel and sell it and continue on with her miserable life. What events and people cause her to change the trajectory of that initial decision?

4. Upon arriving at La Llorona, Irene is introduced to Leila, the owner of the hotel and her longtime employees, Luis, Maria, Elmer, and Mirabel. There are no other guests at the hotel besides Irene, which is not unusual. Why does Leila continue to employ these individuals?

5. La Llorona sits at the base of an active volcano that had not erupted for hundreds of years. Leila says "It will happen one day, of course. But I like to think that living this way, in the shadow of an active volcano, serves as a daily reminder of the preciousness of my days. One day I'll be gone. We all will. Why worry about that? In the meantime, let's make sure the fish is cooked just right and the wine is French." (p. 64) What do you think about Leila's perspective on life?

6. Irene starts to experience the beauty of the town of La Esperanza and La Llorona and describes it to Leila as a peaceful and safe retreat. Leila responds by saying "You remember the story of the Garden of Eden. Every paradise has its serpents." (p.116) Who and what is she referring to?

7. Recently, some authors have been chastised for cultural appropriation, the idea of writing outside of their ethnic heritage and background. Maynard, who is an American, finds this to be a dangerous trend as it limits an essential part of the creative process, which is imagination, and the freedom to express more than what is actually known and familiar. Do you agree?

8. The author initially used her small home in Guatemala as a venue where women writers could come and attend workshops while staying in the local village, which was a haven both for the indigenous workers as well as a tourist venue for "hippies." When the pandemic hit, while the town was not affected by the epidemic, the villagers were because the tourists left. Unemployment skyrocketed so she started a project to employ workers at her home. This work eventually led to the creation of Casa Paloma. What do you think about the author's endeavors and is there a connection to events that happened in *The Bird Hotel*?

9. The cover of the book is from a painting the author commissioned from an indigenous painter. It tells the story of a volcanic eruption that occurred in 2018. There is a volcanic eruption in *The Bird Hotel*. What do you think about the image and this book cover?

10. Jeanine Cummins, the *New York Times* bestselling author of *American Dirt*, wrote that, "In *The Bird Hotel*, Joyce Maynard imagines a glorious landscape where one broken woman, Irene, must lose herself in order to find the hope of survival. Although it's Irene whose heart-stopping tale drives the narrative, this is also a rich ensemble novel about endurance, courage, healing, and the salvation of human generosity—the glittering, unexpected ways we save each other every day, despite all the reasons not to..." Do you find that this book provided a meaningful message about hope and discovery after great loss?

11. Joyce Maynard is above all else a storyteller. She hosts memoir-writing retreats both at Casa Paloma and at her home in New Hampshire. She has posed the question in several of her interviews "Do you have a story you are burning to tell?" She further opines that it doesn't matter if your story ever gets published as long as you have "told your truth." Do you have a story that you are burning to tell, and would you put in the time and effort to write it even if you knew it would never be published?

12. *The Bird Hotel* provides us with a vast array of characters, both good and bad. Who was the character you liked the most and who was the most despicable?

13. Some of the guests who visited La Llorona experienced its natural beauty and left with life-changing experiences. Others viewed the

hotel only for its potential financial windfall. Which of the guests do you believe had the most memorable experiences?

14. Carl Edgar, the hotel businessman from Dallas, is the first guest to arrive seeking to buy the hotel. Leila is in severe financial straits but refuses to sell. She chooses instead to "sabotage" his hotel room by planting scorpions in his bed. It is at this point that Irene realizes that Leila wants the hotel to outlive her. (p.124) Shortly after this, Leila dies. How does the trajectory of Irene's life change from this point?

15. Gus and Dora turn out to be scoundrels, getting control of La Llorona from Irene and previously defrauding Leila as well. At what point did you realize that these two were up to no good?

16. Amalia comes to the town as a dramatic figure; a former activist and prison inmate, with wild curly hair and outfits with fringe and beads that she makes herself. She realizes that there is a huge problem with garbage in the town and she employs a workforce of children to stuff wrappers into bottles as a recycling project with the result of the creation of houses, a classroom and even a health center. (p. 177) Why do you think the author incorporated this character into her story?

17. Jun Lan (Pretty Orchid) comes to La Llorona from China seeking a magic plant that she has been told will allow her to finally become pregnant. She remains at La Llorona for over three weeks and locates the plant. After her return to China, she becomes pregnant. Why do you think the author includes this fanciful tale?

18. Jerome Sapirstein travels to La Llorona simply to study birds. He becomes immediately entranced by Irene and wants her to travel

and illustrate his book on birds, in addition to marrying him. They spend a day and night on the volcano. Sapirstein offers her a life filled with adventure and the possibility of children. She chooses to reject his offer. Why?

19. Jerome reads her a poem while on the volcano "The Lake Isle of Innisfree." Years later, Jerome writes her a letter (p. 314) and references the same poem. Why is this poem important?

20. Helen and Jeff Boggs travel to La Llorona with their daughter, Sandra, in an attempt to reunite with Sandra's birth mother. It turns into a disaster. If you were in that family, how do you think you would have felt?

21. Elmer has been in love with Mirabel all his life, but he steals from Irene and Mirabel rejects him. He later has the chance to redeem himself. Were you rooting for Elmer?

22. Rosella dies in childbirth but delivers twins (Alicia and Mateo). Wade, the father, has difficulty managing fatherhood. How do you see the role of the women who step in to help raise these children?

23. Bud and Victoria Albertson travel to La Llorona from Arkansas to buy property. During their stay, Victoria comes upon Andres, the Mayan astrologer. Her interaction with him leads to devastating consequences and Andres is never seen again. Do you think Bud killed him?

24. Irene eventually accepts an offer for the hotel, but just as the deal is signed, a hurricane hits the area and destroys much of La Llorona, with the seller backing out of the deal. Irene's response to

this turn of events is relief. (p. 277) Why did she initially decide to sell and why did she then have regrets?

25. Dora becomes interested in the "herb" that helped Jun Lan become pregnant. (p. 287) Did you have any suspicion at the time as to why she was so interested?

26. Irene confronts Gus and Dora after she realizes her property has been taken away from her. She thought that these two had been her friends, which is why she signed legal documents in a language she did not understand. Under the circumstances, can you see why Irene would have made such a dreadful mistake?

27. La Llorona and its environs are idyllic. Its inhabitants are, for the most part, kind and generous but impoverished people. However, the Lizard Men (who rape Mirabel) and Andres (who rapes Victoria) are clearly evil. Would you be interested in visiting a place such as this?

28. At what point in the book did you think that the volcano was going to erupt?

29. Did you anticipate the ending of the book and how it would come back full circle to the explosion that took place with the Weather Underground?

Set 2

1. Do you agree with Irene's grandmother's choice to make Irene swear she would never tell what happened to her mother?

2. When Irene first arrives at La Llorona, she barely cares whether she lives or dies. What, for you, represented the turning point for her? Do you believe that a person can endure great tragedy and still find joy and hope in the world? Could you do this?

3. The country in which the novel takes place is never named. Why do you think the author made the choice NOT to name a specific country (for instance, Guatemala, where she owns a home)?

4. How did you feel about Tom when it turned out he had deceived Irene concerning his motives to come to La Llorona?

5. A number of the women in this novel make the choice NOT to marry a man who asks them to be his partner. Do you have thoughts on why the author made this choice in her storytelling?

6. How do you feel about Irene's mother? Would you have forgiven her?

7. Can you understand why Irene never told Lenny the truth about her background?

8. When you first encountered Gus in the story, what did you think about him?

9. Which characters in the novel come across more sympathetically—the gringos or the local indigenous people?

10. Which character in the novel would you most like to have dinner with?

11. If you have read other novels by Joyce Maynard, you probably know that until this one, they were all grounded in very realistic-seeming family drama. Why do you think she chose to insert the element of magical realism in this novel—and how do you feel about that choice?

12. Would you like to stay at La Llorona? Does reading *The Bird Hotel* make you more or less likely to want to travel to Central America?

13. In the acknowledgments of the book, Joyce Maynard writes about resistance in the current world of publishing to her having written a novel located in Central America. How do you feel about this? What does the term "cultural appropriation" mean to you—and did you witness examples of it in the novel?

14. As you may know, Joyce will be publishing a sequel to her novel, *Count the Ways*, in June 2024. Would you like to read a sequel to *The Bird Hotel*, or do you feel it's best to end this story where Joyce left off?